To Pam and Derek. 20/11/98
With all best wishes
Hector Shears (Stephen)

THE CHRISTMAS CLUB

Hector Shears

MINERVA PRESS
LONDON
ATLANTA MONTREUX SYDNEY

THE CHRISTMAS CLUB

ISBN 0 75410 184 3

First Published 1998 by
MINERVA PRESS
195 Knightsbridge
London SW7 1RE

Printed in Great Britain for Minerva Press

THE CHRISTMAS CLUB

To my wife and family
for their understanding, patience and encouragement

About the Author

A textile engineer by trade, and also a father and grandfather, the author lives in the heart of the Yorkshire wool district where he greatly enjoys good food, wine, pursuing his interests of gardening, photography, wildlife and the countryside, and, above all, meeting the people for whom he has had a lifelong fascination.

Chapter One

'What's for dinner?' This question was asked every day by Willie Arkenthwaite. If he didn't ask it in the mill canteen every day at noon, he asked it at home on Saturdays and Sundays at half past twelve. It wasn't that he needed to ask the question, it was just that he did, because more than anything else, Willie liked his food. He asked, 'What's for tea?' every day as well, much to the annoyance of his wife, but she had, over the years, gotten used to it, and for the most part ignored it.

Willie was a smallish, plumpish valley man with a good sense of humour. He was in his early forties (although he looked much older) sporting a fast-receding hair line, a usually overfilled beer belly and, most of the time, a pair of iron-soled leather clogs. There were those in the village who swore he went to bed in them.

He lived in the large village-cum-small town of Grolsby which as everyone knows nestles in the fold between two steep hills to the west of the heavy woollen districts in the West Riding of Yorkshire, and certainly to the east of the customs post on the Lancashire/Yorkshire border.

Willie lived in a small cottage in a row of such dwellings, aptly named Cutside Cottages, on a strip of land close to the centre of the village, with the canal in front, almost close enough to jump into from his front doorstep and separated only by the towpath. At the bottom of his back garden was the river, which was really nothing more than a large stream. The only way to get to Cutside Cottages was along the canal towpath, where at weekends in spring, summer and autumn, a few pleasure craft could be seen chugging along the canal from lock to lock, the occupants trying to see as much as possible of the pleasant countryside interspersed by dark satanic mills. During the week the working barges traversed with their loads of coal and other commodities.

Cutside Cottages were very old, having been built at the time the canal was constructed some one hundred and fifty years earlier. They were built in locally quarried stone, and a headstone in the middle of the row had the year 1803 carved on it. They had at the time of building housed the canal staff, the lock-keepers, the maintenance staff, and the people who worked on the wharf loading and unloading the endless queue of barges which were the main method of transporting goods up and down the valley. They were neat little houses with a good size front living-cum-dining-room, and a kitchen and small pantry at the back. Two good bedrooms and a small bathroom were upstairs. There had been three bedrooms and a stone privy in the garden when they were built, but they had all been modernised after the war when they had been bought from the canal company by Murgatroyd's mill, a quarter of a mile further up the valley, to be used as employee housing.

To say that Number 6 Cutside Cottages was overcrowded would be an understatement of the truth. There resided within its portals, Willie, his wife Thelma, his wife's mother, four children with ages ranging from fifteen to five, two cats and a dog, not to mention a collection of rabbits in cages and hens in a run, which inhabited part of the back garden, and Willie's favourites, his pigeons, in a beautifully white and black painted cote.

Thelma was most of the time somewhat fraught, what with her half-invalided, nagging mother who interfered in absolutely everything, and the four children, especially during the school holiday times. The overcrowded state of the house, the animals inside and out, her part-time job as a cleaner up at the mill house for Mrs Murgatroyd, all the washing, ironing, cooking and general housework, and the thousand and one other things that had to be done got on top of her with frequent regularity.

The old lady, being a martyr to her bad back and always enjoying ill health, had forced herself into being chair-bound soon after she had arrived to live with Willie and Thelma following the death of her husband several years previously. She had entrenched herself firmly in the most comfortable chair in the house, at the side of the cottage range, and demanded a large roaring fire from first thing in the morning until last thing at night, winter and summer alike, as she was 'starved through to the very marrow' at all times. From her well-chosen situation she could see into the kitchen and out through the front window, so that she could nosy in all directions at one and the same time. She knew everybody and everything that passed by the cottage, and much to everyone's dismay she kept up a constant running commentary on the goings-on outside the house. To add to the annoyance of the constant monotonic drone of her voice, she would wave to acquaintances who passed and beckon them in for a chat. She moved from her chair only to eat or sleep or to perform the little necessities of life, and then only with very exaggerated difficulty. In her free time between nosying, she would moan on at Thelma about Willie, the children, her various complaints and illnesses, and was gradually wearing Thelma to a state of nervous exhaustion.

Willie escaped most of the problems with his mother-in-law, although he was fed up to the back teeth with her. He was normally a placid man, but in fits of anguish from time to time he could visualise the old lady swinging from a gibbet, or being tortured by the Nazis, or even just simply being helped to fall into the canal. He once ventured to ask the rag-and-bone man if he would take her away in exchange for a couple of balloons, but the rag-and-bone man took one look at the old lady and declined the offer on the grounds that two balloons was far too dear a price to pay for an old lady, particularly that old lady.

Willie got around the problems of the household because of his daily routine which read: rise on the first sound of the mill hooter, get dressed, go downstairs, pack up breakfast to be eaten at the mill, clean out the range and fill the coal buckets to keep the old lady warm, go outside to talk to the pigeons, check the hens and the garden, and then off to work, dinner in the mill canteen, home for tea, straight out into the garden in summer or the potting shed in winter, back inside about eight o'clock, wash, shave and change, and off to the pub or Club until closing time. With this routine he carefully avoided the majority of domestic conflict. He was happy with his lot, for he was too thick not to be. He hadn't any spare money; it was almost all spent each week, but he was content with life, and lived his daily routine year in and year out.

One bitterly cold day in January 1953, Willie was sitting in his usual place in the mill canteen at Murgatroyds, having enjoyed yet another of Greasy Martha's dinners – for so the canteen lady was affectionately named after the copious quantities of fat in various forms that she served up on a daily basis. He always sat on the same seat at a table for four in a corner of the dining-room, with his three mates from the dyehouse, where they were dyers' labourers. They all wore iron-soled clogs and thick leather aprons that almost touched the floor, even through their dinner break. They were playing cards, a type of cribbage with local variations, for a halfpenny a corner a game. They had played this particular brand of cribbage for as long as any of them could remember, and they played every dinner break as soon as they had finished eating. A stranger watching them could be forgiven for not understanding the game, and it was rumoured in the mill that over the years they had introduced so many local variations that they could not understand it properly themselves. They always talked whilst they played, usually something and nothing about the pubs, clubs, football, horses, dogs, or some other topic of local interest, but today the conversation was of a more serious note, namely the state of their personal finances following Christmas and the New Year.

'I've got nowt left until I get paid on Friday,' said Arthur Baxter, looking glum.

Dick Jordan looked up. 'I think I'm worse than that because I owe the coal man for ten bags, as well as having nowt.'

'What have you gone and had ten bags for all at once?' enquired Arthur.

'Nay, it were the wife, I don't know whatever she were thinking about. I says to her we're running a bit low on coal, see if you can catch coal man and get him to drop a few bags into the cellar, 'cos they'd have carried us over till the cheap coal comes in summer, and beggar me if she hasn't gone and had ten bags put in when I gets home from my work, and it's week before Christmas, and all my money spoken for. I could happen have found the brass for three bags, but not ten all at once. I shall be bound to get some overtime in or stop drinking or summat to pay for that lot.'

He took a deep breath and sat back. He wasn't given to making speeches of that length; it had overtaxed him mentally and physically, and he certainly wasn't ready for the next pronouncement which came from Willie.

'You must have a right big fire if three bags will last you until summer – we burn a bag a week at our house.'

'Aye, it's all right for you, you've got your mother-in-law to pay for it,' said Dick.

'Aye, you're right,' he replied, lying through his teeth, but he never let on to anyone just how the family finances were standing, and as usual he made full use of his audience to expound the virtues of having an over-generous mother-in-law living in, knowing full well that she never spent a penny on them, and also knowing that his lying would catch up with him one day. Building his mother-in-law up to being a saint in front of his pals had become quite an act with Willie, to the point where some of them were beginning to believe him.

Lewis Armitage, being the fourth member of the card school – the philosopher of the group, and the one who said least but made most sense when he did, said, 'You know, Willie, it must be grand to have a kind and generous mother-in-law who buys your coal. What else does she buy for you?'

Willie huffed and puffed a little, then said, 'Er, er, er, groceries, er, yes, er, groceries.'

'Does she hell as like,' retorted Arthur Baxter.

'She does, she does,' shouted Willie.

'You're a liar!' Arthur shouted back.

'I'm not a liar, it's true.'

Lewis Armitage decided it was time to cool things down. 'Willie, I think it's your turn to play.'

'Aye, Lewis, so it is, sorry.'

Play recommenced and they made a couple of rounds of the table in silence until Arthur Baxter claimed victory. Being two pence to the better, he shuffled the cards and dealt another hand.

Whilst the dealing was taking place, Willie started talking yet again.

'A bit of a problem this shortage of money after Christmas you know; these women spend all the money they can lay their hands on.'

'Doesn't affect you, does it?' asked Dick Jordan.

'Why?'

'Well, with your over-generous mother-in-law, all you need to do is hold your hand out and she contributes.'

'It's not just exactly like that,' replied Willie hesitantly.

'Just exactly what is it like then?' asked Dick. 'It sounds like it to me.'

'What does that mean?'

'Well, I can't see why you're complaining – she buys your coal, she buys your groceries – do you ask her for money every time you are getting a bit short?'

Willie was getting worried now; they were cornering him and he didn't quite know what to say next, so he said nothing and went on playing cards seeing that it was his turn to drop.

'Come on Willie,' said Arthur. 'You haven't answered Dick's question yet.'

'Er, er, what was the question Dick?'

'Tha knows full well what the question was, without pretending. Trouble is you either can't or won't answer it.'

'Come on,' said Lewis. 'It'll have gone bedtime and we'll be here arguing all that time; there's nobbut another ten minutes left and it's back to work. So let's get on and finish the game.'

'Have you got a winning hand, Lewis?' asked Willie quickly, very glad of an opportunity to change the subject.

'Never bother about the winning hand, what about answering my question?' Dick persisted, but Lewis countered him with a sharp, 'Shut up and let's get on with the game.'

They played quietly for a while without any further problem when, having just played, and not having a particularly good hand anyway, Arthur said, 'It is a problem is Christmas. You make sure that Father Christmas comes to the kids, you give the wife as good a time as you can afford, you buy a turkey, the in-laws come and eat you out of house and home, you go back there and do the same to them on Boxing Day, you go out and have a drink or two, the kids break their presents, the in-laws moan and groan, the wife's tired out and you've nowt left. It's a right horrible mess.'

'Come on,' said Lewis. 'We've not had as bad a dinner time, as this for weeks, and anyway, I've got a winning hand.'

'You must have, you're making enough noise over it,' said Willie, as play commenced again, and Lewis won easily.

Being the winner it was his turn to shuffle and deal, a job he hated.

'Er, er, don't think we've time for another hand today.'

'Course we have,' said Arthur. 'Come on, get on with the dealing. But you know this shortage of money after Christmas is a bit of a beggar; it happens every year and I can't see how we can do owt about it. It doesn't matter how you try to scrimp and save, you can never get any more money together ready for it.'

Willie belched out loud without any apology.

'Ready for what?' interrupted Dick.

'For Christmas, you daft devil.'

Dick, being a man of few words, stared in wonder at Arthur who was not usually given to making long speeches either.

'Come on, lads, just one quick one to finish with and I've dealt myself a rotten hand, so you can all have a decent go at winning,' said Lewis.

The four of them picked up their cards and examined them. 'Terrible,' 'Awful,' 'Bloody rotten,' were three of the comments that were heard, to be rounded off with, 'A shocking state of affairs is this, you aren't fit to have charge of a pack of cards – don't know why we left you to deal.'

'I don't have to deal again ever if you don't want me to,' said Lewis gleefully. 'Anyway, it's your lead-off, and get a move on, we've no time left.'

They had almost finished when the mill hooter sounded twenty to one, and they rushed to finish the game. Greasy Martha was watching them.

'Come on you lot, hooter's gone and I've to clear up yet.'

She finished the sentence with an indiscreet cough, making the dead ash fall from the remains of her cigarette, which was stuck to her bottom lip. It fell on to the serving counter, making her sweep it off with her hand on to the kitchen floor.

'That's it, nothing but pure cleanliness and hygiene in this establishment,' said Arthur. 'Nothing like a bit of Martha's fag ash mixed with your dinner.'

Willie farted out loud.

'Sod off out of it,' shouted Martha, being at her usual uncouth best. 'And don't bloody well come back again if you don't bloody well like it.'

'Bye, Martha.'

'Bysie wysie, Martha dearest.'

'Adieu, adieu, until the morrow.'

'See you later, alligator.'

They didn't turn around to witness the gesture that followed them, nor to hear the cursing that accompanied it.

'Remarkably fine woman, our Martha,' said Lewis as they descended the stairs to the mill bottom where they worked.

'They don't build them like her any more.'

'No, thank goodness.'

⋆

They arrived back at the dyehouse, laughing and joking, all thoughts of money forgotten.

Work, to Willie, was a monstrous drudge. Not that, in comparison to many more automatic jobs, dyehouse labouring could be classed as monotonous or as a drudge, but to Willie's simple mind it was. He worked fairly hard, always did his best, and did his job well as long as he kept to the well-tried routine, but if the routine was altered for any reason he had difficulty in tuning his mind into something new. The pigeons didn't help – his mind was usually more on them than on his work for they were the number one love of his life.

Five o'clock could never come soon enough for Willie. As soon as the mill hooter sounded, he would take off his thick leather apron and hang it on the handle of the cold water valve at the side of Number Seven dye winch, then quickly wash his hands, put on his heavy, old, thick tweed coat and flat cap, and make his way home as fast as he could.

This particular day was no exception. He rushed along the canal bank towards Cutside Cottages, his iron-soled clogs making a clanking sound on the concrete path, accentuated by the severe frost which had lain there for a few days. Occasionally the noise would reach a crescendo as he broke the ice on top of a frozen puddle lying in a hole in what had at sometime been a good concrete road. His breath hurried out of him as if he were on fire, making a smoke haze in front of him in the bright early evening moonlight.

As he opened the door of Number 6, Willie was already repeating under his breath, 'Your Willie's home, Thelma, get your coat off Willie, your tea will be on the table in a minute.' And sure enough, as he opened the front door which led directly into the living room, and the tremendous heat of the living room fire hit him, his mother-in-law started. 'Your Willie's home, Thelma, get your coat off Willie, your tea will be on the table in a minute.'

Willie was inclined to tell the old lady to shut her cake-hole – he felt like this every day when he arrived home – but as usual he kept quiet, took off his coat, washed his hands again and sat down at the table ready for tea.

Thelma appeared out of the kitchen with the tea, being helped by Josie their eldest daughter.

'We've got your favourite for tea today, Dad.'

'Tripe and onions?'

'Yes, that's right.'

'Goody goody gumdrops, come on, Grandma, and you kids, come and sit down and let's get on with it before it goes cold.'

Josie carried in a huge steaming pan of stewed tripe and onions which she put on the table. Thelma followed with a giant teapot, and a plate with a mountain of bread and butter on it.

'By gum, this looks good,' said Willie. 'Come on, Grandma, you're last again.'

'It's me back, it isn't half giving me some gip today, it must be the cold, I'm starved through to the very marrow, this weather will be the death of me.'

Willie prayed silently for more and harder frosts. Josie served out generous helpings of the piping hot stew, large lumps of tripe, rings of onions, and a beautiful, creamy white sauce with yellow blobs of melted butter in it.

As was the privilege of the family breadwinner, Willie was served the first helping, and immediately grabbed a full slice of bread, folded it in half and dipped it into the creamy sauce in his dish.

'Willie! We haven't got ours yet.'

Willie stopped eating and stared at his wife's mother: if looks could have killed, they would have been sending for the undertaker a few minutes later.

'Yes, my mother's right,' said Thelma, trying to calm what could have been a very tense situation.

Willie turned his stare to Thelma, who met his eyes directly, and Willie, knowing when he was beaten, gave in and sat back until everyone was served.

'But it was so good. Come on, get on with serving it out and let's get to it.'

'Come on, Dad, have some patience, it will be all the better for waiting, you know.'

Willie smiled at Josie, who was the apple of his eye. When everyone was served, she said in a rich American southern drawl, 'Okay, you guys, let battle commence.'

Willie dived in again with his folded bread, slurped noisily and sucked the sauce from the bread, dunked the bread again, greedily wolfed the soggy mess and grabbed another piece. With the bread being dunked by his right hand, and a fork in his left deftly picking out the pieces of tripe and rings of onion, it wasn't long before the dish was empty.

'Is there any more?' he enquired.

'Aye, but you'll have to wait until we've all finished before we start dishing out any more,' replied Thelma, without looking up from her eating.

'Nay, come on, get on with it, it's fair right good, and I could eat another half-dozen platefuls right now.'

Grandma looked up from her half-empty dish.

'Well, I'm not rushing for anyone, especially you; it's bad enough having to eat this sort of thing in the first place, without being rushed.'

'You'd best go out and buy us some fillet steak tomorrow, and then we can all eat in the manner like what you are accustomed to.'

'You know very well that my back won't let me.'

'Thelma can get it for us then – all you need to do is give—'

'Willie,' interrupted Thelma, 'that's quite enough of that.'

'Give us some more tripe then.'

'Oh, all right, pass your dish over here.'

Willie passed the dish over to Josie who, having filled it to the brim, passed it back to Willie, who greedily slurped, slopped and sucked his way through the delicious tripe and onions. Having emptied the dish, he once again enquired, 'Any more?'

'Sorry, Daddy, you've had the last of it, there's none left.'

Upon this, Willie picked up his dish and drank the few remaining drops of sauce, then looking around to see if anyone was watching, and discovering that no one in particular was, he raised the dish to his face once more, this time to lick the dish as clean as a new pin – only to find that someone was watching.

'Willie!' came the cry from Thelma. 'How dare you!'

'Eh, it's so good, I can't afford to waste a drop.'

'I told you when you were insisting on marrying him that he would be no good for you, our Thelma, but would you take my advice? Would you? No you would not. Your dear, late father would turn in his grave if he could see.'

'For heaven's sake, shut up, Mother.'

'Aye, put a sock in it, why don't you. Pour the tea or something,' said Willie who sat back, opened his mouth and belched as loud as he could, saying, 'That's a lot better.'

'See what I said, he hasn't even got the manners of a pig. You might silence me again, but you'll see that I was right; this marrying below your station has got you nowhere.'

'Marrying below her station! By gum, you've some room to talk – you a skivvy, and your husband a cesspit emptier for the council – if marrying me wasn't above her station, I'd like to know what was. Don't forget, we've got an inside toilet here, you nobbut had a brick privy down the garden, you live in the lap of luxury at my and Thelma's expense – we have to have a roaring fire from morning till night, all for your benefit – and you accuse Thelma of marrying below her station, absolute rubbish, poppycock – and I'll thank you to mind your own manners in future. Or else!'

Willie in one and the same breath pointed to the door, and sat back and sighed, more than well pleased and even astonished at his performance, as he wasn't given to making clever speeches. He observed that his mother-in-law was shedding a tear or two, and that Thelma had her arm around her shoulder.

'There, there, Mother, Willie didn't mean it.'

'Oh, yes, I did mean it.'

Willie was trying to develop his masterly control of the situation.

'Unless she keeps her gob tight shut where I'm concerned in future, she can pack her bags and get out.'

More than a tear or two was flooding from the old lady now, and Josie looked reproachfully at her dad.

'Dad, look what you've done now.'

'Josie! Don't interfere in things you know nowt about. Now, Grandma, stop blubbering and listen to me.'

For the first time ever, Willie was beginning to have visions of being the master in his own house, although he didn't quite know how to continue, and a little ball of phlegm in his throat was just beginning to annoy him, but he threw caution to the wind and breezed in.

'Starting with the next lot of coal what we need, you can pay for it, and all that what we buy after that you can pay for, or you can starve, and you can suit yourself.'

He snooked up the phlegm, rolled it around his mouth and swallowed it again, dreading what the reply to his outburst might be. He didn't have to wait long to find out.

'Nay, lad,' she wailed, 'ah can't afford to pay for t'coal and ah need a big fire else ah shall be starved through to the very marrow. Ah don't know what ah shall have to do.'

'Well, suit yourself, but I'm paying for no more coal. Now then, is someone going to pour me some tea or not?'

Thelma poured Willie his pint pot of strong tea, and the others got a cup each. The kids were getting restless and Thelma sent them off to play in the kitchen. Willie drank some of his tea with his teaspoon, ''cos it's hot', and then when it had cooled a little, he noisily drained the pint pot and put it back on the table.

'Right, I'm off to look at my pigeons,' he announced.

He got up from the table and marched as uprightly, masterfully and smartly as he possibly could, away into the kitchen where he belched as loudly as he possibly could, then he took out his hurricane lamp, filled it with paraffin, lit it, pumped up the pressure, and made ready for off to the pigeon cote.

Arthur Baxter knocked on the door of Number 6 Cutside Cottages, and without waiting for a reply he walked in as he did most nights.

'Evening all, is Willie out in the back?'

'Hello, Arthur,' said Thelma. 'Yes, he's out in the back with the pigeons. Getting rid of some tonight, aren't you?'

'Aye, we're setting them off on their long journey tonight. It'll take 'em two days to get there on the train, not every day you send 'em as far as Bristol. No, it's hell of a long way, but they look after 'em well on the railway. Anyhow, I'd best go give him a hand wi'em.'

Arthur lifted the latch on the back door and went out into the cold black night, observing Willie down the bottom of the garden in the pigeon cote, from which shafts of bright light pierced the frosty night air.

'That you, Arthur?' came the muffled voice from within the pigeon cote.

'Aye, have you got baskets out yet?'

'Nay, I were waiting for you coming. Come on, they're at back of the hen run.'

Arthur followed Willie to the back of the hen run, and in the light of the hurricane lamp they pulled away a dirty old tarpaulin to reveal two large wicker panniers used solely for transporting pigeons. They picked up the bottom one of the two, with the other resting on it, and carried them back to the cote.

'Which of them are we sending, Willie?'

'Well, I don't know, we could send 'em all. Tha knows if we put 'em six to a basket they're all right, so there's no problem.'

'Well, why not, it won't cost us any more to send the other two, then at least they can pick which they want and send the rest back in the baskets.'

So the two friends carefully and slowly collected the birds one by one and put them into one of the baskets. Willie had a few words of encouragement for each of the birds.

'Now, Henrietta, you go and be a good girl for your new daddy. Claudine, you will have to pull your socks up if your last race was anything to go by, else you might end up in an oven with a crust over you.'

As he spoke, the birds looked at him as if he was demented, each bird turning its head in small jerky movements from side to side, but he went on giving each one a fond stroke or two. Finally, they were all in, and the panniers placed on top of one another again.

'What train they going on?'

'Oh, not until half past ten tonight, 'cos they're not leaving Leeds while ten o'clock tomorrow,' replied Arthur.

Willie and Arthur were partners in the pigeons. Willie was the works manager and Arthur the company secretary. Willie did the feeding, the talking to, the nursing and the mucking out, and Arthur made the arrangements with the local society secretary, did the necessary paperwork and collected the prize money, not that the latter part of his job had required much effort lately. The pigeons had to live in Willie's back garden because Arthur lived in a house with no garden, and at the year end it was usual for Arthur to pay Willie a substantial sum of money as his share of the running expenses.

They picked up the two panniers, Willie at the front with his hands meeting behind him on the large wide handle of the bottom one, and Arthur bringing up the rear, with his hands on the opposite handle. The only access to the back garden was through the house, and so in they trooped, into the coolish atmosphere of the back kitchen and then the hot temperature of the living room.

Arthur looked firstly at the huge fire burning in the black leaded cottage range, and secondly at the old lady sitting very comfortably in her corner near the roaring fire.

'Willie's been telling us how generous you are, buying all this coal to keep this big roaring fire going, Mrs Woofenden. It's good of you, it is, to keep it so warm. I wish somebody'd buy coal to keep our house as warm as this.'

The old lady was momentarily dumbfounded. Thelma looked uncomfortable and kept quiet. Willie would have liked to have kicked Arthur, or bitten his own tongue out for his earlier stupidity in lying about the coal, but he could do neither from the position in which he was and the latter was only a thought. The old lady found her tongue again after a short but pregnant silence.

'Oh, he has, has he?'

'Aye, he has, I wish my mother-in-law would buy us some coal. You're a very lucky lass, Thelma.'

Willie, even though he was not so bright, decided it was time to change the subject.

'Come on, Arthur, or we shall miss yond train, and there's not another tonight,' and with that he began to march towards the front door.

'Don't forget which day you set off,' said Thelma.

'Aye, don't come back in the early hours disturbing us all,' the old lady growled.

'No, we'll just take the birds up to the station, and have a quick one on the way back. We won't be long.'

'Goodnight all,' shouted Arthur as they entered the cold night air once more.

★

They turned left out of the house and along the canal towpath, the few distantly positioned bright gas lamps casting long shadows on the two friends in the frosty night air. They passed the local wharf and turning circle where there were two barges tied up for the night. One, the local boat, was empty; the other was from St Helens with a load of coal going back to Lancashire. The few dirty windows in the cabin at the stern showed a weak glow from the poor oil lamps. They looked in through one of the windows. The bargee and his wife were having a meal. Both were the colour of their cargo, neither of them having washed since Christmas.

'It would be grand to live on one of them barges, never need to wash, no mother-in-law, nowt to bother about all day but see the scenery and be out in the fresh air and sun,' Willie said thoughtfully.

'You've nowt to bother about anyway, with a generous woman like Mrs Woofenden; life must be five-star all the way.'

'You should come live there and try it, you'd soon change your tune.'

'Nay, I've enough on with what I've got.'

'Aye, you have.'

*

The two figures, walking smartly in time with each other, made their way slowly from the canal towpath, along the village, past the by now darkened shops and the well-lit pubs, up the steep hill to the railway station where they entered the grimy, dimly-lit entrance hall, put the panniers down on the floor by the booking office window, which was closed, and inspected the silent edifice for signs of life. Finding nothing and nobody, they opened the door marked *Station Master*, and walked in, to be met by a bright roaring fire in an old cast iron fireplace. They pulled up two buffets and sat down to get warm. There was a deathly silence over the room, except for the crackling of the fire and the hiss of the gas lamp, until Arthur broke the silence.

'Good heavens, it's Evans!'

'What is?'

'That is,' said Arthur, pointing to a half-smartly attired British Railways employee sat in a rickety armchair next to them in front of the fire.

'It's not!'

'It is, you know.'

'I thought it was a corpse waiting for the next train to Boot Hill.'

At this last exchange, Willie got up, bent over the figure reclining in the chair, and stared intently into the third face. The never-emotive face of Owen Evans, stationmaster, ticket salesman, ticket collector, porter, cleaner, gardener and general factotum of Grolsby Station, remained unmoved. Willie passed his hand slowly up and down in front of the impassive face.

'No sign of life. Told you it was a corpse.'

Suddenly Owen Evans moved, then opened his mouth. 'Noss Dahrr,' He didn't move again.

'What were that?' asked Arthur.

'Nay, search me, it sounded as if it were Chinese, or a pig in labour, or something.'

'Happen it's a Russian spy.'

'What would a Russian spy be doing in a place like this?'

'Waiting for a train?'

Owen Evans moved again, and spoke again.

'Look you, Willie Arkenthwaite, what is it you was wanting?'

'Hey, look Arthur, it's Owen the 'orrible and we've wakened him from his beautiful dreams.'

'I wasn't asleep.'

'You could have fooled me,' said Arthur. 'We were just going to run away with the day's takings.'

'It wouldn't have been worth your while, boyo, you can't get far on 3/4d.'

'You've taken 3/4d already today and it's only half past seven at night. British Railways won't half be paying a big dividend this year.'

'Now look you here, you two, what is it that you was wanting? I'm very busy and I haven't the time to waste on the likes of you.'

Willie looked at Arthur. 'Never, boyo, have I heard the Yorkshire mother tongue, look you, spoken with such a stupid accent.'

'Suit yourself. If you don't tell me what it is you was wanting, I shall shut up for the night, and that'll be that.'

'We've brought two baskets of pigeons.'

'Very kind of you, I'm sure, but I've had my tea already.'

'We've brought two baskets of pigeons to go to Bristol.'

'So why didn't you say so in the first place?'

'We did.'

'Well, you didn't. So, anyway, what are you two reprobates coming all the way on here, with a basket of pigeons each, to send them all the way to Bristol for?'

''Cos we've sold them to a racing man down there.'

'How come an intelligent man from Bristol, which incidentally is nearly part of Wales, has bought two baskets of pigeons from two loonies like you two? Mind you, now, thinking about it, his intelligence I suppose could be brought into doubt. However, I, being but a humble stationmaster, whose sole purpose in life is to despatch all human life and its effects to its chosen destination, have no right at all to question your purpose in sending these pigeons all the way to Bristol on a cold, cold night.'

He finished his speech and smiled at them in eager anticipation of a suitable reply.

Willie and Arthur stared at each other and then at Evans. Arthur was the first to speak.

'The reason we are sending them to Bristol is to keep you in a job for a while longer, to find something to do on a cold Tuesday night, and for the money.'

Owen Evans smiled again.

'You don't need the money, Willie Arkenthwaite. From what I hear, you're living very comfortably off your wife's mother and saving your wage every week, and as for you, Arthur Baxter, it's a well-known fact in the valleys that you're the richest working man around here for miles. Now, let's get on with the all-important job of paperwork for the pigeons, we wouldn't want them running all around the railway system in ever decreasing circles without paperwork, would we?'

Evans got up and walked over to a very old desk in front of the ticket window. Willie, having been dumbfounded for a few seconds, found his voice again.

'How do you know about my mother-in-law?'

'It's all over the village, boyo, it's a well-known fact that she gives you twenty pounds every week.'

'By gum, I wish she did.'

'You mean she doesn't?'

'Does she hell as like,' said Willie, then, thinking of the claim he had made in the canteen at lunchtime, 'well, not quite, anyway.'

'What about the coal?' asked Arthur.

'What about the coal?' replied Willie.

'What's this about what coal?' asked Evans.

'Come on, Willie, Evans wants to hear about how your mother-in-law buys all your coal.'

'Coal and twenty pounds a week, bach, there's a nice situation. Gosh, you must be rolling in it.'

'In what?'

'Money, you daft head. Wish I was a couple of hundreds behind you.'

Willie felt a slight discomfort at the back of his throat, so he had a good snook up, rolled the ball of phlegm around his mouth, walked over to the fire and spat out into the fire, before saying, 'It's not true, I'm skint.'

'You don't need to sell the pigeons, isn't it?'

'We bloody do need to sell the pigeons.'

Willie began to raise his voice just a little bit.

'Ah, well, never mind, have you got the address almost in Wales where the pigeons are going?'

Arthur produced a dirty crumpled piece of paper from his coat pocket, and Evans filled in the paperwork, forms for the pigeons' despatching thereof, and, at the same time, singing 'Land of my Fathers' in a rich baritone voice.

Meanwhile, he smiled to himself whilst stealing a few quick glances at Willie.

'Is the entertainment free, or will you be paying us to listen?' asked Willie.

'Free to you any time, boyo. Will you be paying cash or is it account?'

'Eh?'

'Two pounds six and threepence in money. Now!'

Arthur produced the money. Just then the bell rang to tell Evans that the Leeds train had left the neighbouring station and would arrive in four minutes.

'Best get the baskets on to the platform,' said Evans, reaching for his hat and coat which were hanging on a nail behind the office door. 'Come on, you two, when this one's gone it's locking-up time.'

They carried the two baskets on to the platform, waited for the train, loaded the baskets into the guard's van, and then, with a collection of 'Nohss Dahrrs', 'Bohra Dahrrs', and 'Good Neets', the two pals took their leave of Owen Evans and set out for the village.

They hadn't gone above a couple of strides when Evans shouted after them. 'Don't forget to remind me to charge you for your platform tickets when I see you again.'

⋆

The streets were deserted in the cold midwinter evening, and there was an air of calmness and serenity all around, broken only by the occasional loud belch from Willie.

'Crown and Anchor or t'Club?' asked Arthur.

'Oh, t'Club, ale'll be cheaper there.'

They turned into Albert Street, the main street of the village, and slowly caught up with a solitary figure heading for the Club. Arthur nudged Willie, who saw Arthur put his finger up to his lips to motion strict silence, and speed up to a cat burglar-type quick creep towards the back of the figure. Willie followed the action. As they arrived at the sauntering figure, their paths diverged so that they came alongside, one on each side. Arthur shouted, 'Now,' upon which they picked the man up by his arms and propelled him quickly forward for a few paces, before they tired and put him down again.

The man was too shocked to protest, too weary to bother, and too slow to know what it was all about anyway. Willie and Arthur stood before him, beaming.

'Evening, Eustace,' said Arthur.

'Evening, Useless,' said Willie.

Eustace had by now forgotten about the acute state of shock in which he had been.

'Hello, Willie, hello, Arthur. Are you going to the Club?'

'Yes, are you?'

'Yes. Where have you been?'

'With the pigeons to the station.'

'Have you? With the pigeons to the station? What for?'

'To send them to Bristol.'

'To Bristol? The pigeons? Have you? What for?'

''Cos we've sold 'em to somebody.'

'Have you? Sold 'em, to somebody in Bristol, what for?'

'Come on, Arthur, it's too cold to stand out here listening to him. Let's get off to the Club.'

'Why have you sold your pigeons to someone in Bristol, Willie?'

'Are you going to the Club, Eustace?'

'To the Club, er, yes, to the Club.'

'Come on, then.'

'With you, now?'

'Yes, now, come on, it's cold,' roared Arthur.

They walked along, encouraging Eustace to keep pace with them, and hadn't gone far when Arthur stopped and looked in the brightly-lit shop window of Harry Howard, whom the notice over the shop door pronounced *Licensed to Sell Intoxicating Liquor.*

'Join our Christmas club,' he read out aloud. 'Bit late, isn't it. Still, it's not a bad idea for next year, put a bit away with him each week ready for next Christmas, then at least we shall be able to afford some booze for the festive occasion, not like this year when we had a right dry do.'

Eustace came to life again.

'Would you? Join his Christmas club? Save some money with him? Not a bad idea!'

'Come on,' shouted Willie, 'let's get to the Club before we freeze to death.'

Another two hundred yards along the road and they entered the portals of the Grolsby Amalgamated Working Men's Club Affiliated. Inside, the bright light dazzled them for an instant, and the heat met them, taking their breath for a moment. They hung their flat caps, overcoats and scarves on the row of hooks which lined the cream walls of the mid-brown, lino-floored entrance hall, and made their way through the dark-stained door at the end of the hall into the main bar. The room was filled with men, some playing snooker at two tables, some playing darts, some dominoes, even cards, and others just sitting or standing drinking, smoking and talking. The room was sparsely but comfortably furnished, very warm, and a thick blue to yellowish-brown pall of smoke looked down from above on to the proceedings.

There was a chorus of 'Evening all' or 'Willie' or 'Eustace' or 'Arthur', and the three friends exchanged greetings with everyone in the room as they picked their way through the throng to the bar.

Arthur took great care not to lose Eustace, and as they got to the bar he said in a loud voice to no one in particular, 'What was it Dr Snodbury said in here last week after he'd just become a father again?'

'I know!' cried Eustace. 'It were "drinks are on me".'

'That's very generous of you,' laughed Willie. 'Mine's a pint of the best.'

'Me, too,' followed Arthur.

'Eh, what? You did that on purpose.'

'Did what?'

'Got me to say, "Drinks are on me".'

'By gum, you're generous tonight. Keep me one in, Harry, if Eustace's buying two rounds.'

'Nay, nay, I'm not. I'm only buying one round, you must think I'm daft.'

'You, daft,' said Willie, 'now what do you take us for? We wouldn't take advantage of you like that; we'll just have one round for now, and try another one later, sometime.'

'Oh, yes, right, er, er have you ordered, Arthur? What are you having?'

'A pint, please.'

Arthur held the pint he already had behind his back out of sight. Fat Harry, the Club steward, leaned over the bar and stared into Eustace's face.

'I wouldn't buy these two rogues a spoonful of arsenic, never mind a pint each – you must be mad.'

'I'm not. I'm not. I'm not mad at all. I'm normal, just like you lot. I'm not mad. I'm not.'

'All right, all right, go sit down and enjoy your drinks.'

Fat Harry could see Eustace working himself up to an epileptic fit, which he was prone to having when wound up to concert pitch, and not wishing to let an epileptic fit tarnish an otherwise very uneventful evening, Harry decided to quieten the proceedings. Willie and Arthur, being in the same mind as Fat Harry, took Eustace by the arms yet again, only much gentler this time, taking care not to spill his half of bitter, and were guiding him to a quiet table away from the bar, when Harry hauled his oversized beer-laden belly on to the top of the bar counter, leaned forward, and bellowed at Eustace, 'Hey, you haven't paid for these drinks.'

'Shut up, Harry, and put them on his slate,' Willie shouted back.

'His slate's full as is yours and Arthur's.'

'I haven't got one.'

'Exactly, it's so full it's never going to be opened again, so pay up now.'

'Later on, when we've had another round.'

'What do you mean, when we've had another round. You lot have never ever had another round. You make one last all night, don't you? So, come on, pay up now.'

'Hold your noise a bit, we'll see you right, later on.'

Fat Harry pulled his beer belly off the top of the bar and it sagged earthwards, turning part of the waistband of his trousers over in the process. He looked at the offending trio, sighed, and shook his head in the full knowledge that matters could only get worse before they got any better, as far as these three were concerned.

'Cold night tonight, isn't it? I say, isn't it cold tonight? It's warm in here though, warm isn't it? Lot of smoke about all over, smoke isn't there, lot of smoke?'

Willie broke wind loudly, as usual without apology.

'Glad he works in t'teazin hoil and not in t'dyehouse,' said Willie.

'Aye,' said Arthur. 'Couldn't do with that row all day long.'

'What row? What row, Arthur? I can't hear any row.'

Willie sat back in the hard wooden chair and reflected.

'You know, that idea of a Christmas club isn't so bad. We could do with having one at the mill, then we'd happen have a bit of brass to chuff on next Christmas.'

'You mean, have one of our own?' asked Arthur.

Eustace followed the words but not the gist of the conversation.

'Aye, we could have one at the mill. We'd only need someone to run it, to collect money and look after it, and share it out at Christmas. It's simple.'

'Well, seeing that you're so keen, you'd best start and get one organised. What do you say, Eustace?'

At the sound of his name, Eustace awoke from his usual trance-like state, just as if he'd been kissed by the handsome prince.

'What? What did you say, Arthur? What did you say?'

Arthur grimaced and thought bad thoughts about Eustace.

'A Christmas club at the mill, and Willie could run it. We ought to have one, didn't we?'

'Yes, yes, a Christmas club at t'mill and Willie could run it. We ought to have one, didn't we? Yes, a good idea. Yes, can I join Willie? Are you going to run it, Willie? Are you? Good idea, yes, yes, a good idea. Can I join? Can I?'

He looked at Willie with eager anticipation, as did Arthur.

Willie was still sitting back very relaxed and very reflective. For the first time in his life, someone had asked him to do something important, and he wasn't going to let the opportunity slip by without a good try.

'You're right, Arthur, I had better start and get it organised. How much a week each are you putting in?'

'Hey, it's a bit sudden you know, I'll have to consult Jess about it. I know I can't afford much, for I haven't any spare to start with. What about you, Eustace?'

'Er, me, Arthur, er, what about me, Arthur, what do you mean?'

'How much are you going to put into Willie's Christmas club?'

'Hang on, it's not just my Christmas club, it'll have to be for everyone at t'mill.'

'Aye, I know that. Anyway, what about it, Eustace, what are you going to put in?'

'Well, I've been thinking.'

'You what?'

Eustace managed a feeble grin.

'Well, I've been thinking, Willie, I have, I've been thinking I might put a pound a week in, just a pound, every week, a pound. How much will that be by Christmas, Arthur? If I pay every week, Arthur? How much do you think, I'll get? What do you think? Do you think I'll—?'

He was cut short by Willie.

'I can't reckon that up at this time of night without a paper and pencil; it's a big sum is that.'

He sat upright and began to make sniffing and snorting noises, snooking a ball of phlegm into the back of his throat, and then propelling it, accompanied by a series of noises to the front of his mouth, then spat it out to land neatly by his foot. He completed the move by grinding it with the sole of his shoe into the planked timber floor.

'Oy, you mucky pup,' roared Fat Harry who had been watching the stylish performance.

'Sorry, Harry. Are you going to join our Christmas club?'

'Your Christmas club, you must be joking. I wouldn't come within a thousand miles of anything you lot were organising. I'd lose every penny I put in, with you criminals in charge. It'd be like burning money,' and he turned away, roaring with laughter.

'I'll get him one day,' said Arthur. 'Anyway, have you lot supped up yet, it's getting on for my bedtime.'

'Is it, Arthur? Is it your bedtime already? Had we best go home now then? What time is it? What time do you go to bed, Arthur? Have I to finish my drink, Willie?'

Willie stood up and made for the door.

'Come on you lot, it's another day tomorrow.'

'Aye, you're right, we've got to get to the dyehouse by seven. Come on, Eustace.'

'Wait a minute, Arthur, I haven't finished my drink yet, Arthur. Are you going to wait a minute whilst I drink up? Are you?'

'For heaven's, shut up and get on with it.'

'Yes, Arthur, I shan't be a minute.'

Eustace guzzled the remains of his beer, almost choked, coughed until his face was the colour of a beetroot, then sat back gasping for air.

'Come on, Eustace.'

'Yes, Arthur,' he said, still gasping for air, 'I'm just coming, Arthur.'

He stood up, still gasping, puffing and panting.

'Just coming, Arthur. Are you ready, Willie?'

By this time he was more or less back to normal, and he made his way out of the Club with the others. Having reached the end of Gallipoli Avenue, where Eustace lived, the other two stopped.

'What have you stopped for, Willie, just here? What for?'

'So we can point you in the right direction for your house.'

'It's up here.'

'Aye, we know that.'

'Aye, well then, that's all right then, I'll go get to bed. Goodnight Willie, goodnight Arthur, I'll see you tomorrow at us work.'

'Not if we see you first,' Arthur muttered under his breath. 'He goes worse and worse.'

'Aye, dafter and dafter,' agreed Willie.

Soon they arrived at Cutside Cottages, and Willie turned into his home, leaving Arthur another three hundred yards to go to his cottage.

★

Inside Number 6, the fire was still glowing, and the children were all tucked up in bed, as was Mrs Woofenden. Only Thelma remained up, waiting for Willie.

'Shall I get your cocoa, love?'

'Yes, please.'

Thelma went into the back kitchen to get Willie's bedtime drink. Willie stood with his back to the fire, belched, farted, and finally snooked up a ball of phlegm, turned around and very purposefully spat the contents of his mouth as hard as he could into the fire. Up yours, Mrs Woofenden, he thought to himself, and then Thelma reappeared with his drink. They climbed the stairs arm in arm, taking the steaming hot mug of cocoa with them.

'What sort of an evening have you had, love? Did you get the pigeons to the station?'

'Aye, everything went off all right. Evans, the station master was his usual happy self, and we've spent the rest of the time at the Club with Eustace, so it can't be bad. They're talking about having a Christmas club at the mill.'

'Who are?'

'Oh, one or two of 'em.'

Willie lay awake, thinking how nice it might be to be the big boss of the Christmas club, and although he thought and thought about it, he got nowhere at all with it, and drifted into his usual deep, snoring, troubled sleep.

Chapter Two

At half past six the following morning, Ted Smith, the night boilerman and watchman at Murgatroyd's mill, performed one of the last chores of his nightly routine. It was to him the most pleasurable chore, and quite the hardest, for since the introduction of automatic coal stokers and chain grates into the huge Lancashire boilers that raised the steam for the dyeing and finishing processes, all the hard work had been taken out of his job.

This pleasure was to open the valve which let steam run high up the pipe to the roof of the engine house and blow the mill hooter. The high-pitched wailing sound that ran for thirty seconds, echoed up and down the valley, awakening every living thing within earshot. It was rumoured by those with a more vivid imagination that it also awoke some of the dead in their graves, but this point had never actually been proven.

Generally speaking, Ted Smith hated his job, not just this particular job but work of any type, so it gave him an immense feeling of power and satisfaction to be able to waken everyone in the neighbourhood whilst he was getting ready to go home to his bed.

The thirty seconds of hooter were almost over when Willie Arkenthwaite decided to open his eyes. It took a full five minutes for him to properly enter the land of the living, and to begin to make a move to get out of bed. Thelma and the kids were awake, as they always were, but they habitually stayed in bed until Willie had left for work, because he usually wasn't fit to talk to first thing in the morning, and his personal toilet habits defied description.

The pyjama jacket was removed to reveal an open-necked loose-collared white winceyette shirt with delicate pale red vertical stripes. The pyjama trousers were removed to reveal a pair of almost white long johns. These long johns were then covered by Willie's best pair of light grey working trousers, made from a fent he had got from the mill and which Thelma had sewn up for him. The braces were left dangling at the back until such time as Willie had performed his ablutions. To complete the scene, a pair of dirty well-worn slippers were put on to the feet and Willie, hands in pockets, plodded his way down to the warmth of the living room.

The first job for Willie each morning was to rake out the glowing embers of the fire in the range, take out the hot ashes to the dustbin and stoke up the fire again. Willie enjoyed using the poker on the hot fire to rake out the ashes, for at every thrust and parry he muttered 'Woofenden', visualising driving a stake through the old lady's heart. Needless to say, this was the best-poked fire in Grolsby, and it did him good to take it out on the old lady in this way. Having cleaned out the fire, he fetched a huge shovelful of coal, put it on the glowing embers and moved the kettle on to the grid to boil.

Soon, he was to take the kettle into the back kitchen where he poured the warm water into an enamel bowl in the sink, and, using a long since cracked mirror hanging on a nail over the sink, he proceeded to lather up his shaving brush and to cover his face in the creamy carbolic froth. Then with a quick rub on the leather strap hanging on the back door with his shiny cut-throat razor, he deftly shaved off the stubble from his face. Packing up breakfast to eat at the mill was the next job. The kettle was back on the hob boiling merrily away, and he brewed a pint of tea whilst contemplating the contents of his breakfast pack. Finally, he settled for a buttered currant teacake with a sliced banana within. Having carefully constructed the sandwich, he dropped it from an indiscriminate height into his tin lunch box.

The next, and equally important, operation was to tear a sheet of newspaper into three equal pieces, put two heaped teaspoons of sugar into the middle of each piece, a heaped teaspoon of tea leaves on to the sugar in two of them, and then a similar quantity of coffee grounds into the third one. The three mashings, representing tea for breakfast, coffee for elevenses and tea for mid-afternoon, were then wrapped into neat little parcels and placed carefully into the lunch box. Finally, a medicine bottle, which at some time had held a strong laxative, was filled with milk, and the day's refreshments were packed. The laxative bottle had been a source of constant amusement at the mill for many months past.

Having no pigeons to which to attend, Willie sat back in Mrs Woofenden's chair to drink his pint of tea. Usually it went with him outside, but this morning and until they restocked the pigeons it would have to stop inside with him. The warm liquid quickly loosened the overnight collection of phlegm and it wasn't long before Willie was able to snook up, gather a nice big ball of phlegm in his mouth and spit it into the fire, to be followed by a loud belch and an even louder fart.

Finishing his tea, Willie climbed the stairs to the bathroom, completed his morning toilet and returned downstairs. His clogs were on the hearth keeping warm where they had been all night, and they felt very cosy and warm as he put them on. He took his coat and hat from the hook at the back of the front door, wrapped his red striped scarf around his neck and, picking up his lunch box, he left the house just as the second, five to seven, hooter sounded announcing five minutes to starting time. Ted Smith, attired in cap and coat, really enjoyed operating the five to seven hooter, as this was his home time, and the second he let go of the lever which controlled the hooter, he was away.

The biting north wind blowing straight against the front of Cutside Cottages caught Willie's breath as he left the warmth of his front room. There had been a very heavy frost during the night, the canal was beginning to ice over in small patches, and his clogs made a crisp, fresh, crunching sound as he walked on the frozen puddles of the towpath. As he exhaled, steamy breath disappeared just as quickly as it had appeared, and the frozen air made him cough. The barge from St Helens, into which he and Arthur had peered the night before, chugged slowly by. The bargee, with steaming mug of coffee carefully balanced at his side, gave Willie a cheery wave and Willie waved back. The lady of the barge was nowhere in sight and Willie correctly assumed that she had stayed below in the small cabin where it would be quite cosy and warm.

*

Ted Smith, the nightwatchman, came towards Willie and they met as usual at Coopers Bridge, a by now disused cobbled turnpike bridge of many years ago.

'Morning, Ted.'

'Morning, Willie. Brass monkey weather.'

'Aye, and bloody cold to go with it.'

Ted stared at Willie, not appreciating his little joke.

'Have you left t'mill in one piece, then?'

'Yes, as usual, everything's as usual, absolutely fed up with this boiler house routine, it's too hard a job for a man of my age – going to find a lighter job.'

'But you've got a light job now.'

'Nowt of the sort, it's ruddy hard work.'

'Aye, it must be, sleeping and getting paid for it.'

They were beginning to have to shout now, for they hadn't stopped walking and were getting far apart from each other.

'I'll have you know I don't sleep at my work.'

'You're a liar.'

Willie looked around at Arthur who had shouted the last few words from behind him. He then turned around and caught Arthur up. Ted shouted yet another reply, but the two friends were not listening to him.

'A right miserable sod is that one, carries one half of the world's problems on his shoulders – and he does sleep at the mill,' said Arthur.

'Do you know,' said Willie, 'if I were as miserable as what he is, I'd jump in the canal. He has a bed behind the mill boiler, but it's covered over with old sacks during the day and it just looks like a dirty old pile of muck that hasn't been moved for years. One of these days Anthony Murgatroyd is going to have that area cleaned out, and then the balloon'll go up.'

'Not before time. He's due for his come-uppance and the sooner the better.'

'By gum, but it's cold this morning,' said Willie. 'I think we ought to run to the mill to get us selves warm.'

'You run and I'll watch you. I'm quite prepared to freeze and get warm at the mill when I get there.'

'Nay, it's always cold in yond dyehouse, it's not possible to get warm.'

'Aye, ah know, but it'll be warmer than what it is here.'

They hurried along to the mill and clocked in at the penny hoil door dead on the dot of seven o'clock. They made their way to the dyehouse and exchanged coats and caps for the dyers' traditional thick leather waterproof aprons which they both wore and which were provided by the mill as part of their uniform.

The first round in the dyehouse was always running by ten past seven. Willie and Arthur pushed in a cart of heavy, wet woollen pieces, and threw the first end of the top piece over the top of the huge wooden dye winch. They pulled the lever at the side of the machine. This moved the wide leather driving belt from the loose pulley to the fast pulley, which in turn drove the winch and pulled the heavy piece into the big timber vat sunk into the floor below them. They made sure that the head-end of the piece was laid over the front edge of the vat, and when the whole of the piece was in they caught the tail-end and laid it together with the leading end. They repeated the operation six times, then sewed each leading end to its respective tail-end so as to create six continuous loops of fabric over the winch and into the vat. Having completed the first machine they shouted for the dyer, and moved on to the other five machines they looked after, and fed them with cloth in the same way.

The dyer, a man of some importance in the mill, distinguished from his labourers by the fact that he wore a khaki smock, emerged from his office on hearing Willie's shout. He had a bucket of carefully mixed dye powder and he put it down in front of the first machine. The dyehouse foreman then came along, opened the cold water inlet valve from which he filled the vat, submerged the cloth, and turned on the steam to boil the water. He put the bucket of dye powder under the cold water tap and half-filled it, then transferred it to beneath an open-ended steam pipe to boil up the dye before he poured the boiling colour into the vat. He set the winch in motion with the control lever, leaving the coloured liquid to penetrate the cloth as it boiled. The bucket was returned to the dyer's office to be refilled with dye powder. The dyer was, in the meantime, mixing more powders to carefully prepared recipes for the next machine. And so the daily routine of the dyehouse moved into full momentum.

There were eleven dyeing machines in the room, six on one side and five on the other. At one end of the room, Willie and Arthur looked after three machines on each side, keeping them filled with cloth and emptied when the pieces were dyed. Dick and Lewis looked after the five at the other end; there should have been six but one had been removed in order to facilitate preparations for one of the newfangled, all stainless steel machines with its own electric motor, due to arrive the next day.

Once all the machines were filled and running, breakfast was taken by the dyehouse staff. They sat around an old wooden table in the corner of the room, from where they could keep half an eye on the running of the machines. Willie, as part of his daily routine, had to scald six pints of tea or coffee. This onerous duty entailed collecting the newspaper-wrapped mashings from his workmates, taking six pint pots in a narrow wooden tray with a full-length handle across the yard to the steam-heated water geyser in the entrance to the big mill, and scalding the six pints. On his return to the dyehouse he put five pints on the table and took the sixth one into the dyer's office for the dyer, who through his own self-importance always dined alone.

Willie sat down with the rest of the staff, opened up his sandwich box and extricated the currant teacake with banana. Walter Smith, the foreman dyer, stared at Willie's breakfast.

'Your Thelma stayed in bed again this morning, has she?'

'What does tha mean?'

'Well, just look at that currant teacake. No woman alive would plaster a currant teacake with so much margarine.'

'It's best butter.'

'Never in this world. If that's best butter I'm the Emperor of China, and I'm not, so it isn't.'

Willie being quite used to this kind of ribbing took no offence at the matter and began to trough by dipping the teacake into the pint of tea, having the obvious effect of making the teacake soggy, but also leaving a considerable quantity of margarine to float and melt into yellow globules in the tea. He then noisily sucked the soggy end of the teacake, and prepared to repeat the exercise.

Lewis Armitage, one of the other four around the table and eating a far more conventional jam sandwich, asked, through a very full mouth, 'Have you ever seen a more disgusting sight than that?'

Willie grinned. 'Hey, these teacakes are grand. You should make yourself one, Lewis.'

'No thanks, I'd rather die of starvation. It'd make me puke up eating that.'

'Well, it's not going to make me puke,' said Willie.

Arthur, who had been quietly eating his bread and dripping, said, 'Willie and me passed Ted Smith again as usual this morning. He's getting worse touchy about sleeping behind the boiler during the night.'

Dick Jordan, the fourth member of the dyehouse labouring team, said, 'You know it's right, he sleeps all night here, wakes up in time to get steam up, then blow the mill buzzer, then has his breakfast, waits until Walter Holroyd comes to take over for the day shift, then goes home, waits until his wife goes off to t'co-op, where as we all know she works, then goes and beds down with Walter Holroyd's wife for a few hours, getting back home before his wife comes back from t'co-op. Mind you, he has to ruffle up the bed sheets to make it look as if he's slept all day at home, and it's rumoured that on more than one occasion, his missus has been a bit suspicious about the state of the bed, but he's had a lucky run so far.'

Willie belched out loud without any attempt either to conceal it or to excuse himself, then dipped what remained of the teacake into the tea, sucked out the juices, ate the remains, drank the rest of his tea, and to round off a good breakfast, stuck his finger up his nostril, removed a rather large piece of green slimy snot and ate it with great enjoyment.

'You know he nearly didn't get away with it a fortnight since,' said Lewis.

'How do you mean?'

'Well, his missus had forgot summat and when she were halfway to t'co-op she bethought her about it and went back home to get it, only to find Ted as throng as hell, washing, shaving and generally sprucing himself up. "What are you getting yourself all donned up for?" she asks. Of course, Ted can be a quick thinker when the need arises, so he says, "I were just going off somewhere." So she says, "Somewhere like where?" "It's a secret." "What sort of secret?" she asks. "Well, it's a secret, and I can't tell you if it's a secret, can I?" Anyway, like all good women she wheedles it out of him eventually that he's going off to look for a surprise birthday present for her, and she believes him and goes back off to her work, leaving him to visit Margery Holroyd.'

'So, what's he going to do about this here surprise birthday present then?' asked Dick Jordan.

'Well, I don't rightly know what he's going to do, and neither does he, except he knows he's going to have to get her something good, and he also knows he can't afford to get her owt at all.'

'No, that's a problem we have at birthdays and Christmas,' Dick thought out aloud.

'Aye, well, Willie has a solution for that problem,' said Arthur.

'What's that then, Willie?'

'It's nowt much.'

'Come on then, let's know what it is you have in mind.'

Willie snooked up, turned his head and spat a ball of phlegm into a nearby drain.

'Well, it's like this. Arthur and me and Eustace were talking last night and were saying as how as we ought to have a Christmas club.'

'Not useless Eustace from t'teazin hoil?' asked Walter Smith.

'The very same.'

'Well, if he's having owt to do with it, count me out from the start.'

'He's not having owt to do with it. Anyway, we were thinking we ought to have this here club for anybody that wants to join it from t'mill. So we could each put a bit away each week then pay it back out at Christmas.'

'Bloody good idea,' said Lewis. 'Count me in. How are you going to organise it, Willie?'

'Nay, it were only an idea like, I'm not going to organise it.'

'Why not, you ought to, didn't he lads, it was your idea.'

The other three nodded their assent.

'Well, that's settled then,' said Lewis. 'Tell you what, I'll help you a bit, Willie.'

'Now hang on a minute, lads, it were nobbut an idea. Somebody else ought to do it, somebody what understands it.'

'Now look, Willie,' said Arthur, 'it was your idea and you ought to do it – we'll all give you a helping hand with it.'

Willie was no longer listening to Arthur. He was having visions of grandeur as the head of a large club, with people putting vast amounts of money in his hand, and he putting it in his pocket. He was brought back to reality by Arthur tapping his arm.

'Er, er, what, Arthur?'

'I was just saying we should ought to have a meeting in the canteen at dinner time.'

'Aye, well, happen we did, and there again, happen we didn't.'

'Getting cold feet already, are you?' enquired Lewis.

'No, I am not, it's just that doesn't tha think we should think about it a bit first?'

'Nay, there's no time like the present, so let's get on with it. I'll make a notice to pin on t'canteen door, then all them what's there can join in and you can give a speech, Willie.'

'Not on your Nellie.'

'You'll have to.'

'Why me?'

'Because you are the secretary of Murgatroyd's Christmas club,' said Dick, with the satisfied grin of a Cheshire cat.

'Since when?' enquired Willie.

'Since just now,' said Dick, and Willie looking around his workmates, realised there was no future in protesting.

Arthur left the assembled throng sitting at the table, and went into the dyer's office, where Seth Whitehead, the dyer, was enjoying his breakfast in peace. He looked at Arthur, just like a man who didn't want to be disturbed.

'What the hell do you want?'

'I want to borrow a big piece of paper and a pencil.'

'What for?'

'To write out a notice about us new Christmas club.'

'What new Christmas club?'

He began to take notice of the question.

'The one that Willie's running.'

'I didn't know nothing about no Christmas club.'

'Neither did Willie until two minutes ago. Have you got a big piece of paper and a pencil what I can borrow?'

'You can use back of one of them old daily piece record sheets there.'

He pointed to a pile of old sheets of paper that he had indiscriminately thrown into the corner over a period of years so that they had come to form an abstract heap which any modern-thinking art gallery would have been pleased to exhibit.

'Can I borrow your pencil as well?'

'You'll want me to write the bloody thing for you next.'

'You can if you want.'

'Bugger off out of it,' he shouted as Arthur moved out of the office, paper and pencil in hand, and then by way of an afterthought, 'And be sharp about it, it's almost time to start work again.'

Seth carefully put his foot behind the office door, and it swung to as if it were not going to stop at the frame, sat down again and shut his eyes, well content with the few minutes of pleasantries he had exchanged with a member of his staff.

Arthur sat down again with the others and began to write:

MURGATROYD'S CHRISTMAS CLUB

SECRETARY WILLIE ARKENTHWAITE

FIRST MEETING TODAY

MILL CANTEEN

QUARTER PAST TWELVE

Willie continued to protest but the others just told him to shut up, and Arthur nipped across the yard, up one flight of stairs to the canteen which stood over the wool warehouse, where he pinned the notice on the door so that all attending diners would see it.

Chapter Three

As the morning ambled along, Willie's thoughts turned more and more often to the Christmas club. Usually he didn't have any thoughts worth speaking of, but this day was different. Each time he turned his attention to the club the first thought was of a huge table laden with all the trimmings of a Christmas dinner surrounding a giant turkey and a rather large Christmas pudding sitting side by side in the middle. These two main items were so big that he couldn't see across the table to Mrs Woofenden who was seated behind them. He could, however, see Thelma and all the kids well attired, all dressed up with party hats, boxes of crackers ready to pull, streamers, decorations, holly and mistletoe, presents by the score, and everything that they had never been able to have on Christmas day before.

Following the best part of the vision, he then began to think about such things as when he would collect the money. How would he make a record of the money received? Where would he keep the money? When would he pay it out? How would he know how much to pay out and to whom? All these and a thousand other questions went unanswered.

Dinner time came and Willie, as was his normal habit on hearing the midday hooter, dashed across the yard and ran up the canteen steps to be first in the queue. He never washed his hands at dinner time, as this would make him miss his first place in the queue, a position he had held for many years with only the very occasional loss, and one which he wasn't going to give up lightly. In order to make sure of the front position he didn't even remove the thick leather dyer's apron, but dived out of the dyehouse like a hare in front of the hounds.

His iron-soled clogs made a hollow ringing sound on the stone steps, and sure enough he was first once again, and able to read proudly the notice calling the meeting, which was pinned on the door outside the canteen. He was so engrossed in reading the notice that he was unaware that Sarah Anne Green, who was almost always second in the queue, and upwards of two hundred other people were queuing behind him, and it was only when one of the more impatient weavers dug his finger into Willie's ribcage that he awoke with a start from his dream-like trance.

'Come on, Willie, what's up with yer?' they were shouting from below.

'All right, all right, hang on a minute,' and he still admired the notice.

Sarah Anne Green whispered in his ear, 'Take it down and pin it up again in t'canteen, else it'll get hidden at the back of the door and that'll be the last you'll see of it.'

In the midst of the catcalls, boos and shouts, Willie carefully took out the drawing pins. With the notice in hand, he opened the canteen door, and was propelled forward by the seething human tide to the servery hatch.

Greasy Martha never opened the hatch until such time as the hungry mob made so much noise with banging and shouting that she was forced to do so. Her motto was 'let 'em wait', and in true tradition the hatch was closed when the disorderly queue presented itself to be served. Sarah Anne Green showed Willie where to pin the notice for greatest effect – on a flat part of the dividing partition between the cooking and eating areas, near the serving hatch.

'Aye, a good spot that, Sarah Anne,' and as he went through the motions of pinning it up he asked, 'Are you going to join the Christmas club then?'

'I don't know, I can only afford half a crown a week at most. I'll have to see, I'll think about it whilst I have my dinner.'

★

'What the bloody hell's that then? And whatever it is you can just take it down again right now.'

Willie and Sarah Anne had been so engrossed in conversation that they had not noticed the hatch open and Greasy Martha look out at them.

'Nay, Martha love, it's about the meeting here after us dinner. It's about us new Christmas club and we're having a meeting here to sort out the job a bit like.'

'Well, first of all Willie Arkenthwaite, we'll have a bit less of Martha love, and secondly, you can take it off there here and now.'

'Nay, aren't you going to join?'

'What! Me! Join owt you lot have ought to do with? Nay, credit me with some sense if you please.'

She snuffled, snorted and grunted to herself, making Willie, not for the first time, have visions of her and a lot more, round, pink-bodied, short-legged, curly-tailed animals in a sty together, with their trotters in a trough, lunching.

Her rasping voice awakened him from his dreams.

'What about this dinner? Do you want it or not? And get that poster off my wall.'

Willie picked up his dinner and moved away a few paces, turning to Martha. 'I'll shift it when I've had my dinner, Martha love.'

'I've told you before I'm not your love,' but Willie was out of earshot on his way to the corner table.

Sarah Anne always sat with her cronies on the next table to Willie, and when she arrived with her dinner he was tucking into his like there was no tomorrow.

'You'll have to move that there notice, Willie.'

'Nay, Sarah Anne, I shan't, just you wait and see,' and he turned his attention to the more pressing matter of devouring his dinner. His eating habits were no better when out than they were at home. He noisily guzzled what had loosely been described as beef stew with boiled potatoes and carrots, and by the time Lewis Armitage arrived, he was just in the act of picking up his plate and drinking the gravy from it, before licking it clean.

'Martha's playing hell about yond notice,' observed Lewis.

'Take no notice of the old bag. What's for pudding?' he replied in one breath.

'Manchester tart.'

'Eh, great, one of my favourites; ah'd best get into t'queue.'

Away he trotted to join the end of the by now diminishing queue where he came upon his old friend Eustace, who was as usual last in line for first course.

'Hello, Willie, what's that notice by the serving hatch? What's for dinner? Are you playing cards after dinner?'

'Which question shall I answer first?'

'Eh?'

'Which question shall I – oh, never mind. That notice is about the new Christmas club. We're having a meeting here after dinner.'

'A meeting, are we Willie? A meeting? What for? What about? Are you going to stand up and say summat, Willie?'

A sudden horrible thought hit Willie like being smashed with a sledge hammer, and then acute panic set in. 'A speech! A speech! I couldn't make a speech! What about? It's all Arthur's fault. Nay, I can't make a speech. Not in public.' He was awakened from his state of panic by the mellow tones of Eustace once again.

'What are you going to say, Willie? Can I join Willie? Can I?'

Before Willie had time to answer they had arrived at the serving hatch and Eustace took his dinner. Willie gave Martha a nice smile.

'Now, Martha my dear, what's for sweet to-day?'

'You don't deserve no sweet, sticking notices up on my wall.'

'Come on, fair does, it's only till after dinner, and then we're having a meeting here, then it can come down again.'

'Who says you're having a meeting here? I've got to wash up and clear up and clean up. You're delaying me and it's not good enough. I'm overworked now without any monkey business from you lot."

'Aren't you going to put anything into this Christmas club then, Martha? It'll be a proper do you know, not a twopenny halfpenny affair.'

'It might not be a right bad idea you know. That's if it is all above board. I'll think about it and see what happens at meeting.'

'Well, whilst you're thinking about it, just cut us an extra big slice of that Manchester tart. I aren't half hungry.'

'Was there ever a time when you weren't, and anyway, what makes you think you can have a bigger slice than anyone else?'

'I've a lot to do, sorting out this here Christmas club, and I need all the strength I can get, besides which I always do.'

Martha, grunting and grumbling, cut Willie an extra large slice of tart and put it on a meat plate for him. Dick Jordan put down his knife and fork and sat back, absolutely amazed at the spectacle before him. There was Willie with the biggest piece of Manchester tart he had ever seen, holding it up to his mouth, fingers in the cold custard and jam, thumbs supporting the pastry base from beneath, taking big bites without putting it down or having time to enjoy one mouthful before the next. As if this wasn't enough, the piece of tart suddenly collapsed into one thousand bits and cascaded all over the table, the diners and the floor.

'Bloody hell,' said Willie.

'You nasty, horrible little bugger,' said Dick. 'You must have left your manners in your mother's womb.'

Arthur Baxter was laughing uncontrollably and was in imminent danger of spitting out his mouthful of stew as he watched Willie collect bits of Manchester tart from other people's dinners, from the table and from the floor, to assemble them on his own plate, where he dived in again with fingers and thumbs.

'Why don't you use a spoon?'

'What for?'

'To bloody well eat your pudding.'

'Nay, it's just as easy with me fingers,' and with that he continued to guzzle his pudding.

Whilst the others were getting and eating their pudding, Willie was doing just that to his pint of tea which he slopped on the floor on his way back to the table. Having arrived there he slurped as loudly as he could, much to the disgust of those around him – they should have been used to it but never quite were. Having emptied and replaced the pint pot on the table, Willie proceeded to get out the playing cards from the window ledge where they resided when not in use.

'Hang on a minute, Willie, we've no time for cards this dinner time,' said Arthur.

'Why not, Arthur?'

'Because,' then he pleaded, 'Give me strength!' Then, 'Because we're having the opening meeting of this here Christmas club, aren't we?'

'Oh, aye,' replied Willie, replacing the cards on the window ledge.

'Right, let's get on with it then.'

'Wait till I've finished my dinner. I shan't be a minute now, and then we'll have a bit of a go.'

When he was ready, Arthur stood up, looked around at the assembled diners and banged his pudding spoon hard on the table to get everyone's attention.

There was a spontaneous show of quietness by all assembled except Greasy Martha, who called out, 'Oy, watch what you're doing with my spoon.'

She was howled down by the rest of the crowd, and the silence returned as the attention of all turned back to Arthur.

'Er, ladies and gentlemen, er, friends, er, we, er, that is to say, Willie Arkenthwaite has proposed—'

He got no further.

'We hope you'll be very happy.'

'Who to?'

'He's already got one wife, a mother-in-law and a horde of kids.'

Arthur waited for the audience to settle and began again. 'Ladies and gentlemen, Willie Arkenthwaite has suggested—'

He was stopped again.

'Nay! Shame!'

'The dirty old bugger.'

'I'm never going near him again.'

Once again the uproar subsided and Arthur continued.

'That we, er, should have a, er, Christmas club. The lads in the, er, dyehouse think that it's happen a good idea, and, er, so, er, I give you Willie Arkenthwaite.'

A lone voice shouted, 'And we give him straight back again.'

Arthur sat down to thunderous applause. He looked at Willie who studiously avoided his glance, but Dick Jordan was already pushing Willie to try to get him to stand up.

Willie refused to move. He sat stiffly, holding the edge of the table, and just wouldn't budge. The combined persuasive powers of Arthur, Dick and Lewis failed to shift him – they pleaded, cajoled and threatened, all to no avail. Sarah Anne Green came over and tried to reason with him, without success. Eustace had a try but gave it up before he started properly, then Arthur had a brilliant idea. He walked around the back of Willie and pulled his chair from under him, taking the chair a safe distance away.

Willie came down to earth with a bump and lay flat out on the floor, much to the amusement of the audience who responded to this fine bit of acting with another round of applause. He then picked himself up and turned to face the crowd. Carefully, he removed a dewdrop from the end of his nose by wiping it on his shirt sleeve, then belched out loudly yet again, to the amusement of the assembled crowd.

Having taken a deep breath he began to speak. 'Ladies and gentlemen...'

He stopped as he didn't know where to go from there. There were boos and catcalls at the delay, and even applause from one corner, and then finally he started again.

'Arthur says we want a Christmas club.'

'Nay, it were your idea, not mine,' shouted Arthur.

'Well, happen it were,' retorted Willie who secretly liked to accept the thanks for putting up the idea in the first place. 'Well, me and Arthur were talking last night and we thought we needed a Christmas club for all of us here at t'mill so as we shan't be short next Christmas same as what we were this Christmas, so me and Arthur mentioned it to t'lads in't dyehouse this morning and they thought it were a good idea too.'

He stopped to come up for air and because he had dried up, but not for long.

'It's come on us a bit sudden like, and none of us has any idea how to go on so if any of you lot knows, let's be hearing from you.'

He sat down to tumultuous applause, as pleased as punch with himself. When the applause had died down and Arthur had finished congratulating him, there was a long pregnant pause, following which there were quiet moans and groans from the crowd of diners as Daniel Sykes rose to his feet. Daniel was a tall, thin, intellectual type of chap who was a foreman weaver and a well-known pain in the backside. Arthur had been known on several occasions over the years to remark that Daniel should have had a first class honours degree in boring people. Daniel began to speak.

'It appears obvious to me that we should elect a steering committee to administer the affairs of the Christmas club – even set up a trust in order that the full value of any tax advantage to be gained from such a move can be obtained to our benefit.'

At which point he sat down and everyone stared in his direction.

'We aren't having him on t'committee,' Arthur hurriedly pointed out to Willie.

'No, he can have his own club,' said Lewis.

'Hold on a minute though, he might have a point and know summat we don't,' said Dick.

'Well, I think we ought to elect a committee, then ask Mr Anthony Murgatroyd what to do next – he's bound to know,' Willie replied thoughtfully.

'You're excelling yourself today, Willie,' said Lewis.

'Aye, it's that Manchester tart, I could just eat another big slice. Do you think there might be one? I think I'll go and see.'

'Sit down and stay here,' said Dick. 'This is serious stuff we're at.'

Nothing much at all happened next. The four people at the centre of the discussion stared at each other, and the rest chatted amongst themselves. Eventually, after what seemed to Willie to be a lifetime, Sarah Anne Green stood up, banged her pudding spoon on the table and bellowed for silence.

'By look of things, these men are a bit lost as usual with something a bit more complicated than normal, so I think we ought to take a vote to see if we want or even need a Christmas club.'

She was rudely interrupted as Willie sprang to his feet.

'Yes, yes, that's it, let's have a vote to see if we want a Christmas club. Now then, all those in favour raise—'

'Hang on a minute, Willie Arkenthwaite, shut your blathering and sit down. You wouldn't have known ought about having a vote if I hadn't suggested it, so I'll carry on with it. All those in favour?'

There were a very limited few who didn't vote.

'All those against?'

Only Greasy Martha put up her hand. There were boos and catcalls, but she loved them all and rose to the occasion with a series of well-aimed gestures.

'Well, it looks as if we've got ourselves a Christmas club, or the beginning of one at least. Now I'll hand you back to your master of ceremonies, Mr Arthur Baxter.'

Sarah Anne sat down to wild applause. Arthur slowly rose to his feet.

'Er, I would like to thank Sarah Anne Green for her, er, very valuable, er, contribution to the, er, er, proceedings. Now, er, it looks as if we shall have to elect a committee, and I, er, suggest that, er, Sarah Anne Green becomes, er, chairman.'

There were murmurs of approval from around the room, except from Willie who began to see his chance of stardom slipping away from his grasp, so he tugged Arthur's sleeve.

'What about me, Arthur?'

'Oh, you can be treasurer, yes treasurer, that's the most important job of all.'

'Treasurer, eh, oh yes, treasurer,' and a smile lit his face from corner to corner.

Arthur continued. 'Now, we should, er, take a vote on chairman, er, Sarah Anne Green, but first we should, er, ask her, er, are you, er, willing?'

'Course she's willing,' came a shout from the crowd.

'Er, er, are you willing to become the chairman of Murgatroyd's Christmas club for the next twelve months?'

Sarah Anne stood up. 'Yes, Mr Baxter, I am willing to become chairman for the next twelve months.'

'Mr Baxter? Who the hell's Mr Baxter?' came a shout from the crowd, which was ignored by the dignitaries.

'Now, er, ladies and gentlemen, er, can we have a, er, vote for Sarah Anne Green as chairman, er, those in, er, favour?'

Almost all hands were raised.

'Er, er, those against?'

There were no votes against.

'Er, right, Sarah Anne Green is elected, er, chairman. Er, come over here lass, tha'd best take charge now, come over here.'

Sarah Anne walked over slowly. She was a small woman with a grim determination, and with anything she did, she worked hard at it. She had had little thought as she had read the notice at the top of the canteen steps that she could possibly be actively involved in the Christmas club, and had as yet not come to terms with what was happening. However, she put on a brave face and looked at the audience. She paused for a few moments, then began.

'Ladies and gentlemen, I would like to thank you for the confidence you have expressed in me, in electing me to be your chairman. I shall do my best to ensure that the club runs smoothly and that we do the best for all of you that invest your money with us. Now, in common with all other clubs, we need to elect a number of officials, namely secretary, treasurer and a committee. It would seem to be appropriate that Arthur Baxter and Willie Arkenthwaite should be involved as it was their idea in the first place. Lewis Armitage and Dick Jordan should I think be elected to the committee as they have been involved from the beginning, and probably two others from amongst you, which would give us a good strong committee to sort out the club during the year.' At this point, she sat down.

Arthur leaned over to Sarah Anne. 'I say, Willie wants to be treasurer and I'll be secretary if that's all right with you.'

'It's all right with me as far as you are concerned, but I'm not so sure about Willie. Let's see what the rest of them say.'

She rose to face her audience again. 'Arthur Baxter has kindly volunteered to act as secretary, and Willie Arkenthwaite as treasurer. Now can we please take a vote on these two very important positions, firstly for Arthur Baxter as secretary.'

She watched a total show of hands.

'Thank you, that was unanimous. Now for Willie Arkenthwaite as treasurer.'

At this point the number of hands that were raised did not constitute a majority.

Come on now, friends, it was Willie's idea, after all.'

More hands were raised than for the first vote.

'Those against?'

Greasy Martha's hand went up once more, but that was all.

'Motion carried, Arthur Baxter is elected secretary, and Willie Arkenthwaite is elected treasurer.'

She sat down and leaned over to whisper to Arthur.

'What about Willie? Is he to be trusted to keep the books in order? He's not dishonest, I do know that, but when it comes to his ability to keep the books in order, well, quite frankly it worries me.'

'It worries me, lass, as well. We shall just have to keep our eyes on him, that's all.'

'Right, we'd best get the election of the committee over and done with whilst there's still time, then we can get down to sorting out the details.'

She stood up again.

'Ladies and gentlemen, we now would like to elect four committee members. As I said earlier, Dick Jordan and Lewis Armitage are willing to offer their services, and therefore I would like you now to vote for them. Those for?'

She watched as ninety-nine per cent of the hands went up.

'Good, the motion is carried, now we need two more. Any nominations?'

Daniel Sykes stood up once more and addressed the gathering. 'In my opinion, for what my opinion is worth around here—'

'Here, here,' came an interruption.

Daniel frowned in the direction of the lone voice. 'As I was saying before I was so rudely interrupted, in my opinion, this committee needs someone to join it with a knowledge of how business matters are carried out, and one whose voice can carry some weight in various circles as and when it might be needed—'

He was interrupted yet again by the same lone voice shouting, 'Does tha mean somebody what's a bit top-heavy upstairs like?'

Daniel rose to the challenge. 'If you mean someone with a good business brain, then yes I do, and, furthermore, I have much pleasure in offering myself for election as I am sure I can be of real value to this committee.'

'There's nowt like a bit of cheek,' Willie observed to Arthur. 'What are we going to do now?'

'Nay, I don't know, except fix everything before the meetings so that he's bugger all to do with it when we do have a meeting, and not have so many meetings either. What do you say, Sarah Anne?'

'It will be very difficult with him, but we can't just ignore him. Let's get a vote taken.'

She rose again.

'Right. Ladies and gentlemen, Daniel Sykes has put his own name forward for election. Can we please take a vote. Those in favour?'

There was a mixed reception.

'Those against?'

Yet again a show of hands.

'I think we'd best have a count – it looks pretty even to me.'

So they took a count, with Arthur as secretary counting, and he produced a majority of five votes in favour.

Daniel stood up again. 'I would just like to express my thanks to you all for the confidence you have shown in me, and I will serve you all to the best of my ability.'

He sat down again.

Willie groaned. 'We're for it now with him on t'committee, it should have been five votes t'other way,' and he sat back, happily picking his nose and eating the contents.

Sarah Anne whispered to Arthur, 'Now, there's just one more to elect. Who shall it be do you think?'

'Well, I know he's a bit daft but I should have thought that Eustace Ollerenshaw would do as he was told, without question.'

'Let's see if there are any volunteers first,' said Sarah Anne, and she rose yet again.

'Now, we need just one more committee member. Have we any volunteers?'

She carefully scanned the blank disinterested faces in front of her, then leaned over to Arthur.

'Well, shall we ask Eustace?'

Arthur consulted Willie, who by now had finished his snot sandwich. 'What about asking Eustace?'

'Asking him what?'

'Asking him if he'll be on t'committee.'

'Aye, go on, he'll be all right.'

Arthur turned to Sarah Anne. 'Yes, ask Eustace.'

Sarah Anne faced the audience again.

'It has been suggested that Eustace Ollerenshaw be asked to join the committee.'

There was a low level of murmuring and a few laughs and sniggers were heard. Sarah Anne looked at Eustace and continued.

'Eustace Ollerenshaw, are you willing to stand?'

'He couldn't be willing if he tried,' came the interruption from the same source as before.

'I will ignore that very rude interruption and ask the question again. Eustace Ollerenshaw, are you willing to stand as a candidate for election to this committee?'

Eustace looked at Sarah Anne, then Arthur, then Willie. 'On the committee? Me? On the committee? Yes, please! Yes, please.'

'Right, Eustace Ollerenshaw is willing to stand as a committee member. All those in favour?'

There was a unanimous show of hands, not because they favoured Eustace but because they didn't want to get involved themselves.

Whilst Eustace was being elected Willie had collected a large ball of phlegm in the back of his throat and was embarrassed with its presence. Finally he decided to quietly lean forward and deliver it to the canteen floor under the table, which he did, and then ground it into the floor with the sole of his clog.

'Eustace Ollerenshaw is elected to the committee.'

The three of them held a short discussion and Sarah Anne stood up again.

'Ladies and gentlemen, the committee will meet within a very short time and we will put a notice on the canteen wall to inform you all of the progress or otherwise we have made, and the way in which we shall be collecting the money from you. Thank you all.'

She sat down to a round of good solid applause, and the workforce of Murgatroyd's who had been present at the meeting drifted away in ones and twos as it was just about time to start work again.

'When and where shall we be holding the inaugural meeting of the committee?' enquired Daniel Sykes, when the group of elected officers had all gathered around the corner table.

Arthur Baxter spoke up. 'Speaking as secretary, I think we should hold a meeting in the Working Men's Club at eight o'clock.'

'Women isn't allowed in,' quipped Willie.

'They are into t'committee room, and seeing as it's Tuesday there'll be nowt on, so we can have it. I'll call and see Fat Harry on my way home and fix it up. Does that suit everybody?'

There were murmurs of assent except from Daniel Sykes. 'I am not altogether in favour of holding meetings on licensed premises.'

'Well, where would you have it then?' snapped Lewis.

'I don't exactly know, probably the church Sunday school, but I suppose I shall have to bow to the decision of the majority. Where exactly is the committee room in the Club?'

'Yes, I was wondering that,' said Sarah Anne.

'First door on the left as you go through the front door of the Club. You can't miss it. Anyway, Sarah Anne, I'll call for you so that you won't have to go in by yourself,' said Arthur.

'Thank you. Right, that's it, time for work again. See you all at the Club at eight.'

The meeting broke up and they all went back to their respective departments.

Chapter Four

As Fat Harry moved sideways along the bar to serve Willie and Eustace, the polished edge of the bar counter became more polished than it was before as his guts pressed on to the corner of the long wooden top.

'So they've dragged you on to this committee then, Eustace, have they? You'll have to watch 'em, they'll give you nowt but mugging jobs, mark my words. I've known 'em for a long time,' said Fat Harry in one of his more jovial moods.

'Oh, I don't think... I, er, don't think they'll, er—'

'Who else is on t'committee then?' asked Harry, neatly quietening Eustace.

'Er, er, er, oh, yes, er, er, Sarah Anne Green, Willie Arkenthwaite, er, er, me and, er, Arthur, Lewis Armitage and, er, er, er, Dick Jordan. Oh, yes, there's, er, Daniel Sykes. That's, er, let's see now, there'll be, er, that's a difficult one, Willie, how many of us is there then?'

'Nay, Eustace, I haven't counted 'em yet. Let's see now, there's me and you and Arthur, that's three, and—'

'Seven,' said Harry.

'Seven what?' said Willie.

Fat Harry, very patiently for him, replied, 'Seven of you on this here committee.'

Eustace started talking again. 'Seven of us is there? Is there, Willie? Seven of us on the committee. Hey, won't it be good, won't it Willie? Eh, won't it be good?'

Fat Harry asked, 'This here Daniel Sykes, that's him what lives up Rougher Brow?'

'Aye,' said Willie.

'Not one of my better customers.'

'That's right.'

'Well-known locally as a self-opinionated twit, thinks he knows all there is to know about everything and its cousin.'

'The very same.'

'Knows nowt about owt when it comes down to it.'

'Exactly.'

'Heaven help the rest of you. We shall just have to hope we can lace his drink and get him rolling blind drunk.'

'Not a cat in hell's chance, he won't even drink a free glass of water, for nowt.'

Arthur put his head around the door.

'Evening all, a pint for me, Harry, please, and a gin and tonic for the chairman.'

'Nay,' said Willie. 'He won't have any tonic – nobody's wanted tonic in here since goodness knows when.'

'Just a minute, just a minute, Willie Arkenthwaite, I'll thank you not to make ill-founded allegations on these premises.'

'Tha what?'

'We do have some tonic I'll have you know, just a couple of bottles we keep for visiting dignitaries and the like, and as your chairman is one of these, she can have one.'

'Well, you've fair surprised me, Harry, I've never seen soft drinks in here before.'

'You've got the Club committee to thank for the soft drinks; it was their insistence that we always keep a few assorted bottles for emergencies and that sort of thing.'

'Come on, Harry,' urged Arthur, 'can't keep the lady waiting like this, we need to make a good impression for our visitors.'

He took the two drinks from the bar after paying for them, and looked at Willie. 'Are you and your friend coming into the committee room sometime tonight Willie, or not?'

'Aye, we'll just have another one in before we come, won't be a minute.'

Arthur took his two drinks down the corridor towards the committee room.

Lewis and Dick opened the front door and came in out of the freezing cold.

'Cor, it isn't half cold out there, proper brass monkey weather. Is everybody here?' asked Dick.

'All apart from Daniel Sykes, and he's got three minutes to be late yet, and he won't be!'

'Right, we'll just get ourselves a drink and catch you up in a couple of minutes,' said Lewis.

Arthur entered the committee room for the second time that evening. It was a small room with a dark brown painted oak panelled bottom half and a dirty cream top half. In the middle was a table to seat eight people, with what had been a good quality green baize cover in its day. A large, carved oak sideboard stood at one side of the room, holding old records, old minute books and numerous other important articles concerning the Club. There was a blackleaded fireplace on one wall, with a huge fire roaring away in it, and over the top of it was a hideous clock with a monotonous tone, donated to the Club by a local widow in loving memory of her husband, sadly (for the club's profits) departed, for the many happy (and, unknown to her, blind drunk) hours her husband had spent there before she had put him finally to rest. Over the table was a single, dirty, sixty-watt light bulb, and the room was completed by a multitude of glass ashtrays.

'Here you are, Sarah Anne, one gin and tonic which incidentally took a bit of getting as we don't have many lady guests or soft drinks for that matter. Sorry about the state of this room and the hard chairs, but it's only used the odd night in any week at the most, and then, apart from the Club AGM, only for short committee meetings.'

'It's not so bad, it's just the smell of stale beer and cigarettes that make it uncomfortable. Still it's better than nowhere and at least we can get started here, although we shan't need many committee meetings during the year. It's only at year-end time and pay-out time that we need a proper meeting.'

Daniel Sykes walked in and took off his scarf, gloves, mac and cap which, having stowed the scarf, gloves and cap in the pockets and sleeves of the mac, he hung carefully over the back of a chair.

'It smells foul in here. I object to these sort of stale odours, they numb your brain and give you a feeling of nausea. Can't we have the windows opened and let in some fresh air?'

'No you can't!' said Willie who had entered the room very quietly. 'You can't because it's bloody cold outside, and anyway, there aren't any windows in this room what'll open.'

'Well, I think it's disgusting having to sit here inhaling this sickening atmosphere all evening, it's not good enough.'

'Tha can always go home. Tha knows there's nowt to stop thee.'

Willie was always at his broadest when confronted with a person like Daniel Sykes.

'Now then, you two,' said Sarah Anne, 'give over bickering and let's get the meeting under way, it's eight o'clock.'

'Yes, I believe we have a quorum present,' said Daniel, and with great satisfaction he stared at Willie.

'Well, where is it?'

'Where's what?'

'Where's this here quorit thing what you're on about?'

'This here quorit thing happens to be a quorum. Now to explain it in simple terms—'

'Hey, not so much of the simple.'

'I mean no disrespect to yourself Willie, I mean that so as to keep the matter the least complicated.'

'Oh, yes, very well then.'

'As I was saying, to keep it in its simplest terms, a quorum is having a large enough minimum number of members present in order to have a meeting. We have five out of seven and that is quite enough.'

'Actually, we do have seven out of seven. Dick and Lewis will be here in a minute, they are only in the bar getting a drink,' said Arthur.

Daniel started to talk again. 'I do think we should find a better meeting place than this, such as the church hall or somewhere.'

'Are they licensed?' asked Willie.

'Certainly not.'

'Then that's a waste of time even talking about it.'

Willie took the opportunity to have a good loud belch which everyone chose to ignore.

'Willie, can you go to the bar and ask Dick and Lewis to come in here so that we can start the meeting, please,' asked the chairman.

'Aye, I can do that right now.'

He disappeared to reappear two minutes later with the two by now late arrivals.

'Right,' said Sarah Anne. 'Please be seated, everyone. In order that we can keep the meetings as informal as possible I will not stand up to speak. Arthur, have you got pen and paper at the ready to take a note of the minutes?'

'Yes I have.'

'What's he want to make a note of the time for?' asked Willie.

'Some committee this is going to be,' said Daniel Sykes.

'Now Daniel, please keep all personal remarks to yourself in future, and Willie, the minutes are nothing to do with time, they are a write-up of the meeting so that a record of the proceedings can be kept by the secretary.'

'What's he want a record of the proceedings for?'

'So that we can refer to them from time to time if we need to, and so that as time goes on, a true record of all that has taken place with the Christmas club can be kept.'

Daniel Sykes sat quietly sulking, having been ticked off by Sarah Anne.

'Now, as duly elected chairman of Murgatroyd's Christmas club, I declare the meeting open at 8.10 p.m.'

Arthur made a note on his pad, and Willie leaned over to see what he was writing.

'What have you written 8.10 p.m. there for, Arthur?' he whispered.

'So that I can write it in the minutes.'

Sarah Anne ignored the interruption and continued. 'I have worked out a short agenda so as to give us a basis to work on, starting with who is eligible for membership of the club. Has anyone any thoughts on this matter?'

Lewis was the first to speak.

'Well, seeing as it's Murgatroyd's Christmas club, it seems only right and proper that only folks as works at Murgatroyd's should be able to join.'

'Yes,' said Daniel Sykes. 'That is a very good idea and very much along the lines that I was thinking. It would make administration that much easier than if folk from far and wide were to join.'

'What happens if Fat Harry or some of the lads from the Club want to join, or some of the folks from the pigeon association or—'

'Now, Willie, as chairman I have to tell you that as treasurer it will be your job each week to get all the money in, and it will be a hard enough job at Murgatroyd's without a lot of outsiders to think about.'

Eustace, who had up until now uttered not one syllable as he was dozing, not able to follow the conversation, suddenly came to life.

'Will it? Will it, Willie? Will it be your job to collect all the money every week? Will it? Eeh, won't that be grand,' whereupon, having made his first worthwhile contribution to the event, he went back to his dozing.

Arthur then had his turn.

'Yes, I agree with Lewis, we should only admit folk who work at the mill. It's not fair for strangers from far and wide to join, and as Sarah Anne says, you've enough on your plate, Willie, at the mill, without making more work for yourself.'

'I weren't talking about strangers joining, just folk what we know.'

'I used the word 'strangers' to cover people that we know that don't work at the mill.'

'Oh, yes, but there might just be a few of us mates what'll happen want to join, like Fat Harry and them.'

Sarah Anne addressed Willie.

'Have you actually asked Fat Harry, as you call him, and whomsoever he might be if he wants to join?'

'No, Sarah Anne, but I was going to do tonight.'

'And what if he doesn't?'

'Doesn't want to join our Christmas club? Nay, they'll never not want to join.'

The secretary said, 'Well, I think we ought to put it to the vote.'

'Yes,' said Daniel Sykes, 'it's about time we stopped all this useless chatter about Fat Harry and got on with something more positive.'

'Right,' said the chairman. 'The motion is "All those in favour of keeping the Christmas club to the employees of Murgatroyd's alone". Those in favour?'

There was an almost unanimous show of hands, then Willie reluctantly raised his. About this time, Willie began to have the urgent need to snook up and spit out.

'Good, unanimous, motion carried. Right now, the second item on the agenda is—'

'Hang on a minute, I can't write that fast,' said the secretary.

Willie belched out loud and said, 'Time for another round I think.'

He got up and walked to a bell-push set in the wall adjacent to the sideboard. He leaned on the bell for longer than necessary.

'Fat Harry'll just be saying, "There's no peace working at a Club like this. Why can't they hold a meeting without me having to keep walking around there to fetch them another round of drinks." Then he'll come clomping round the bar and walk down here, clomp, clomp, clomp, any time now. Listen for him, here he comes, clomp, clomp.'

Sure enough the door opened and Fat Harry's huge, beaming face appeared around it.

'Did you ring, sir?'

Willie was just about to make his usual reply of, 'No, it was probably a giraffe having a fart that disturbed you, but now you're here we might as well have another round,' when he remembered that there was a lady present and checked himself. Instead, he said, 'Yes, steward, we'd like another round of drinks, please.'

'Hey, you what? You've never asked for ought politely before.'

'No,' agreed Willie. 'But you see, steward, we've never had a lady present before either.'

Fat Harry turned his head and let his gaze rest on Sarah Anne at which his manner changed visibly.

'Well, Sarah Anne Green, I haven't seen you in years, nobody told me it was you that was coming to this meeting. Well, I never did. How are you, my love?' and he stood with a broad grin on his face and stared at Sarah Anne.

Sarah Anne, being in her early forties and still carrying a model-like figure, felt herself slowly turning the colour of a well-pickled beetroot, and was for once lost for words.

'Er, er, hello Harry, I didn't know you were steward at the Club.'

'This could prove to be very interesting,' whispered Lewis to Dick.

'What did you say, Lewis?' said Eustace. 'I couldn't hear you, what did you say?'

'I coughed in French.'

'How do you do that, Lewis? How do you cough in French? Can you teach me to do it? Can you, Lewis? Can you?'

'What on earth possessed you to bring along an imbecile like him?' asked Fat Harry of no one in particular.

Daniel Sykes stood up and addressed the meeting.

'As you are all aware, I was against this meeting being held on licensed premises, but if it has to be, can we please get on with it?'

Sarah Anne had by this time composed herself again.

'Yes, does everyone want the same again? It looks like it. Will you please bring another round, Harry.'

'Certainly, for you, Sarah Anne, with the greatest of pleasure,' and he left the room.

Sarah Anne now took complete control of herself and the meeting.

'We have already decided that Murgatroyd's Christmas club will be open only to those who are directly involved as Murgatroyd's employees, so the next item on the agenda is how best and when to collect the money that people will pay into the club.'

'Well, I think I shall put it in an old biscuit tin – I can happen get one from t'co-op.'

'That is exactly the type of stupid remark one expects to hear from our treasurer,' said Daniel Sykes.

'Oh, and what's wrong with what I said, Mr Ever-so-high-and-mighty, pray?'

'All right, all right, you two, that's enough,' said the chairman. 'We are not here so that you two can have a verbal battle, we have a job to do, so can we get on with it please. The next question is when to collect the money – has anyone any suggestions?'

Eustace, from whom no one in the room expected any sensible contribution to the debate, suddenly came to life.

'Friday dinner time, yes, that's it, Friday dinner time, isn't it? Isn't it? Friday dinner time, yes, that's the right time, Friday—'

The other members of the committee were gobsmacked and sat staring at him in total silence. Only Arthur had the presence of mind to pull himself together and stop what might otherwise have been a very long utterance.

'Why Friday dinner time?'

Eustace looked blank for a few seconds, and Arthur asked the question again.

'Why Friday dinner time?'

'Because I've just been paid and I'll have enough money to pay with, shan't I, Arthur, shan't I? Just have been paid and I'll have some money, won't I, Arthur, won't I?'

'Yes, Eustace, you will, and so will everyone else in the mill as long as they've been to collect their wages from the penny hoil, when the hooter's gone.'

'It looks as if Friday dinner time in the canteen might be the right time,' said Sarah Anne, and looking around it seemed that everyone was in agreement. 'Good, that's settled. Now, how about—'

'Hang on a minute, what about them as goes home for their dinners?' asked Dick Jordan.

'They'll have to come back a bit earlier that usual and come up to t'canteen to pay their dues,' replied Arthur.

'Yes, there's no reason why they shouldn't return to the mill five minutes earlier than usual to pay up,' confirmed the chairman. 'Now, how to collect the money – any bright ideas?'

Willie could contain himself no longer. He indiscreetly snooked up, then brought a ball of phlegm into his mouth. The chairman remonstrated with him. Through the phlegm Willie made a noise that sounded like an apology, then got up from his seat, walked over to the fire and spat the contents of his mouth into the fire, where it sizzled away.

The chairman remonstrated with him yet again.

Daniel Sykes made a discreet coughing noise which drew everyone's attention.

'If Willie was to be seated at a table by the piano, those who were intending to pay could form an orderly queue past the servery hatch, and he could deal with each of them in turn, collecting their money and making an entry in his book.'

'I haven't got a book.'

'A minor detail – you only need something very basic and straightforward, either one page per week or one page per person, something which is easy to control. I think one page per week would be easiest – in fact, if it were sorted out properly on a large sheet of paper, you could probably organise three or four months at one time on the one sheet.'

Willie looked baffled. All this talk of pages per week, pages per person and three or four months per sheet had made him think that possibly he had bitten off more than he could chew. His thoughts, such as they were, were interrupted by the arrival of Fat Harry with a tray of drinks.

'Now, here's your G and T, Sarah Anne love.'

He placed the glass in exactly the correct position in front of her – very correctly.

'Do you know, it's done me a power of good seeing you again after all these years. I hope you'll have a lot more meetings here. No doubt you have got married since last I saw you?'

Sarah Anne, although colouring up again, remained as calm as possible, concealing the flutterings and stirrings inside her.

'Yes, Harry, thank you, happily married with two grown-up children – and you?'

'No, not me, a bachelor by profession. Matrimony never came my way. Still, there's time yet and I live in hopes that—'

He was interrupted by, 'Aye, and we all live in hopes that we might get a drink sometime,' from Willie.

Harry dropped the tray into the middle of the table with a loud bang, stared threateningly at Willie and bellowed, 'Right, who's paying for this round then?'

There was a deathly hush, not a sound from anywhere, until Arthur spoke out, 'Don't worry, Harry, I'll sort it out and let you have the money when we've finished.'

'Right-oh, you know how much it is, so make sure you bring the right amount.'

With a wicked grin and wink at Sarah Anne he clomped out. They all sat quietly drinking their pints of beer. Willie was picking his nose and eating the contents thereof when Sarah Anne enquired, 'Not had enough tea tonight, Willie?'

'Yes, plenty, we had bacon and egg with black pudding, with acres of dip and tons of bread – it were great. Why?'

'Nothing really, it was just with you eating again now I wondered if you hadn't had much tea.'

'I weren't eating, only drinking my beer,' he said very seriously.

'What were you eating, Willie?' enquired Eustace.

'Shut up,' said Lewis.

'Can we please get on with the meeting and then I can return home. As you know, I make nothing of having to attend licensed premises.'

'Why don't you go home then,' said Willie, but Daniel chose to ignore him and not reply.

Sarah Anne, by now composed yet again, took the meeting in hand.

'We were discussing ways of recording the amounts of money paid into the club each week, and I think it would be an excellent idea if we were to let the secretary and treasurer sort it out between them and arrive at the best way of dealing with it.'

'Hear, hear,' said Daniel Sykes. 'Now, the more important question to my way of thinking—'

'Which way is that?' enquired Dick Jordan.

'Why I ever got myself involved with a bunch of ignoramuses like you lot, I'll never know.'

'Who are you calling an ignoramus?' asked Dick Jordan, rising to his feet. 'I've a good mind to come round there and alter the shape of your face.'

'Now, now,' said Sarah Anne, 'we can't sort out matters of this importance with all these senseless interruptions. Now please sit down, Dick, and let's hear no more of this stupidity. Please carry on Daniel, you were saying?'

'I was saying that the more important question is what to do with the money once Willie has collected it.'

'Yes, that was the next item on the agenda. Has anyone any bright ideas?'

'I were thinking of taking it home and keeping it in a tin under the bed,' said Willie.

Arthur frowned at him. 'Nay, lad, I should think we ought to put it in the bank.'

Daniel put his spoke in again.

'Very definitely the bank is the correct place to keep the money. We can use the Northern Counties Bank down Station Lane.'

'Do you bank there, Daniel?' enquired the chairman.

'Er, no, that is I, er, don't possess a bank account.'

'Does anyone have a bank account?' she enquired.

There was no response, then Willie, suffering a minor brainstorm said, 'We could ask Mr Anthony what to do about a bank account – he goes regularly to the Northern Counties.'

'How do you know?' asked Lewis.

'Because I've seen him when I've been dashing on to Sweeny Todd's to get me hair cut, at dinner times.'

'I'm surprised you bother going to Sweeny Todd's with the bit of hair you've got,' continued Lewis.

'Yes, he does, he does bank at Northern Counties bank, he does, he goes regular he does. I've seen him when I've been to Sweeny Todd's haven't I, Willie, haven't I?'

Sarah Anne decided that she had better bring the meeting to order again before it got completely out of control.

'Well, now, what about this money? It seems to me that Willie, as treasurer, had best get in touch with Mr Anthony and ask him if he will fix us a meeting with the bank manager so that we can open an account. All in favour?'

All present raised a hand.

'Very good, motion carried. Willie, will you make the necessary arrangements please. Now, if there's no other business it's half past nine and time for home. I declare the meeting closed. Arthur, how much do you want for the G and T?'

'Nay, Sarah Anne, if I can't buy you a drink, then I don't know.'

'That's very nice of you, Arthur, at least you do it from a gentlemanly and friendly angle, and not because you're a lecherous, leering lout like Harry Howard. Are you coming along home, or are you staying here drinking with the rest of them?'

'No, I think I'll walk along home and make sure you are all right. You should be safe enough through the village but you never know, and, in any case, I could do with an early night myself.'

They were just about to go and fetch their coats when Daniel Sykes walked over to them.

'Ah, Sarah Anne, please allow me to escort you home on this most horrible of nights. It can't be very pleasant for a lady on her own in the dark.'

A cold shiver ran down Sarah Anne's back but she managed a smile.

'Well, that's very good of you, Daniel, and I appreciate the thought, but Arthur is going to drop me off on his way home, and anyway, it's out of your way to come past our house.'

'Yes, I know, but I just thought I might be of assistance, so, seeing I can't, I'll bid you all goodnight,' and he proceeded to wrestle with his coat to be finally reunited with the cap, scarf and gloves which he carefully placed on his person in the correct position, precisely, shouted 'goodnight' again and left the room to a chorus of goodnights which were soon changed by a lone voice shouting, 'Flippin' good riddance.'

'Willie, please don't get personal again,' begged Sarah Anne.

'Well, he's a pain up the—'

'Willie, give over, live in peace with your fellow man.'

'But he's not my fellow man, he's not even a man at all,' following which he belched out loud, without apology, and Sarah Anne, half-smiling under a stern face, said, 'No, and neither are you at times.'

'Come on, Sarah Anne, get your coat and we can go.'

Sarah Anne put on her coat which had been resting over the back of her chair all night. Arthur collected his coat and cap from one of the hooks in the cold draughty corridor, and they both prepared to enter the cold night air.

'Any of you lads coming with us?' ventured Arthur.

'Nay, not on your nellie, there's a good hour's drinking left yet,' retorted Lewis.

'Come on then, Sarah Anne,' and to a chorus of goodnights they left the Club.

⋆

They walked quickly in the bitter frosty air.

'Thank goodness I got out of the Club without Harry Howard seeing me. No doubt he'd have been all over me again.'

'Yes, he can be a bit of a nuisance. I think he's harmless enough – in fact I'm sure he is – but you never know, do you.'

As they walked through the village shopping centre Sarah Anne stopped outside Mossop's Electrical and Radio shop staring at a wireless set.

'You know, that's what I'd like to get with my Christmas club money next Christmas. It doesn't say how much they are though, does it? I'd best remember to go and ask on Saturday, and I'd best remember not to bring Bill, he might not approve.'

'Why? I would have thought Bill would have wanted a new wireless set like we all would.'

'Yes, he probably does, but he'd still sooner buy himself a new set of wooden bowls.'

They walked on, laughing together. Arthur left Sarah Anne at her garden gate, and made his own way home.

*

Back in the Club the remains of the committee made their way back into the bar.

'Weren't a bad meeting,' said Willie as they were selecting their dominoes from the face down pack on the table. 'Mind you, I couldn't understand a lot of it.'

'Couldn't you, Willie? Couldn't you understand it? Couldn't you? I couldn't either,' chimed in Eustace.

'It was simple enough,' said Lewis. 'Surely you could follow what was going on. Who's got double six?

'Not me,' said Dick. 'I understood it perfectly. There was nowt not to understand, it was all very straightforward.'

'Aye, but it were all that about how to book it down and what to do with the money that's left me a bit flustered. Anyway, happen Arthur'll help me with it when the time comes.'

'Time'll be here by Friday, it's not so far away,' said Dick. 'Have any of you decided how much a week you're going to put into the club yet? I think I shall go for five bob.'

'Five bob!' said Lewis in astonishment. 'I were nobbut thinking of half a crown. It's a lot of brass is five bob out of our pay.'

Fat Harry came over to the table where the four friends were getting the dominoes session under way.

'Has him with the constipated gob gone home then?' he bellowed.

'Who's him with the constipated gob, then?' asked Lewis.

'Him from Rougher Brow, Sykes, tha knows, him what's been at your meeting.'

'I wouldn't say he had a constipated gob.'

'No, more like verbal diarrhoea he's got. It's a bloody purgative he needs rubbing on his throat, not a laxative,' confirmed Willie. 'Knows all there is to know about everything. There's nothing at all that he doesn't know, but he hasn't got a bank account and he didn't know a right lot about the bank either. That shut him up in double quick time.'

Eustace, who had been sitting quietly not following the conversation too well, suddenly came to life.

'What do you want to rub his neck hoil with a laxative for Willie? Hey, Willie, I say, what do you want to rub his neck hoil with a laxative for?'

He looked to Willie for an answer.

'You dunderhead. It was a purgative on his throat to stop him talking, not a laxative on his neck hoil – a fat lot of good that would have done – it would probably have made his clack drop out. Come to think of it, happen I might just put a laxative on his neck hoil tomorrow and shut him up for good.'

Fat Harry bellowed again.

'Where's Sarah Anne Green? Has she gone home? By gum, she's a bonny lass it ever I saw one, could do a man good she could. Why didn't you bring her in here with you when you came in?'

'You're a randy old sod,' said Lewis.

'Not so much of the old. Randy I might be but old I definitely am not.'

'That's a matter of some opinion,' said Willie.

'Now, listen here you, I'll sling you straight out of here and over yond hedge in the back if I have any more of your lip.'

'Come on, then, come on,' shouted Willie, getting excited. 'Come on, then.' He stood up, shadow-boxing with clenched fists.

'Sit down, for heaven's sake, and both of you act your age,' said Lewis. 'You're both as daft as one another, and can we get on with our game of dominoes?'

Fat Harry laughed.

'Can I join your Christmas club, then?' he asked of no one in particular.

'Just a minute,' said Willie sternly and trying to look efficient. 'I am sorry to have to inform you that it was this evening decided, under rule three, that no one who does not work at Murgatroyd's Mill can join the Christmas club, and furthermore, seeing that you do not work at all but spend all day lounging about here, drinking beer and talking, you are definitely not allowed to join.'

He completed the speech with a good loud belch which true to form he did not excuse. There followed a stunned silence, during which four pairs of eyes were trained on Willie. The silence was eventually broken by Fat Harry.

'You big, stupid, foul-mouthed—'

He was interrupted by Lewis.

''Willie's right, Harry, in as far as if you don't work at Murgatroyd's you can't join. About the rest of the conversation I am not in a position to express an opinion, and by the way, steward, we are all ready for another round of your most excellent ale, so be a good fellow and cut along to your bar where you may prepare and serve the said beverages.'

Harry opened his mouth and closed it again, stared at Lewis, then Willie, then Dick and then Eustace. Only Eustace wasn't staring straight back – the others were levelling their gaze straight at him, without expression, and he stomped away to the bar.

As soon as he was out of earshot, the four friends broke out into loud uproarious laughter.

'How the hell did you manage to speak like that, Willie?' asked Dick.

'Nay, I don't know what came over me, it were simple like when I concentrated a bit,' and Willie sat back, letting forth yet another ear-shattering belch.

'Why don't you get your over-generous mother-in-law to tip a bob or two into t'club each week Willie?' asked Dick.

''Cos it's not allowed under rule three,' said Willie, sarcastically.

'Aye, well, that's probably as good a reason as any for me not to bother asking the old cow. Mind you, if we could prise a few bob out of her it might not be a right bad do. I might have a words with our Thelma and see what she can do about it.'

'Aye, you want to – the more you put in the more you'll have next Christmas. I'm going to try mine for a contribution,' observed Dick.

'How about you, Eustace?'

'Oh, yes, er, oh, yes, er, how about me what Dick?'

'How about getting your mother-in-law to put a bob or two into the Christmas club each week?'

'But she can't, can she Willie? Can she? She can't. You said so, didn't you? Willie? Didn't you say she can't? Nobody can what doesn't work at Murgatroyd's.'

Willie, who had been sitting quietly biting his finger-nails, muttered under his breath to Dick, 'See, he does listen sometimes, this proves it.'

Then aloud to Eustace he said, 'If you get the money from her each week, add it to yours, and pay it to the club in your own name – no one will know the difference, and you can sort it out with her next Christmas, can't you?'

'Oh, yes, I see, yes that's it, at least I think it is, isn't it? Yes, yes, that's it.'

'Thank God for that,' said Lewis to no one in particular.

Willie turned his attention to the bar and shouted, 'Steward, steward my good fellow, kindly trot this way with our drinks, we're bloody parched.'

But the only response he got was bellowed back, 'Shut your noise and wait your turn, you noisy little twerp.'

The attention of the whole of the club was focused on Willie as they awaited his reply, but he disappointed everyone by not taking the bait. Instead, he remarked to the assembled throng that it was nice to know they were all still in good hands at the club.

The remainder of the evening passed on much as usual: a few more pints, more coarse humour, dominoes, senseless comment, farting and belching and finally, Fat Harry's well-known cry at half past eleven, 'Right, you can all sod off home, I'm shutting.'

At this point he slammed down the new rolled front of the bar, and herded all the flock into the bitter freezing outdoors. They all wended their weary way home, some to be met by wives asleep in bed, others by wives sitting up waiting with supper prepared or for explanations as to where they had been, but irrespective of the greeting, they all crawled into bed, contented and tired.

Chapter Five

Mr Anthony Murgatroyd made two tours of inspection around the mill each day, the first at about half past nine in the morning after opening the post and seeing to the day's incoming orders, to be back in his office by ten to take coffee from his silver service. The second tour was made sometime after lunch, as and when it became convenient, but usually between half past three and four o'clock. Many a time, Mr Anthony would have visitors with him, more often than not buyers from the great British fashion houses, and, occasionally, from abroad.

The tour of inspection always took on the same form – out of the back door of the office block, across the yard and into the lift to ascend the six floors to the top of the big mill where there were to be found two long pairs of spinning mules with their hundreds of gleaming spindles flashing in the light as they revolved at hundreds of revolutions per minute, drawing out the thick carded yarn into a strong spun thread. Then a slow walking descent of the mill, through the various floors, passing more mulegates, and then lower down the big heavy carding machines with their giant flat belt pulleys hurtling around, driving the fancy rollers, swifts, hopper feeds, condenser belts, peralter burr crushers and other magical names associated with the carding of wool. The carding engines were in places so close together that it was necessary to turn sideways to pass between the belt pulley drives. All these machines were driven from overhead line shafts, by wide flat leather belts, the drive to each floor being by a vertical shaft up the mill wall, through giant, noisy, cast-iron bevel gears, running in huge bronze bearings oozing oil and grease.

From the big mill, the next shed he visited was the blending department, a step backwards in processing order, but more convenient in terms of the tour. In here were to be found people walking around covered in fibre and hair from the wool being processed, looking for all the world like giant teddy bears on off-white days. Huge bales of wool already dyed to shade were emptied by hand and put into large hoppers, from where the fibre was sucked by fans and blown down long circular tubes to the blending room. Here it was mixed with wool of different shades and qualities, then sucked by other fans into the willying machines, garnets and fearnoughts, all with big sharp teeth on huge revolving drums, which one by one mixed the various colours and qualities even further to produce an entirely new and special blend to go to the carding department.

Next the tour went through the weaving shed with rows and rows of Dobcross looms clattering away, weaving cloths of all colours and designs. Here some of the looms had been converted to the new electric motor drives but many were still driven by the overhead line shafts. The tour concluded by passing through the greasy piece warehouse, the dyehouse, the wet finishing and dry finishing departments, to end in Mr Anthony's office by way of the finished piece warehouse. Throughout the tour, Mr Anthony would stop and pick up a handful of wool or a piece of cloth, and look at it, smell it, and rub it between his fingers, for he was one of a rare breed of men, a wool man who knew wool inside out and upside down. What he didn't know about wool wasn't worth knowing. He would stop and talk with all the departmental managers and foremen, both about cloth and socially. He would also stop and pass the time of day with any of his workforce who happened to be around, for he always took a deep interest in the well-being of his employees.

*

On the day following the first committee meeting of the Murgatroyd Christmas club Mr Anthony was on his morning tour, walking through the dyehouse with a visitor, when Willie saw him. Dick saw him as well and nudged Willie. 'Go on, go and ask him whilst he's here.'

'Nay, I can't, he's got a visitor with him.'

'Go on, get a move on else he'll have gone.'

Willie watched Mr Anthony and the visitor as they took hold of a sopping wet piece of cloth which was going around and around in a dye vessel to make a close inspection of it. The dyehouse foreman, Walter Smith, was with them, and Willie was not so sure about interrupting them.

'Go on, Willie, move yerself on.'

Dick pushed him towards the little group where he stood hovering indiscreetly. The group took no notice of him, and he swayed from one leg to the other, changing the weight balance of his body from one clog to the other; he put one hand behind his back and scratched his bottom, then he pushed the same hand backwards and forwards across his bald head; he stuck his finger in his left ear and cleaned out the wax which he sucked off the finger, and turned around to look at Dick who was motioning him to move forward; he was just about to start picking his nose when Walter Smith saw him.

'What do you want, Willie?'

'Want a word wi' Mr Anthony like.'

'Can't you see Mr Anthony's busy?'

'Aye, but I've need of a word wi' him.'

'Well, you can't just interrupt him; this here's a very important customer and you'll have to come back another time when he's not so busy.'

'Aye, but tha sees it's like this.'

'Now look, Willie, I'll tell him you want a word with him, so get back to your work.'

Willie walked sadly back to Dick and the round of pieces they were just changing.

'He hadn't time to see me. It's no good, we'll never get this job going.'

'Hang on a minute, Willie, Mr Anthony's all right, he'll see you when he has time, I'm sure of it.'

'Aye, happen you're right.'

They got on with unloading and reloading the machine.

*

The same afternoon, Anthony Murgatroyd came into the dyehouse and walked straight over to Willie.

'Now then, Willie, Walter Smith told me you wanted to have a word with me this morning, but unfortunately I was tied up with a very important customer at the time. Anyway, now I am here, what's it all about?'

Actually coming face to face with Mr Anthony to discuss something serious somewhat flustered Willie, and he was not quite coherent when he began to speak.

'Well, it's about the bank account, like.'

'The bank account?'

'Er, yes, can you help us get one?'

'Who's us?'

'The committee, it's us what needs it.'

Mr Anthony was well-known for his patience.

'Which committee?'

'Murgatroyd's Christmas club.'

'So, we have a Christmas club, have we?'

Willie wanted to belch but didn't dare.

'Aye, and we need to have a bank account, like.'

'Willie, come with me to the private office where it's quiet, and let's sort out what you want.'

Willie had never been to the private office before – he'd been to the enquiry window in the general office a few times but never, ever, to the private office, and until this moment had never expected to either. So it was with some awe and trepidation that he followed Mr Anthony. They walked through the back door of the office block, and Willie's clogs made a peculiar ringing noise on the linoleum covered floor. They made even more noise on each tread as they climbed the stairs and, finally, they made no noise at all as they walked side by side along the thick-carpeted, oak panel-lined corridor to the office which said PRIVATE in big black letters on the door.

All the time they had been walking, Mr Anthony had been talking to Willie, enquiring about Thelma and the children, about the prospects for Grolsby AFC in the local league, and about the trouble Willie had been having recently with a neighbour over his back garden always being fouled by his neighbour's dog. They talked so much that by the time Willie was motioned into a comfortable leather chair he was much more relaxed than when they had set off.

Willie had heard of bosses' private offices before, and on the way up had imagined that he would be taken into a very large room with a roaring fire, a desk in the middle that looked as if it stretched to Manchester, large crystal chandeliers, very deep pile carpets, a private bathroom concealed in the oak panelling, a large and well-stocked bar, and a very pretty young secretary. Instead, the reality was indeed very different – it was a very plain room, small with an average executive desk, a couple of steel filing cabinets and half a dozen leather chairs. A single light bulb hung on the end of a flex in the centre of the ceiling, and the carpeted floor had holes here and there. The desk was strewn with papers as were the tops of the filing cabinets, two of the chairs, the window sill and various parts of the floor. The only luxury was a painting of Mr Anthony's grandfather, the founder of the firm, himself called Anthony, and another painting of his father, Mr Joseph Murgatroyd. Willie looked around, surveyed the scene, and eventually spoke.

'Well, tha's fair sluffed me and no mistake, Mr Anthony. I allus thought that you'd a right posh office up here, with big cocktail cabinets and a private bathroom and great big comfortable armchairs, and you've nowt, no cigars, no whisky, no nothing.'

'I'm sorry to have disappointed you, Willie, but you see I only use this office when I'm bound to. I prefer to spend my time either in the mill or in the sales office, and anyway I can't thoil to spending hard-earned brass on a lot of frivolous and fancy gadgets for an office. Now, what's this about a Christmas club?'

'Well, it's like this – a few of us have got together and decided that we ought to have a Christmas club here at t'mill, for them what works here.'

He stopped to uncross and recross his legs.

'We had a meeting in the canteen the other dinner time, and they made me treasurer, Arthur Baxter secretary, and Sarah Anne Green chairman, then we had a few on the committee. I think there's seven of us altogether.'

'Yes, I heard from Martha, nattering and grumbling, that you'd had a meeting regarding the proposed club.'

Willie had taken the opportunity of Mr Anthony's interruption to poke his ear, uncross his legs, play with his trouser belt and generally fidget.

'Aye, well, we had a meeting on at the Club last night to settle some of the details.'

'Was Sarah Anne Green there?'

'Yes.'

'What, actually inside the Club?'

'Aye, why not?'

'Why not indeed, but a very brave yet foolish woman.'

'How come?'

'Not exactly the place for a lady, I would have thought.'

'Well, we only let her go into the committee room, so you see everything's sort of settled now.'

'Good, good, so what do you want me for?'

'Eh?'

'What have you come to see me for?'

'About the bank.'

'What bank?'

Willie decided that Mr Anthony must be a little bit stupid, so he thought it best to explain.

'Well, it's like this. We decided we need to be able to put the money what I collect on Friday dinner time into the bank so as we know where it is like. I said I'd keep it in a tin under my bed but they weren't having none of that – instead I've got to take it to the bank.'

He stopped for breath and to collect his thoughts.

Mr Anthony intervened. 'So, where do I come into it?'

'For flippin' crying out loud,' shouted Willie, 'we want you to get us a bank account.'

'Why me?'

'Because none of us knows owt about bank accounts.'

'Ah, I see, you want me to use my good offices to help you to open an account at the bank.'

'Aye, that's about the strength of it.'

'Right, I'll do it tomorrow morning when I take the cheques in. Incidentally, can I join the Christmas club?'

'Of course you can, you work here, don't you?'

In order to prolong the agony of the interview no longer, Mr Anthony suggested that it was time for work once again, and the two of them walked back together to the dyehouse, he promising to Willie that he would let him know what happened at the bank as soon as he arrived back at the mill tomorrow morning.

⋆

The next day, Mr Anthony followed his usual morning routine of opening the post, checking the order book, and then touring the mill. He made an unscheduled stop at the counting house to tell the company secretary not to take the cheques to the bank as he had to visit there himself shortly. The secretary gave Mr Anthony the paying-in book, and thanked him for saving him some time so as to attend to other pressing matters.

Immediately Mr Anthony was out of earshot of the counting house all hell let loose as the secretary kicked the living daylights out of whatever or whoever he could find to kick, as part of his daily pleasure was to get away from the mill for a few minutes to visit the bank, to place an odd bet or two, and to spend time talking to the many ladies of the village who were very much of his acquaintance. Today, through no fault of his own, he had been denied that pleasure.

⋆

It was a very foggy, frosty cold morning, and it didn't take Mr Anthony long to walk from the mill, through the village and halfway along Station Lane to arrive at the Northern Counties Bank. The building stood out as a perfect example of the soundness and rock solid nature of the bank, and even though by city bank standards it was indeed tiny, it still imposed itself on Station Lane and made all the other buildings including the station itself and the Railway Hotel, come a very poor second. Mr Anthony conducted the mill business at the counter and then enquired if the manager was free.

Douglas Sharples, the manager of the Grolsby branch, was free for Anthony Murgatroyd. He might not have been free for anyone else, depending on whom that might have been, but with Anthony being a near neighbour, and their families being very friendly, he was free.

Normally, Sharples was a man of few words, most of which were very much to the point, and he was also blessed with the idea that he was a few degrees better than anyone from the West Riding of Yorkshire, with certain exceptions, Anthony being one of these. Sharples was ex-Shropshire, ex-public school, ex-army and proud of his own capabilities.

*

Anthony entered the rather ornate office.

'Come in, come in, nice to see you.'

Anthony took the outstretched hand of Douglas Sharples and shook it warmly.

'Sit down, won't you. How's the family?'

'Well, Douglas, thank you. Well, how's yours?'

'Just the same, thanks. Now, are you here on business or pleasure? Bloody good party up at Johnson's last Saturday night, eh? My word, his daughter isn't half developing into a nice young woman – couldn't keep my eyes off her.'

'Yes, she's a pretty little thing, isn't she – turned a few heads she did.'

'Not so little either. I managed to get myself wedged in a doorway with her, face to face as it were. I wish I were eighteen again. So what was it you wanted, eh?'

'I'm only here to do a favour for some of our work people. A few of them have decided to open a Christmas club ready for next Christmas, and they intend to collect each Friday lunchtime after we have paid the wages, then bank the money straight after lunch.'

'So, what has that got to do with you?'

'Well, they asked me if I could fix it for them to have a bank account, and I promised to see what I could do for them, so that's why I'm here. Of course, you must understand I want to do the best possible I can for them.'

'How much money are we talking about?'

'That is the question of the year. Let's see now, we have close on two hundred and fifty employees – if they all put ten shillings a week in, and they won't all, and a lot of them won't join, then think of the number you first thought of, helped along by a following wind and the moon in the third quarter, let's say sixty to seventy pounds a week, perhaps, but I could be miles out.'

'Three to three and a half thousand a year, a tidy little sum. The best thing we can do is to let them have a special high interest savings account. It's supposed to be for fixed, regular weekly or monthly investments, and we can assume that if the club works correctly, the weekly amount will be fixed. We need one month's notice of withdrawal, but we can fix that now when the account is opened, or near enough anyway. I have the power of discretion in cases like this to allow a cheque book on a savings account, and that can be dealt with, leaving only the questions of who is going to run the show or sign the cheques, or pay in the money, etc., etc.'

'As far as I can tell you, Willie Arkenthwaite is.'

'Who?'

'Willie Arkenthwaite.'

'Never heard of him, not one of our clients.'

'Probably not, but you will have heard of him by the time you've got him sorted out.'

'Who is he?'

'He's a dyehouse labourer who lives at Cutside Cottages on the canal bank halfway between here and the mill. He's been elected treasurer of the club, but how he's going to go on with it I do not know. I've always found him to be very honest but he's difficult to hold a serious conversation with, as he can't follow most normal matters. Anyway, you'll have to judge him as you find him.'

'One of those, eh. Would you say he could be described as being a bit thick?'

'As good a description as one could have asked for. Mind you, he's all there when he wants to be.'

'Yes, I know the type, leave him to me. When can I have him here?'

'Today after lunch, say two o'clock.'

'Yes, that's fine. Thanks, Anthony.'

'No problem, Douglas, no problem.'

The two men rose from their padded chairs. Douglas put one hand over his mouth to try and discreetly hide a somewhat loud embarrassing belch and hurriedly started to talk again.

'Are you going to pay into the Christmas club then, Anthony?'

'I haven't given it much thought, though I might just risk a half a crown a week.'

Anthony Murgatroyd stared aghast as Douglas Horatio Sharples laughed out loud, for, in keeping with many of the bank managers of his day, Sharples made it a solemn rule never to laugh during office hours.

'You've laughed during office hours.'

'Sorry, couldn't help it. It was the thought of you shelling out half a crown a week – you'll only have about six pounds by Christmas at the most. You could afford six pounds a week and not notice it; it's well worth a laugh even during office hours. Just wait until I tell the chief clerk about it.'

'Now then, Douglas, do you want to chip into the club?'

'No, not at all, I can't afford anything at all on my salary.'

This time they both burst out laughing, and as Sharples showed Anthony to the front door many people noted, and talked for years afterwards, about the day that Douglas Horatio Sharples laughed during office hours.

*

Mr Anthony arrived back at Damside mills, so known because his grandfather had built the mill at the side of an existing mill dam many years earlier. This towering building was erected much to the consternation of the owner of the mill on the opposite side of the dam, because old man Murgatroyd had managed by means never disclosed to get a right to draw water from the existing dam rather than build himself a new one nearby, and in the process of so doing had saved himself a fortune.

The owners of Tansy Mill on the other side of the dam had never forgiven the Murgatroyds, and three generations on, there was still an uneasy calm in their relationship.

*

After leaving the bank paying-in book with the company secretary, Mr Anthony took a walk down to the dyehouse where he sought out the foreman dyer, Walter Smith.

'Now, Walter, you know this business about a Christmas club, and Willie Arkenthwaite's involvement with it.'

'Yes, Mr Anthony, I'm going to join the club on Friday.'

'How much are you going to put in, Walter?'

'I don't exactly know. I've been trying to figure it out all morning – happen ten bob a week, don't know exactly just yet – better ask the wife tonight.'

'Yes, you would more than likely be better to ask your wife before making a decision of that sort. Anyway, Willie's going to need a bit of time off every Friday, just after lunch, so that he can take the money to the bank. It will only take an odd half-hour or so, can you spare him?'

'Oh, yes, I can cover for him for half an hour, no problem.'

'Good, good. Now he needs to go to the bank this afternoon, so I suggest we let him go straight after lunch to let him smarten himself up somewhat, and then he should be back by three o'clock. Can you manage that?'

'We'll have to, won't we.'

'Yes, you will, won't you.'

He made his way over to Willie who, ever since he had seen Mr Anthony enter the dyehouse, had been on tenterhooks, waiting to see if he could go to the bank.

'Now, Willie, I've had a talk with Mr Sharples the bank manager, and he wants to see you at two o'clock to discuss matters appertaining to the Christmas club money. He suggests you put the money in a special high interest deposit account, so that the fund will gain in value as the year rolls along.'

'Very good, Mr Anthony. Ah'll go when ah've had my dinner.'

He had no idea exactly what Mr Anthony was talking about.

'Yes, Willie, that's just fine, but do pop in home and put something more suitable on, you're not exactly dressed in bank attire, and Willie...'

'Yes?'

'Do try to speak a little bit more refined when you get to the bank.'

'Eh?

'Speak posh in the bank.'

'Oh, aye, Mr Anthony, I will.'

*

Willie took his usual front place in the canteen queue, to be closely followed up the steps by Sarah Anne Green.

'Have you seen Mr Anthony, Willie?'

'Yes, I have, I had a talk with him this morning, then he went to t'bank and saw the manager, and now I've to go see the manager after dinner at two o'clock, and I've got to go and get myself washed and changed, and I have to talk poshish like, and he were going on summat about high interest what I couldn't understand and—'

'Hang on a minute, Willie, is Mr Anthony letting you have time off to go to the bank this afternoon?'

'Aye.'

'With pay?'

'Well, well, nay, I don't know. Well, now you come to mention it, I never thought to ask him.'

'Here save my place in the queue a bit, better still get my dinner for me whilst I come back – here's the money.'

She thrust a two-shilling piece into his hand and disappeared down the steps, pushing past the queuing throng. Sarah Anne walked over to the offices and asked the young lady receptionist if she could see Mr Anthony on a matter of some urgency. The young lady, who on getting the job of receptionist had instantly risen four steps up the social ladder, looked at Sarah Anne and spoke in a snotty haughty manner.

'And whom shall I say wants to see Mr Anthony?'

Sarah Anne was not put off by such people and blasted forth, 'Now, look here young woman, you know who I am as well as I do, and I'll thank you to mind your manners when you speak to me or I shall have a thing or two to say to your mother and father the next time I see them.'

The young lady blushed and mellowed and ran out of the room in one and the same breath. She did not appear again, but Mr Anthony was not long in coming to the reception area.

'Now, Sarah Anne, what can I do for you?'

'It's about the Christmas club. You know I'm chairman, and Willie Arkenthwaite, for all his sins, was elected treasurer, and I understand he's been to see you about going to the bank, and in fact he tells me he's going after dinner.'

'Yes, that's right, I have made arrangements with the dyehouse foreman to cover for him whilst he goes about his weekly duties of the Christmas club, and also for him to go to the bank this afternoon.'

'Are you going to pay his wages whilst he's doing his treasurer's duties?'

'Do you know, I've not given it as much as a minute's thought yet. Should I, do you think?'

'Well, we are sort of doing it voluntary like for the benefit of those that work here and only those that work here, not anyone else, and I think you ought to pay his wages if I guarantee to keep his club activities to the bare minimum each week.'

'Sarah Anne, of course I'll pay his wages for that period each week. I think it's a good thing for the mill, and I'm looking forward to being able to join. When are you collecting the first instalment?'

'Friday this week, in the canteen, at dinner time.'

'Good, I'll be there, and please tell Willie that all will be all right with his wage.'

'Thank you, Mr Anthony, I'll go and tell him.'

She made her way back to the canteen, half-walking, half-running. Meanwhile at the canteen, Willie was having not just a little bit of trouble, firstly with Greasy Martha in trying to convince her that he really did want Sarah Anne's dinner as well as his own, and then trying to work out how he was going to carry two plates of dinner and two lots of cutlery over to his table. However, he was soon relieved of any further worries by the reappearance of Sarah Anne who carried her own food and utensils.

'By gum, I'm glad you're back, I were just wondering how I were going to carry my dinner and yours over to the corner table. Did you see him?'

'Yes, he says it's all right, he'll pay your wages whilst you attend to the duties of the Christmas club providing you don't overdo it.'

'Good, then I can have my dinner and then geroff to the bank.'

Willie sat in his usual seat at the corner table and was joined by his three pals from the dyehouse. He ate with his customary well-known zeal and noise, using knife and fork occasionally, fingers regularly and tongue finally to lick the plate clean, stopping only long enough for a loud belch also customary. He headed back to the servery for his pudding with which again he dispensed in his own inimitable style. Having consumed the pint of tea in one long swallow he got up to leave, belching out loudly yet again.

'Hold on, Willie, it's card time,' said Dick.

'Nay, not today, I'm off to the bank.'

'Come on, you can go after we've played, we can't play a three hand.'

'Well, get somebody else to play for me today – how about Eustace?'

'Nay, we'll not play if it's got to be that bad,' said Dick.

'Well, suit yourselves, I'm off to the bank, it's a very important job what I'm doing.'

With that he walked away leaving the other three staring after him, making useless comments.

Willie went back to the dyehouse to take off his thick leather apron, replace it with his cap and coat, and then away to leave the mill through the arched front gate. The gate was closed as it was only opened at twelve noon to let those who went home for dinner out in a hurry, and then closed until a quarter to one when it was opened again to let the workforce who had been home back in again in a hurry. In order to get out at any other time it was necessary to go through the penny hoil, or gate lodge, so named because it was where the gatekeeper or penny hoil man paid out the wages through the little opening window or penny hoil, each Friday morning.

George Schofield had been the penny hoil man at Murgatroyd's for as long as anyone could remember. It was part of his duty to stay at his post throughout the dinner break and keep an eye on the comings and goings through the gates. In summer he would stand across the road, leaning on the wall overlooking the canal, but in winter he had a roaring coal fire in his office, and he usually took the opportunity of the lull in traffic at dinner time to have forty winks.

As Willie approached the penny hoil he could see George, slumped back in his chair, one of the drawers in his desk a quarter open, and his feet off the floor resting on the edge of the open drawer. The fire was blazing away merrily and George was fast asleep.

Willie stopped hurrying so that his feet gave over clonking, and instead, he was to be observed making a very careful and stealthy approach to the penny hoil. He opened the door without a sound, crept inside very quietly, closed the door, then very slowly and stealthily made his way over to George Schofield's feet resting on the drawer. He took very careful aim and swiftly kicked the drawer back into the desk, causing George's feet to crash to the floor, and

George to sit bolt upright at a speed far too great for a man of his age.

'Oh, you are still alive then, George? I thought you were dead when I walked through the passage and saw you lying there.'

'You bloody stupid sod, you could have killed me, I could have died of heart failure, you might have set my palpitations off again. You can make folk have a growth with a physical shock, you can make them lose their memory – it is possible to do.'

'Now, George, it was just my little bit of fun.'

'Bit of fun! Bit of fun!' His mood changed instantly for the worse. 'And what the bloody hell were you doing in my office anyway? My inner sanctum is barred to all and sundry except the chosen few and management.'

'Like Mary Barhead?'

A slight reddening around the cheekbone was to be observed.

'It's got absolutely nothing to do with you, William Arkenthwaite. Who comes in here is my affair and my affair alone.'

'Well, first of all, my name's not William, it's Willie, Mr High-and-Mighty, and, secondly, we all know it is your affair. Anyway, a nod's as good as a wink to a blind horse, so I'll be on my way.'

'If it's not a rude question, where are you going?'

'To the bank.'

'What for?'

'Same as thee, it's my affair and my affair alone, but it's not called Mary Barhead.'

With this Willie escaped into the cold half-foggy midday January air, and half-walking, half-running he made his way to Number 6 Cutside Cottages.

*

Willie opened his front door to be met by Mrs Woofenden, sitting almost in the big roaring fire.

'Is that you, our Willie? Thelma, your Willie's home, whatever can have happened? What are you doing home at this time? Have you had your dinner? Is't mill on fire? Have you had an accident or summat?'

She stopped only long enough for a sharp intake of warm air giving Willie no time to reply, then started screeching at the top of her voice.

'Thelma, your Willie's home, where are you? Come and have a look, what can have happened? Has t'mill engine run out of control has?'

Willie chose to ignore the old lady and to make his way upstairs to find his best dark grey three-piece suit. Thelma opened the back kitchen door, came into the living room and confronted her mother.

'Now, what on earth is all this loud noise about?'

'It's our Willie, he's come home.'

'Well, where is he, he's nowhere in sight.'

'He's gone upstairs.'

'Well, what's it about?'

'I don't know, you know what Willie's like, he never said a word, just walked in and went upstairs. I told you not to marry him, you could have done a lot better for yourself, but would you take any notice? No, you would not, you would only do—'

She gave over as she realised she was talking to four walls and a roaring fire. However, she was highly delighted as she had got her spoke in about her son-in-law once again.

Thelma entered the bedroom to find Willie busily getting changed.

'What are you doing?'

'Going to the bank to see about yar new Christmas club.'

'But you should be at your work.'

'Mr Anthony's let me go, and he's paying my wages. I've got to go see the manager at half past one to see about new account, so I can bank money every Friday after t'dinner.'

'So what are you getting changed for?'

'Well, Mr Anthony said as I wasn't fair well enough dressed to go before the bank manager in my dirty working clothes and I'd best go home and change.'

'You don't need your best suit, you could put your sports jacket on and your new brown trousers. It's not a funeral or a wedding.'

'No, but it's a bank manager and I'd best look right and then.'

'Why are you going?'

'I am the treasurer and in my official capacity I have to go to see the bank manager about our money.'

'Are you sure you know what you are doing?'

'Yes, well no, well happen. I know a bit about it and I shall have to learn the rest of it as I go.'

'Well, do take care love, it's a lot of money you'll be handling, and it's somebody else's, and Willie—'

'Yes.'

'Do try and be civil to my mother – she's very upset that you walked in and ignored her and wouldn't tell her why you were home.'

'Well, you know what she's like, straight into the attack, spitting fire and venom as soon as I walk through the door – it's easier to shut up than have a row with her.'

'I know it's difficult, but you could try. It makes it awkward for me – she'll go on all afternoon about it.'

'Specially for you, I'll be nice to her when I come downstairs.'

Thelma left Willie with a hug, a kiss and a smile, and he continued to change into his best white shirt, red polka dot tie, grey suit and highly polished black shoes. He then applied a very generous helping of hair cream, combed it straight, put on his best grey overcoat, new cap and scarf that he'd had as Christmas presents, and descended the stairs.

'Coming with me then, Mrs W?' he said with a grin as he faced his mother-in-law.

'You know very well I can't, my back's playing me up something shocking. If I'd been a bit younger there'd be no stopping me. Where are you going?'

'To see the bank manager about Murgatroyd's Christmas club.'

'What's it to do with you?'

'I'm treasurer, I'm in charge.'

'There's no answer to that.'

Thelma straightened Willie's cap and brushed his collar.

'Come on, love, you'll be late, it's almost a quarter past one.'

'Yes, all right, I'm on my way. So long.'

'Good luck,' shouted Thelma as he walked down the canal towpath.

She closed the door to the strains of, 'Shut that door, the cold's going through my back like the blade of a sword cutting it. You'll have to keep an eye on him you know, there'll be no good come of this Christmas club, just you mark my words. I told you not to marry—'

'Oh, for heaven's sake shut up mother,' stormed Thelma as she walked back into the kitchen and slammed the door hard, tears in her eyes. Mrs Woofenden stared at the fire with an expression which was blacker than the coal that was burning on it.

★

Willie walked quickly towards the village, in the sure knowledge that he had a half-hour to spare to pop into the

Club and have a quick drink before his meeting with the bank manager. He passed the canal wharf where a barge was unloading bales of wool and on through the village past the shops, most of which were closed for lunch, and on to the Club. He carefully hung his outer garments on the hook rail in the entrance hall with the other few coats that were there from the usual small lunchtime crowd and opened the door into the bar.

'Awe, my Gawd, what do we have here?' rang out the dulcet tones of Fat Harry. 'Is it a well-dressed dummy from Fifty Shilling Tailor's window, or is it a fairy what has just fell off the Christmas tree? No, no, it must be the new manager from the brewery what we haven't met before. Good afternoon, sir, somewhat cold for the time of the year, even the brass monkey's put his clothes back on. What can I get you to drink sir?'

'Give us a pint.'

'A pint, sir, certainly, sir.'

He poured the drink, chuckling under his breath but saying nothing. When the glass was full of the frothing bronze liquid he handed it over the bar to Willie.

'That will be one shilling and sixpence, if you don't mind, sir.'

'Get stuffed.'

'I beg your pardon, sir.'

'Get stuffed, you invited me to have it, so you pay for it. I only came in to show you that I do have a best suit, just to prove to you who have often claimed differently that I do in fact have one, so thanks for the drink.'

'I shall take the greatest of pleasure, sir, in walking to that end of the room there,' he said pointing to the far end of the bar, 'Turning ninety degrees, walking three paces forward, turning ninety degrees again, walking up to where you are leaning on my recently highly polished bar top, sir, picking you up by your ears with my left hand whilst at one and the same time helping your teeth to pass through your body at great speed with my right hand, if you don't pay for that pint bloody quick.'

Although Fat Harry was much taller, rounder and wider than Willie, he didn't make any impression with his well-dressed client who replied, 'Thank you my man, I'll not forget your generosity in a long time,' and went on drinking his pint, adding a rather loud fart just to close the proceedings.

'That doesn't suit one who is dressed like a right dandy. Have you made a will yet?' enquired Harry.

'Have I heck. I've nowt to leave and anyway it's nowt to do with thee.'

'It's everything to do with me. I need to know that your Thelma's well provided for before I rip your insides out slowly piece by piece. By the way, what are you doing here dressed like a dog's dinner when you should be grovelling for your master up at Murgatroyd's?'

'I'm going to the bank at two o'clock.'

'What for?'

'To see the manager.'

'What for?' shouted Harry.

'To see about Christmas club.'

'What about Christmas club?'

'We need an account.'

'Why?'

'To bank the money.'

'So what's with the new-look Willie, then?'

'Anthony Murgatroyd said I'd best get changed and look posh for the manager.'

'Ah, well, good luck. Do you want another pint in there which I am definitely not paying for?'

'No, not just now. I'd best stay sober for the manager, and anyroad it's time I were on my way, it's ten to two and I don't want to be late.'

'Well, take care. Are you coming in tonight?'

'Might, might not, see how the mood grabs me.'

'You know you will be, you never miss. Are you going to pay me for that pint or not?'

'Not, and thanks.'

Willie closed the door behind him, put on his coat and cap and went out again into the bitter cold. It wasn't far to the bank, perhaps three hundred yards, and Willie set off at a brisk pace. He was passing the end of Mafeking Street when he almost stopped dead in his tracks as he saw what he took to be Daniel Sykes trying to make his escape from a house halfway up the street. Obviously, he didn't wish to be observed, and gave furtive glances to all sides, but he didn't see Willie.

Couldn't be him, he should be at his work, thought Willie. But it was him, I'm sure. Wonder who lives there and what he were up to? Aye, I wonder; and he wondered all the way to the bank.

Chapter Six

The Grolsby branch of the Northern Counties Bank was a foreboding building standing between the railway station and the railway hotel. It was built of local millstone grit, not the common rough-finished house stone but the carefully machined and bevel-edged stone, so popular with those architects who worked for clients with a money no object building fund. To Willie Arkenthwaite it represented something akin to a prison or courthouse, or somewhere to beware, as he stood before it and viewed it on this particularly cold and drab winter's day. He decided he would not be a coward and miss his appointment; he therefore counted up to three then three and a half, then started again – two and a half, two and three quarters, three – and marched straight towards the revolving front doors.

⋆

Willie was just about to give the nearest segment of the doors a push when he stopped, turned around and walked back to the pavement edge. He searched for an iron grate over a street drain and observed one on his right. He walked towards it and stood on the pavement edge over it with head bowed forward. Willie lightly pinched the end of his nose between the thumb and first finger of his right hand, then blew with all his might. A torrent of snot flew towards the grate, and trailers from his nose waved gently in the low breeze. These trailers were soon dispensed with on the sleeve of his coat, and declaring that he now felt a lot better he retraced his steps to the bank. One little old lady who had been passing at the time that Willie was clearing his nasal passages heaved all the way home and was as sick as a drunken duck in the sanctity of her own kitchen sink. Her neighbour wanted to call the doctor but the little old lady, although she was unable to explain why she was sick, steadfastly refused medical help.

Having pushed through the revolving doors and, in so doing, helped one of the bank's regular clients to leave the building at a far faster rate than he would usually have done, Willie stood back dumbstruck, admiring the majesty and luxury of the interior of the building. Never in his wildest dreams had he imagined the oak panelling, thick pile carpets, large ornate chandeliers, central heating, and the air of quietness and calm. It is fair to say he didn't know just what to expect and he stood back for a few minutes to take it all in. People came and people went, some queued at counters, others went through various doors and he could see people working, sitting at desks behind the counters. No one bothered him or talked to him, they just left him to study his surroundings.

Eventually a young lady he almost recognised said, 'Good afternoon,' to him as she walked past, and he returned the greeting, but even she didn't ask him what he wanted or why he was there, and so he began to look around for someone to ask as to where he might find the manager. Seeing no one who looked important he ventured a little walk around to see what he could find, and his wanderings eventually brought him into contact with a small opening window at the far end of the counter, which had a notice above it in gold lettering saying ENQUIRIES.

At the side of the window was a brass bell-push with a small notice reading PUSH FOR ATTENTION. Willie was just about to press the bell-push when he began to have cold feet about how much noise the bell might make. He looked around carefully to see if anyone was watching and, finding no one, he plucked up courage and leaned hard on the brass button. Nothing happened; there was no sound at all. He decided that perhaps it rang in a place where it could not be heard from the counter and so he decided to wait a few minutes before leaning on the button again. Once again there was a painful silence.

Willie could see people walking about behind the barrier that separated the counter from the commercial section of the bank. He wondered what to do to attract their attention. He could have hammered hard on the window with his fist but even to Willie, who wanted to belch and dare not, this did not appear to be seemly behaviour. He could have done his locally famous monkey impression but he decided that this was not the place for that type of exhibition. He finally decided to try and repair the bell. It was almost a dead certainty in his own mind that the trouble lay with the bell-push rather than the bell itself because he could see the push button and not the bell.

Willie fumbled in his back trouser pocket until he found the twenty-seven-implement Swiss army penknife which he always carried with him. He selected the medium width screwdriver blade of the three available, and carefully unscrewed the cover plate of the bell-push, which removed the push contacts as well. The screwdriver blade was then folded away and the multi-purpose file was opened. He carefully cleaned the contacts in the housing on the counter with the file, having first gently probed them to make sure they were low voltage, and then filed away at the push contacts until they were bright and shiny.

He worked away quietly, concentrating hard on the job in hand, and did not notice the enquiry window open quietly, and he almost jumped out of his skin when a voice close to his ear asked, 'And what do you think you are doing?'

'Mending your bell, it's bust. Nobody came and I'd rung it twice, because it didn't ring, so I thought that I'd mend it, then ring it.'

'This is a most unusual state of affairs, we don't usually allow this type of occurrence in the bank you know. A further question, sir, whilst I am here, what business do you have in the bank?'

'Eh?'

'What do you want?'

Willie smiled proudly. 'I've come to see t'manager.'

'Have you an appointment, sir?'

'Aye, of course I have, lad, why else do you think I'd be stood here?'

'What is your name, sir?'

'Willie.'

'Willie who?'

'Arkenthwaite.'

'Right, Mr Arkenthwaite, what did you want to discuss with the manager?'

'It's none of your business, and if it were I wouldn't tell you, cause you ask too damned many questions, so be a good lad and trot along and tell him I'm here.'

The smartly-dressed young man stood back and gave Willie a good coat of looking at. Never in his short career at the bank had anyone spoken to him in this manner before. He just stood and watched as Willie finished cleaning the contacts of the bell-push and began to screw the brass top plate back into position. He grimaced as Willie snooked up out loud and then looked for somewhere to spit out the phlegm, finally swallowing it, jumped in surprise as Willie pressed the bell-push and it rang out loudly all over the bank, and frowned as Willie belched out noisily without an apology. Willie looked up and observed the young man standing staring at him.

'Get on with it then, give over staring at me and go tell t'gaffer I'm here.'

The young man turned and walked away, Willie pressed the push button again making the bell ring once more and ring out loudly throughout the bank. The young man turned back to Willie who shouted, 'And get a move on, I haven't all day to wait whilst you dawdle about, I've some work to do.'

The young man glared at Willie, then went towards the manager's office. Once out of sight he turned to where Willie was standing and generously pulled out his tongue at the unseeing new customer. He knocked on the manager's office door and waited for the shout, 'Come in,' then opened the door and entered.

'Mr Sharples, there is a most uncouth and ill-mannered person to see you by name of Willie, sorry, Arkenthwaite, who says he has an appointment with you. A most unsavoury character if you want my opinion.'

'Quite frankly, I do not want your opinion, and, for what it's worth, this Mr Arkenthwaite is soon to become one of our clients, so show him in and bring me the file you opened this morning after Mr Anthony Murgatroyd had been in to talk about the Christmas club. Mr Arkenthwaite is the treasurer of the club and as such will be in here banking the club funds at least once every week.'

'Very good, Mr Sharples, but I wouldn't trust him with my last farthing. I don't like the look of him at all.'

With that the young man closed the door and walked back over to the enquiry window where Willie was waiting patiently and watching the young ladies working behind the counter.

'Mr Sharples will see you now, Mr Arkenthwaite. Please go to the door marked PRIVATE at the opposite end of the counter where I will meet you and escort you to his office.'

'Ah telled you ah'd an appointment, lad,' said Willie in reply.

He walked across the carpeted floor to the door marked *private*. He was wishing he was out in the street again, for he could just feel a ball of phlegm gathering in his throat and he wanted to have a right good snook up and spit out but just at this minute he dared not do so. The door opened and Willie entered a long oak panelled corridor. The young man walked silently in front until they came to a large solid oak door bearing the sign MANAGER in big gold letters. He knocked discreetly and opened the door announcing as he did, 'Mr Arkenthwaite, sir.'

'Nay, lad, you needn't call me, sir, after my name, thanks all the same.'

'I was referring to Mr Sharples as sir, not you.'

Having closed the door he once again enjoyed the luxury of sticking his tongue out at Willie, with the door firmly between them.

Mr Sharples rose from his chair, walked around the desk and shook Willie warmly by the hand, much to Willie's surprise.

'Hello, Mr Arkenthwaite, I'm very pleased to meet you. Anthony Murgatroyd has told me a lot about you. Please sit down in that chair.'

He motioned to a big, black, leather padded armchair in front of his desk.

Willie was a little nonplussed by all these posh-speaking people and he blurted out, 'Hello, Sir Sharples, I'm pleased to meet you as well.'

'No, not Sir Sharples, just plain Mr Sharples, I haven't hit the dizzy heights of knighthood yet.'

Willie had not grasped the basic fundamentals of this conversation so far and as he was sitting down he said, by way of apology for something he didn't understand, 'Nay, yond young lad called you "sir" and I got a bit flummoxed.'

He was still wanting to snook up.

'The term "sir" is used by staff to managers in the banking profession.'

'Oh, yes, I see,' said Willie, trying to sound convincing.

'Now, I understand you are intending to run a Christmas club for the benefit of the employees of Murgatroyd's Mill.'

'Aye, that's right,' following which they stared at each other, Willie waiting for Mr Sharples to continue the questioning and Mr Sharples waiting for Willie to elaborate on his plans.

Mr Sharples watched Willie who was staring all over the room, and decided to break the silence. 'Can you briefly elaborate upon your proposals for the initial organisation of the club?'

'Eh?'

'Er, can you er, er, can you tell me how you are going to run the club?'

Mr Sharples had, whilst they were talking, been slowly and quietly opening a drawer in his desk, standing upright a half-bottle, flat in appearance and containing a deep golden bronze French seventy per cent proof liquid, and in his well-practised method, so as not to arouse the suspicion of the client, had been unscrewing the cap. Whilst Willie was thinking of a suitable reply to the last question, Mr Sharples ducked down behind his desk out of sight of Willie and took a quick slurp from the bottle, replaced the cap, laid the bottle flat, closed the drawer and surfaced again, only to realise that Willie was leaning over the desk watching him.

'Are you all right, Mr Sharples?'

'Er, yes, I er, er, er, just dropped something, but I have located it now thank you. Are you ready now to tell me all about the club?'

'Oh, aye, it's simple, me and Arthur'll—'

'Who is Arthur?'

'My mate, Arthur, he's secretary.'

'Yes, but Arthur who?'

'Arthur Baxter, he works in the dyehouse with me and Lewis and Dick. Anyroad, as I were saying, me and Arthur'll collect money every Friday dinner time in the canteen, then I'll bring it straight on here and give it to you.'

'Well, now, you won't exactly give it me, you will have to hand it over to one of the clerks behind the counter. What will be the weekly subscription rate for the members, er, no, er, how much will each member pay into the club each week?'

'Well, that'll depend on what they can afford when it's time to pay. It might be different every week depending on how skint they are.'

He was stopped short by Mr Sharples again. 'Skint?'

'Short, tha knows, short of brass.'

'Oh, yes, please carry on.'

'Well, like I were saying, it might be different every week but I shall keep a record of what they all put in, in my little red book. It's got lines and columns for cash you know. Myself, I shall put three pounds a week in when I have it to spare and nowt at all when I haven't.'

'What do you know of banking procedures?'

'Nowt at all.'

'Do you not even know how to go about paying your money into a bank account?'

'No, I was just going to give it to you.'

'Firstly, we need to open an account for the Christmas club. We did that in anticipation this morning after

Anthony Murgatroyd had been in to see me, and all that we need to do now to complete that particular part of the operation is for you to give your specimen signature on this card just here so that you may legally transact the business of the club.'

Willie gave Mr Sharples a funny look. 'Why do you want me to pee into a little bottle?'

'I beg your pardon!'

'Well, the last time the doctor asked me for a specimen, I had to pee into a little bottle but I can't think what you want that for at the bank.'

'It's a specimen of your handwriting we want, not a medical specimen,' roared Mr Sharples, visibly upset.

'Now, don't you go having a bad turn, Mr Sharples, it were just a little misunderstanding on my part.'

Mr Sharples passed the card over to Willie for signature, and at the same time began slowly to open the drawer in his desk again – for medicinal purposes. Willie took a grubby pencil from his pocket, licked the lead to make it nice and juicy to write smoothly, and was about to write his name in his best possible hand when Mr Sharples intervened.

'Er, no, Mr Arkenthwaite, in ink if you please. Here, use my pen.'

He took out a fine gold fountain pen which was his pride and joy and which certainly looked expensive, or at least Willie thought it did as he lovingly felt it, rubbing his fingers up and down it and staring at it in disbelief. A diplomatic cough from Mr Sharples brought Willie back to the real world again and he began very carefully to write his name. He managed the 'W' without any difficulty, but then in forming the 'A' he somehow twisted the two points of the nib, scratching the card, producing a blot the size of a garden pea and permanently damaging the nib.

'Oh, my God, shouted Mr Sharples. 'My best gold pen, you've ruined it, ruined it, it will cost a fortune to repair.'

'Nay, it's nowt, it only wants twisting back into place again. Give us your pliers and I'll do it now.'

'No, no, you may not, it will require very special attention.'

'Suit yourself, give us a biro, I'm not used to a fountain pen.'

So, Willie, believing that Mr Sharples was making a lot of fuss about nothing, took the proffered ballpoint and, after being given a new card, completed his signature without further incident.

'Next, you will need a paying-in book, which is here.' He held it up for Willie to see. 'I have had your current account number written into the front cover to make it easier for you and—'

He was rudely interrupted. 'What's a current account number?'

'It's the number of Murgatroyd's Christmas club current account, so that we can keep a check on and record of all transactions, and make an observation on the name and number of each transaction as a cross-reference. Every bank account everywhere from Timbuktu to Jefuf has a number, it makes the posting of entries so much easier for the staff.'

Willie was floundering again with this explanation, so he had a little belch and asked a question in a different direction.

'What's t'paying-in book for then?'

'The paying-in book is for you to use every Friday when paying money into your club current account. You fill in all these columns including the account number and total the money in this square here.'

Mr Sharples pointed to all the relevant sections in the book whilst Willie took a half-hearted interest.

'When you have paid over the money to the cashier and handed him the book he will stamp this small section known as the counterfoil, then sign it, and that will be your record that we have received your money. The transaction will then be entered into your account by one of the staff on the accounting machine, so that each payment is entered on to a large sheet which is our record of your account. Once a month we shall send you a statement of that account.'

'What's a statement?'

Mr Sharples was becoming seriously exasperated but he counted to ten and took himself in hand. At least he would have if Willie hadn't, without apology, belched out loud.

'What do you say?'

'Ah didn't say nowt. I were waiting for you to tell me about this here statement thing.'

Mr Sharples composed himself once more.

'The statement gives details of all the money you have paid in during that particular month, and then gives you a total of all the money you have got in your account. It is of course in your own interest to check the statement with your paying-in book to ensure that all payments to your account have been entered and recorded. Now, about the cheque book, it is usual in such cases as this to have at least two signatories to a cheque so that there can be no fraud. Furthermore it is advisable to have a third signatory if either of the other two should be ill or away from home at the time the cheque needs signing.'

Willie had been about to ask what a signatory was when he had a flash of inspiration and realised the answer.

Mr Sharples continued. 'Now, have you any nominees?'

He observed Willie frown and look up.

'Can you tell me who the other signatories are to be?'

'No, I'll have to think about it.'

'Well, please let me know as soon as possible. The cheque book will be about a fortnight in being prepared, so I suggest you ask for it at the counter about that time.'

Mr Sharples felt that he was well overdue for another nip from his bottle, so he carefully opened the drawer again whilst trying to appear to sit perfectly still. He stood the bottle upright, unscrewed the cap, and stared straight at Willie who was staring straight back at him. A short diversion was necessary.

'Have you seen that rather fine print of the Canaletto hanging on the wall behind you, Mr Arkenthwaite?'

Willie turned to look at the painting. Sharples knocked some papers to the floor and dived down behind the desk for a quick swallow of the brown nectar, put the cap back on the bottle, laid it down again, slammed the drawer to very quietly, picked up the papers and sat upright again just in time to see Willie turning back to face him.

'Do you mean that painting there?' asked Willie pointing to the Canaletto print.

'Yes.'

'It's horrible. I wouldn't give it t'wife's mother for her birthday, it's that bad. Is there anything else then?'

'Yes, Anthony Murgatroyd has suggested that you should also open a deposit account so that you can, for the benefit of your members, accrue some interest before next Christmas.'

'What does that mean?'

'For every pound you have invested we will pay you four and a half per cent worked out on a daily basis. That means we will pay you eleven pence in the pound. You will need to hold an audit before you pay out the club funds because you could be liable for income tax on the interest depending on just how much interest you have received. This of course always depends on current interest rates to depositors, and by the way, when I use the term 'you' I mean the club and not you personally, if you know what I mean.'

Willie didn't. All he wanted to do now was to get out of the situation in which he found himself, and away to the big outdoors where he could have a good snook up and spit, not to mention a giant fart he was just about containing. He sat quietly for a few minutes, then said, 'Do we get this eleven pence for nowt?'

'Yes in one sense, and no in another. The bank lends your money to someone else who in turn pays interest for borrowing it, and the bank then gives you some of the interest it has received as a payment for lending it to us in the first place.'

'Well, I don't know so much about that, if you're going to lend our money to someone else how do we know we'll get it back again?'

'Your money goes into a big pool and we lend out of the pool. Your money is always available on demand, no problem in that respect. The big advantage is that all your members will get more than they paid in when you have your Christmas pay-out. We have made arrangements to leave fifty pounds in the current account and to put the rest on automatic transfer to the deposit account. If you find it necessary to have more money in the current account, you will have to come in and see one of the cashiers to make the necessary arrangements, by signing a transfer form. Now, is everything perfectly clear?'

Mr Sharples hoped and secretly prayed that it was.

'Aye, I think so,' said Willie very unconvincingly.

'Well, in that case here is your paying-in book. We shall expect to see you on Friday with your first payment, and don't forget two things, to collect your cheque book and to nominate two more signatories.'

With that, Mr Sharples rose to his feet, walked around the desk to Willie who stood up, and they both walked out of the office together down the long corridor and back to the customers' side of the counter.

'When you come in with your money on Friday just take it to one of the windows and give it over to one of the cashiers. Goodbye, Mr Arkenthwaite, and thank you for calling.'

'Goodbye, Mr Sharples, and thank you.'

They shook hands and Willie walked out of the bank into the cold air. He snooked up a big ball of phlegm, spat it out on to the pavement, carefully spread it with the sole of his shoe so as to kill it, turned to face the bank, stuck out his tongue at it, farted as loud as he could and muttered, 'Up yours, Mr Sharples,' and, feeling much relieved, he headed for home.

Back in the bank, Mr Sharples dashed back to his office in desperate, need of another nip of brandy to calm his nerves.

Chapter Seven

Banking matters were soon forgotten as Willie passed the bottom of Mafeking Street. 'Hey up, hey up,' he said to himself as he turned up the street, and when he got to the house out of which he thought he had seen Daniel Sykes come, he couldn't decide whether it was Number 17 or Number 19, but he was sure it was one of them.

He retraced his steps to the main road, and was soon back at the Club and there being still another quarter of an hour of official drinking time left, he went in without hesitation, work conveniently ignored.

'Good afternoon, sir, yet again, sir, it's not often we have the honour of welcoming you to our humble institution twice in the same afternoon, sir, particularly when you should be slaving your guts out at the mill, sir, instead of out on the razzle, sir.' Fat Harry had a grin as wide as his stomach.

'Shut your gob and give us a pint.'

'Certainly, sir. Well, not exactly certainly, sir.' His grin got even wider and his quiet attitude continued. 'If sir will kindly show me the colour of his money I will oblige.' Then he roared, 'Cause you're not having another bugger till you do and that's a fact.'

'Just pour one and I'll pay. Come on, I've got one hell of a thirst and so would you have if you'd been to see that Sharples fellow.'

'He's all right, just a miserable sod, he can't help it, there's nowt wrong with him really.' He gave Willie his pint. 'At least no worse than any other bank manager.'

Willie's countenance changed into a wicked grin. 'I say, Harry, who lives at either 17 or 19 Mafeking Street?'

'Don't know. Why?'

'When I'd left here before to go to the bank, as I crossed the bottom of Mafeking Street, I saw Daniel Sykes come out of one of them two but I couldn't just tell you which and he should have been up at t'mill and he doesn't live there.'

'No, no, you're right he doesn't live there. Now let's think a minute, is it the new painted one, 17, or is it the one – hey, I know it's yond blonde woman.'

'Not her what's?'

'Aye, her, her with the big—'

'Well, I'll be blowed – and Daniel Sykes.'

'Aye,' said Harry, 'Daniel Sykes, Daniel holier than thou Sykes, a walking encyclopaedia of useless information, never put a foot wrong in his life and having his wicked way with her. Are you sure it was him?'

'Well, I thought it was, but I'll try and check when I get back, and talking about getting back—'

'Hey, you can't go yet, what about Daniel Sykes?'

'I never thought I'd live to see the day! I wouldn't have thought he were capable of owt like that. By gum, wait until his missus finds out, there won't half be a row and three quarters for she's got one hell of a temper, or so they say on at Strict and Particulars where she's the boss. I wonder if he knows what to do when he gets behind her locked door?' asked Harry.

'He might just because he has got three children. I wonder what excuse he's given at the mill for not being there. I bet he hasn't got a proper one like me. Anyroad, I'd best be on my way else I might not have any excuses left.'

So Willie left the cosy warmth of the Club and ambled along the main street towards the mill. The street was filled with shoppers all going about their business, many stopping to speak to Willie, then stepping back to admire and question the smartly-dressed man they never normally saw.

Len Charrington, the local retail purveyor of high-class meats and home-cooked pies, brawn a speciality, known to one and all as Porky, observed the smartly-dressed figure of Willie across the street and went to the shop door to shout across, 'Hey, Willie, come over here a minute.'

Willie crossed the street and entered the shop. 'Can't stop more than a minute, I'm on my way back to work and I'm late now.'

'Why? Where have you been?'

'To the bank.'

'What for?'

'Eh?'

'What for?'

'To arrange about Christmas club.'

'Which Christmas club?'

'Ours up at mill.'

'What's it got to do with you?'

'You have the honour to be speaking to the honorary treasurer.'

'What, you? How the hell did you get that job then?'

'I were voted on – anyway, it were my idea to start with.'

'It was!'

'Well, me and Arthur and one or two others.'

'So, you're in charge then,' said Len, thoughtfully. 'Running it like?'

'Well, it isn't starting until Friday but you could say that I were in charge. Yes.'

Len looked around to make sure that no one was eavesdropping.

'Listen, Willie,' he talked in a hushed voice, 'I might just be able to do you a big favour in return for another one from you, seeing that you're in a privileged position as it were, and it'll put a few bob in your pocket.'

Willie's ears pricked up at this half-whispered statement from Len. 'Oh, aye, tell me more.'

'Well, if you can persuade your club members to come shop here for all their Christmas meat and turkeys I'll offer five per cent discount to encourage them and I'll give you an extra five per cent in pound notes or meat on all that they spend. The only thing is, no one has to know about the last bit and it depends on you bringing me a fair bit of Christmas trade. So remember, and very important, keep it to yourself.' Len was pointing to the side of his nose. 'So what do you say?'

'Sounds all right to me,' said Willie. 'How much is it worth?'

'How many members have you?'

'Nay, I can't fair tell you yet because we haven't fair started properly yet. Ah can happen let you know on Friday when we've had a bit of a do at it, on my way to the bank like.'

'Well, let me know how many as soon as you can and I'll tell you how much you can expect. Now don't forget, mum's the word.' He pointed yet again to his nose.

Willie pointed to his own nose as he left the shop. 'Might just be a bit of all right this here Christmas club,' he thought as he made his way along the village, snooking up here, spitting there, and occasionally breaking wind. He was deep in thought, so deep in fact that he didn't know he had said out loud to no one in particular, with a huge grin on his face, 'By gum, I never knew Len Charrington had such a big nose.'

Len Charrington never knew either why a little old lady, not one of his regular customers, spent the whole of five minutes staring at him through his shop window.

★

'Be sharp and shut that door! There's a right draught when it's open and it gets into my bones right through to the marrow. This cold weather will be the death of me yet.'

I ought to leave it wide open, thought Willie, but he shut it again just like Mrs Woofenden knew he would.

'Now, how have you gone on at the bank? What's the manager like? Have you sorted him out and got your Christmas club sorted out? Are you going back to your work again? We can't afford to lose a whole afternoon's pay. Have you—'

She gave over as she realised she was interrogating an empty room.

Willie went into the kitchen to Thelma. 'Have we a mantrap what'll fit your mother?' he enquired. 'I nearly left the front door wide open to let the cold get through to her marrow. She's had the bloody cheek to tell me to get back to my work because we can't afford to lose a full afternoon's pay. We could if she contributed a bit towards the running of the house. It's not fair, I've kept her for more years than I care to mention, and she's kept me poor all that time.'

Willie belched out loud.

'Willie!'

'Sorry, love, that was for your mother. Have we owt to eat? I'm starving.'

'You can't be starving, by the smell of your breath, and you can manage until teatime without. Now I know it's difficult and I know she goes on a bit, but can't you try to live in peace with her? It does make life awkward for me.

As soon as you've gone back to work she'll be on at me about how she pleaded with me not to marry you, etc., etc.'

'It's just like having the Gestapo living here. Anyhow I'd best go get changed and get back to the mill, they'll wonder where I am. Hey, do you know what? You know Daniel Sykes? I saw him coming out of Number 19 Mafeking Street where yond blonde woman lives.'

'Which blonde woman?'

'You know, her what always wears low-cut dresses and a lot of make-up. Nice figure, different feller every night whilst her husband's away at sea.'

'How do you know so much about her?'

'I hear folk talking.'

'Are you sure that's all, only hearsay?'

'Aye, that's all, I don't know the woman personally.'

'Not Daniel Sykes! Why wasn't he at the mill?'

'Nay, I don't know, but I'm sure as hell going to find out when I get back.'

Willie went upstairs to get into his working attire again. He went into the kitchen to give Thelma a kiss, then into the front room where he stopped in front of Mrs Woofenden who was tuning up for a good squeak.

'Well, it's about time, I thought you were never...'

'Shut your foul gob for a minute and listen to me.'

Willie was amazed by his own courage.

Mrs Woofenden looked somewhat startled, if not angry.

Willie continued, 'If you say one word about me to Thelma after I've gone back to my work, when I get back again I'll have you out of that door and on your way for good as fast as it's bloody well possible. Do you understand?'

She thought about replying but, thinking he just perhaps meant it, she decided to turn the tear taps on at full flow instead. Willie straightened his cap, opened the front door, went out into the icy, biting half-fog and set off with a determined stride, leaving the door wide open. He heard her shouting, 'Thelma, Thelma,' quickened his stride and laughed out loud.

*

The big wrought iron gate was open but Willie made a slight detour through the penny hoil to speak to George Schofield who saw him coming.

'Oh, it's you again.'

'Hey, that rumour that you sleep in here all day isn't true, then?'

'Huh.'

'Hey, I say, has Daniel Sykes come back yet?'

'No, and he won't be. His mother's popped her clogs for the last time and he's off sorting out the funeral arrangements. Anyway, what's it to you?'

'Nowt, I just saw him in the village when he should have been here, and I wondered what he were doing. Well, thank you for your assistance my man, you may go back to sleep now.'

'Bugger off and get some work done.'

Willie made straight for the dyehouse.

'How've you gone on then?' enquired Arthur as soon as Willie had put on his leather apron.

'Not bad, not bad. I've sorted it out with Sharples the bank manager. I just have to take the money in every Friday after t'dinner, and that's all there is to it. Hey, guess what, I saw Daniel Sykes coming out of Number 19 Mafeking Street.'

'So what, apart from why was he there when he should have been here.'

'His mother's died.'

'So what,' said Arthur.

'Well, he's out making arrangements for the funeral but I saw him coming out of 19 Mafeking Street.'

'What's so bloody significant about 19 Mafeking Street?'

'She lives there.'

'Who's she?'

'That blonde woman with the big bust, her what's husband's away at sea and her what displays her favours all over for any man what'll have her.'

'Aye, I know who you mean. Happen she's related.'

'Never in a month of Sundays, not a miserable sod like him related to a woman of easy virtue.'

'Why not?' asked Arthur.

'Well, it doesn't seem right, him being like he is and her being like she is, they couldn't be related.'

'Happen it's her husband.'

'Happen what is?'

'Happen it's him what's related.'

'I never thought of that. It's more likely, 'cos them two can't be off of the same breed. It's not possible.'

'Hey up,' said Arthur, 'we'd best get some work done. Walter's coming over.'

'Let's ask him about it, he might know.'

Walter Smith hurried over to see why the two friends were not working.

'Have you got nowt to do or what?' he bellowed.

'Hey, Walter, come here a minute,' said Willie motioning him to attend, which he did. 'You know yond blonde woman what lives at Number 19 Mafeking Street?'

'What about her?' asked Walter, beginning to redden up around the neck.

'What relation is she to Daniel Sykes?'

'Nay, I don't know and anyway, what is it to you?'

'I saw him coming out of her front door when I went to the bank.'

'His mother's died. Perhaps they are related and he'd gone to tell her. Still, I don't think they are related; in fact, I'm fairly sure they're not, so what would he be doing there at that time of day?'

'I wonder,' said Arthur.

'I've been wondering ever since I saw him,' said Willie.

'Anyway, give over worrying about Daniel Sykes and get some work done for a change.'

They started work again, Arthur pouring a bucket of black dye liquor into a dyeing machine and Willie pulling a big cartload of pieces up the dyehouse to another machine.

As he passed Arthur, Willie stopped briefly and said, 'Did you notice how Walter began to blush when we mentioned her what lives at 19 Mafeking Street.'

'Yes, I had noticed. It makes you think doesn't it.'

'Aye, it does that.'

'It makes you think', said Arthur, repeating himself, 'that we ought to go round by Mafeking Street on our way to the Club, if we go there that is, just to see what, if owt, is happening there.'

'Aye, we could do, it might make life interesting for a change.'

And so the late afternoon's work in Murgatroyd's dyehouse continued at its usual hurried pace. Willie confided in Arthur that he would probably be in terrible trouble when he arrived home, following his brush with his mother-in-law, and Arthur interrogated Willie closely on what had transpired at the bank, not that he managed to get a lot of sense out of Willie about that matter.

★

As Willie, Arthur and Eustace were walking home at five o'clock, the ice was crunching under their feet, as they walked on top of the frozen puddles which lay perpetually through the middle of most winters in the ruts and troughs of the canal towpath.

'Now, are you sure that you are fully prepared for the first session on Friday dinner time?' Arthur asked Willie.

'First session of what?'

'First session of people bringing money for the Christmas club.'

'Is it on Friday? Is it Arthur? Is it on Friday? First time is it?'

'Yes, Eustace, it is. Have you decided how much you are going to pay in?'

'No, no, not yet, I've no idea, none at all, no, none at all, I don't know how much to pay in, I don't know. How much do you think I should pay in?'

'Well, I can't answer that for you, but a pound wouldn't be a bad idea.'

'A pound, I might, a pound. Yes, I might. How much would that be at Christmas?'

'Well, how much is fifty times a pound?' Willie asked him.

'Fifty times a pound. Fifty times a pound, that's a difficult question to answer. I don't know. Now let's see, it's, er, er, er, er, er, fifty.'

Willie and Arthur walked on in silence as Eustace wrestled with the mathematical problem, discussing it with himself.

'It's a bit of a poor do when you can't reckon up something as simple as that,' observed Arthur.

'Aye, it is,' agreed Willie, who was having serious private doubts about his own ability to cope with the task that lay ahead of him. 'Mind, you've got to be daft not to be able to reckon up a simple sum like that.'

'Fifty pounds, fifty pounds, it was easy wasn't it? Wasn't it, Willie? Easy, wasn't it,' and he walked on with a contented smile.

They arrived outside Willie's abode at Cutside Cottages, both Arthur and Eustace living nearer the centre of the village.

'You coming to the Club later, Willie?'

'I think I'll go now. Look she's staring out of the window, sat in front of the fire. She won't ever let Thelma draw the curtains till I've got in from the mill. Mind you, that's only so she can nosy. What she can see of the outside in the pitch black dark from where she sits, I do not know. I think I might go and move her on to the towpath where she can freeze to death, and then there'll be peace in our house. Anyroad, I'm having no more of her nonsense ever again – I've made my mind up – so I'll call for you at half past eight.'

'Make it nine, will you? She wants a bit of a shelf putting up in the scullery.'

'Can I come to the Club? Can I, Willie? Can I? Can I?'

'Yes, Eustace, you come with us. Of course, you can, you be at t'Club at quarter past nine.'

Arthur and Eustace moved off towards their respective homes leaving Willie standing staring at his front door. He took a deep breath and marched smartly up to the house, forcefully opened the front door and marched in, slamming it hard behind him.

*

'You're late again,' cackled Mrs Woofenden.

'Shut up and don't ever interfere with me again.'

'Willie, don't you ever speak to my mother like that again,' shouted Thelma from the kitchen.

He looked at his mother-in-law with a withering look of utter contempt then turned his attentions to the kitchen door, walked smartly over to it, put his head through to see Thelma preparing tea and said in a voice loud enough to carry back to his mother-in-law. 'Now, listen here, I've just about had my bellyful of your mother. I've had enough of her moaning and groaning about her bad back and the cold getting through to her bones. There's nowt wrong with her back that a lot of hard work wouldn't put right and she's not as starved as she makes out either.'

'But Willie—' started Thelma, but he silenced her.

'But Willie, nothing. You shut up a bit as well and listen to me. She has sat in front of that roaring fire for that long now that she can't do without it, but it's all of her own making, so, starting tonight, you can start and cut down on the amount of coal that we burn. She sits there in front of that fire all day long never contributing a penny piece to the running of this house. She expects you to wait on her hand and foot and there's nowt wrong with her. She has an appetite like a horse, eats like there's no tomorrow but never pays for any food. She never gives the kids owt except something and nothing at Christmas and birthdays, and, finally, she's a rotten, tight-fisted, miserable old woman.'

Willie was delighted with his performance so far. He turned away from Thelma, who had stopped preparing tea in the face of his tirade, and returned to the front room where he addressed himself to Mrs Woofenden.

'I hope you heard that lot, Woofenden.'

It was obvious she had for he observed the waterworks in operation.

'I see you did. Right, you can stop scriking now and listen to me. I've had enough of your moaning, groaning and interfering, so you can either agree to stop it here and now for good, or pack your bags tonight and leave my house for ever.'

'Where will I go?' she wailed. 'I've nowhere else to go to.'

'That's up to you,' he said. 'And in addition to all that, if you are stopping and behaving, you can start forking out each week. Five pounds a week will do nicely for a start.'

'Five pounds a week, five pounds a week. I can't afford five pounds a week.'

'Well you can and I know you can, so you can start this Friday. In fact I'll put one pound of it into our new Christmas club every week.'

Josie and the other younger children had been watching the proceedings with awe. They had on very few occasions seen their father as cross and masterly as he was now and were frightened of him, because they knew that when he was in this kind of mood he meant every word he said, so they kept very quiet. Even Josie, who was very prone to getting involved in any domestic argument that was going on, kept well out of this one.

Willie continued the tirade at Mrs Woofenden. 'You can also start and help Thelma around the house. It's wearing her to a frazzle looking after all of us, so I'll give you twenty-four hours to decide – either you do as I say or you pack your bags and get out of my house for good.'

'It's not your house, it belongs to the mill,' she began.

'I might not own the house, but it's still my house and if I say so, you'll go. I only need to mention it to Anthony Murgatroyd and he'll have you out as well.'

He turned to face the kitchen and asked, 'What's for tea Thelma?'

Thelma looked at him, then decided she'd better answer. 'Sausage and chips.'

'Good. Now get it ready and on t'table. I'm starving.'

They ate tea in a somewhat strained atmosphere, almost in silence except for the sound of Willie and his performing table manners. He, for his part, enjoyed his tea more than usual.

After tea and a couple of hours of pottering around between the kitchen and the now empty pigeon loft, Willie went upstairs to get washed and changed to go to the Club. Thelma came upstairs into the bedroom, put her arms around Willie, gave him a big hug and then a long loving kiss.

'Thanks, love,' she said, and went back downstairs again.

Willie smiled, glowing inside, knowing he had done what he should have done a long time before.

*

Willie knocked at Arthur's door promptly at nine o'clock. It was opened by Arthur's wife Jessie, a good-natured, well-built woman who always made him feel at home.

'Come in, Willie, how's Thelma? Arthur's not hardly ready yet. He's been fixing me a new shelf in the back scullery and it's taken him a bit longer than he thought. He gets a bit muddled over a job like that – he's very good at decorating but he's not at all clever with woodwork and bits of repair jobs.'

Arthur came through from the back scullery in time to save his reputation from any further demolition, already changed and ready to go.

'Now, behave yourselves you two. Are you taking Eustace with you?'

'Yes, he said he'd come along,' said Arthur.

'Well, don't lead him into any trouble, you know he can't cope.'

'Don't worry, Mrs Baxter, we always look after him.'

'When will you start to call me Jess?' she asked Willie.

'I've told you before it doesn't sound right,' he replied.

'Well, I wish you would, I hate Mrs Baxter from a friend.'

'Right-oh, Jess,' said Willie grinning. 'Come on, Arthur, let's be having you,' and the two of them set off walking to the Club.

On the way Willie said, 'Why don't we go round by Mafeking Street and see what's doing at Number 19?'

'It's too cold,' said Arthur.

'Aye, it is, but it's not far out of us way, just to see if she's in mourning or not.'

So they walked along, Willie playing football with a stone, imagining himself playing for Manchester United in their front line, and helping it along with a belch here and a spit there. Arthur, being by this time somewhat worried as to what might happen on Friday lunchtime when they opened the Christmas club, tried his best to cross-question Willie as to just exactly what he might be going to do, but as usual he could get not a lot of sense out of him and he was no wiser when they arrived at Mafeking Street.

'We can't just walk up here and back for no good reason or folks'll think us potty,' said Arthur.

'We have a good reason.'

'Yes, but you know what I mean.'

'Aye, but we can look like two plain clothes beat bobbies about their speed, nice and steady.'

So they walked up the hill to the top, past the terrace of neat clean houses all with well-scoured front steps and tidy gardens. Number 19 was a blaze of light. There were lights upstairs and in the front passage, but no one came and nothing happened. When they reached the top of the street Arthur moaned about how cold it was and how it would be a lot warmer at the Club, but Willie insisted on walking down the street steadily. They passed the front door of Number 19 again and Arthur, moaning again, observed what a waste of time it had been and it was only when they were a couple of houses lower down the street that they heard a door open and the sound of people talking. They turned immediately around to observe Walter Smith coming out from within. Unfortunately for Walter there was a street light just outside and, as he made a quick and furtive glance up and down the street, his eyes came to rest on Willie and Arthur.

He stepped back quickly inside and slammed the door.

'That's flummoxed him,' said Willie. 'Quick, around the back.'

'There's a through passage two houses up,' said Arthur, before they set off, running like rats out of a trap towards the back door, arriving there just in time to see Walter step out, observe them and step back in again.

'What now?' asked Arthur, beginning to enjoy himself.

'Nay, I don't know. Which door do you think he'll try next?'

'I don't know. Tell you what, you stay here and I'll nip around the front again.'

Arthur set off running as fast as he could and arrived at the front door just in time to see Walter look out and slam the door again. Willie observed the curtains at the back of the house part and Walter leer into the black darkness of the icy night. It was beginning to snow, just a few light airborne flakes but enough to tell Willie that it was time to go to the relative comfort of the Club. He walked back through the passage to the front of the house to tell Arthur it was time to go.

'Hold on a minute,' said Arthur. 'We've got him trapped in there. We could make him very late home and in certain trouble with his missus.'

'Didn't I tell you he blushed when I mentioned Daniel Sykes being here. By gum, we couldn't half have some fun here, but I reckon we'd best let him be for now, so let's get off to the Club.'

'Go on then, it's not fair to leave him in there, and just think, we can hold it against him for the rest of his life.'

It smelt warm when they opened the front door of the Club, and even warmer when they went into the brightly-lit bar.

'My word, well look who's here for the forty-third time today. Can't keep away, it must be my overly pleasant personality that pulls him in. It can't be the beer nor the decorations, so it must be me. What will you be purchasing for your own consumption this evening, oh, truly valued customer?'

'At the next committee meeting I'm going to recommend a new steward.'

Arthur whispered to Willie, who took up Fat Harry's challenge. 'It's not the beer, it's not the decorations and it's certainly not you, foulbreath. It's because it's warm in here and the landlord at the Woolsack won't put much coal on his fire that we had to come in here.'

He took a breather to break wind, which created much coarse comment from those seated in the airstream, but contrary to the threatening no one moved away.

Fat Harry was the first to react. 'They reckon there's going to be a farting contest over Penistone way this summer. Can I enter you, Willie, as the club's official farter?'

'Nay, I think not, I'll have more than I can cope with with this Christmas club.'

'What are you having to drink then, you and your sidekick here, eh? And your other sidekick what's just walked in?'

They turned to see Eustace approaching.

'Sorry I'm late, Arthur, Willie, sorry I'm late. My mother wanted a few jobs doing and they took me a bit of doing, they did, they took me a bit of doing.'

'You're lucky you've just come in in time as it's your turn to buy a round,' said Arthur.

'Is it? Is it my turn to buy a round, is it? Is it, Willie, my turn to buy a round? Is it?'

'Yes, it is, Eustace,' said Dick who, accompanied by Lewis, had crept in behind the other three.

'Well, what yer having then? Treble whisky all round?' asked Fat Harry.

Eustace was a bit taken aback by this. 'No, no, not whisky, no, not whisky, no, no, not—'

'Go on, treat us all,' said Dick.

'No, no, just a pint each, just a pint, can't afford whisky. No, no, can't afford, not whisky, just pints, yes, just pints.'

Fat Harry pulled the pints and Eustace, after searching through several pockets to no avail and having been offered the job of cleaning out the none too salubrious lavatories in exchange for the drinks, found some money and paid.

Willie began to tell the tale he'd been dying to tell. 'Saw Walter Smith on the way here.'

'Oh, aye,' said no one in particular, very uninterestedly.

'Aye, he were coming out of Number 19 Mafeking Street.'

'Where that blonde tart lives?' asked Fat Harry. 'Her what—'

'Aye, her,' and amid uproarious laughter he related the events of his visit to Mafeking Street earlier in the evening.

Dick said, 'Wait till I get to work tomorrow.'

'Nay, don't say nowt at all to him,' said Arthur. 'Let's see what he says to us first of all, so don't any of you say owt at all to him – not nowt at all.'

'You can hold it against him for t'rest of his life,' said Lewis. 'You two should be able to have a right nice steady carry-on from now on. You want to make most of it.'

'Ee, I never thought about that, but I'll work on it, won't we, Arthur. Hey, you lot, I've had a right do with t'wife's mother. I've told her she can either get off her fat backside and get some work done, pay her fair share and burn less coil on the fire or pack her bags and go.'

'Did you, Willie? Did you? Did you tell her that?' Eustace smiled with admiration.

'What did she say?' enquired Dick.

'Nowt. She just sat there and blubbered and wailed.'

'Good lad, Willie, I'm proud of you,' said Fat Harry.

There followed a chorus of praise for him, but privately they all assumed he was lying and it was just wishful thinking again.

Chapter Eight

Friday morning arrived with a flurry of snow which lay three or four inches deep on the canal towpath. Wearing their wellington boots, Willie and Arthur trudged towards the mill head on into the driving snowstorm coming on the back of a north-east wind.

'I hope it won't be so deep by ten o'clock that they can't fetch our wage money from the bank, or else we shan't be able to start the Christmas club at dinner time, because nobody'll have owt to put into it, where's Eustace?' said Willie all in one breath.

'Nay, I haven't seen him this morning. Probably digging a path from his front door to the gate.'

'Aye, that's the beauty of having a front door straight on to the towpath, I've nowt to dig.'

'Yes, you're right, it's taken me ten minutes to dig out. I can't have Jess late for her work. Willie, have you brought a book or anything to note down who pays us what, when you collect the money?'

'No, I never thought about it. Do I need one do you reckon?'

'Of course, you do, a book and a pencil to note down who pays what, and then after the first week you can make up a series of columns across, with names in the first vertical and the amount they pay. It will be very simple after that, and then any of us can do it if you can't for any reason.'

Willie was once again floundering in understanding Arthur's very straightforward explanation, but said, 'Yes, I'll do that. Happen I can borrow a piece of paper from Walter Smith, it's the least he can do under the circumstances.'

'Yes, it wouldn't do him any harm to give us a piece of paper or two.'

They arrived at the penny hoil and went to clock on and to say good morning to George Schofield.

'Brass monkey weather,' said George, dryly.

'It is that,' agreed Willie. 'Just the day for taking your pet elephant ice skating.'

'Don't be so daft, I haven't got any skates what'll fit my elephant and, anyway, it can't skate.'

Eustace arrived, decidedly out of breath. 'I've run all the way in the snow, I have, all the way, run, in the snow, all the way.'

Willie looked at him and said, 'George's elephant can't ice skate.'

'Can't it, George? Can't it? Can't it ice skate? Your elephant, can't it? Can't it...?' He paused for a few brief moments then said, 'Which elephant, George? I didn't know you had one, have you? Have you an elephant? Have you, George...?' He paused again, then smiled. 'You're having me on, aren't you? Having me on, aren't you George?'

Arthur interrupted the proceedings saying, 'Come on or we'll be late.'

'It's all right, he can't say nowt,' said Willie.

'Who can't say nowt?' enquired George Schofield.

'Walter Smith.'

'He can't because he hasn't clocked in yet, but why can't he not say nowt?'

'It's nowt to do with you. Are you putting owt into our Christmas club? It's at dinner time today, you know.'

'Aye, I do know and no I'm not. You're not having my brass and that is for sure. I'll never see it again if you lot get a hold of it. You won't have seen Ted Smith on his way home this morning will you? He's had to stop behind and help Walter Holroyd dig a load of snow off coal stack, or else we shan't have enough for today. He won't half cop it when he gets home more than late.'

'Do him good to cop it,' said Willie. 'Come on, let's get that dyehouse into life.'

⋆

They hadn't been working for long when Walter Smith walked in. Willie beamed at him saying, 'We've got things moving all right, so you needn't have worried about it.'

'Thanks, Willie, I wasn't worrying anyway. No problems?'

'Well, me and Arthur haven't any. Can I have a piece of paper?'

'What do you want a piece of paper for?'

'For our Christmas club what we're starting this dinner time. Are you putting ought in?'

'No, I can't afford just now, I've a lot of commitments at home, you understand.'

'Oh, aye, I understand all right. Can I have a piece of paper then?'

'Yes, how big a piece do you want?'

'Oh, er, well, er, a big one and a pencil.'

'And a pencil?'

'Aye, I've got to write down a list of all them what's paid and how much.'

'How many are you expecting to join?'

'Nay, I haven't a clue. Can I borrow a pencil then?'

Walter, having decided he was very lucky to get away without a cross-questioning regarding last night's activities, went away to get Willie his paper and pencil.

When break time came around Arthur and Willie told Dick and Lewis about 19 Mafeking Street. Walter must have heard the uproarious laughter, as he turned around from his mug of coffee and newspaper several times to stare at them. Dick was more than surprised to hear that Walter had said nothing about the affair to any of them.

'He could have apologised for his behaviour or played war with you two for spying on him or summat, but to say nothing at all, it's brazen.'

They chatted about the same subject throughout break time without getting it any further, just turning it over and over.

Dinner time arrived. Willie was halfway up the canteen steps when the hooter sounded. Sarah Anne Green, who not for no good reason was worried about Willie, was close behind him.

'Hello, Willie, have you everything prepared?'

'Aye, I think so, I've got a big piece of paper and a pencil.'

'And what are you going to do with the paper and pencil?'

'Going to write down everybody's name what pays and how much they pay.'

'Then what?'

'Then I'm going to the bank with the money, then I'm coming back here to my work.'

'What are you going to do about making a permanent week by week record of payments?'

'Eh?'

'What are you going to do about making a list that you can use every week so that it's easier, a bit like a school register, only for money?'

'Well, me and Arthur's talked about it and we're going to do it after today and before next week.'

'Where's the paying-in book?'

'What paying-in... Oh, hell, I've gone and left it at home. Mind you it's nowt because I shall pass our house on my way to the bank, so I can get it then.'

Fortunately for Willie the serving hatch opened and Greasy Martha stuck her ugly head out. 'Fish,' she stated, or possibly asked.

'What about it?' asked Willie.

'Do you want some or not, it's all the same to me.'

'Aye, I might as well as not. Has it got worms in it?'

'Do you want parsley sauce? Worms's good with parsley sauce.'

'Well, in that case happen I'd better have some. Put plenty of chips on, I'm starving.'

'Never known you not to be.'

'Is there any parsley in the parsley sauce?'

'No, it's my own special recipe made with fresh green mouse droppings.'

'Great stuff, shove a great big dollop all over it, long time since I had green mouse dropping sauce.'

Willie walked over to his usual corner table carrying an unusually generous helping, which he devoured at great speed, partly with his fork, partly with his knife and partly with his fingers, making more than his fair share of noise in the process. He had almost finished his first course when the others arrived with theirs, and they had no sooner started to eat than Willie was on his feet heading for the dirties trolley to stack his licked-clean plate. He was soon at the back of the queue to the serving hatch, those in front of him still awaiting their first course, and as Willie arrived at the hatch he was handed a plate of fish and chips.

'Bloody funny pudding.'

Greasy Martha looked at him and said, 'Oh, it's you. By gum, you've pigged that lot, sweets isn't ready yet.'

'Well, get a move on, I've a lot to do this dinner time.'

Martha went on preparing to serve the sweets. 'Are you ready for the big rush, then?'

'Do you reckon there's going to be a big rush?'

'Yes, there well might, there's a lot talking about joining. Anyway, your sweet's ready.'

She placed a dish of Manchester tart in front of him and then gave him the huge jug of custard so that he could pour on as much as he liked. In the meantime, Martha dodged into the kitchen, out of sight of the diners, to have a quick drag of her cigarette and a cough.

On his way back to his table, Willie passed Eric Tanner who was eating his first course.

'One of them, aren't you, Eric?' said Willie at the top of his voice.

'One of which?' retorted Eric in a very offended manner.

'You know, one of them there,' said Willie as he winked.

Almost at a scream Eric shouted, 'One of which? I don't know what you mean I'm sure, and I'll sue you if you say any more, and anyway, what are you talking about?'

'One of them from Manchester.'

'Yes. So what?'

'So what? We're only having your pudding, that's what.'

'What sort of pudding?'

The whole canteen was by now watching and listening to the proceedings.

'Manchester tart. You were brought up on it, and that's why you are as you are.'

'I've a good mind to give you a good hiding.'

'No fighting in here,' shouted Martha. 'Outside, if you're going to fight, I've got to clear up.'

Eric Tanner turned his back on Willie in the hope of offending him, but Willie wasn't in the least bothered. He had upset haughty Eric and that was good enough for him.

Willie's portion of Manchester tart was soon dispensed with in a few deft movements of spoon, fingers, and tongue to lick the remaining custard from the plate. The pint of tea was downed as if it were a spoonful and his dinner was rounded off in time-honoured tradition by the usual loud belch which everyone expected and ignored.

Soon after Willie finished his dinner, Sarah Anne Green came over and asked, 'Are we just about ready?'

'Yes, I think so, as soon as Arthur's finished eating.'

'Won't be two minutes,' said Arthur.

Sarah Anne sat down to wait for Arthur and, as soon as he was ready, she banged on the table with Willie's dirty spoon. Eventually some sort of order was established and she began to give the assembled diners a short lecture.

'Ladies and gentlemen, as you all know, today is the first payment day for the Christmas club. Willie Arkenthwaite will take your money at the corner table, ably assisted by Arthur Baxter. Thank you.'

She sat down on a free seat nearby making ready to watch and assist, if required.

*

The rush to join was slow to start – in fact, for a few minutes it was non-existent, then slowly, first one, then another, then a few more, and finally a lot more, until there was a sizeable queue weaving in and out amongst the canteen tables, all wanting to give Willie their money.

Willie carefully laid his piece of paper on the table, got out his pencil and licked the point, began to write the name of the first person in the queue and promptly broke the point. There was a slight delay whilst he sharpened the pencil with his Swiss army knife, and he started to write again. He carefully wrote down the name of each person that paid and the amount they paid as well as taking the money.

Arthur began to realise that it would take them far longer than the allotted dinner break to deal with the queue, so he started to take the money in order to try and speed things along and to give Willie more time to deal with the writing down bit.

In order to speed up the system even further, Willie began to note some people by initial only, then he lost control of the situation completely by getting some names in full, some as initials, missing out the money they paid, getting the money and not the name, and slowly losing track of what was happening.

Mr Anthony Murgatroyd appeared at the head of the queue and paid over a five pound note, which Willie handled longingly before Arthur nudged him and removed it to add to the ever-mounting pile.

By the time the mill hooter sounded again to herald the start of the afternoon work session, they still had a sizeable queue but they continued until they had dealt with every one of them.

'Right,' said Willie. 'That were a right good do. We've had loads of them, now I'll get off to the bank.'

'How many have we had?' asked Arthur.

'A lot. A right lot.'

'Yes, but how many's a right lot?'

'Well, I'm not right sure. I got a bit confused halfway through so I don't know just how many we had.'

'Haven't you got a full list?'

'Well, nearly, but I missed a few. Anyway, we can get them next week.'

Arthur examined Willie's piece of paper. 'Who's that?' he asked, pointing to the initials *J.C.– 10/-*.

'J.C., that would be, er, let's see now, er, it would be, er, came with, er, let's see now, it would be, er—'

'Jasper Collins.'

'Yes, that were him, Jasper Collins.'

'How many more are like that?'

'Like what?'

'Initials, no name.'

'A lot.'

'Do you know who they all are?'

'Well, I did, but I might not now, and there's some with no name, just money.'

'Do you know who they are?'

'A few of them and there's some with just name and no money.

'I'd best come around to your house tonight to see if we can sort this lot out before we go to the Club. It's a good job Sarah Anne's gone back to her work. Now, you'd best take this money to the bank.'

He handed over to Willie a mountain of coins and notes.

'What am I going to carry all this lot in, and how much is there?'

'You'll have to count it, then roll the notes up and put them in your pocket along with the change.'

'I'll count it when I get home,' said Willie, then he made a scruffy roll of notes, pushed them into his trouser pockets and went off to find his coat, scarf, cap and gloves.

★

'Where are you off?' shouted George Schofield from the warmth and comfort of his little office behind the penny hoil.

'What's it got to do with you?' came the reply.

'Nowt, I were nobbut asking. Mind you, I couldn't care less and in this weather you'd be a fool to go anyway.'

'Well, in that case I'm telling you nowt at all, except that I'll be back later. So long.'

He went, just hearing George's shout of 'So long.'

★

The snow was still falling heavily and there was a deep covering by the time Willie left the mill for his cottage. There had been no one along the canal towpath for ages, and certainly the local snowplough had not, as it never did clear as far as Cutside Cottages. He struggled gamely through the deepening snow, each footstep being an effort and becoming worse by the minute. As he approached the cottage he assumed that Mrs Woofenden would still be sitting by the huge roaring fire, and he resolved to give her another talking-to on the subject. Imagine his surprise when, on entering the front room, she took the initiative and attacked him.

'Thelma, our Willie's home,' she screeched and then she turned her attention to him. With a self-satisfied smirk on her face she asked, 'Have you had to come home to get changed to take the money to the bank, and you needn't ask, before you do, because I've been up on my two feet all morning helping Thelma, and I've only just sat down for a rest and I'm tired out. So you just trot off to wherever it is you're going and I'll have a short sleep to recover all that lost energy.'

Willie said nothing but walked into the back kitchen where he took hold of Thelma and gave her a big hug and kiss.

'Stop it, my mother'll be watching and, anyway, what are you doing home at this time again? It's getting too much of a habit, is this.'

'Have you any idea what I have done with the paying-in book?'

'No, none at all. Have you lost it?'

'Not so much lost it as can't remember where I put it. I forgot to look for it last night, so I didn't take it with me this morning. Hey, we've had a heck of a lot joined and I've stacks of money to take to the bank.'

'How much have you, then?'

'Don't know, I haven't counted it yet, thought I'd count it at the bank.'

'If you don't know how much you have, how do you know who has paid and if so what they've paid?'

'It's all on a piece of paper what we got from Walter Smith.'

'I wonder he's even talking to you after last night.'

'He's no option. Anyway, Arthur's coming round after tea to help me sort out a proper list of members, so where's the paying-in book?'

'Did you ever take it out of your best suit when you'd been to the bank the other day?'

'Hey, no. It might be there, mightn't it.'

He dashed upstairs to try to find the missing book and returned to the kitchen with it two minutes later.

'Has your mother been good, behaved herself, and helped you like I told her to and like she says she has?'

'Yes she's washed up and done some ironing. Mind you, it's tired her.'

'It would have tired you if you'd done nothing for more years than you could remember, but at least she must have taken heed of my warning.'

'You scared the living daylights out of her; I'd a terrible time with her when you had gone back to work. You'll never know, or care, how much you upset her. Anyway, are you going to fill that paying-in book in?'

'No, I'll fill it in at the bank. So long, I'll see you at teatime.' He had no need to speak to the old lady as he passed her for she was fast asleep in front of the fire.

★

Willie had taken no more than two strides into the ever-deepening snow when Thelma called out from the front door, 'Willie, love, it's too deep for me to go out, fetch me two pounds of sugar from the co-op please.'

Willie waved and nodded, then he heard her voice again. 'Oh, and Willie, don't forget, straight there and then back to the mill.'

'But of course, my dear,' he said mockingly, and went on his way.

★

The Club looked strange with no one in it. The big fat steward was half-asleep, lolling on the bar counter, and there was a general air of gloom about the place. Willie crept very quietly and stealthily to the bar where the grotesque form of Fat Harry lay. He thought once of picking up a soda siphon and squirting Harry in the ear, but then decided that it might be very unsafe to do so, taking into account Harry's size and temper. The next thought was for him to pour himself a pint without Harry's finding out he'd got it, but decided against that idea also for more or less the same reasons, and Harry was touching the pump handle. He looked around for some other form of mischief and suddenly an idea came, the sheer brilliance of which amazed him, and he spent a few moments in silent self-congratulation. He would pull out the peg that held up the roll shutter in front of the bar, and this would come clattering down making a terrible noise, and narrowly avoiding Harry. He walked around the bar to where he could see the peg above his head and began to outstretch his hand.

At this point in time, Willie's back was facing Harry and he jumped a mile as he heard a whisper in his ear. 'Now listen carefully, fart face, if you as much as touch that peg they'll find you hanging from the bar.'

'Pour us a pint, Harry.'

'What the hell are you doing here again?'

'Taking the Christmas club money to the bank. Will you help me count it?'

'You mean you haven't counted it yet?'

'No, it was a bit busy when they were paying it over and there were a hell of a lot of them, so I thought I'd count it here or at the bank.'

'Come on then, let's have a pint each and count it. It's dead in here, glad you came in, there's been nobody at all. It's only in weather like this. It's usually busy on a Friday. It's rotten when it's quiet. Where's the money then?'

Willie tipped out a handful of coins from his left trouser pocket, then another handful from his right one, a few from his jacket, then a big scruffy roll of notes.

'Is that it? By gum, you've a lot. Do you know how much there should be?'

'Nay, they were coming that fast it were getting out of hand, so we lost track a bit, and me and Arthur's going to sort it out tonight. I'd best pay for the pint whilst I bethink me.

'Nay, nobody'll never know, get it supped, give over bothering and say nowt.'

'You're a good pal, Harry. Now, let's get this money counted so that I can get on to the bank with it before they close.'

It didn't take them long to count it and arrive at a grand total of sixty-four pounds three shillings and sixpence.

'Good do,' said Harry. 'There's a good few paid.'

'Yes, over a hundred and fifty, I bet.'

'Not so many. There can't be a lot more than that as works there.'

'There's over two hundred goes there every morning, but how many of them actually works is a good question.'

'You silly beggar, you know what I meant.'

'Aye, I do, about two hundred.'

'Well, isn't it time you were off, they'll wonder where you are if you don't turn up.'

'Yes, I'm just going. I'll finish my beer first, though.'

Willie made another scruffy bundle of notes which he put back in his trouser pocket. He put the coins in his other trouser pocket and took his leave of Fat Harry.

'Go straight to the bank,' shouted Harry. 'Do not pass go, do not collect two hundred pounds and do not go up Mafeking Street.'

Harry heard the 'Shut up' part of whatever it was that Willie said, and then the door slammed, leaving him to go back to sleep after the rude interruption.

⋆

A rather large pompous lady was at the head of a long queue in the bank. She wore a fur coat and hat and spoke posh. She was arguing with the cashier in a very loud commanding voice that her account was not overdrawn and under no circumstances whatsoever had the young girl to say so ever again. In fact, she wished to see the manager immediately and if she did not see the manager immediately she would close her account and take it elsewhere. Willie was inclined to shout out some words of encouragement to the woman to take her account elsewhere, and quickly, but feeling a bit like a fish out of water, he kept quiet and waited for his turn to come. He had prepared for his entry to the bank with a quick snook up and spit on the pavement, and now waited patiently for his turn.

The young lady behind the desk said, 'Yes, sir.'

'I've, er, er, brought the, er, money.'

'Yes, sir. Well, are you going to pay it over?'

'Er, yes, er, here it is.'

Willie put the bundle of scruffy notes followed by handfuls of coins on to the counter, then stood looking absent-mindedly at the grid.

'Have you got your paying in book, sir, please?'

'Yes, here it is.'

Willie handed it over.

'But you haven't filled it in, sir.'

'Have I got to fill it in then?'

'Yes, sir. Haven't you paid in any money before?'

'No, and I don't know how to fill the book in.'

He didn't like to admit it to the young lady but he realised he had no alternative, as she was very bright and knew he hadn't paid in before. So the young lady painstakingly gave him a lesson in the finer arts of filling in the various boxes and columns, including sorting out the various denominations of notes and coins.

'It's going to be a hard job is this every Friday. Have I got to sort out all these different things?'

'Yes, sir, every time you pay some money into the bank.'

'Well, it's going to take me a long time. I shall never get back to the mill before finishing time.'

'You can come in here and sit at one of those small tables to sort it out.'

She indicated a row of writing tables beneath the wall behind Willie.

'Very nice. Yes, I'll do that,' said Willie as he watched the young lady stamp the page and counterfoil before tearing the page out of his book to leave the counterfoil.

*

He couldn't decide whether or not to go back to the mill. However, after a quick snook up and spit just to change the colour of the snow in one tiny area, common sense overruled his heart and he headed back through the snow which had started again following a brief respite.

Not given to being a deep thinker, Willie was somewhat surprised to find himself thinking about the mess he had made of listing people's names and monies paid to him. So deep in thought was he that he could remember nothing of the events leading up to his head feeling cold and wet, his body splayed out in the snow and a warm rough tongue licking his left ear. Several of the inhabitants of the village well remembered the 'Bloody Hell' they heard floating down the main street that horrible snowy day, and Willie remembered well enough the number of hands that picked him up and brushed the snow off him. He also remembered hearing the voices around him.

'Who is it?'

'It's Willie Arkenthwaite.'

'What's he doing out here in the middle of the afternoon?'

'You'll have to look after this here dog better than that, Sam.'

About this time, Willie had recovered enough of his senses to look around and see a collection of familiar faces gathered around him, along with Sam Garside and his Lakeland terrier.

Willie stared at Sam. 'What the hell happened?'

'Nay, it were thee. I said, "Good afternoon, Willie" and yer took no notice, just walked on with yer head down as if yer hadn't heard me and then bang, yer walked straight into the dog lead and went straight over it with yer head in the snow and yer arse uphill. Josh here took a liking to yer ears and kept 'em warm for yer. What's up wi yer, it's not like yer to be like that?'

'Sorry, Sam, I'd my mind on other things. Is your dog all right?'

'Oh, aye, there's nowt up wi t'dog, he's had many a worse do ner that. Anyroad, what were yer thinking about? Is it this here Christmas club what rumour has it yer the big boss over?'

'Aye, summat like that, just a few problems. Anyway, if your dog's all right, I'm all right and there's no harm done. I'd best be on my way, so I'll see you later. In fact, when I do see you, you can buy me a pint for causing the accident.'

'Nay, it weren't that bad an accident, not worth a pint and, anyroad, it weren't yer fault.'

'So long, Sam.'

'So long, Willie.'

Willie trudged away, heading for the mill, fuming with inner rage at his own stupidity. The onlookers had moved on one by one, all laughing at him behind his back and it was this that was making him angry. He vowed not to tell a soul about his fall, and after carefully observing what he could see of himself and removing a few lumps of snow that were stuck to his clothes, he kept on walking with his mind back on the money problem.

*

He passed through the penny hoil passage without even looking in to see George Schofield who was looking out and staring at him aghast, for never, ever, in all the years they had both worked at the mill had Willie passed by without a few words of idiotic wisdom. It wasn't until Willie had vanished from sight around the corner of the big mill that George gave over staring after him, and even then it was quite a while before he resumed his normal gormless expression. He then began to muse as to why Willie's coat back had been covered in snow.

★

'Has tha been rolling in t'snow, then?'

Willie ignored, or maybe didn't hear, this proffered gem from the far side of the dyehouse. Similarly, the 'Hey up, he's back. By gum, lad, you're nobbut just in time, we were about to send St Bernards out looking for you,' didn't receive the verbal return it should have.

In fact, no one could get a word out of Willie for the rest of the afternoon. He buckled down and worked harder than usual, ignoring everyone around him.

When five o'clock came Arthur asked him, 'What time shall I come around to your house?'

'Straight after tea, I'm a bit worried about this money business.'

'You're not on your own, I'm scared stiff about it. I'll be around at half past six.'

'Thank heavens for that.'

The two of them and Eustace walked together as usual to Willie's cottage. Eustace was most concerned about Willie, and Arthur tried his best to explain the difficulties they had with the club money. They parted company outside Cutside Cottages with their customary 'See you later' and 'At the Club, Willie.'

'The Club, are you going to the Club, Arthur? Are you? Are you going—'

'Shut up.'

Arthur and Eustace plodded on through the deep snow, still arguing.

Chapter Nine

The warmth of the front room at Number 6 Cutside Cottages relieved Willie's sombre mood somewhat. Mrs Woofenden was at her usual post in the corner, the young children were playing on the peg rug in front of the roaring fire, Josie was laying the table and Thelma was busy in the kitchen. Most of the snow had melted from Willie's wellington boots into small pools on the front room carpet by the time he got to the kitchen where he gave Thelma his usual hug and kiss.

'Willie, have you let all the snow from your boots melt on to the living room carpet as usual?'

'Sorry, love.'

'Where's the sugar?'

'Oh, sorry, I forgot to get it.'

'Oh, Willie, I wanted to bake tonight. Can you go now and get it?'

'Co-op shuts at half past five, it's too late. Mind you, Freddy Nevershut will still be open. I could go there, only his sugar is a halfpenny dearer than t'co-op's. Hold tea up for ten minutes and I'll go get a bag.'

He went out into the bitter cold night and headed for the village. The wind had dropped by now and there was just a steady downpour of big white flakes. The bell over the door sounded as Willie entered the emporium of Freddy Nevershut.

'By gum, William Arkenthwaite, as I live and breathe. You haven't graced your presence on my establishment since I don't know the day when. How are you?'

A quarter of an hour later Willie was still sitting on the edge of an upturned lemonade crate telling the tale with Freddy.

'Before I forget, can I have two pounds of sugar, I'd best not go home without it.'

'Is that all you've come for on a night like this?'

'Yes, our Thelma hasn't been out today.'

'She wouldn't have been in here if she had.'

'No, she likes her divvy from the co-op. Er, Freddy, getting back to this here Christmas club, what's in it for me if I try and get as many as I can of 'em to get their Christmas orders here? Can you do stuff a bit cheaper for them, and what can I get out of it for nowt?'

'Nay, Willie! That's corruption! You know full well that I'm an upright and sober law-abiding citizen and a true Christian. Pop back in a fortnight, I'll have had time to think about it by then.'

'Thanks, Freddy. Give us a quarter of aniseed balls for the kids. Now how much do I owe you?'

Willie picked up the sugar and the sweets, paid Freddy, and trudged off into the deep snow again. The bargees were tying up a barge at the wharf as he went past, and he stopped to exchange a few words with them before returning to the cosiness of his cottage.

*

'What's for tea?'

This must have been Willie's favourite question throughout his married life.

'Neck of mutton stew and dumplings with bread and butter pudding for afters,' said one of the youngsters who had as big a liking for food as his father.

'Great stuff,' said Willie rushing to wash and find his carpet slippers.

He sat down at the table to watch Josie take a big, steaming, time-blackened pan from the hob of the range and carry it to the table, where she proceeded to serve the contents into a pile of hot dishes.

'Put plenty of dumplings on mine, Josie,' ordered Willie as he got up from the table and walked over to stand with his back to the fire to get warmed through before he ate. He was still standing there when Thelma came out of the kitchen to ask the children and her mother to sit around the table.

'Come on, Willie love, your tea's out.'

'Nay, I can't, I shall have to get warm, it's the weather you know, it cuts through to my bones, I'm starved to the very marrow.'

Mrs Woofenden looked at Willie, then at Thelma, shed a tear or two and then said, 'Nay, Thelma lass, tell your Willie to stop imitating me will you?'

'See, Willie, you've upset my mother again.'

'Not half as much as I shall if ever I hear any more of her trouble,' he said, and with a smile of great satisfaction he sat down at the table again where he gave a demonstration of troughing with sound effects of which any right-thinking pig would have been proud. The youngsters were struggling to finish their big bowls of hot stew, and Willie suddenly had an idea as to how to get them to eat up.

He said, 'I've got a very special present for after tea and those who don't eat all their stew can't share at it.'

'What is it?' came the chorus.

'Wait and see.'

'Oh, Dad, come on tell us.'

'No, you'll have to eat all your stew and dumps first.'

'Oh, Dad, come on, tell us what it is.'

'No. Eat your tea.'

The children tucked in again, resigned to the fact that they would have to eat all their stew before they could enjoy their surprise. Thelma, who had joined into the spirit of the events, doled out large portions of bread and butter pudding, skimping Willie's usual pudding mountain in favour of the children. He realised why and didn't complain, just ate with his usual fervour.

As soon as the pudding was finished the children started again. 'Come on, Dad, let's have our surprise now.'

'No, not yet, I want my mug of tea first, in peace.'

'Oh, go on, now, now,' the chant began, 'now, now, now—'

'All right,' he said, and smiling, went into the kitchen to retrieve the bag of aniseed balls from his coat pocket and transferred it to his trouser pocket. He walked back into the front room to sit at the table again, picking up the steaming pint pot of tea that Thelma had put there in his absence.

The children stared at him and shouted, 'Dad, Dad!'

'Oh, go on then,' he said as he handed them the bag of sweets. 'Give one to your mum and gran.'

'Super. Thanks, Dad. Do you want one, Mum?'

'Don't talk with your mouths full,' said Willie, happy in his children's joy.

'You shouldn't spoil them like that,' said Mrs Woofenden.

Willie stared her straight in the eye and she retreated into silence again.

'Now, you young 'uns, Uncle Arthur's coming around tonight because me and him's got a lot of office work to do and we need some quiet whilst we work, so I want no noise whilst he's here. So, if you want to play you'll have to go into the kitchen. Okay?'

'Yes, Dad.'

*

Half past six arrived, and Arthur, with his usual promptness, knocked on the door.

Josie opened it wide and beaming at him said, 'Come in, Uncle Arthur, out of the cold snow. Here, let me take your coat and hang it up. How's Aunty Jess?'

'Jess is fine, just fine. Where's the young 'uns?'

'They're playing in the kitchen.'

Arthur walked through into the back with the greeting, 'Hello, Thelma, hi, kids.'

'Hi, Uncle Arthur.'

'I haven't seen you all since Christmas. Did you have a good time? What did Father Christmas bring you?'

'He brought me a new dolly and a pram for my new dolly,' said little Margaret, who was seven, and Peter, who was ten, joined in the conversation with, 'He brought me a clockwork train set but that's upstairs in my bedroom. Do you want to come up and have a look at it?'

'Later on when me and your dad's finished our business. Now, what about you, Thelma, what did you get from Father Christmas?'

'You know full well what I got from Father Christmas, don't you? A couple of pairs of nylons same as last year, and the year before, and the year before, and—'

'What did you get, Uncle Arthur?' asked young Peter.

'A bag of coal and a string of onions,' he said, laughing.

'What have you got in your case?' continued the ever-inquisitive little boy, for Arthur had brought along his briefcase.

'Dolls' eyes, mill chimneys and other things for grown-ups,' he said seriously.

'Can I have a look, please?'

'No, not until you're a big man like me.'

'Now, now, Peter,' scolded Thelma, 'let Uncle Arthur and your Dad get on with their business.'

Arthur returned to the front room and sat down at the table with its cloth cover, where Willie joined him. He proceeded to open the case and take out a foolscap pad. Willie placed his single sheet of paper on the table in front of him and stared at it, waiting for Arthur to begin. Arthur then picked up Willie's piece of paper and studied it for a while.

'I can't make head nor tail of this. There's a few names with money, there's a lot of initials, there's a lot of amounts of money, we know how much money you took to the bank, so let's try and make a sensible list of members for a start. We know there were a heck of a lot of folk who paid, don't we, so we might take quite a long time to sort the list out. Now then, Willie, let's write down on this pad a list of names of all those that paid.'

He took from his waistcoat pocket a very expensive-looking fountain pen.

'By gum, that's a very fine pen,' said Willie gazing at it jealously.

'Yes, Jess gave it me for Christmas.'

'Can I try it out to write the list with?'

'No, you can't. You should know that a fountain-pen's a very special pen and only its owner should use it. Haven't you got a pen of your own?'

'Aye, I've got an ordinary pen and a bottle of ink what we use for special occasions, but usually I use a pencil. Anyroad, a pencil'll do this job.'

He walked over to the range and took a pencil from the mantelshelf.

When he was seated again, Arthur enquired, 'Are you ready, now?'

'Aye, I'm ready, let's get cracking.'

Willie carefully wrote out the list of names he had written out in full earlier in the day, as Arthur looked on. Willie was painfully slow, and Arthur was almost losing patience with waiting for the list to be written out in almost joined up writing.

'Good, now, what about these here?' he asked pointing to the original dinner time list. 'These initials here, do you know who they all are?'

'Some of them.'

'Right. Write those that you know out in full, then let's see if we can decide who the rest are.'

'Can't we stop now, my writing arm's tired.'

'No, we can not, not for a long time, not until we've sorted everything out.'

'But I'm not used to all this writing and it's rotten difficult.'

'By heck, but you're a lazy sod, Willie Arkenthwaite. Come on, get on with it or we shan't get a drink tonight.'

So Willie studied his list of initials and wrote out the names of those he could remember, adding twenty-one names to the list making twenty-seven in all. He sat back, heaved a huge sigh of relief and, for good measure, farted *fortissimo*.

'There's a hell of a lot of initials there yet,' said Arthur as he began to count them. 'Thirty-seven yet left there. Don't you know any of them?'

'No, I can't think of one more.'

'It's a good job I got a full list of employees from Tom Sykes this dinner time. He was a bit reluctant to let me have it at first but when I explained to him what a cock-up you'd made of the official list, he gave it me without any bother.'

'I didn't make a cock-up of it. It were all them folk what came too quick for me, I couldn't keep track of them. Anyroad, let's have a look at this new list then, where is it?'

Arthur, in his amateur clerical/administrative roll, always the perfect professional in these matters, opened the briefcase with a flourish of arms and wrists, busied himself pretending to search for the piece of paper, found it, snapped the clasp of the case firmly closed and laid the sheet of paper smartly on the table.

Willie observed the exhibition with interest and said silently to himself and anyone else who might happen to be listening, 'Bloody show-off.'

'Right, let's examine this matter more closely.'

Arthur carefully unscrewed the lid of the new fountain pen and began to point to each name on the list in alphabetical order. Willie followed with keen interest, not the names, but the fountain pen, and his mind strayed to owning such a pen. He was awakened from his daydream by Arthur's voice.

'Well, has he or hasn't he?'

'Er, who?'

'Sid Beaumont, did he pay us any money?'

'Yes, Sid did.'

'How much?'

'Well, if he isn't on the list and his initials aren't down either we can't tell, can we?'

'But you're sure he paid?'

'Yes, I'm sure.'

'Okay, so we've got one Sidney Beaumont with no known amount of contribution, so let's put his name on a separate sheet of paper and see how many names we can get on the list.'

It was a good half-hour before they had a comprehensive list of names, and all initials were crossed off except one. For Arthur it had been a difficult half-hour trying to keep Willie's mind on the job. For Willie it had been a very boring half-hour with his mind constantly straying to any subject other than name listing. For Mrs Woofenden, sitting in her corner chair by the fire it, had been an amusing half-hour, confirming her thoughts that Thelma was too good for Willie. For Thelma it had been a very routine half-hour darning and mending the children's clothes.

'Now, who's the owner of this last pair of initials that we can't find? I just can't understand it, we've no one that we can apply these last pair to.'

'Nay, I don't know. Oh, yes, I do, hang on a minute, it's Greasy Martha.'

'Greasy Martha, G.M. What's her proper name?' asked Arthur.

'Who's Greasy Martha?' enquired Thelma.

'Fag ash Lil from the canteen, her what slops fat all over and drops cigarette ash in us dinners.'

'I know, she lives down Ashbourne Road,' said Thelma. 'She's called Martha Gregson.'

'That doesn't sound right,' said Mrs Woofenden. 'Gregson was her maiden name.'

'She's never married, nobody'd marry her.'

'Our Thelma married you.'

'I've warned you already, tonight,' said Willie, but this time she didn't shed a tear; instead she sat silently, pleased and contented.

'It's Martha Sykes,' said Thelma. 'You know, she married Hector George Sykes; his mother kept the sweet shop by the church for years and years.'

'Oh, you mean horrible Hector – well, they didn't spoil two couples, did they,' said Willie.

Arthur was beginning to get agitated.

'Can we please get on with the matter in hand? This idle chatter is getting us nowhere at all.'

'It is, we've got the answer to G.M.'

'Well, time's pressing on, so let's get this job finished. Now, we've still got a list of names with no money against them and a list of monies with no names. So where do we go from here?'

'How about the Club?'

'First sensible suggestion you've made all night,' said Arthur.

'You're both raving mad, in this weather,' said Thelma.

Arthur, maintaining his professional manner, packed away the papers in his briefcase, then they both donned their outdoor clothing and disappeared into the cold wintry night.

*

Mrs Woofenden started on to Thelma again as soon as Willie and Arthur had vanished through the front door. 'I told you not to marry Willie Arkenthwaite, I warned you, I did my best but you would take no notice. No brains, that's his trouble. He's got this Christmas club into a right mess and it isn't above started proper yet. You'll live to mark my words yet, he's no good at all, not one bit of—'

She was rudely interrupted by young Josie who had just had enough of her grandmother.

'That's my father you're talking about and I'll be obliged if you'll give over right now. You never have a good word for him, in fact, you never have a good word for anyone and I for one am fed up of it. He's provided you with a good home to which you never contribute one penny piece. You are the most ungrateful woman I have ever met. He's my dad, my favourite dad, and I won't hear another wrong word said against him.'

She stood staring at her grandmother, shaking with rage and frightened of the consequences of what she had just done.

A tear or three came to the old lady's eyes. She looked at Thelma and said appealingly, 'Are you going to sit there and let your Josie talk to me like that?'

'Yes, Mother I am, because like the other two I also am fed up of hearing you moan and groan. You are making this into a very miserable house. We were a very happy family before you came to live here, and now you're slowly driving a great big wedge between us all, making all of us very unhappy. So, I think it's time you thought about things a bit and for once keep quiet whilst you do so.'

Thelma nudged Josie and they went into the kitchen to join the other children. The old lady sat by the fire wetting her handkerchief as she wiped her red eyes.

*

Willie and Arthur trudged along the towpath through the deep snow.

'Do you reckon they'd sentence me to death if I threw the old cow into the canal with a weight tied around her neck?' asked Willie.

'I reckon they would be bound to.'

'Even if I explained to them it was a mercy killing.'

'How can you possibly make out it's an act of mercy?'

'Well, it'd be very merciful on me and Thelma. Summat'll have to be done about her, she's been staring me out all night.'

'Aye, I noticed she never took her eyes off you, not even for one minute, and they are evil eyes, horrible evil staring eyes. It makes a shiver run down your spine thinking about her, doesn't it. Yes, you've a right problem there and no mistake. Anyway, let's change the subject. It seems to me that we've need of a committee meeting. We ought to have it on Wednesday evening in the Club, there'll be nobody in the committee room on Wednesday evening. I'll fix it up tomorrow. We just need to review progress so far, or lack of it, and to see if anyone has any bright new ideas.'

Willie nodded in agreement as he always did when Arthur was speaking. However, his mind was on two more imminent pressing matters. The first was to have a good belch, and the second was to suggest that they should go to the George Inn instead of the Club, it being a lot nearer in the bad weather and they had no particular reason to go to the Club. Arthur readily agreed, looking forward to seeing one or two people they hadn't seen for quite some time.

The George Inn was named after George IV, in the days when it had been a large elegant posting inn on one of the many turnpike roads connecting Yorkshire with Lancashire. Many a wealthy traveller and many a highwayman had graced its portals in years gone by but now it was somewhat different. Instead of a thriving post inn it was now a local pub frequented not too frequently by a largely lethargic and apathetic clientele. It was dowdy and drab in appearance. There were concert and meeting rooms, lounge and public bars, tap rooms and snugs, but only the lounge and public bars were in use. No one ever met there, no one ever held a concert there. A few brave ones drank there and occasionally people like Willie and Arthur would drink there when, for various reasons, they couldn't or wouldn't find anywhere else to go. Just before and during the war it had been a very popular place to meet, but the present landlord whom the brewery had installed had seen to it that the regulars, and therefore sales, had dwindled.

They stood on the doorstep of the George and surveyed the dismal scene.

'Ten past nine and not a light on,' said Willie.

'Door's locked as well,' observed Arthur, trying the handle.

Willie stood back and looked up. 'One miserable low light in the far end room yonder,' he pointed. 'The miserable bugger can't even put a decent size of bulb in his living room light.'

Willie read the sign over the front door. ' "James Richard Wood, licensed to sell intoxicating liquor etc." He ought to be licensed to hang for crimes against the human race.'

Willie took a breather to have a good old-fashioned loud belch, without apology.

'Ring the bell, Arthur.'

Arthur pressed the bell and waited for nothing to happen. Willie enjoyed himself picking his nose and eating the contents. Arthur rang the bell and waited again. Willie snooked up, took careful aim and spat into a street grate, being well satisfied with his directional control. Arthur leaned on the bell and remained leaning on it.

Two minutes later an upstairs window opened and a curler-bedecked head poked its way out. A coarse female voice shouted, 'Shut that bloody racket! What do you want?'

'What do you mean what do we want? We want a drink, that's what we want.'

'What time is it?'

'A quarter past nine, it's nearly closing time.'

'You'll have to wait a couple of minutes.'

The head disappeared and the window slammed shut.

'Ignorant cow,' observed Willie. 'She makes it sound as if she's doing us a bloody great favour, opening up.'

'Yes, it's a sad reflection on what a good pub it was when we were under-age drinking all those years ago,' said Arthur.

'Aye, it were a good pub for under-age and after-hours drinking were this.'

By the time the various locks and bolts were withdrawn three more people had gathered in the door to wait. They had rapidly dispersed for a brief interlude when Willie broke wind but they were back again by the time the door opened.

James Richard Wood himself opened the door to let his guests into the cold of the public bar. He slouched away in front of them, heading for the back of the bar. He was wearing a loose shirt with no collar, part of a two-tone suit, black trousers and brown checked waistcoat. His well-used carpet slippers slid across the floor in a steady mechanical rhythm and he kept his hands firmly in his pockets.

'Can't think why you lot can't let a fellow have a bit of peace. Didn't think anybody'd come tonight. Bloody cold i'nt it. What do you want?'

Willie didn't know which statement to answer first, so he plumped for the sensible one. 'A pint of bitter and a pint of common. Can we have 'em served outside where it's warmer?'

'What do you mean, outside where it's warmer, it's perishing out there.'

'Aye, it is, but a brass monkey would be hard done by to survive in here. Haven't you lit the fire today?'

'Couldn't see much point in it. Can't see why you had to come in here tonight.' He continued to serve the other customers, muttering, 'There was me looking forward to a nice cosy night in front of the fire, listening to the wireless, then a nice early night, then you lot come along. It wouldn't be so bad if you were regulars but you only come in here when you can't be bothered to go as far as the Club. You haven't half upset the wife, she'll go on at me something awful when you've gone home. Life won't be worth living then.'

'I can't think why your good lady should be upset,' said Arthur. 'After all, you wouldn't have taken any brass at all if we hadn't turned up.'

'There's some others here as well, you know, I haven't opened up just for you two.'

'No,' said Willie, 'but they wouldn't have rung the bell like we did.'

Just then a vision of loveliness, still with her curlers in her hair, torn cardigan, dirty dress and worn-out slippers, shuffled in behind the bar and surveyed the throng before her eyes.

'All that bloody fuss just so that you two can have a drink, I might have known. Why couldn't you go to t'Club like you usually do?'

'Don't worry, Edith, we will tomorrow,' said Willie.

'Yes, I think you can be assured, madam, that we shall not grace your hovel again for many a long night to come,' said Arthur.

Edith looked at Arthur, made an unladylike noise accompanied by a gesture directed at him, and disappeared again to the upstairs living quarters where it was much warmer.

'Good riddance to bad rubbish,' said Willie.

'Don't you speak about my dear wife like that behind her back, Willie Arkenthwaite,' said James Richard.

Willie stared him straight in the eye and ceremoniously belched as loud as he could.

'You've got the manners of a bloody pig,' said James Richard.

Willie downed the rest of the pint at one swallow, stared yet again at James Richard and belched even louder, concluding the performance with a solitary fart and one solitary word, 'Arseholes.'

'Time for an organised retreat, I think,' said Arthur.

'Yes, let's go somewhere, where we're more welcome,' said Willie and just for good luck he finished with, 'And somewhere where it's warm.'

James Richard had the final word. 'Just to use one of your well-known phrases or sayings, good riddance to bad rubbish.'

He might have had the last word but not quite the last of the noise, as Willie responded with yet another loud belch and a gesture. Finally, just for good measure, as he was walking through the front door he broke wind as forcefully and as loudly as he possibly could.

Unknown to Willie and Arthur, James Richard had another final word.

*

The snow had abated a little by the time the two pals emerged from the pub and on to the street.

'Come on, let's go and have one at the Club for good measure,' said Willie.

'Right, you're on, and you're paying.'

They trudged on the few hundred yards to the Club. There was no talking; it was too cold.

*

'Am I glad to see you two,' boomed out Fat Harry.

'Well, that makes a change, for a start,' said Willie.

'Why, what's up?' enquired Arthur.

Harry pointed into the corner of the Club room. They turned around in the direction of Harry's pointing finger and observed Eustace sitting bolt upright at a table, his usual happy countenance looking every inch like death warmed up. They stared at him for a few minutes, then turned back to face Harry.

'What's up with him, and two pints please?' Willie asked.

'Please! Please! Coming from you! There's more than him acting a bit queer tonight.'

Fat Harry proceeded to pull the two pints and go on talking. 'He came in here just after seven and started heavy drinking, pint after pint, it's not like him. He's said nowt to nobody, just gone on drinking, it's not like him, he's got me worried.'

'Well, when Willie's paid for these two pints we'll go over and have a word with him.'

'Oh, yes,' said Willie as he paid reluctantly.

They picked up the two pint glasses, ambled over to the table and sat down, one on each side of Eustace who remained motionless, staring into his beer. Willie gave a rather loud belch which produced a frown from Arthur but had no effect on Eustace.

'I've just won two hundred quid,' Willie announced to no one in particular, and still there was no response from Eustace. Only Arthur looked up and frowned again.

Arthur then tried with more success, taking hold of Eustace's hand and saying, 'What's up old friend? We don't like to see you down in the dumps like this.'

Eustace looked up, his eyes were watering.

'It's rotten, Arthur, it is, it's rotten, absolutely rotten, Arthur, it is, it's—'

'What's rotten, Eustace?' he enquired.

'It's Claribell, that's what it is, it's Claribell, she did it, she did, she bloody well did it, the stupid little twit. That's what she is, a stupid little twit, that's what, a stupid—'

Willie interrupted. 'It must be bad, your language is shocking for you. Who the hell's Claribell, and what did she do?'

'I'll ring her ruddy neck if I get hold of her, wring her neck, aye, that's it, wring her bloody sodding neck, that's it, I'll wring—'

'Pardon,' said Arthur. 'This is not the Eustace we know and love. Who is Claribell, and what has she done to get you into this state?'

'The bloody cat, our bloody cat, the stupid sod, our cat, the stupid cat, she's eaten Tweety Pie.'

'Who's Tweety Pie?'

'Tweety Pie, Tweety Pie, my old pal, my beautiful budgie, Willie, Arthur, my old friend. He could say "Hello Eustace, Hello, Eustace", he could say that, he could, he could say that, "Hello, Eustace", he could say that, Arthur, he could, Willie. Trained him myself I did, trained him, I did, trained him, took me years, years and years, always said "Hello, Eustace", always, it did, Arthur, always said "Hello, Eustace". Then that bloody daft cat, it's eaten him, all of him, just left a few feathers and bits, just a few feathers, eaten him all, he has, Willie, all of him, a few green and yellow feathers on the table, that's all, just a few green and yellow feathers, on the table, that's all. Nothing left, eaten all of him, best pal a fellow ever had, a real pal, a real friend and he's been eaten. It's that bloody sodding stupid Claribell, that's what, it's—'

'Well, Eustace, we are really sorry,' said Arthur.

'I hope it gets indigestion, Willie, yes, indigestion, that's it, indigestion, no, diarrhoea, yes, that's it, bad diarrhoea, Arthur, I hope its diarrhoea's so bad it blows its brains out.'

'Not to mention other parts of its anatomy,' said Willie.

'Where did you learn a big word like that, Willie?' asked Arthur.

'It's nowt to do with you,' replied Willie, who just for good measure and bearing in mind the effect the recent conversation concerning diarrhoea had had on him, ended with a loud fart.

'I'm going to give it to next door's dog. That's what I'll do, give it to next door's dog, that'll teach it, that'll learn it a thing or two, that'll teach it, there'll be nowt but skin and claws left of it, nowt but skin and claws, just like my darling Tweety Pie. It's buggered, Willie, it is, Arthur, proper buggered,' said Eustace, following which he crawled back into his own little state of depression.

Willie stared at Eustace then observed, 'Well, there's a how-do-you-do and no mistake.'

'Yes, it throws our little problem of names, no names, money and no money into complete insignificance. By the way, Willie, whilst I am talking, it's your round.'

'Nay, it's not my round again, it can't be, not yet, I've only just paid, are you sure? Nay, it's not, I bought this round we're just finishing.'

'So you did, Willie, sorry it's my round. I'll hail the steward, we might get waiter service for a change.'

Arthur turned to the bar and gesticulated. 'Ahoy there.' There was no response from the bar, so he shouted, 'I say there, bar steward.'

Fat Harry looked up.

'Two more glasses of your best ale over here for me and my friend, if you please.'

Fat Harry mouthed an answer and diverted his gaze from them.

'What did he say?' asked Arthur.

'I don't exactly know, but I don't think you're going to get the waiter service you want.'

Arthur walked over to the bar and quietly clattered the glasses on the stained bar top.

'Two pints of the usual.'

Harry grinned. 'Not so much as an if you please, by your leave, or even kiss my—'

He was cut short.

'Now then, Harry, there are deeply troubled people in here tonight who can well do without your coarse humour.'

'Have you found out what's up with him?'

'Yes, it appears that his pet budgerigar, answering to the name of Tweety Pie, has fallen victim of a dark, foul and dastardly deed.'

'What's happened to Tweety chuffing Pie, then?'

'He has met his maker in a most unfortunate fashion.'

'Eh?'

'He has been the subject of a feline's refectorious delight.'

'Eh?'

'Claribell's eaten him.'

'Ho, ho, ha, ha, ha,' Fat Harry's large frame roared with laughter. 'Flippin' heck. Who the hummary's Claribell?'

'Their cat.'

'Ho, ho, ho, best I've heard this week. Hey, you lot, come over here and listen to this.'

'I think we'd best drink up and get poor old Eustace home.'

'Yes, you're right,' said Willie. 'Come on, sup up, last to finish buys tomorrow's first round.'

'You've no need to bother racing, I can't win against an ale can like you, Willie.'

Willie grinned and downed his pint in one long swallow. He was at the door with Eustace before Arthur had finished his.

They walked Eustace home and left him on the front doorstep. Conversation was not in evidence, and little was said after they left Eustace other than for Willie to remind Arthur whose turn it was to buy the first round tomorrow.

Chapter Ten

The committee meeting was finally called for the Wednesday evening in the committee room at the Club, half past seven sharp. It had to be Wednesday as it was the only night of the week that the room was free of other functions.

Willie, having had a heavy tea of home-made steak and kidney pudding, chips and peas, with apple roly-poly pudding and custard for afters, was in good form as he called for Arthur. Jess opened the door after Willie had just about flattened it with the big brass knocker.

She gave him a big broad welcoming grin and said, 'Come on in out of the cold. How's Thelma? Arthur tells me your mother-in-law's being her usual obnoxious self.'

'If you want to have a pleasant few minutes whilst I wait for Arthur, please don't mention her again.'

Jess looked startled and Willie continued, 'Sorry if I were a bit sharp, but tempers in our house are just about at breaking point over her – even Josie played war with her yesterday. She'll have to go, there's nowt but trouble and strife in our house with her there, and it used to be such a happy place before she moved in.'

'I saw Thelma today and she told me all about it. You're having a rough time of it just at present.'

'Yes, I might not be the world's brainiest bloke, nor the richest, but we've a nice little cottage and a right grand family. We were all very happy until she came along, sticking her oar in, complaining about me, and how her

Thelma should have married somebody better. That's all that she does, complain and moan. If it's not one thing it's another.'

Jess decided it was time to change the subject, asking, 'When are the new pigeons coming?'

'We haven't decided yet, probably when the weather gets a bit better; young birds'll settle better in warmer weather, and then they'll have bags of time to get used to home and homing before the next racing season.'

'I'll be glad when they do come,' said Jess. 'Arthur's getting a bit irritable without his favourite hobby. Mind you, this Christmas club is taking his mind off them, and talking of Christmas clubs, where is he, I wonder.'

She walked out of the living room to the bottom of the stairs and shouted up them, 'Arthur, Arthur, are you ready? Willie's here.'

Willie took a good look around the living room, as he always did when he was there, and felt his usual pang of jealousy. The room was very similar to his, very neat and tidy, unlike his, but no children to make a mess, and best of all, no Woofenden.

Jess reappeared saying, 'He's lost his clean socks again.'

'Has he lost them before?'

'He loses them almost every time he wants them. You men are quite incapable of looking after yourselves. I wonder where you'd be without us women?'

'I wonder,' said Willie. 'Particularly one in particular.'

Arthur descended the stairs, well groomed as usual, for an evening out.

'Do you want to borrow a pair of my socks, or have you found your own?'

'Up yours,' said Arthur, with a wide grin.

'Now, now, you two,' said Jess, 'please leave the Club talk to the Club, this is a clean and respectable house and we're keeping it that way. Come on now, you'll be late, especially if you're calling for Eustace.'

'Calling for Eustace, are we? Are we, are we, Arthur, calling for Eustace? Are we, are we, are we, Arthur, are we—'

'Willie, that really isn't very kind of you to mimic Eustace like that,' said Jess.

'No, but it's good, isn't it?' said Willie.

'Come on, let's be having you on your way – there's a good programme on the wireless I want to listen to.'

She gave Arthur a peck on the cheek and he carefully tucked the ends of his scarf into the smart vee cut of his thick tweed overcoat. Jess opened the door to let in the icy cold north wind. Arthur picked up his case and they exited into the night, heading for Eustace's abode.

*

It meant a slight detour to collect Eustace, but as the snow had been cleared from most of the streets and all of the pavements it was an easy walk.

Eustace lived in the middle of a long terrace of stone houses which Willie always reckoned must be, at the least, the longest terrace in the world, owing to the time it took to walk from one end to the other. The road behind the terrace had not been cleared and the snow was still very deep, much of it flattened into hard-packed ice with people walking over it. Willie knocked on the back door, which faced the road, and it was answered promptly by Eustace's dragon-like wife, Joan.

'Come in, he'll be ready in a minute, won't you?'

'Yes.'

'I can't think what use he can be to you on a committee, he's no use to me around the house, completely useless.

Are you ready yet? Arthur and Willie are waiting,' she bawled upstairs.

Arthur ventured some polite conversation. 'I understand the cat has eaten the budgerigar.'

'Best thing that ever happened to it. It was like him, Sitting there going tweet, tweet, all day long. At least it's shut that horrible row up.'

Arthur didn't try polite conversation again and there was then a very pregnant silence for two minutes. Willie thought that Eustace was a poor sod with a wife like the woman who was standing with them, then, because he couldn't think of anything better. 'Poor sod', he thought, and he was just going to think it again when his thoughts were disturbed by...

'Hello, Willie, hello, Arthur, isn't it cold outside, isn't it? Have you got your wellingtons on? Have you, Arthur? Willie? Oh, yes, yes, you have, I'll put mine on. Yes, I'll put mine on. Where are they, Joan? Where are they?'

'Cor, you'd lose your head if it were loose. They're in the back kitchen where you left them.'

It always took a couple of seconds for things to dawn with Eustace, so, seeing that he wasn't going to move immediately to fetch the wellingtons, she said, 'I'll go fetch them, it's no good bothering waiting for you.'

She stomped off into the back kitchen and returned in a trice, wellingtons to hand.

'Here, get them on and get going, you'll be late. All of you,' she added.

The three men almost became wedged in Eustace's front door in their eagerness to get out. Even the cold night was preferable to being any longer in the company of Eustace's wife.

'Are we going to be late, Willie? Are we?'

'Not so you'd notice, Eustace. Is your Joan always in such a bad frame of mind? She always is with me and Arthur.'

'Oh, it's not just you two, she's gone off men in general, she has, she's gone off men. She reckons, she does, that they cause her more bother than they're worth, she does. She does.'

'Aye, we've noticed we're nowt better than a nuisance to her, several times now,' said Arthur as they made their way slowly along the front of the terrace. 'I take it she's a bit more gentle with other women.'

'Not a lot,' said Eustace, 'not a lot. They get in her way as well, they do, they get in her way. Come to think of it, it's only that bloody, stupid, sodding cat that doesn't. Just that bloody, stupid, sodding cat. It's always, "Who's Mummy's little pet then?" it is, it is, Willie, "Who's Mummy's little pet then?" and then, "Come to Mummy, little darlikins," it is, Arthur, it's "Come to Mummy, little darlikins," all day, all sodding day long. If I just get the chance, if I could just get the chance, just once.'

A wicked gleam came into his eyes as he said, 'I'd shove its little darlikins right up its little—'

'The thought's too horrible to contemplate,' said Arthur. 'It's not that I don't entirely agree with you.'

'Speaking personally,' said Willie, 'I might come along and help you.' He was sore at the verbal mauling he had received from Joan. 'Anyway, here we are at our number two residence.'

*

It was twenty-five past seven when they arrived at the Club, so they first went into the Club room for a drink.

'Your round, Eustace,' said Willie.

'Is it? My round? Is it, Willie? My round?'

'Put your money where your mouth is,' shouted Fat Harry. 'It's good to see you're better. Thought you were a goner on Monday night, at least on a slow decline, thought we'd be having to have a collection for you. As it is here you are, hale and hearty and talking again with a vengeance. Three pints is it?'

'Yes, please, yes, three pints, Harry, yes, yes, please, that's it, three pints of best bitter—'

'Coming up,' said Harry with a smile, cutting off Eustace in mid sentence, for as anyone in the Club could tell you, if you didn't cut him off he might go on all night.

'Committee room's ready for you, gentlemen, given it a special quick flick-over seeing that we're going to have a lady present, and talking of ladies, here she is.'

Fat Harry's grin broadened perceptively. 'Hello, Sarah, love, what can I get you to drink?'

'I'll have a gin and tonic if you're paying, Harry.'

Arthur leaned over and whispered in Willie's ear. 'Just look at him playing up to Sarah Anne, the big stupid fool, she thinks no more about him than she does the station platform.'

'Aye, but he's smitten,' said Willie. 'Just look at him.'

The fact that Harry was smitten with Sarah Anne would have been obvious to anyone who happened to be there at the time, by the way he was prancing about behind the bar, wiping the bottom of her glass even if the tea towel was filthy, the way he kept making short smiling glances in her direction, and the change in his general attitude.

Eustace very bravely enquired as to when he might expect to get served, but Harry just quietly whispered in his ear, 'Shut your gob and wait your turn.'

'Right you lot, it's half past seven,' Arthur announced to the assembled throng, 'time the meeting began. Can we please move into the committee room.'

'I've lit the fire so you'll all be nice and warm in there. Here you are, Sarah Anne, your very good health.'

He gave her the gin and tonic and out of politeness she stayed to have a few words with him. 'What about my three pints?' asked Eustace.

Harry turned to face Eustace and was just about to verbally tear him apart when Sarah Anne said, 'Yes, please Harry, get him his drinks, we should start the meeting on time.'

*

Arthur lead the procession along the corridor, unintentionally at a funeral pace. Sarah Anne was next followed by Eustace, Willie, Dick and Lewis, in no particular order.

Willie piped up from the rear to no one in particular, 'What time's the interment?' But Arthur wasn't to be drawn and carried on walking.

Eustace, who wasn't normally to be credited with being observant, asked, 'Where's Daniel Sykes?'

Dick Jordan, who was quick on the uptake, said, 'Probably still feeding the lions.'

'What lions?'

'The lions in the den. From the Bible. You know, Willie, Daniel in the lion's den.'

'Oh, aye,' said Willie, only to be agreeable.

Sarah Anne, as chairman, stood up and called the meeting to order. 'Good evening, gentlemen, thank you all for coming along on this ever so horrible night. Have we any apologies for absence?' She looked around but there was no response.

'That's unfortunate,' Dick whispered to Willie. 'He must be coming.'

'Right then, if there are no apologies, we will get straight on to the second item on the agenda, the reading of the minutes of the last committee meeting held here at the Club last week. Arthur, can you oblige, please.'

Arthur rose to the occasion. 'Yes, certainly, madam chairman.'

He stood with the minute book in hand like a soloist at a concert, read the minutes and sat down.

Sarah Anne rose again. 'Can we have a proposer and seconder for the minutes, please?'

Three or four hands went up, and Arthur made a few notes.

Sarah Anne continued. 'Now for the reason we are here tonight, a report from Arthur and Willie to give us an up-to-date picture of events so far. Which of you would like to begin?'

As the others were waiting for some response from either the secretary or the treasurer, the door was opened with some force and Daniel Sykes dashed in, gasping for breath, trying to say something. He remained firmly holding the door handle whilst he regained his composure.

'Have you been running, then?' enquired Willie.

'Yes, yes, of course I have been running,' he said very crossly, then he smiled at Sarah Anne. 'My apologies for my lateness, madam chairman.' He removed his thick tweed coat and sat down.

'Now, can we please begin this report from, yes, the secretary, I think.'

Arthur rose slowly to his feet. 'Er, yes, well, as you know, the initial response to the Christmas club was somewhat overwhelming and took both Willie and myself by surprise. In fact we were totally unable to cope with the onslaught. There were so many people wanting to join the club that we lost control of the situation. We managed to get the first few names and the money they paid, then we fell behind and finished up with a list of names without how much they had paid, a list of money without names, and we had some more money without either names or amounts.'

'I think it is absolutely disgraceful that you could not cope with the situation,' interrupted Daniel Sykes.

'Please allow the secretary to continue, Daniel Sykes, and give over interrupting; you can have your say later.'

'Thank you very much, madam chairman. You will all be pleased to know that we have now rectified the situation, by asking almost everyone that works at the mill if they had joined the club and how much they all paid. Now you could be forgiven for thinking that it is almost impossible to get the truth from everyone regarding money, especially where there is the opportunity to be on the make, as it were, but without any problems we have been able to match names with money, to account for all the money paid in and to balance the first week's account.'

Daniel Sykes interrupted again. 'Well, that's an improvement, but I still say that the whole matter is absolutely disgraceful.'

Sarah Anne didn't bother to intervene again.

Arthur glared, then continued. 'We have now been able to devise a system whereby we can tick off each person's name against our master list as they pay, and that side of things should run smoothly hereafter. That concludes my report for this meeting.'

Eustace gave a solo performance of clapping and then said, 'That was good, Arthur, it was, it was good, it was, Arthur, good it was, it was—'

Daniel Sykes interrupted him, almost shouting at Sarah Anne, 'Madam chairman, I would be very much obliged if you would kindly ask our treasurer to refrain from picking his nose and eating the contents thereof. I can think of nothing more revolting and despicable than to sit here watching him carry out this vile and indecent act.'

Willie stared at Daniel Sykes. Sarah Anne was too embarrassed to comment.

Finally, Willie spoke directly to Daniel Sykes, 'Do you want a lick then, it's right good, nice and salty, super stuff.'

'You nasty little man,' was all Daniel could reply in his rage.

'Now, you two, let's have some order to the meeting.'

Sarah Anne was about to ask Willie for his contribution when Dick Jordan put his fourpennyworth in. 'Can we get on and have the treasurer's report, please?'

'Yes, I was just about to announce it. Willie, please.'

Willie stood up and stared through the wall opposite, played with his pencil and finally, after an indeterminable pause, said, 'Er, aye, well, er, yes, well, it's like this, like, er, yes, well, same as what Arthur says like, we, er, got everything sorted out like.' He stopped and another long pause followed, then said, 'Oh, aye, I went to t'bank.'

He was saved from further immediate trouble by Fat Harry opening the door and walking in with a large tray of drinks.

'Now, Sarah Anne, love,' he said with his usual smile, 'I thought as how you'd all be thirsty by now, so I brought another round of drinks just as the last.'

'Are these on the house?' enquired Lewis Armitage.

'No, they bloody well are not,' said Harry, and looked at Sarah Anne in embarrassment.

'My apologies for the foul language.'

He carried on placing the drinks carefully on the mats on the green baize cover of the committee room table until he arrived at Daniel Sykes.

'Hey up, it's the Lucozade king himself. What will you be drinking then?'

Daniel Sykes turned five shades deeper of purple and looked ready to burst, but restrained his anger and ordered a tomato juice. Willie took the opportunity of Harry's timely intervention to ask Arthur what he should say next.

'Tell them about your visit to the bank, how much money you paid in, how many paid, and anything else that's relevant.'

'I didn't think I'd have to speak.'

'You'll have to give a report at every committee meeting, same as anyone else who has a special job.'

'If I'd have known that before, I wouldn't have had a special job.'

Willie lapsed into silence, meditating as to how he had got into this mess. He had served on committees before at the Club. He had been on the management committee one year and the racing trip committee another time, but only as a general member, not anything special as it were, and now here he was the treasurer of Murgatroyd's Christmas club. He came back to life with a start as Sarah Anne was digging him in the ribs.

'Come on, Willie, it's time to continue with your explanation of events.'

He looked around. Where was Fat Harry? He must have gone, everyone had a drink, including Daniel Sykes – he must have been deep in thought for far longer than he thought he had. He stood up again, picked up his pint glass, took a long, slow swallow and with difficulty stifled an urge to give a good loud belch, especially in the direction of Daniel Sykes. He began to address the meeting once again.

'Nah, then, we had a bit of a rush on Friday dinner time, but when it were over and we'd had time to reckon up, we'd had one hundred and twenty-seven people paid.'

'Eeh, that's marvellous,' said Dick Jordan, and a low murmur of voices accompanied by a nodding of several heads agreed with him.

Willie was glad of the short break to collect his thoughts before continuing, 'We took sixty-four pounds three shillings and six pence, all of which I took on to the bank.'

At this point he began to dry up again.

'Er, we, er, well, we, er,' and then he had what for him was a brilliant idea, so he steamed on again at top pace. 'The highest amount of money what we took from any one person were five pounds and I might as well tell you who it was.'

He was interrupted by Sarah Anne standing up and saying, 'Willie, I don't think that it's quite ethical to divulge the details of individual members to the committee.'

'Eh?'

'You mustn't tell who pays what – it's confidential.'

'Aye, but this five pounds one doesn't matter because everybody knows it were Mr Anthony himself.'

Sarah Anne gave up trying and sat down again.

'And the lowest what we had were half a crown. Mind you, we'd a few of them and I'm not telling you who they all are. Now, er, er, I can't think of anything else to say except next week it'll go like clockwork.'

He sat down, well contented with his performance.

Sarah Anne rose to her feet yet again. 'I can't think that we can take this matter any further tonight except to thank Arthur and Willie for what must have been a far more difficult task than we had appreciated last Friday and to wish them good luck with future collections. Now, is there any other business before I declare the meeting closed and we adjourn?'

Daniel Sykes, to the accompaniment of several groans and moans, rose to his feet and began to address the meeting in his familiar, somewhat austere manner.

'Madam chairman, if we are to bank the princely sum of sixty-four pounds three shillings and sixpence each week except holiday week until the week before Christmas, this is going to mean something like two thousand nine hundred pounds being banked by that time. Now, can I, through the chair, ask the treasurer whether this money is being kept on current account?'

Arthur dug his elbow into Willie's ribcage, to awaken him with a start from his own private little world.

'What?'

'Answer Sykes's question.'

'What question?'

'Just answer, "yes".'

'Yes.'

Daniel continued, 'It seems to me that it would be advisable to transfer this money into a deposit account where interest could be gained on the capital. With there being a regularly increasing capital it is more than difficult to estimate the final yield over the year, but every little helps and the interest could be divided up at Christmas, pro rata to the amount each member has paid in. Could we please have the treasurer's feelings on this most important of issues?'

Sarah Anne and Arthur were the only two people in the room who had fully understood Daniel's speech. Willie was baffled, Eustace had been baffled even before Daniel had started to speak, Dick had a mild interest, and Lewis couldn't have cared less.

Arthur whispered in Willie's ear, 'Go on then, get up and answer him.'

'Answer him, I couldn't even understand him let alone answer him. You answer him.'

Arthur stood up. 'Madam chairman, may I please answer the question on behalf of the treasurer?'

Sarah Anne was very relieved to see Arthur stand up as she had been dreading Willie's answer. She was just about to nod her assent when Daniel got there first.

'Why can't he answer for himself?'

'Because he has asked me to answer on his behalf.'

'He can't because he knows nothing about it. He's thick, he is, thick. He's not fit to be our treasurer.'

Willie, who had been trying his best to stifle the almost overwhelming urge to break wind for a long time now, lost his temper – and the wind – loudly, looked at Daniel Sykes, and shouted, 'I'll come over there and smash your gob straight through your teeth and down your throat if you say one more wrong word about me.'

'Willie! Please control yourself,' ordered the chairman.

'Well, he's always picking on me, and I'll pick on him with my fist if there's any more of it.'

'May I continue?' enquired Arthur looking at Daniel Sykes whose silence was taken as confirmation that he could. 'Thank you. Now, the idea of banking the money on deposit or some other interest bearing fund must be one that appeals to us all. I do believe that everyone in this room tonight would support a motion in favour of such a move, but there is the one small stumbling block of taxation to consider. We have not before talked about this matter but it would appear to be worthy of some further consideration, and I would like to thank Daniel Sykes for bringing the matter to the attention of the committee. Might I ask Daniel if he has any thoughts himself on this matter of the taxation of the interest.'

Arthur sat down, pleased with his oration, as was Sarah Anne.

Willie was bored, this conversation was beyond him, and his glass was empty. He yawned, picked his nose and savoured the contents, then just as Arthur sat down again he said to no one in particular, 'I could do with another pint.'

Sarah Anne looked around to find several empty glasses and observed that five minutes' break wouldn't go amiss, but only five minutes, and quicker if possible. The room emptied as if the plague had entered when the announcement of the break was made. Even Daniel Sykes, feeling the urge, took himself off to the gents.

Around the bar the conversation between Dick, Eustace, Lewis and Willie centred around the fact that the intricacies of high finance were beyond them and, with the exception of Willie, they might just as well not be there, or even on the committee for that matter. However, Willie, in need of moral support, persuaded them to stick with him, so they returned to the committee room suitably refreshed and replenished. Sarah Anne opened the proceedings once more. 'Daniel Sykes, you were about to give us your thoughts on the problems of taxation with regard to a deposit account.'

Daniel rose to the occasion. 'Quite frankly, madam chairman, the fact that the interest we would receive on a deposit account would be liable to taxation had not crossed my mind at all. However, as I have had time during the interval to give a brief glance at the problem, initially it looks as if the income would be treated as unearned income and taxable, therefore causing a problem, albeit a minor one. On the other hand, it could be that the income is so small when broken down into individual pay-outs that it would be negligible in taxation terms. I would not like to see us becoming embroiled with the Inland Revenue, with long meetings and arguments ensuing, but, like any other man not wishing to look a gift horse in the mouth, I would very much welcome some bonus, as it were, on my contributions. So my advice, for what it is worth, and I hasten to add for the benefit of those who know me well, not a course of action I recommend lightly, is that we place the money on deposit and completely ignore the tax man. If we get done by him later we get done, plead total ignorance and pay up.'

As Daniel sat down Eustace began to clap and the others joined him. Daniel was visibly moved.

Sarah Anne asked, 'Can we have a proposer and seconder for the motion that all contributions to the Murgatroyd Christmas club should be put into a deposit account?'

Daniel proposed the motion, Lewis seconded it, and it was carried unanimously.

The chairman continued. 'Right, Willie, will you please make the necessary arrangements.'

' Eh?

'Give me strength,' she muttered. 'Willie, will you please go to the bank and make the necessary arrangements to open a deposit account and keep all the money from the Christmas club in this new account except for a few pounds we need to keep in current account for contingencies.'

Willie leaned towards Arthur and asked, 'What's contingencies?'

'Well, let's see now, it's like if you were just going to buy the last pint of the night and you decide not to, instead putting your money back into your pocket to save it for if you might need something else.'

'But I never do.'

'Well, if you did it would be.'

'What?'

'A bloody contingency.'

The rest of the committee turned at Arthur's raised voice.

'Oh, yes, I see,' he said, trying to sound convincing.

'Willie,' asked Sarah Anne.

'What?' asked Willie.

A note of exasperation entered Sarah Anne's normally calm voice. 'Go to the bank and open a deposit account.'

'Yes, I will, but I'll have to get Mr Anthony's permission.'

'I'm sure he'll allow it. Right, if there isn't any other business I'll close the meeting, leaving you gentlemen with plenty of drinking time, and it's home for me.'

'Won't you come and have a quick drink before you go?' asked Arthur.

'No, not tonight, I've some housework to do.'

With that, the meeting, with the exception of the chairman and Daniel Sykes, adjourned to the bar.

*

Fat Harry as usual was first off the tee with his sarcastic wit. 'Where is he, then?'

'Who?'

'Why, the Lucozade king of course.'

'Gone home to be miserable there because he's better being miserable there than here.'

'He might have gone up to 19 Mafeking Street,' said Willie.

'Well, she's welcome to the miserable sod. Never could abide him and his supercilious attitude,' observed Harry.

'Why don't you pour some ale and keep your customers happy?' asked Arthur.

Harry decided to change the subject. 'Are you feeling better, Eustace?'

'Me, feeling better, me? I haven't been poorly, not me, no, not me, Harry, no not—'

Harry was beginning to regret his mistake. 'No, but you were a lot off it when you were in here the other night. You sat in that corner and said nowt to nobody for nowt all night. Even the terrible two couldn't get a word out of you, it were just as if you was dead, or nearly dead.'

'That was after Claribell had eaten Tweety Pie, poor old Tweety Pie, he had, he'd eaten Tweety Pie.' Eustace shed a tear. 'That poor little bird's gone. Gone, he has, Harry, he's gone. Eaten by her ruddy stupid cat, eaten by—'

He was rudely interrupted by, 'Give him another pint, Harry.'

Willie had cut him short to the relief of the people in the bar. Harry pulled a pint and gave it to Eustace, but Eustace accepted it without any sort of acknowledgement. He sat down in the corner nearest the bar and quickly drank the pint, looking down in the dumps and lost in his own little world of budgerigars, cats and domineering wives. The others watched him, and Lewis asked Harry for another pint for him.

'Nobody's offered to pay me for yond last pint yet, but I'm not forgetting who ordered it in a great hurry.'

'Here you are,' said Willie, as he handed over the money. 'Don't let me be the cause of your distress. It's bad enough having one distressed person without any more.'

The evening rolled on, the conversation followed its usual pattern of football, weather and sex. Daniel Sykes figured large in the latter subject, particularly the bit about Mafeking Street and, as usual, several rounds of beer were consumed by all except Eustace. He drank considerably more than the others, at their expense, right up to and beyond closing time, at which time he began to serenade the crowd with an endless rendering of 'Nellie Dean'.

Fat Harry donated a double whisky as a nightcap for Eustace, working on the theory that it was a very rare occasion when he could be seen to be drunk, and it would be a good idea to help him along a little.

Arthur, who was ready for home by this time, pointed out to Willie that they couldn't very well leave Eustace at the Club in his present state, so they agreed to take him home although it meant a short detour for them both.

'The Club won't miss another drop of whisky, will it, Harry?' asked Willie.

'Not if it's for a good cause,' he answered, laughing. 'Here, fill his glass to the top.'

He passed the whisky bottle over the bar to Willie who filled Eustace's glass right up to the brim. Eustace needed a little encouragement to finish the final glassful, for he was in such a state by now that he couldn't find his mouth with his glass and was in need of assistance from others.

When the glass was empty, Willie and Arthur helped him to stand up. They didn't have to help him to sit down again quickly, and they lifted him up again. They then, all four of them, struggled to put on his gloves, scarf, coat and cap. It wasn't that he was uncooperative, it was more that by now he was so relaxed he was just like the India rubber man with no control over his movements. He was ushered outside, and it was when the cold night air hit him that the trouble really started. 'Nellie Dean' was rendered at full volume, it wasn't in tune, pitch or time, but it was loud. They tried to quieten him, but to no avail. Dick, in a mood of desperation, put his hand over Eustace's mouth to silence him but removed it very quickly with a loud scream as he studied the teeth prints in it.

Willie and Arthur managed, by each getting hold of one of his arms, to drag him along home. Dick and Lewis came along for the fun of it. As they made their way along the road, past rows of houses and cottages, the very tuneless strains of 'Nellie Dean', caused windows to open, curtains to be pulled back, dogs to bark and cats to flee. They came to an abrupt halt outside Eustace's abode.

'What shall we do now?' enquired Willie of the general population.

'You go knock on the door,' said Dick.

'It'll happen be for the best if you do it,' said Willie.

'Yes, go on Dick,' said Arthur. 'We'll just continue to support Eustace whilst you get the door open.'

As it happened, Dick didn't need to go and hammer the knocker – for two reasons. Firstly, Eustace began to fight with Arthur and Willie to free himself of their support. They let him go and he immediately attempted to force his way through the neatly trimmed privet hedge that surrounded his garden rather than take the usual route through the gate and up the path. Secondly, the door opened anyway, and Joan, disturbed by the kerfuffle outside, looked out. With the exception of Eustace who was still fighting the hedge and singing, no one moved a muscle and no one spoke.

Joan was the first one to break the deadlock.

'What are you lot staring at?' she snarled.

'We've brought Eustace home,' Arthur said lamely.

'Why couldn't he bring himself home?' she demanded.

'Well, er, well, er, well, it's like this, he's had too much to drink and he's not in a fit state to see himself home,' Arthur was never so glad in his life to finish a little speech.

'No thanks to you lot, I imagine.'

'Now, look here, it wasn't our fault.' Stroppy women were beginning to get to Willie. 'I don't mind being blamed for what I have done, but I strongly object to being accused of what I haven't.'

Joan realised that there might be someone in Willie who, unlike Eustace, would face her and argue her out, so she pulled in her horns and looked at Eustace.

'Leave him there, I'll deal with him later.'

They left Eustace still fighting the hedge, and hurried away along the road before she changed her mind or something. They hadn't gone far when they heard the singing stop, the plaintive cry of a drunken man as a woman's heavy hand descended hard upon his head, the rough end of a woman's tongue and more cries from the man.

Chapter Eleven

Mrs Amelia Smythies, with a 'Y', changed her voice up from third gear to top. 'And furthermore, I have been on this earth a long time.'

'That's true,' agreed Willie.

She glared, as only a woman of breeding can glare, and continued, 'But never, ever, have I had the misfortune to meet such a horribly rude, disgusting, filthy, mannerless, little man as you. What Gerald would have said had he been with me, I shudder to think.'

Gerald Smythies, not bothered about a 'Y', was the president of the cricket club, the president of the bowling club, chairman of the brass band committee, member of this, sponsor of that, churchwarden, rural district councillor, junior school governor, etc., etc., and when he found the time he ran his old family firm of corn millers and agricultural supplies distributors.

Mrs Smythies was also a member of every association, committee and gathering of which she could in some way manage to become a member. She was one of those peculiar breeds of women who could possibly have been acceptably good-looking in her early twenties, but now, forty years on, was fat, bloated and ugly to the point of being able to scare young children with just a glance. Her extravagantly superfluous mode of dress combined with her extra-loud, commanding voice made her to be very well-known, if not on a personal level, in every nook and cranny throughout the length and breadth of the village.

The shopkeepers of the village lived in dread of her next visit for, unlike the vast majority of the female half of the local upper crust who were pleasant enough people to deal with, Mrs Amelia Smythies, with a 'Y', was a sod. She examined each individual piece of fruit or vegetable in the greengrocers before consenting to purchase. The butcher was in danger of suffering a double strangulated hernia every week, lifting carcasses of meat from fridge to slab, in order to locate a suitable piece of meat for her Sunday roast. She watched Freddy Nevershut weigh out each pound or half-pound of whatever it was she was buying, to make sure it was not underweight. Her favourite saying was, 'You have got to carefully monitor the activities of the tradesmen, you know, for they are sure to try and profit from your visit.'

It was precisely this extra careful control of her weekly grocery order, which Freddy's lad had to deliver, once approved, that was occupying her mind so intently when Willie entered the shop, belched out loud and made a very loud fart at one and the same time, without excuse either before or after.

Amelia Smythies had just finished tirading Freddy about the quality of last week's cheese when the offence happened, and it was at that point that she turned her attention to Willie, with the verbal barrage.

Willie attacked, saying, 'Your Gerald wouldn't have given a monkey's chuff if he had been here. Couldn't have cared less.'

'My husband would have been distraught.'

'Dis what?'

'Distraught.'

'Oh, yes, I thought that were what you said.'

'Your command of the English language isn't very good either, is it?'

'What?'

'Pardon, my man, pardon.'

'Why, what have you done? You must have done it quietly, I didn't hear it, did you Freddy?'

'I beg your pardon,' she screamed.

'Nay, I just wondered if you'd had to fart as well.'

'I have never, never, never, ever, been so insulted. Well, that does it, I'm not stopping here one moment longer whilst he's here. I will be back later to complete my order when he's not here. Good day, Mr Ogley.'

With that, and a long stony stare at Willie, she left. The bell on the shop door clanked, the door slammed hard and all was once more at peace in the little shop which, true to its nickname, very rarely shut.

Freddy Ogley looked at Willie who was looking just a little bit sheepish.

'I suppose you'll be a bit cross with me, Freddy?'

'Well, I ought to be absolutely livid but, to tell you the truth, I fair enjoyed it.'

Willie relaxed a little at this unexpected answer and Freddy continued. 'That woman, if that's what she is, gets on my wick. She spends a fair amount of brass in here every week, but boy, oh, boy, does she put you through it. "Just another couple of currants on there to make the pound up I think, Mr Ogley; please make sure you close the sugar bag up tightly, one and a half grains had come out last week because you had not taken sufficient care," and so it goes on, week after week after week. She's so ugly as well, I sometimes think she might petrify me when she stares hard at me.'

'Aye, she's a face a bit like a camel's bottom,' said Willie who was busying himself poking the wax out of his ear with his little finger and wiping it on his trousers. 'And she dresses like nobody I've ever seen before or want to again.'

'Yes, how her Gerald puts up with her I'll never know.'

'Oh, he doesn't, he's never in to put up with her, neither is she for that matter.'

'Anyway, Willie what can I do for you this bright and merry evening?'

'There's nowt bright and merry about this evening – it's bloody freezing out there and blowing a howling gale. It's cold enough to freeze a monkey's tonight.'

'A monkey's what?' enquired Freddy.

'A monkey's you know what. I called in to see if you had had any more thoughts about what we were talking about last time I called.'

'You mean about the Christmas club?'

'Aye, that's it.'

'Well, it all depends like – how many members have you?'

For once in his life Willie had come prepared with all the facts and figures he could muster to do with the Club. He commenced with the usual good old belch.

'Well, we had one hundred and twenty-seven members paid the first week, but then we had six more join the second week and another thirteen joined last week so that makes a total of one hundred and forty-six. Mind you, we reckon a few more could join yet.'

'That's not bad, not bad at all,' said Freddy, more than suitably impressed. 'How much money are you banking each week?'

Willie exaggerated the answer just a little, thinking, and rightly so, that Freddy might be even more impressed. 'About eighty pounds.'

'Eighty pounds, eighty pounds eh! Very good, very good indeed. That's four thousand in the year, about.'

Willie was pleased that Freddy knew it was four thousand so quickly, because he wouldn't have been able to reckon it up without a piece of paper and a pencil and then only slowly.

'So, hey, that's all right, that is. How much do you reckon you'll be able to persuade them to spend here, then?'

'Nay, that's a daft question if ever I heard one. You'll know far better than me how much folk spend here. How much do you reckon, then?'

'Not enough, however much it is. You see, food's usually the main item at Christmas, that and presents, say half and half happen, hey, that wouldn't be bad, two thousand, that would boost my takings all right, by gum, it would that. Eeh, well, I never thought, hey, it might be a right good do yet.'

He continued to enthuse and Willie began to enjoy it, for, every word that Freddy uttered Willie began to feel far better about the whole job. Then suddenly Freddy went quiet and his countenance changed.

'Hey, some of that brass'll have to go to other food shops, butchers, greengrocers and the like, so that's going to cut it down a lot, by at least half again. Still, one thousand isn't bad, in fact it's good.'

Willie's good and warm feelings had rapidly vanished at Freddy's temporary change of mood but they began to come back again.

'It's probably a thousand more than I would have had if I hadn't, if you see what I mean.'

'Dead on, there, Freddy lad.' Willie was absolutely baffled. 'So what do you reckon then?'

'What do I reckon about what?'

'About what it's worth to me and the members if I promote your shop at the club.'

'Well, it's got to be done proper like, official you know, none of this behind the backs of the committee. It's more than my future trade's worth if any smell of anything a bit bent got out.'

'No problem.'

'Right then, five per cent discount for all orders specifically for Christmas from paid-up club members – as long as I have their orders two weeks before Christmas, and a free box of groceries for yourself to the value of twenty-five pounds.'

Willie was over the moon.

'Twenty-five pounds, eeh, that's great, I'll get 'em all to come, eeh, that's smashing.'

'There's just one thing, however,' said Freddy. 'There's nowt doing under a total of five hundred pounds. I'll still give five per cent discount to club members but your free box of groceries won't be there if they don't spend a minimum of five hundred pounds.'

'I'll make sure they spend far more that five hundred pounds.'

'You still having the usual bother with the wife's mother then, Willie?'

'Not hardly as much as what I were. I put my foot down with a firm hand with her and it's quietened her off a bit. She's still a nasty old bugger but quieter with it. Anyroad, it's time I weren't here, my tea'll be ready so I'll see you later.'

With a good loud fart for good measure he headed off for the comfort of his cosy warm cottage and, more importantly, his tea.

*

Willie had, as requested by the committee at its second meeting, organised the deposit account at the bank. He had asked Walter Smith's permission to be absent in order to go to the bank for a while on the Friday afternoon and this had been readily granted, especially when Walter had learned that he might get a bit of divvy on his Christmas club account. Willie and Arthur had collected the money properly from the members, in the canteen. Willie had collected the money and Arthur with his new list had made a note of who had paid what. He had also added the new members to the list and they had got through the whole procedure in not much longer than the allotted time. Even Greasy Martha had been in an affable mood and had not tried to clear them out of the canteen before they had finished their task.

'We'll balance it later,' Arthur had advised Willie when the last member had paid and Willie had pushed and shoved the money into his various pockets.

The only balancing that Willie had ever seen was at the Palace theatre as a young lad when his parents had taken him to the music hall, where he had sat riveted watching the feats and antics of the balancing act on the slack wire. So he couldn't quite work out what Arthur was on about balancing.

He plucked up courage to ask, 'Balance what?'

Arthur couldn't make his mind up whether to strangle Willie or just ignore him, and, being a peaceful sort of fellow, he told Willie to wait until that evening for an explanation. He also pointed out to Willie that it was time he was heading for the bank.

The Club held for Willie what was to become a regular Friday after-lunch magnetism. It was always quiet at this time of the year, and over the next few months it was to become a quick counting house for the Christmas club money, with liquid refreshment.

'Hey, up, make way, Lord Moneybags is here again to thrill us all once more with one of his Friday displays of his knowledge and dexterity in the world of high finance.'

This solemn announcement was made by Fat Harry from behind the bar as Willie entered. It was to no one in particular as there was almost no one there to hear it.

The reply came swift and sure: 'Piss off', then, as an afterthought, 'Give us a pint.'

Harry's permanent grin broadened at Willie's reply but then he looked solemnly back and said, 'No sir, as usual I will not give you a pint. I am not a charitable institution. However, I will sell you a pint of our best bitter for the usual small consideration.'

'Small what?'

'Pay up and enjoy it.'

'I might pay up but I shan't enjoy it.'

'How dare you say you will not enjoy a glass of our best bitter beer.

'I shall enjoy your beer, it's paying for it.'

'What is?'

'What I shan't enjoy.'

'Oh.'

Two minutes later there was money all over the bar counter, as Willie emptied his pockets, narrowly avoiding mixing his own half-crown with it. He and Harry carefully counted it all, separated it into its various denominations, pocketed it and entered it into the paying-in book. This being a job that required a degree of concentration, Willie subconsciously belched and farted his way through it. He finished his pint, pocketed the money again and headed for the bank.

*

The passers-by observed Willie emptying the contents of his nasal passages into the grate outside the bank, then, after one extra loud public belch, he went inside.

There was a long queue inside, composed mainly of local businessmen and shopkeepers all attending to their usual business, with the odd local wealthy widow asking long and awkward questions of the staff. There were just one or two other people who, like Willie, were there for other slightly different reasons.

After what seemed to be an afternoon of waiting, Willie's turn finally arrived and across the counter he faced a smart young man, who sat smiling, waiting for Willie to make the first move. Willie stood expressionless, staring blankly at the young man waiting for him to kick off.

It was a few moments before the young man decided to speak and then it was only, 'Yes, sir?'

Willie, who was delighted to have won the war without words answered, 'Ah've come to pay in.'

There was another somewhat pregnant pause before it dawned on the bright young lad that this could be Mr Arkenthwaite from the Christmas club at Murgatroyd's mill, about whom they had all been lectured long and hard by the manager, so he decided to act dumb and play it by ear.

'What have you come to pay in, sir?'

'Money,' then as an afterthought Willie said, 'From the Christmas club,' and, as a final afterthought, 'From Murgatroyds mill.'

The young man's worst fears were realised but he carried on calmly and correctly.

'Where is the money, sir?'

Willie pulled out a few crumpled notes from his right-hand jacket pocket, two handfuls of coins from his left-hand jacket pocket, a few coins from the left-hand trouser pocket, followed by a large handful from the right-hand trouser pocket. Accompanying this he extracted his half-crown, a sometime white handkerchief covered in hard and dried up snot and his Swiss army twenty-seven blade penknife.

The sight of the handkerchief was just about enough to put the young man's light out for ever but he carefully counted the money and put it into one pound piles.

'Can I have your paying-in book please, sir.'

'Oh, aye, here it is, all correct. Tha'll have no need to count it, it's right, sixty-eight pounds, six and sixpence.'

'Sixty-eight pounds, seven shillings to be exact, sir.'

There followed a long and bitter argument which was finally won by the young man counting the money again and still arriving at the same answer. Willie reminded himself not to forget to thump Fat Harry when he next visited the Club.

The paying-in book was returned to Willie and the young man was pleased that his turn was finished, looking forward to a more normal banking customer to come next in line, when his hopes were short-lived.

'Now, then, we want to open one of them other sort of accounts.'

The young man began to look crestfallen.

'Which other sort of account, sir?'

'One of them what pays us to use it. You know, a what do you call it? A doings, a... oh, hell, I can't remember what you call it.'

'A deposit account, sir,' volunteered the young man.

'Aye, that's right, a deposit account.'

'I'll get the necessary forms for you to sign, sir.'

'Ta,' he said as he belched out loudly.

The young man winced and left Willie leaning on the counter, staring at his surroundings. He was not normally known for making a detailed study of his environment but having nothing to do he began to look around. The very ornate and delicate plasterwork of the ceiling rose in the centre was the first thing to take his attention, closely followed by a not quite so ornate spiral effect around the perimeter.

'By gum, Albert Absolom's had a good order here,' he said quietly to himself. 'Mind you, it'd be beyond him, would this.'

From end to end, he next investigated the floor covering.

'Better bloody carpet than what we have at home, is this,' he would have been heard to mutter had anyone been listening.

He turned his attention to the fixtures and fittings behind the counter and was about to give himself a few more mutterings when a sharp pain struck him between the shoulder-blades making him gasp for air as his head pitched forward towards the counter top.

'Ow do, Willie,' said a deep, rich Yorkshire voice.

Willie gasped into sufficient life to turn and see the smiling face of Joshua Greasly, the proprietor of the local newsagent, books and fancy goods shop.

'Haven't seen you in weeks how are you I've seen your Thelma when she comes in to pay for your papers her mother's all right I hear what are you doing here have you come into brass or summat?'

Willie was trying his best to get a few words in to tell Josh in very un-banklike language what he thought of people who knocked seven bells out of him without letting him know what was coming, but he couldn't even get a word in edgeways as the verbal tirade continued unabated.

'Ow's things at the Club I haven't been for weeks too busy you know it's a ten day week job is running a paper shop and nowt for it at th'end of the day nowt at all if yer make owt government takes it up early late to bed tired all day nobody in their right mind'd have a paper shop still it's a job hey up it's my turn well I'd best get on been nice talking to you see you sometime.'

He turned his attention to the clerk at the position next to Willie.

All this time Willie had been recovering his breath in short sharp gasps and was just about back to normal, having broken several lots of wind owing to the shock he had received, when the young man returned.

'Well, all we need is your signature on the form and everything is sorted out.'

There was no response from Willie, and the young man looked up to observe him, fairly red in the face and still gasping for breath, although much improved by now.

'Are you all right, Mr, er, er, er,' he asked and looked at the paying-in slip, 'Arkenthwaite?'

'Aye, lad.' Willie straightened up. 'Aye, as right as rain, thank you.'

The form was pushed over the counter to Willie, who signed it and pushed it back.

'Now, Mr Arkenthwaite, how much do you wish to open it with?'

'What?'

'How much do you want to open it with?'

'What do you mean?'

'You have just opened a deposit account on behalf of the club and you must therefore be desirous of putting an amount of money into it.'

'Oh, aye, that's right.'

'Well, how much?'

'Don't know.'

The young man was becoming exasperated.

'Well, nobody said. Why don't you ask your manager, he'll know, he's a friend of Mr Anthony.'

'You mean Mr Sharples?'

'Aye, that's him, him what drinks a lot.'

'I don't think that Mr Sharples is a heavy drinker.'

'I didn't say he were, he just drinks a lot.'

'I don't think we need to disturb him with such a minor problem. Now, it seems to me that you would need to put all of the money you bank each week into this deposit account so that you can earn interest on it right up to Christmas. What do you think, Mr Arkenthwaite?'

Willie was just about to agree when his train of thought was diverted with an interruption.

'Are you having nowt but a lot of bother, Willie?' Josh Greasly, not waiting for an answer, said, 'Don't let this lot in here give you any hassle give 'em some more back if necessary play hell with 'em and sort 'em out you're the customer you're the master of the situation put your foot down with a firm hand well I can't stop here talking all day must be off customers'll be waiting they're my masters see you Willie so long.'

The young man was waiting patiently for Willie's decision, and Willie was wishing he was the master of the situation. Finally he decided.

'Yes.'

'You mean we bank all of the money into the deposit account each week?'

'Aye.'

'Right, we shall have to fill in a standard automatic transfer form. You pay into the current account every week and we will then automatically transfer the amount into the deposit account, leaving a working balance in the current account of say, ten pounds, for contingencies.'

Willie was about to enquire as to what were contingencies, yet again, but having decided not to show his ignorance he signed the form, left the bank, cleared his body of all the nasty inner feelings and went back to the mill.

On his return to the dyehouse Willie immediately sought out Arthur, reported on the progress he had made, and asked one very important question, 'What's contingencies?'

Meanwhile, back at the bank, the young man was busy consulting his colleagues as to their knowledge of their manager's heavy drinking habits.

*

It was so cold on that Friday evening as Willie and Arthur hurried home from the mill that they didn't stop to exchange the usual pleasantries with their workmates, neither did they say much to each other. It was only when they reached Cutside Cottages that Willie said, 'Club tonight?'

'Of course,' agreed his best pal.

'I'll call for you,' Willie shouted as he dashed inside.

*

'By gum, mend that fire sharp, Josie, for it's a cold 'un.'

'Aye, it is Dad, I've been frozen all day at school.'

'Where's your grandma?' he asked as he suddenly realised there was something missing from the room and particularly the corner by the fire.

'She's poorly, me mum's upstairs with her now, and tea's a bit late on account of her being ill.'

Willie, who liked to get his priorities in the correct order, first of all enquired, 'What's for tea?' and secondly, 'What's up with her? Nowt serious, I hope,' hoping it was something very serious.

'She's been sick all day and she's got diarrhoea as well.'

'Oh, a both ends job, eh,' then under his breath he said, 'With a bit of luck she might pass herself away', and then out loud, 'Well, happen I'd best go look at her.'

He climbed the narrow staircase with the bend at the bottom and went into her bedroom. He was met with a scene of buckets and towels all over, Mrs Woofenden in bed and Thelma mopping up the bedclothes. The air was heavy with the stench of vomit.

Willie pulled his face at the smell, then looked at his mother-in-law and said, 'Coming out at both ends at once by all accounts, isn't it? You won't know which direction to go first, will you?'

Mrs Woofenden burst into floods of tears.

'Willie!' said Thelma. 'It's bad enough having to cope with this situation without your stupid comments.'

Willie ignored Thelma's rebuke. 'How long will tea be?'

'Oh, you go and have yours with the children and I'll have mine later when I can find the time.'

Now Willie, for all his faults, worshipped his family and liked them all to sit together for tea.

'Nay, I shan't lass, I'll wait for you as soon as you've done. Have you had the doctor to her?'

'No, not yet, she's only been like this for about an hour.'

'Well, happen you'd better, she might disappear up her own whatsit at this rate.'

Mrs Woofenden heaved and brought back the remains of her dinner into the bucket at the side of the bed.

'Just like the vomitorium at Throstle park is this. I see you had carrots for dinner.'

He returned downstairs to the children.

'What's for tea, Josie?' he enquired.

'Stewed liver and onions with mash and cauliflower, followed by chocolate pudding and custard. Will that do?'

'Aye, it'll do fine if we ever get it.'

"Do you want yours now?'

'Nay, lass, I'll wait for your mother. If hers has to be ruined then mine can be too.'

'It'll not ruin, Dad, but the custard might have a thick skin on it.'

'Good, I like custard skin. Listen, we's never get our tea again by the sound of that lot.'

They both looked up at the ceiling to listen to the sound of much puking, honking and farting which was penetrating the ceiling from the room above.

Tea was eventually taken after Thelma had settled her mother and got her off to sleep. There wasn't much conversation over tea except for a couple of very useful comments from Willie, both of which brought a stern rebuke from Thelma and Josie: 'Why don't you take your mother a big dish of prunes up for her tea?' and, 'I reckon the undertaker'll have one hell of a job getting a coffin around the bend at the bottom of the stairs.'

⋆

Willie didn't stay long at Cutside Cottages in view of the circumstances. He quickly washed, changed and disappeared to Arthur's. Jess as usual made him welcome, and when he had explained the situation at home she was soon putting her coat on to go and see if she could help Thelma. The two men arrived at the Club somewhat earlier than usual.

⋆

They hung their coats on the hooks in the corridor and walked into the bar. Arthur stared as Willie took up the pose of a Christmas fairy, standing on tiptoe and holding his hands above his head. He advanced into the room singing to the tune of the Blue Danube waltz.

'Honk, honk, honk, honk, honk, puke puke, puke puke. Honk, honk...' and he continued right up to the bar.

Fat Harry observed his coming with an unusually sombre expression. 'If that's best tha can do, then I'm not entering you for the talent show at the summer fête. Next door's cat could give a much better performance.' Then he burst out laughing, saying, 'Have you gone off your crock or something?'

'No, it's the wife's mother.'

'There's no answer to that.'

'There is,' said Arthur, and he struck up again. 'Honk, honk—'

'Shut up, it's early yet and I for one cannot stand the noise any longer. It's a rotten job this is, putting up with you lot, don't know how I do it on my wages, any lesser mortal would have perished by now. Anyway, what's up with your wife's mother?'

'She's been just a little bit sick.'

'A little bit sick and you make all that stir?'

'Well, not just a little bit sick, a bloody hell of a lot sick, acres and acres of vomit, honking and puking up all over – they had carrots for their dinner.' He stopped for a good old belch. 'Coming out of both ends at once as well. Delightful smell in our house, and the noise she's making whilst she's doing it, never, ever, heard anything like it.'

'Aye, well, she's had a good tutor at the noise bit, hasn't she,' said Harry.

'Who?' asked Willie.

'I can't think,' said Arthur.

'So what's the form then?' asked Harry. 'You stopping out till the early hours so as not to get involved or what?'

'Don't know. Mind you, if she goes on going like she were going when I came out there'll be nowt left of her by the time it comes closing time – I hope.'

'Come over here and I'll explain to you about these contingencies,' said Arthur as he began to make his way over to the table in the corner by the fire where Dick, Lewis and Eustace were getting the dominoes out ready to start a game.

'What contingencies?' asked Harry innocently.

Willie looked at him and tapped the side of his nose with his forefinger.

'Bugger off,' said Harry, and Willie went laughing.

Willie snooked up and spat a nice round ball of phlegm into the fire, where it sizzled.

'Bullseye,' he was heard to remark, then sat down.

'Now, what about these contingencies?'

'Now,' said Arthur, 'I explained all about them last week, don't you remember?'

'Can't say as I do.'

'What's a contingency, Arthur? What is? A contingency, what is it?' enquired Eustace, whilst Dick and Lewis abandoned their game of dominoes to listen in.

'A contingency is like an insurance, it's as if, er, let's see now, as if you were going to spend the night in a tent on a mountain and you only had enough rations with you for one evening meal. Rather than eat it all you'd save a portion of it for breakfast, just in case you couldn't get back to base in time. That's an insurance, a contingency, it's like being prepared for what you hoped might not happen. Does that explain it for you?'

'Well, aye,' said Willie. 'Except that I wouldn't go on to the mountain without enough food in the first place.'

'I don't understand, Willie. I don't. I don't understand it at all. None of it. Not any of it. I don't, Arthur, I don't,' Eustace bleated.

Arthur was well into the process of making a monumental decision, whether or not to try and explain the matter further to Eustace, when the decision was made for him.

'Good evening, brethren, it is very inclement outdoors. May I join you to share the benefit of this splendid fire which our host has very kindly kindled for our comfort?'

They all turned their heads to observe the tall, round figure of the Reverend Clifford Tunstall MA, vicar of St Cuthbert's-on-the-Hill, the local parish church.

'Aye, sit yourself down, vicar,' said Dick, who was well acquainted with the vicar as his wife was a regular worshipper at the Church.

They all hutched up to make room for another chair which the vicar fetched from the next table, then with a broad jovial beam he put his pint glass on the table and sat down.

'I am given to understand, by Mr Anthony Murgatroyd, who, as you all know, unlike present company, is a regular worshipper at my church, that you have opened a Christmas club at the mill.'

'Yes, that's right, vicar,' said Arthur. 'In fact we are holding a half of a committee meeting right now. Mind you, we're seven-eighths of the way through it.'

'How does one hold a half of a committee meeting?'

Willie answered, 'Why, you daft bugger – sorry vicar – there's nobbut half of us here. Well, no, we're nearly all here, but two main 'uns's missing. Sarah Anne Green, who's chairman, and that well-known self-opinionated twit, Daniel Sykes, who'll do nowt but moan if he isn't here to criticise whilst we make the decisions.'

'You are probably right, Willie, I am a daft bugger, I should have realised what Arthur meant. Now, Daniel Sykes, is he the one that visits that lady up Mafeking Street?'

They all looked at one another, then back at the vicar.

'Yes, that's him,' said Dick.

'Can't say that I know the said gentleman but his reputation goes before him.'

'Anyway, what brings you in here, vicar?' asked Lewis.

'Well, it's Friday evening, we have no meetings or socials at the church demanding my attention, for a change, so I decided to come out to the Club for a drink and to see how the other half of my congregation, that I never see on a Sunday, was faring. Now, don't get worried, Willie, I am not here Bible thumping, just gently recruiting without ramming it down anyone's throat. By the way, my glass is empty. Does anyone need a refill, and perhaps afterwards we could have a game of dominoes?'

Ten seconds later the vicar, well known for his generosity, ordered six pints and when he returned with a tray of glasses the dominoes were shuffled.

'Shall we play for a shilling a corner?' asked the vicar.

'No, thank you, vicar, we don't gamble,' said Arthur.

It wasn't long before the vicar had won the first game and, as the evening progressed, almost every other game.

'I think the almighty has guided me this evening,' he was heard to remark.

'Nowt o't sort,' said Willie. 'You win every time, you're a ruddy professional.'

'Well, no, Willie, not a professional, but I freely admit to having some small amount of skill at the game.'

As well as winning, the vicar had also consumed copious quantities of best bitter which they had allowed him to buy for himself, as none of them could keep up with him financially. He was drinking three to one of theirs.

'Well, shall we just try one last hand?' he enquired.

'No, vicar, I think we've all had enough for one night and may I say that I for one am very glad we were not playing for money,' said Arthur.

'Yes, no doubt you are. Now, Willie, how's Thelma and the rest of the household?'

Dick nudged Lewis, whispering, 'Wait for it, round three.'

'Thelma's as right as rain, so's the kids, but her mother, she's not well, honking and puking all over the place, coming out of both ends at once it is, can't tell whether to sit on the lavatory or stick her head down it. Smells awful in the house and noisy with it too, belching and farting as well in between. Thelma's looking after her – don't know how she copes with it.'

'Perhaps she'll be better when you get back. Well, it's half past ten and high time all good men of the cloth were tucked up safely in bed, so I'll just have a quick whisky chaser to see me home.

He hurried off to the bar.

Arthur watched him go.

'You couldn't ask for a better vicar even if you wanted one, equally at home with us in here as he is with Anthony Murgatroyd and his set. Very posh and proper but no side on him at all.'

Clifford Tunstall MA returned from the bar and stood with his back to the fire, sipping his double malt whisky nightcap.

'Now, then, gentlemen, what chance is there of a poor vicar like me joining your Christmas club?'

Eustace was the first to answer. 'Are you a bit short of money like we all are? Are you? Are you, vicar? Short of money? Are you?'

'Well, no, not exactly short but I thought it might be an interesting exercise.'

Willie was the next to speak. 'Sorry, vicar. Under rule one you can't. The club's for them what work at Murgatroyd's and nobody else.'

'Oh, I see.'

'Yes,' agreed Arthur. 'Willie's right, it's only for us and it's only fair to refuse you as we've already refused others.'

'Oh, well, never mind. It's time I was away to prepare the communion wine.'

'What, for Sunday?' asked Lewis.

'Yes, it takes a lot of preparation. Well, goodnight.'

He stood up, warmed his back on the fire, walked over to Fat Harry for a few words, bid everyone goodnight and left.

'I can't understand why he has to prepare the communion wine on a Friday night, can you? Can you Dick? Can you understand it? I can't, can you Arthur?'

They all turned to stare at Eustace. Was he having a brainstorm or what? He normally didn't think enough not to understand anything.

'Course I can understand,' said Willie. 'He wants a nightcap. Mind you, I wouldn't fancy communion wine after what he's supped in here tonight.'

'How do you know whether or not you'd fancy communion wine? You've never tasted the stuff in your life,' said Dick.

'Aye, but I wouldn't fancy wine after all that beer. Anyway, I fancy a pint of tea. Are we having one for the road before we go?'

'Nay, I'm skint already and it's nobbut Friday night,' said Lewis. 'I've spent enough for one night.'

'You shouldn't hand all your wage packet unopened over to your wife every Friday teatime,' said Willie.

'It's all right for you, you get subbed by your mother-in-law.'

'I've told you before, it's nowt to do with you what I get from her, and talking about her, I wonder if she's still honking and puking all over. I'd best stop here all night. Still, I'd happen better go and see how Thelma's going on with her.'

The gang of five exited the Club to the vile farewells from Fat Harry and suitable replies from themselves, and as usual parted company by arranging to meet at the Club the following evening.

*

Willie arrived home to witness a scene of domestic chaos. Josie was washing Mrs Woofenden's bed sheets in a bucket in the kitchen, the fire in the living room was almost out, and Thelma was upstairs with her mother. Willie climbed the narrow stairs, examining the tight bend near the bottom, wondering how they would get a coffin both up and down. He put his head around the old lady's bedroom door, the room being still heavy with the stench of sickness and diarrhoea. Thelma was busy tidying the bedclothes and his mother-in-law was sitting up in bed looking very poorly.

'Still performing then, are you?' Willie enquired.

She burst into floods of tears. Thelma came around the bed and escorted Willie downstairs where she scolded him yet again for his callous behaviour towards her mother.

'Come on, let's have a pot of tea and some cake, then we can go to bed,' he said, and Thelma dutifully brewed up.

They drank it, and retired to bed in anticipation of a rough night ahead with the poorly old lady.

Chapter Twelve

The horrible, freezing cold weather of winter slowly turned into the more temperate days of spring and summer. With it, the gang of five's thoughts turned to bowls and cricket. The long winter evenings spent in the Club were now a thing of the past, and were spent either on the super turf of the crown green behind the Club or at the other end of the village at the cricket field, when there was anything to watch.

*

The Christmas club rolled uneventfully along with the seasons except for a few new members joining. Willie had become a regular Friday lunchtime visitor to the Club, where he and Fat Harry counted the money before he deposited it at the bank where the new normal procedure was to transfer the weekly payments straight into the deposit account.

*

The strife between Mrs Woofenden and Willie rolled along apace with everything else, his mother-in-law becoming slowly more bedridden and Willie becoming more and more stroppy with her. Thelma despaired of the situation and she became equally more crotchety.

*

As well as the time spent on his interests of bowls and cricket, Willie also put a lot of time and effort into his fairly large garden at the back of the cottage. Vegetables were his primary interest – potatoes, beans, peas, carrots, cabbages, cauliflowers, Brussels sprouts and onions were all to be found growing in profusion in neat orderly rows. Willie had won several prizes over many years at the local flower and vegetable show. Josie helped her father in the garden whilst Arthur and sometimes Eustace were to be found sitting on an old garden seat watching Willie at work, and giving moral support.

It was on one such evening in early May, not far from Whitsuntide, when the youngsters of the village were looking forward to the Whit Monday walks from the various churches and chapels, culminating in the village tea and junior sports at the cricket field, that Willie was busy hoeing and weeding the vegetables. Arthur was in quiet and happy contemplation with the rest of the world, sitting on an old upturned bucket and leaning backwards against the pigeon loft, smoking a pipe of twist. He was staring at Willie but seeing through him as his thoughts wandered from this to that to the other. Eustace was sitting on an orange box next to Arthur, not leaning back and relaxed, but hunched forward and fidgeting. He rubbed his hands together, scratched his ear, ruffled his hair, rubbed his hands again and was never still, for Eustace was never still, never relaxed, never at ease.

'What on earth's that?'

Arthur had come back into the land of the living very quickly and was staring at Willie who was holding a large orange-brown squelchy object between his thumb and forefinger at the end of his outstretched arm.

'What is it, Willie? What is it? Tell us, Willie, what is it?'

'You had your tea, Eustace?' Willie enquired.

'Yes, Willie, I've had my tea. Why, Willie? Why?'

'Just thought you might like this delicious morsel.'

'Why, what is it? What is it, Willie?'

Willie walked over to Eustace who, on observing a big, fat, juicy, orange-brown slug approaching, got up and hurriedly removed himself to the bottom of the garden.

'You know I don't like slugs,' he shouted. 'You're horrible, trying to frighten me like that, you know I don't like them, you're horrible you are, rotten with me you are, rotten, rotten. You know I can't stand slugs and creepy-crawlies like that.'

'That'll do your cabbages a power of good,' said Arthur as he observed Willie lay the slug on the ground and cut it in half with his spade so that all the inside came oozing out as a black sticky liquid.

'It'll not do them a lot of harm now,' said Willie.

'Has it gone?' shouted Eustace.

'Yes, it's fallen in bits.'

'How can it have fallen in bits? How can it? How? How can it have fallen in bits? It can't have. Can I have a look? Can I?' He walked slowly over to it. 'Gosh, it's horrible, I think I'm going to be sick. I am, I'm going to be sick. I am, it's horrible it is, it is, it's all over, I think I'm going to be sick.'

'Get over by the river,' said Willie. 'You aren't getting on with it so quick. If you're going to honk, get on with it and get it over and done with.'

'I'm feeling much better now, much better. I am, I'm feeling much better.'

He was sitting down again, leaning on the shed, the pale white of his face contrasting with the dirty old creosote of the shed wall.

'When's the new pigeons due?' asked Willie.

'Could be any day now. I'm expecting to hear about them very soon,' said pigeon secretary, Arthur.

'Are you getting some new ones? Are you, Willie? Getting some new ones?'

'Yes, Eustace, and tell you what, I aren't half ready for the twice-yearly battle of wits with Owen Evans at the station. Anyway, Arthur, we shall have to be clearing out the loft for the new ones.'

'Yes, Willie, we'll do it one night next week. Now then, if you've finished, let's get along to the Club.'

They ambled slowly away for a pleasant evening with Fat Harry and their other pals.

★

'Willie's cut a great big slug in two, Harry. He has, cut it in two. It was all over, oozed out it did, all over. It made me feel sick, sick it did, sick.'

'Did you vomit in Willie's garden then?' enquired Harry.

'No, no I didn't, but I felt like doing.'

'Was it all liquidy and sticky and nasty? Did all its inside come oozing out, just like blood out of a cut?'

'Give over, Harry, you're making me feel sick again, sick, you are, you're making me feel sick.

'Well, don't bloody throw up here. Get off to the gents and get your head down the pot and don't forget to flush it before you get up again.'

'I can't Harry, I can't reach the chain if I'm bending down. I can't Harry, I can't—'

Arthur chipped in. 'You should have seen him, Harry, as white as a virgin bride's wedding dress he was. It's a wonder he wasn't sick, just looked like death on legs.'

'Talking about looking like death, Willie, how's your mother-in-law these days? We haven't heard a lot about her in recent times?'

'Confined to bed, she is. Not a lot to tell. Very quiet, she is. Thelma and Josie's worn out trailing up and down stairs after her. She's still very demanding, it's fetch me this, bring me that, carry me the other, still eating as much as two pigs, forever knocking on the bedroom floor. There's not a lot of peace with her around.'

'What's exactly up with her then?' asked Lewis, who had been at the Club when they arrived and was two pints ahead of them already.

'Clapped out and knackered,' said Willie.

'Has she long in yet then?' asked Harry.

'Don't rightly know, Doctor's given her up, more or less. Her legs have gone, but she's not lost her appetite, or her temper, and she's still a martyr to her back.'

'So, you don't reckon it'll be long now before you and your Thelma's very rich then, eh?'

'Nowt o't sort. She has no brass, that's the trouble.'

'What is?' asked Arthur.

'Oh, for crying out loud! Why the hell don't you take notice when I'm talking to you? What I said was that she has no brass to leave and that's the trouble.'

'Just as I said,' replied Arthur. 'What is? There is no trouble. What you've never had you'll never miss. Will you?'

'Well, yes and no. Yes, you're right, but no, I've always had high hopes of having a bob or two to make us a bit more comfortable when she is gone and it'll be a big let-down to find there is nowt.'

He let out an absolutely enormous fart.

'But that's what I've been saying,' said Arthur as he backed away from the general vicinity of Willie. 'It won't be such a let-down if you know she has nowt before she dies, will it?'

'No, but it's not fair, is it? We've looked after her all these years and cared for all her needs, even the nasty little unmentionable ones, and how has she repaid us?'

'With bags and bags of coal,' chimed in Harry. 'She's kept you all lovely and warm through every winter for years and years.'

'I've told you before, she hasn't paid for the bloody stuff.'

'I'll thank you to moderate both the tone and volume of your language in this establishment, but, begging your pardon, you have always informed us that the old lady has purchased all of your coal, so either you are a liar or demented.'

'Demented,' replied Willie. 'Anyway, she has nowt and never did have owt. Mind you, we keep living in hopes that a miracle might happen.'

'Did her husband leave anything?' asked Lewis.

'No, not him, drank all he ever had. Seem to remember we had to pitch in to give him a decent burial, so there's nowt left from that direction either.

'Never mind, Willie, have another pint on me to drown your sorrows,' said Arthur.

'Is everything prepared for tomorrow night's committee meeting?' asked Lewis.

'Is Sarah Anne coming here again?' asked Harry with his usual big broad grin at the mention of her name.

'Yes, she is, you lecherous old bugger,' said Arthur, 'so you can start polishing the glasses right now and clearing out the committee room.'

'It'll be a pleasure.'

He hummed away to himself with the grin still in place as he began the task of polishing all the glasses. The rest of them, including Eustace, who had all been having some difficulty following the conversation, went outside into the late evening sunshine and played bowls until they could see no more.

*

The following evening, Arthur, as secretary of Murgatroyd's Christmas Club, was in the committee room of the Grolsby Working Men's Club Affiliated shortly after seven o'clock, preparing for the committee meeting. Just exactly what he was doing was difficult to determine, as the room was always kept at a high state of alertness, ready for any quickly-called meeting. All he was doing, Harry had been overheard to tell one or two of the other regulars, was fussing, about nowt in particular, just fussing.

The other drinkers in the bar could, at the same time, be overheard discussing Harry's mode of dress. He looked smart, was even wearing a tie, shoes were highly polished and hair brushed straight, not the Harry they knew and loved, but there again they didn't need to ask why, for as one of them observed, 'He's in cloud-cuckoo-land tonight – his favourite bird's coming to the committee meeting.'

Sarah Anne Green was the first to arrive, not long before half past seven, and soon she was enjoying a large gin and tonic, a gift from the steward, in fact a gift from Club funds but what the Club committee never knew, never hurt them. Fat Harry was all attention for her, wiping her chair before she sat down, wiping the table before she used it and generally flitting around like a lamb in springtime. Sarah Anne was secretly enjoying it but trying to appear not to notice it, for she had a soft spot for Harry, which was getting softer with each subsequent visit to the Club. The regulars were lapping it up, trying not to stare too hard at them.

Dick and Lewis arrived together, followed closely by Willie who immediately lowered the tone of the evening by breaking wind very loudly and without apology. Harry was just about to make a crude observation about farting in public when he remembered that he had a distinguished visitor present, and so checked his tongue.

He had to keep his opinions to himself again shortly afterwards when Willie, having had several quick, long swallows of beer, belched out loudly and again without apology.

Arthur appeared in the bar, called the members to order, and processed them at funeral speed along the corridor to the committee room. Eustace just scraped in at the last second at the end of the procession.

★

Sarah Anne, as chairman, opened the meeting and asked if there were any apologies for absence. There being none, Willie enquired as to where the hell Daniel Sykes was and the only suggestion that came back was Mafeking Street.

'Right, let's get on,' said the chairman, not wishing to prolong that particular subject. 'Secretary's report, please.'

Arthur stood up. 'Not a lot to report, madam chairman. Everything is going according to plan. The membership has increased quite considerably since the last meeting and is still doing so in penny numbers.'

'In what?' asked Dick.

'Just an odd new recruit now and then. We have now got the banking of the money off to a fine art and that concludes my report.'

'Thank you, Arthur. Can we now have the treasurer's report, please, Willie?'

Willie stood up, and sat down again as a very out of breath Daniel Sykes rushed in.

'Sorry I'm late, madam chairman,' he blurted out as he gasped for air. 'I was most unfortunately delayed.'

'At Mafeking Street,' said Lewis quietly to no one in particular.

'I will not stand for this type of insinuation,' said Daniel.

'Well, sit down then, and let's get on with it,' said Arthur.

The chairman intervened, saying, 'Yes, Daniel, do sit down please and let us get on as quickly as possible. The chair accepts your apology for lateness. Now, Willie, can we start your treasurer's report, please?'

Willie had been brushing up on procedural matters and he was determined to present his report correctly. Daniel Sykes's untimely interruption had somewhat unnerved him but by the time he was seated, Willie had composed himself sufficiently to start correctly, so he rose to his feet yet again and commenced.

'Madam chairman, it gives me great pleasure—'

He stopped as the door opened and the beaming face of Fat Harry surveyed the meeting.

'I thought you'd be wanting a fill up by now. Mind you some of you latecomers might want to buy your first drink of the evening.'

Daniel Sykes, who was just about to argue the point about his having walked into the committee room without buying a drink, was quietly cautioned by the Sarah Anne.

'Harry,' she said, 'will you quickly get your orders then leave us to get on. We'll pay you for the drinks after the meeting.'

'Certainly, Sarah Anne, it'll be a pleasure.'

He flitted, surprisingly deftly for his size, from one member to another to collect the glasses and take the orders.

'Willie, please continue with your report.'

For the third time, Willie rose to his feet.

'Madam chairman, it gives me great pleasure to present the treasurer's report. The club continues to function well each week. Arthur Baxter and I collect the money in the canteen every Friday dinner time and then I take it straight to the bank. We've now got the weekly takings up to seventy-one pounds four shillings. Mind you, I don't think we shall get many more new members now, as it's coming up to the middle of summer. However, I do think we would get more members if we were to run the club for a second year.

'Now, I have an important announcement to make—'

He was rudely interrupted by Daniel Sykes who said, 'You don't know anything important to announce. You never did.'

'I do. At least I know which house I go to bed in, which is more than some folk do.'

'Are you accusing me of sleeping around?'

'Nay, lad, I'm not accusing anybody of owt, but if the cap fits, wear it.'

The chairman intervened yet again. 'We all know what you were saying, Willie. Will you please both be quiet and let us get on.'

Willie had taken the opportunity of Sarah Anne's little speech to remove a particularly annoying piece of snot from his nose with his finger and to eat it.

'Just look at him now, not fit to be called a human being, ought to live in a sty with the rest of the swine.'

'Oh, for heaven's sake! You two sort out your differences after the meeting, and Willie, will you please get on and make your important announcement.'

Willie took a very noisy slurp of beer.

'I don't exactly know how to begin. I had the idea that we might do a bit better for ourselves than just have a Christmas club, so I asked one or two of the local tradespeople if we could get a bit of discount for club members with their Christmas orders. For instance, I asked Freddy Ogley, you know, Freddy Nevershut, what he would do for us if we were to give him a fair lot of Christmas orders, and he said five per cent discount on owt we order providing there's a minimum total of five hundred pounds spent there, and he'd want to know two weeks before Christmas.'

Daniel Sykes interrupted. 'My wife shops at the co-op and she'll not want to change; neither will a lot of them because they all wants their divvy.'

'Aye, but you can get five per cent at Freddy Nevershut's, you know.' He leaned over to Arthur and whispered, 'What's five per cent?'

'What do you mean, what's five per cent?'

'You know, how much in the pound?'

'Oh, yes, I see, it's a shilling.'

Willie straightened up and addressed the meeting again. 'It's one shilling in the pound. Co-op divvy's nobbut sevenpence, so my idea's better.'

'Yes, but it's only five pence better, I still prefer the co-op.'

'So, you go to the so and so co-op and let's see what anyone else thinks about it.'

'Which other establishments have you arranged discounts with, Willie?' asked Sarah Anne.

'Well, there's Mouncy the greengrocer, he said he'd do five per cent on orders up to five pounds and seven and a half per cent on orders above that providing we put a notice up at the mill recommending him. Mossop's, the electrical shop, said they might but they didn't think it'd make any difference to their trade.'

'It's still the co-op for me. Haven't you asked a butcher?'

'Of course, I have, I were coming to that.'

Willie snooked up, rolled a nice ball of phlegm and swallowed it.

'I asked George Tweed what he could offer us and he said he'd knock a penny a pound off turkeys and twopence a pound off pork and sausages, but there again his minimum is two pounds for each order. Ted Hardy at the newspaper shop said he'd give us five per cent if we could get him one hundred pounds extra orders from the club. So tha sees, if we can sort it out right, there's no problem, everybody can win plus, of course, the interest on the deposit account. It should be a good Christmas all round.'

Willie sat down to a round of genuine applause and he drained his pint glass. He was the first to speak again.

'I think we'd best have another round.'

'Yes,' said the chairman, 'it's getting warm. I could do with a long drink this time and, anyway, it's my round. You're always buying me drinks, so I'm going to stand my corner tonight. Press the bell for the steward please Eustace.'

Eustace got up and fumbled with the bell-push which refused to return to its usual place of rest.

'Oh, dear, it's stuck. It is, Willie, it's stuck, it is, Arthur, Lewis.' He was beginning to panic. 'It's stuck all right, stuck. What shall we do? Willie, what shall we do, Arthur? What ever shall we do?'

Sarah Anne was about to ask Arthur to assist when she was upstaged by the door bursting open and Fat Harry coming panting in.

'What the hell's going on? Is there a fire or summat?'

Then he looked at Eustace, the bell-push, and Eustace again.

'I might have known, you bloody daft lummock, you aren't fit to be let out. Come out of the way and let me have a look.'

He pushed Eustace roughly to one side and began to fiddle with the bell-push, to no avail, as it was still stuck in and went on ringing.

The meeting temporarily broke up in confusion with ten willing hands trying to stop the bell ringing in the bar, and Eustace whimpering to himself, 'I'm sorry, Harry, I am, it just stuck, it wouldn't come out, it wouldn't, I am sorry, I am...'

Willie took the opportunity to relieve himself of certain elements of wind which had been gathering in the four corners of his body for some time, making him feel very uncomfortable. Sarah Anne took the time to confide in Arthur that she thought they could very well do with replacing both Daniel Sykes and Eustace on the committee with two more able, amiable and clear-thinking people. Arthur in return pointed out that if they were to run the club into a second year they would have to hold an annual general meeting sometime in January, and that would be the time for a change.

Sanity was eventually restored, the bell was silenced, a round of drinks was served, and the meeting was brought to order by the chairman.

'Now, as I see things,' said Sarah Anne, 'we are in the enviable position where we can obtain certain discounts from selected village shops if we can produce a guaranteed volume of trade in the week leading up to Christmas.'

'Yes, that just about sums up the situation nicely,' said Arthur.

'So, how do we know who is going to buy what and how and when and where and if?' continued the chairman.

'Well, to answer you, as I see it we are going to have to ask each member about his or her shopping intentions,' said Willie.

'That is a gross intrusion into their private lives, which has nothing whatsoever to do with us,' argued Daniel Sykes.

'Act your age, you silly bugger, we only want to get them to the same set of shops for one week of the year,' said Willie.

'Well, I'm having nothing to do with it at all. In fact, I think I shall go home, as I can see no useful purpose being served by my staying.'

There were choruses of, 'Hear, hear.'

'Well, if that's it,' he shouted, 'I shall go,' and rose to leave.

'Shall I help you on with your coat?' enquired Willie.

'Certainly not, it's summer; I don't wear a coat in summer.'

He stormed out, slamming the door behind him.

'Good riddance to bad rubbish,' said Willie, making an impolite gesture to the door.

'Well, well,' said Sarah Anne. 'That takes the biscuit. Anyway, has anyone any idea as to how we can put the matter into practice? Or even if we want to? Would someone like to make a formal proposal on the issue?'

'Yes, I would,' said Arthur. 'As you all know, I had prior knowledge of Willie's investigations and I have been giving the matter a lot of thought. I do envisage some difficulties ahead, but even so, on balance I have no hesitation in proposing the scheme. I would, however, like to hear some further discussion on the subject before I propose a formal motion and, incidentally, I do think that Willie should propose the motion as it was his idea in the first place.'

'All right, Arthur, I think the committee as a whole can accept that, but can you give us some indication as to what lines you are thinking along?'

'Well, it is difficult. On the one hand, we have a series of local tradesmen all willing to offer us discounts if we can get to a minimum order level. On the other hand, we have a club full of members who all shop at different shops, who would not wish to tell us what they are going to buy for Christmas or to tell us how much they are willing to spend whether in total or broken down into groceries, greengroceries, meat, etc. However, I do think that the only way we can get the scheme off the ground is to put it to the members and ask them the questions we think they won't answer, and then see what happens. But how we actually question them, I do not know.'

'We could just ask them when we see them,' suggested Lewis.

'No, I don't think that would do. For one thing, we never see most of them from one week to the next, and for another, they won't know the answer when we ask them without thinking about it for a few days.'

At this point in the proceedings an unknown spark of hitherto unexplored imagination suddenly reared its ugly head as Eustace pronounced, 'We could, yes, we could, we could you know,' following which he became silent again.

'We could what?' shouted Willie.

Eustace started to speak again. 'We could, yes, we could, we could pin a notice up in the canteen, a notice, in the canteen, we could, on the wall, where everyone could read it, they could, they could read it, Willie, they could, near the serving hatch, that's it, near the serving hatch, they could read it, we could, near the serving hatch, we could—'

The committee in general had been so taken aback by this outburst, that it was a little while before anyone of them had recovered sufficiently to reply, but Sarah Anne decided that it was time to put an end to Eustace's tirade which was still continuing. He was getting no further than pinning a notice on the canteen wall by the serving hatch, but nevertheless he was still going on, so she tactfully intervened.

'Well, Eustace, I think we can probably discuss your proposal in more detail now.'

Eustace became quiet, happy with his idea, and he sat contentedly with a broad grin on his face, looking around the room at the other members.

Sarah Anne took the initiative, asking, 'Has anyone anything to say about Eustace's proposal? Personally, I think it merits serious consideration.'

Lewis was the first to reply. 'I think it's a good idea. We could put it up as soon as possible and give them all time to think about it.'

Willie said, 'There's a big snag.'

'What's that?' asked Lewis.

'Greasy Martha. The silly cow's not let us put up a notice on her canteen wall. She'll be as awkward as possible about it.'

Just for good measure, Willie belched out loud, whilst thinking of Martha.

'Willie, please!' said Sarah Anne.

'Oh, yes, sorry.'

'Now,' said Arthur, 'if we may continue. The problems associated with Greasy Martha and her cantankerous ways are too varied and awkward to be discussed here tonight. However, I do think that if we were to enlist the help of Mr Anthony, most of the problems associated with it would disappear quickly. After all, he is a member of the club.'

'Now, there's another good idea,' said Sarah Anne. 'Now, I think that it's time I did a résumé of events so far, and that we take a vote on the issue. Basically, Willie has proposed that we adopt a scheme where bulk buying from local tradesmen with our Christmas orders means that certain financial inducements of benefit to us all can be had. Secondly, Eustace has proposed that in order to test the feelings of club members on this issue we should outline the scheme on a notice to be pinned on the canteen wall and await comments. Thirdly, Arthur has suggested that we should enlist the help of Mr Anthony Murgatroyd in overcoming the difficulties which could arise in pinning the notice on the canteen wall.' She paused for breath. 'Has anyone any alternative suggestions for consideration?' She paused again. 'No? Good, any objections?' She paused again. 'No? Again, therefore, I think we should consider all three items to be carried by the meeting for further discussion and adopted as basic principles for the committee to work on. Well, Eustace, are you pleased with that result to your suggestion?'

'Yes, Sarah Anne, yes, I am, I am, very pleased, yes pleased, very pleased, good idea, yes, pleased—'

Willie decided it was his turn to speak.

'Talking about basic principles, I think it's time for another drink.'

'Hold on a minute,' said Arthur. 'These motions haven't been officially passed.'

'No, you have a point,' said the chairman.

'Right then, I'll propose them, you second them, Sarah Anne. Can we have a vote please?'

All hands were raised.

'Unanimous. Motions carried. Now, what was that about a drink, Willie? Ring the bell, please.'

'Nay, let's have a stretch and a walk into the bar for five minutes, just to clear my head of all this technical stuff.'

There being no objections to this proposal either, the room emptied at a gallop, not at all like the earlier processed entrance.

*

'Meeting over then?' enquired Fat Harry. 'Miles and miles of hot air gone up the chimney. Can't see what you've got to talk about with a Christmas club, except how to line your own pockets without the rest of them finding out.' Then his attitude changed. 'Here, Sarah Anne, love, sit yourself down on this bar stool. What will you have? Another G and T?'

'Yes, please, Harry.'

'My pleasure, my pleasure,' he said as he hurried about his business just as happy as a pig in clover. 'Won't be a minute. You'll be needing this after dealing with that lot, I reckon. Well, it's grand to see you again, fair grand. I hope you're going to hold your meetings here more often.'

He was interrupted by Willie.

'Ow, get a move on, we haven't got all night to wait for you.'

Harry fired a stare at Willie and walked over to him, putting his nose end almost on Willie's nose end.

'I shall tell you once and once only,' he whispered. Then he bellowed, 'Shut your gob and wait your turn.'

Then he turned his attentions back to Sarah Anne.

Willie leaned on the bar, idly picking his nose and devouring the contents thereof. Sarah Anne sat back laughing at events, and the others all looked glum, waiting patiently for their drinks.

The door of the bar opened and Mr Anthony Murgatroyd walked in. He was very smartly dressed, out of keeping with the company in which he found himself. He walked over to the bar and ordered a whisky and dry ginger.

'Be with you in just a moment, Mr Murgatroyd, sir, got a bit of a rush on. Don't usually see you in here, nice to see you.'

'Thank you, Harry, I heard on the grapevine that there was a committee meeting of the work's Christmas club and I thought I would like to see for myself what progress they are making, that is, if no one objects.'

Sarah Anne said, 'No, Mr Anthony, you're very welcome.'

'Have you already completed the formal part of the evening? Am I too late?'

Harry presented Mr Anthony with his whisky and dry before he served Willie and friends, much to their disgust.

'Nay, Mr Anthony,' said Willie, 'we're only halfway through. We just stopped for a drink, that is, if we ever manage to get one.'

'You'll get one right over you in a minute if you don't shut up,' boomed Harry as he prepared their pints.

Mr Anthony turned to Willie. 'I'm sorry if I jumped the queue, Willie, I had no idea you were waiting.'

'Think nothing of it, Mr Anthony, it weren't your fault, it were this big, fat lummock behind the bar.'

'I think we ought to be getting on with the meeting,' said Sarah Anne.

'Yes,' replied Arthur. 'Time, being the proverbial enemy, marches on. Bring your drinks.'

Once again he led the procession to the committee room where they all took their seats.

'You might as well have Daniel Sykes's chair, Mr Anthony. He's taken the huff and buggered off,' said Lewis.

'Why?'

'Because he's of low intelligence and a loony,' said Willie.

'Oh, I can't believe that of him.'

'Well, actually,' said Sarah Anne, 'there has been an ongoing clash of personalities between Daniel and some members of the committee, Willie in particular, which came to a head earlier this evening. As Lewis has said, Daniel took umbrage and left, since when the atmosphere in here has warmed considerably.'

'Yes, I can see that a better atmosphere can come into existence without Daniel, not the easiest of people even at the best of times.'

'Well, now,' said Arthur, 'I think that for Mr Anthony's benefit, and our own, it would be sensible if I were to outline progress so far.'

He proceeded to give a detailed résumé of events up to drinks time. When Arthur had completed his résumé, Mr Anthony was about to speak when Willie got his turn in first.

'Can you do owt about Greasy Martha then, Mr Anthony? Can you cut her tongue out or summat, to help us so that we can put up a notice on t'canteen wall?'

Mr Anthony looked at Sarah Anne.

'With your permission, madam chairman.'

She nodded, and he continued. 'Firstly let me say that I have not come here tonight to interfere in any way in the affairs of the Christmas club. I have come out of a sense of interest only. If you do not wish me to stay you have only to say the word and I will go, without being offended in any way. On the other hand, if I can be of any assistance, I shall be pleased to give you any help I can.'

He stopped momentarily as Willie yet again gave out an almighty belch, then apologised strangely.

'Now, as regards putting anything on the canteen wall, there is no problem at all, in theory. However, there is, as you rightly point out, a problem with Mrs Sykes. How to get around this problem is more often than not a problem in itself. However, you leave that one with me and I will sort something out for you.

'You seem to me to have got the club well organised on a sound basis. I particularly like Willie's ideas for getting the Christmas provisions at a cheaper rate than normally and I look forward to making full use of these facilities myself. So you can be sure of at least one supporter and if I were you I would hammer the tradespeople for even more discount, or shop around until you can find the best available deal by playing one off against another.

'I think I have stolen the show for long enough now, so with your permission I will sit back, shut up, enjoy my drink and listen to the remainder of the meeting. Thank you for listening to me.'

Sarah Anne was the first to speak. 'Thank you, Mr Anthony, particularly for your advice and encouragement. If you feel like joining in again, please feel free to do so. So, Willie, seeing that it was your original suggestion, how do you feel about talking to the other shopkeepers in the village about their discount rates?'

Willie extracted his second finger from a nostrilectomy he was performing and stared at Sarah Anne for a while.

'Well, yes, yes, why not? I can ask them all in the village, then play them off one against the other until we've got the best deal we can.'

'Might I suggest', said Arthur, 'that we discuss this matter with as many people as possible and then select the best ones nearer Christmas.'

'All very well is that,' said Lewis, who had just begun to get over his fear of opening his mouth in front of Mr Anthony. 'But folk'll want to know where they're going to get their Christmas stuff a long time beforehand, and if we don't make a decision for weeks and weeks it'll happen cause a problem.'

'Aye, we'll have to do it quicker than that,' said Willie.

'Than what?' enquired Eustace. 'Than what, Willie? Quicker than what, Willie? Willie? What? Quicker than—'

Anthony Murgatroyd intervened. 'I think, Eustace, that what they are all trying to say is that the shopkeepers will have to be contacted very soon now, if the committee is going to suggest a particular shop where the provisions are going to be very cheap at Christmas, before the various members start to put their orders down elsewhere. Does that explain it for you?'

'Yes, Mr Anthony, thank you, Mr Anthony, yes, thank you, yes, yes—'

Arthur decided to quieten Eustace.

'What about the notice then for the canteen wall?'

'Forget about it for now, until we have a clearer picture of where we are going,' said the chairman. 'Is there any other business?'

No one spoke for a while, then Mr Anthony asked, 'Has any thought been given to the distribution of the money?'

'What do you mean?' asked Willie.

'When and how are you going to pay out the funds?'

'Well, I expect that we shall be ready to pay out the money at dinner time on the last Friday before Christmas. Mind you, Mr Anthony, I shall have to have an hour off to go get t'money from t'bank.'

'That isn't quite what I had in mind when I asked you the question. I had been thinking it might be very good if we were to have a Christmas party for all the members of the Christmas club, at which we could then distribute the money. Before finishing, I must apologise to you all for the use of the 'we' bit; it doesn't infer that I wish to interfere or to press my will on your committee, but I thought it might be a good gesture to the members.'

Mr Anthony sat down to look at a somewhat stunned audience.

Sarah Anne was the first to speak following a fairly long period of silence.

'What sort of party had you in mind, and where would we have it and who would organise it, and how much would it cost, and what would? Oh, I don't know what, it's all come out of the blue so sudden like.'

Arthur said, 'Well, I think we ought to discuss whether or not we want a party to start with, and then, if we do, sort out the details later.'

'A very good idea, Arthur. Do you mind if I continue to sit here and join in occasionally?'

'No, Mr Anthony, you're very welcome, and anyway, it was your idea in the first place so you should stop and see it through.'

'I think it's a bloody good idea.'

'Language, Willie, language,' cautioned the chairman.

'Sorry, but I still think it's a bloody good idea.'

He belched.

'Right, the question is, do we want to hold a party or not? I think we will take a quick vote on the issue. Can I have a seconder?'

'Yes,' said Willie.

'The committee therefore proposes that a Christmas party be held to distribute the club funds. Those in favour?'

All hands were raised.

'No need to ask those against to vote. A unanimous vote in favour. Motion carried. Where and when is it to be held?'

Arthur had been studying the situation.

'It seems to me that the Friday night before Christmas would be best. We could get the money from the bank just before it closes and, seeing that Christmas Day is on a Wednesday this year, it just fits right.'

'What about Saturday?' asked Lewis. 'Saturday's always good for a party.'

'No, we should have then far too long to look after the money, because the bank shuts at twelve on a Saturday. No, Friday's best.'

Dick agreed. 'Friday's fine with me, and if we give 'em plenty of notice they'll all be able to come.'

'Any objections to Friday?' asked Sarah Anne.

No one offered any resistance to that idea, and so 'Friday night is party night' became the slogan of the committee.

'So, where shall we have it?' asked the chairman.

'Here,' replied Willie, without a second's thought.

'Yes, here,' said Dick, Lewis, Eustace and Arthur.

Even Anthony Murgatroyd nodded his assent.

Arthur, being the only Club official present at the meeting, aired his views on the subject.

'We could use the Club room. We'd probably get two hundred or so to the party and they'd all fit in there without any problem. I can use my influence with the Club committee to hire the room for that night.'

Sarah Anne spoke again. 'Well now, we've had a very long meeting tonight and a very fruitful one. However, it is getting late and I for one am getting to be tired. I think we can settle the details of the party later and, if there are no objections I will declare the meeting closed.'

Mr Anthony stood up.

'Before we go, I would like to thank you all for putting up with me, so much so that I would like to offer a contribution to the cost of the drinks at the party, and I would also like to attend the meeting to fix the details of the party, if that is possible.'

'Well, Mr Anthony, as chairman of the Christmas club committee, I would like to thank you for and accept your most generous offer. I would also like to say that you are more than welcome at any of our meetings. I declare the meeting closed.'

'Come on, let me buy you all a drink,' said Mr Anthony.

Willie farted, belched and sang half a chorus of 'For He's a Jolly Good Fellow'.

Fat Harry was his usual subservient self when Anthony Murgatroyd ordered the drinks. It was, 'Yes, Mr Anthony, sir, no, Mr Anthony, sir, yes, Sarah Anne, love.'

'Just listen to the big fat twit,' whispered Willie in Arthur's ear. 'He's got both Mr Anthony and Sarah Anne to bow and scrape to. We've certainly got the all-singing and dancing model tonight.'

Anthony Murgatroyd was standing at the bar next to Eustace, who was feeling very uncomfortable standing next to The Boss and not knowing what to say. However, he didn't need to worry as Mr Anthony spoke first.

'Well, now, are you looking forward to the party, Eustace?'

'No, Mr Anthony, no, I'm not, not, Mr Anthony, no, I'm not, it's my Joan it is, shows me up in public she does, my Joan, shows me up in public, I'm not looking forward to it at all. I might not tell her about it, might not, then it'll be better, it will, be better, be better if I don't tell her Mr Anthony, then I won't come, won't, will I?'

'Well, you voted for it.'

'Yes, Mr Anthony, it's a good idea, it is, a very good idea, I like it, I do, but not with my Joan, not with her, no, not with her.'

Mr Anthony realised it was no use pursuing this particular line of discussion, so he asked, 'Will you come to the party yourself, Eustace?'

'Oh, yes, Mr Anthony, oh, yes, I will, yes, but not with Joan, no, not with Joan, not with her, but I'll come. I'm on the committee I am, yes I am, I'll come.'

Anthony Murgatroyd decided he'd had enough of Eustace for one night so he quickly finished his drink and said goodnight to all concerned. Willie looked at Arthur and Sarah Anne.

'Not a bad sort, our Anthony, is he, not a bad sort at all. Blooming good do, a party, eh? Just what we need, a right good do.'

Sarah Anne laughed and said, 'Yes, Willie, let's have a right good do.'

Arthur had the presence of mind to go and examine the Club appointments book. With good luck, he found that the Friday before Christmas was free and so he pencilled it in as Murgatroyd's Christmas party from seven o'clock. He also, as a mark of respect, mentioned it to Fat Harry, whose only question was, 'Will Sarah Anne be coming?'

'Yes, with her husband.'

The only reply from Harry was, 'Oh.'

They all departed the Club by eleven o'clock. Dick and Lewis escorted Eustace home. Arthur and Willie walked Sarah Anne to her house where they got a mug of tea, and then they took themselves off to their respective homes both highly delighted with their evening's work.

'How's your mother?' Willie asked Thelma as he was getting into bed.

'Just the same, love, no better.'

Good, good, thought Willie as he fell asleep.

Chapter Thirteen

'England six, Wales nil,' Willie shouted through the station booking office window, although he could see no one inside.

There came back a suitable but completely foreign reply in pure Welsh from somewhere within. There was a shuffling and muttering from the room, then a pointed face appeared at the window.

'Oh, it's you two comedians, is it? Hang on a minute and shut your gobs, won't you.'

Evans searched for his keys to lock the booking office door and join his two friends on the platform from where they had come to collect their new pigeons.

It was the height of summer and light until late which accounted for why they had not arrived at the station until eight o'clock.'

'Late tonight you are, isn't it,' observed Evans.

'Not shut, are you?' enquired Arthur.

'No, last train half past ten to Manchester. Got to stay open till she's been through. Come on with me, boyo, pigeons waiting on number two platform, been doing a bit of train-spotting they have, waiting for you two. Been here since yesterday morning. Knew you'd be coming, so I didn't sell them. Gave them a few biscuit crumbs this morning so they're bound to be ravenous by now though. Holiday week next week, isn't it? Going away are you?'

'No,' said Willie, 'can't leave Thelma's mother, worse luck.'

'How about you, Arthur?'

'Scarborough.'

'By train, I hope.'

'Of course.'

'Change at York, no through trains. Where'll you be staying?'

'A nice little boarding house up behind Peasholm Park. What about you, Evans?'

'As ever, back to the valleys, land of my fathers. Change at Stockport and Cardiff.'

'Free rail travel,' said Willie. 'Sponging on the relations. Free holiday in fact.'

'That's right, boyo, can't beat it, can you? Well, here they are. Little beauties, aren't they? Hope they'll be back for flying later on.'

'Yes, they will,' said Willie, 'just as soon as we've trained them locally.'

Arthur and Willie picked up the pigeon basket and began to carry it out of the station.

'Thirty bob,' said Evans.

'Thirty bob what?' enquired an incredulous Arthur.

'They arrived carriage forward, so it's thirty bob you owe me.'

Willie looked at him. 'Carriage forward rubbish, we've never had to pay for any before.'

'Well, whatever, it's thirty bob and that doesn't include the biscuit crumbs that I gave them out of the goodness of my own heart.'

'I can't believe my own ears. Are you absolutely sure?' asked Arthur.

'As sure as sure's sure.'

Arthur found the one pound and ten shillings they owed and paid it over.

'Thanks. British Railways biscuit crumbs come free.'

They left the station wishing each other a good holiday and, just as they were going, Evans enquired as to the health of Willie's mother-in-law. He didn't, unfortunately, quite catch the reply he got, but took it to mean that she wasn't very well.

★

Willie spent the holiday week gardening, playing with the children, watching the barges on the canal and occasionally giving Thelma a helping hand with her mother who was slowly getting worse but also mellowing a little as old age and illness took a tighter grip on her. He was missing his annual trip to Blackpool, he was missing Arthur in Scarborough, Lewis in Bridlington, Dick in Morecambe and Eustace who had been taken to Llandudno and who had been told he was going to enjoy it whether he liked it or not.

He enjoyed the break from the mill but wished he had been away on holiday. He took Thelma to the pub for a drink on three nights that week but he missed the certainty of his normal local life. Inevitably, his thoughts turned to the Christmas party and the free drink to be provided by Anthony Murgatroyd, or to be more precise, Murgatroyd's mill. As ever, left to his own thoughts, he had not made any plans, just daydreams of more and even more free beer. The formulation of precise plans was left until a committee meeting in September.

★

It was during the latter part of August that Mrs Woofenden put her clogs under the bed for the last time. Thelma was overcome with grief. Willie had mixed emotions, for the old lady had been so ill for such a long time that Willie had eventually held some compassionate feeling for her, but on the other hand he was pleased that his house might now return to the peaceful place he had almost forgotten existed. For the children, this was the first taste of death in their household: funerals, grieving relations, darkened rooms with drawn curtains all day, preparations for the traditional ham tea, and they were quiet and overawed. Even Josie, who could just remember one other grandparent's funeral, didn't quite know what to expect next.

The old lady plagued them even after departing this life, with Sedgwick the local undertaker having a more than difficult time getting the coffin around the bend at the bottom of the stairs when he came to fetch the body, and even more so when he carried it back downstairs with the body in it. Willie had to give them a hand to get it into the front room, and Sedgwick whispered to him that he shouldn't let anyone else die upstairs in that house or he could get himself a different undertaker.

Events leading up to the funeral had found Willie having to stop in during the evening, much to his disgust, in order to comfort Thelma and to greet the never-ending number of people who called to express their sympathy to the family. There were, as ever, the genuine ones and then there were those who were nosying, who wanted more than anything to have a look inside Cutside Cottage, and who inevitably left saying that they were sorry they would not be able to come to the funeral and that by gum, she were a grand 'un were Mrs Woofenden.

'Two-faced buggers,' were Willie's words to them from behind his closed door, when they had departed.

There were also the few morbid ones who came to look at the body.

'Doesn't she look at peace with herself,' or, 'He does a good job on a body, does Sedgwick, doesn't he?'

Taken all in all, both Thelma and Willie were pleased when the funeral hour arrived. Sedgwick was very much the professional at his job. The two funeral coaches led by the hearse came smoothly and quietly to a stop outside the cottage. Thelma, Willie, Josie and Aunt Bertha, who was Mrs Woofenden's spinster sister, travelled in the first coach, with another aunt and three cousins in the second one.

There was also a private car belonging to a lifelong friend of Mrs Woofenden. Arthur and Bess travelled in that car, Arthur being one of life's professional mourners who could make himself available at the first scent of a funeral.

Aunt Bertha described the service at the chapel as 'very moving', and produced copious quantities of tears throughout. She continued with the crying right through to the graveside and only dried up when the funeral tea was mentioned.

As the vicar had scattered the handful of earth on the coffin, Willie had felt obliged to help him, over-zealously in fact, as he threw a rather large handful of stones and soil which rattled on the top of the wooden box, making all those present stare at him for a couple of seconds. However, the vicar continued and the incident was more or less forgotten except by Thelma who, at the first convenient moment, gave Willie an earful.

They returned home to a ham salad, trifle and cakes tea at which, as is usual, they ate the old lady down, only finishing when there was nothing left to eat or drink. Willie observed that the vicar had eaten far more than his fair share and certainly more than was good for him. However, he was well known for performing this trick at all such functions and really it didn't cause any comment.

After tea, which they had eaten at three o'clock, they settled down for the long chat. The cousins from Sheffield did not need to catch a train until half past seven, and Aunt

Bertha could go with them as she lived only a couple of stops down the line.

Willie listened half-heartedly to how well they were all doing in steel city, how well they were going to do, and how Willie would do well to move to steel city – he would do a lot better if he were to move than if he stopped where he was, and it wasn't surprising that at seven o'clock, with five minutes' walk to the station, Willie said, 'It's time you were getting ready to catch the train.'

'Oh no, they've plenty of time yet, Willie love,' said Thelma.

'Aye, but they don't want to miss their train, do they?' butted in Arthur.

He also had had enough of them.

In the end the argument carried on about trains and times to get to the station until it was time to go. The children, who had been exceptionally good, thanked their relations for the sweets and treats they had brought, then Willie, Thelma, Arthur and Bess walked with them to the station to wish them all a safe journey home.

Owen Evans expressed his sympathy to Thelma and stayed talking to them for a while, holding what was for him a very rare type of sensible conversation.

As they walked back along the village, Willie said to Thelma, 'By gum, your cousins are a boring lot with all their airs and graces. I wasn't half glad to see the back of them.'

'They're not that bad. Anyway, come along into the Crown and Anchor and I'll buy you all a pint up to my mother's will.'

'Why, she had nowt at all,' said Willie.

'That's more than you know,' said Thelma as she guided a somewhat inquisitive and bemused Willie into the snug. Arthur and Jess, who had been walking behind had not heard the conversation but nevertheless followed on into the snug. It was a pub they didn't frequent very often, but none of them were too proud to refuse a drink if someone else was paying.

★

The next committee meeting was held at the Club in September, as arranged. Willie was sporting a new cap which drew comment from everyone there including Anthony Murgatroyd who ventured to enquire as to whether or not Willie was really spending his mother-in-law's inheritance.

This in turn prompted Lewis to use one of Willie's by now more familiar phrases: 'She couldn't have, she had nowt.'

Willie turned a blind ear to this comment as he had been doing throughout the weeks since his mother-in-law had passed on. He just belched out loudly to tell everyone he couldn't care less.

The meeting took its by now usual form: drinks at the bar with Fat Harry dancing attendance on Sarah Anne and Mr Anthony; Arthur's procession to the committee room at funeral pace, all members in attendance; Willie being his usual foul self, belching, farting, scratching his bottom, picking his nose, getting the wax out of his ears and any other thing of which he could think to absent-mindedly amuse himself.

The formal agenda for the meeting took the well-tried route: apologies for absence, minutes of the last meeting, matters arising and then the proposed Christmas party.

'I've written down a list of items I think essential for a successful party,' said Sarah Anne. 'I'll read them out if no one has any objections: One – Venue, Two – Band, Three – Food, Four – Drink, Five – Distributing club funds.

Regarding the venue, are we all agreed that the Club room here will be as good, if not better, than anywhere else?'

Only Daniel Sykes dissented, for in his view they ought to use the church hall where there would be no alcoholic refreshment served, but this suggestion was ignored by the rest of the meeting.

Willie confided in Arthur, stating, 'Daniel Sykes should be taken to a brewery, chained to a chair, mouth forced open and beer poured into him continuously for hours until he converted to a human being. Mind you, they'd have to put the chair into a big tank, because if it's going in continuous at one end it'll be coming out continuous at the other.'

So, it was agreed that Friday 20th December, in the party room at the Club would be the date of the party, to start at half past seven. Arthur had already cleared the date with Fat Harry; the room was free and everything was in order.

The next item to be discussed was the band. Unfortunately, no one had given any particular thought to this item. It was suggested that a gramophone with a selection of dance music might be the answer, and one of the committee could put on the records.

'Malcolm Siswick has a set of drums.' said Lewis. 'All we need is a good pianist to play with him.'

'That's no good. What we want is a right band,' said Willie.

At this point, Eustace had one of his very rare brainstorms.

'What about Sid Sidebottom's Sextipating Cinctet? What about them, eh? Sid Sidebottom's Sextipating Cinctet? What about them? Sid—'

'What the hell's Sid Sidebottom's Sextipating Cinctet?' asked Dick.

Willie thought for a minute. 'I think he means Sid Sidebottom's Syncopating Sextet, and there's only five of them anyway.'

'They used to be a good band at one time,' said Mr Anthony, 'but I haven't heard them for years.'

Arthur, being better informed than his colleagues, told them, 'I think you will find that they are in fact a quartet and only play occasionally nowadays, but as Mr Anthony says, they used to be good and for anything I know still are. As well as that they used to be reasonably priced. I suggest we give them a try.'

This item was accepted by all, even Daniel Sykes, and it was left with Arthur to sort it out.

'Food now,' said Sarah Anne.

'Bloater paste sandwiches and jelly and custard and trifle and pork pies and cakes and—'

Sarah Anne ignored Willie's outburst and continued. 'I had been thinking that perhaps we ought to ask the Club ladies' committee if they wanted to cater.'

Willie lost interest after being ignored, and turned his attention to relieving his body of ear wax, phlegm, wind and snot, whilst the discussion continued.

Arthur soon countered the Club ladies' committee suggestion by stating rule thirty-two: ' "The Club will cater for its own functions only and all other users must provide their own food by whatever means they may decide. The Club facilities will be available to them during the period of use." In other words, no, and we can do whatever we want.'

Lewis said that his wife and Dick's could cater – they were well-known for catering for small functions – but as there'd be rather a large number of people there it would be asking rather a lot of them.

Anthony Murgatroyd suggested a faith supper.

'A what?' asked Willie, who by this time was listening again.

'A faith supper,' replied Mr Anthony. 'You know, everyone brings something, just enough for themselves. Say if four people were coming from one house they would bring sandwiches for four, or pork pies for four, or trifle for four, or cakes for four, or something for four. It would need sorting out into half to do savouries and half to do sweets, then perhaps the committee wives could make the tea and coffee. That way it wouldn't add much to the price of the tickets.'

'What a bloody good idea,' said Willie. 'I'll have half a dozen.'

Fortunately, everyone ignored him yet again, and the chairman wisely suggested that Lewis and Dick, along with their respective wives, might like to take on the job of catering. They agreed readily to this suggestion, and the chairman moved speedily to the next item.

'Drink, now,' she said. 'I think that this item will answer itself. No doubt the steward will arrange the bar? Arthur?'

'Yes, all taken care of, madam chairman.'

'Can we get an extension until half past eleven?' asked Mr Anthony.

'I hadn't asked about it but I will. I don't foresee any big problem; we've done it before.'

Daniel Sykes was moping, wishing he could give a tirade on the evils of the demon drink, but with Mr Anthony at the meeting, he didn't dare.

'Next item, distribution of club funds. Over to Willie, I think.'

'Well, well,' said Willie, who had come to the meeting totally unprepared, 'I don't know really, I haven't thought about it. I, er, well, I, er—'

'Fortunately, madam chairman, I have given the matter a lot of thought,' interrupted Arthur, and Willie gave a silent prayer of thanks. 'Mind you, I haven't got very far except to realise that we've got to have the money here for the party and we've got to have it distributed in an orderly fashion before we go home.'

Sarah Anne put her spoke in. 'You do, of course, appreciate that every member of the club will know exactly how much he or she is entitled to on pay day, so surely that will make life a little easier.'

'Yes, but we do have the money in a deposit account, and they will all be getting more than they had reckoned on and half of them will argue it's wrong.'

There was a short pause in the proceedings and Willie took the opportunity to have a jolly good old loud belch.

Anthony Murgatroyd decided it was his turn to interfere.

'Thank you, Willie, for that timely interruption. Now, it seems to me that there are only two or three problems with this money, all of which are very easily solved. Number one, the money has to be fetched from the bank. This is no problem as Willie, without belching, and Arthur can go to the bank just before closing time, with my permission, collect the money and bring it around here to the Club. Number two, the money has to be looked after at the Club until distribution time. This is also no problem as Willie, without farting, and Arthur can sit here, with my permission, and guard it. Is there a safe in the Club?'

'Yes, Mr Anthony, there is,' said Arthur.

'Even better, then. You can lock the money in the safe and stay to look after it. Number three, the money has to be distributed. Even yet no problem. Whilst Willie, not picking his nose, and Arthur are looking after it, they can also be counting it and putting it into wage packets which they can obtain from the wages office, with my compliments, if they care to climb the office stairs at the mill and ask for some. All your problems are solved easily.'

'Well, Mr Anthony, that sounds most acceptable, and speaking from the chair on behalf of us all present I would like to offer you our most grateful thanks.'

'Hear, hear,' said Willie, followed by the rest of the committee and a belch for good measure.

'I said, without, Willie,' said Mr Anthony.

Willie gave him a knowing grin.

'Has anyone any other business?' asked the chairman.

Daniel Sykes had. He had a lot to say on the evils of drink, on the bad influence Willie's manners had on the proceedings, and on the fact that Mr Anthony was in some way aiding that bad influence, but he daren't, for he reckoned it was more than his job was worth.

'No, then I declare the meeting closed at half past eight, a sensible time to close a meeting and just the right time for an early nightcap, if it isn't too busy in the bar.'

'What influence does the crowd in the bar have on your decision?' asked Anthony Murgatroyd.

'It is a men's club, not quite the place for a lady, but if it isn't too crowded I might just have a quick one before I go home.'

'Come on, you'll be all right and, anyway, I'm going to buy you all a drink. I am highly delighted with the way you've all buckled down and worked so hard to get this Christmas club off the ground. Margaret and I are both looking forward to the party night – it's a long time since we had a social event at the mill.'

'Are you coming to the party, then?' asked Dick, somewhat taken aback.

'Of course I am, wouldn't miss it for the world. Don't forget, I pay into it, and I shall want my fair share of the proceeds like anyone else.'

As the rest of them made their way to the bar Arthur held Willie back in the committee room.

'Where's the safe key? As far as I know it's been lost for years. No one knows what's in it or anything about it.'

'You know it's no good asking me about it, I've no idea at all, it's never been owt to do with me. We'd best ask Fat Harry.'

They went along to the bar and were each presented with a pint of best bitter by Mr Anthony. They couldn't get near Fat Harry who was as ever attending to the wants of Sarah Anne at the far end of the bar. Arthur, just for one fleeting moment thought he saw them holding hands around the end of the bar, but decided he was seeing things and dismissed the idea from his mind.

Arthur eventually called Fat Harry over.

'Where's the Club safe key, and leave Sarah Anne alone,' he added as an afterthought.

'Man has to take his pleasures where and when and how he can get them,' said Harry, with a wicked smile. 'Now, about the key, no idea, it hasn't been opened for years, so don't know. There's a bag of keys that no one knows what they are for in a drawer under the bar. Do you want it?'

'Yes, let's be having it and we'll give them a coat of looking at.'

They took the bag of keys into the small Club office which was between the bar and the committee room and they emptied the contents on to the desk.

'There's dozens of them,' observed Willie. 'We shall never find the right one.'

'Shut up moaning and show me a safe key. These small ones won't do.'

Arthur sorted out all the small ones and put them back into the bag.

'There's keys here that look to be hundreds of years old. Look at this big one here.' He held aloft a giant brass key. 'Church clock type, I shouldn't wonder. Ah, here's one that might do the trick.'

He selected a medium-sized, age-blackened, iron key and gave it to Willie, who tried it in the safe lock. Willie struggled to fit it into the keyhole but it wouldn't go.

'It's too big. Let's have another look.'

He selected one which looked to be the right size and tried it. It went into the hole but wouldn't turn. They tried three more without success then Willie, partially in desperation, tried to turn the safe door handle. It wouldn't turn, but then in a last defiant gesture he tugged the door and almost fell flat on his face as it swung open towards him. He only remained upright by holding on tightly and swinging out with the opening door. They both stared at the wide open safe, then cracked out laughing.

'After all these years', said Arthur, 'it wasn't bloody well locked. Well, I never. The trouble it's caused! Well, I'll be blowed.'

'Not as much as you will be next.'

Willie walked over to the safe and picked up a bright shiny key from the top shelf. He held it up for Arthur to see, then inserted the key in the keyhole, turned it, locked the safe and gave the key to Arthur.

'Well, I'll be buggered. I wonder who was responsible for that. I've been treasurer for eight years now and we've never been able to find the key. Probably during the war when it was done. The poor sod who did it's more than likely in a box in the cemetery now. Open it up again and let's see what's inside it.'

Willie opened the safe again, only this time using the key. Arthur reached inside.

'By gum, just look at this.'

He picked out a silver cup and read aloud the inscription. ' "Eli Seddon Memorial Dominoes Cup. Presented to the Grolsby Working Men's Club by Mrs Elsie Seddon in fond memory of her husband killed in action 18th September 1916." Hey, look here, last presentation was Herbert Halliday, 1941. It must have been in there for over ten years. What else is there in that safe?'

Willie removed a pile of old books and papers which he gave to Arthur.

'Nothing but old Club records and accounts. Come on, let's take this cup next door.'

'Well, I'm fair flabbergasted,' shouted the Club steward. 'We thought this were a goner. Well, I never did. I take it you found the key.'

'It wasn't locked.'

'It what?'

'It wasn't locked.'

'Nay, not after all these years. We knew there were nowt important in it else we'd have had a professional breaker at it before now. But fancy, not locked. We shall look a right load of nuppits when the tale gets around.'

'Best to say nowt about it and just start the dominoes trophy up again,' said Willie.

'Committee decision is that,' said Arthur.

Fat Harry agreed.

'To hell with the committee,' said Willie. 'Let's get it set up and going again soon.'

Fat Harry enquired as to what else there was in the safe, and having been informed that there was nothing of value except old Club documents, he swallowed his pride and made the magnanimous decision to buy Willie, Arthur and Sarah Anne a drink by way of a little celebration. Shortly after, Willie and Arthur left the Club to go home, but Sarah Anne declined their invitation of an escort home.

'I foretell just a little bit of trouble brewing there,' said Arthur.

'Aye, but for who?' asked Willie.

*

A few days later, Willie was pushing a heavy cartload of dripping wet pieces along the dyehouse to the wringing machine, when Arthur stopped him and suggested that they should go and find Sid Sidebottom and his 'Sextipating Cinctet' as soon as possible. They agreed on the next evening, and Willie enquired of Arthur if he knew where they might find him. Arthur replied that he did.

The following evening, Thelma demanded of Willie as to why he was getting ready to go out so early. She was missing the company of her mother and she tried to keep Willie at home as much as she could.

'Me and Arthur's off to find Sid Sidebottom and his Sextipating Cinctet, for the Christmas club do.'

'You're off your rockers, the pair of you. Sid Sidebottom's Syncopating Sextet as it was properly known, died with the outbreak of war and it was a poor band then.'

'It's a committee decision.' Willie took a leaf from Arthur's book by way of reply. 'Anyway, it's Arthur's problem. I'm just going with him for moral support.'

'Alcoholic support, more like.'

'Well, perhaps just one quick one on the way back.'

'Quick five or six, more like. Anyway, don't be late back.'

Willie escaped as soon as he could, thinking that perhaps having had the old lady living with them might have had its compensations after all, and beginning just a teeny weeny bit to mourn her passing.

*

The terrible two walked briskly through the village and were approaching the area of Mafeking Street when Willie nudged Arthur and pointed ahead to the figure of Daniel Sykes going in the same general direction as they were – 'Mafeking Street, Number 19.'

'A pound to a penny,' said Arthur. 'Let's keep well back, then put a spurt on to catch him up just before Number 19.'

As Daniel Sykes turned the corner of Mafeking Street, Willie and Arthur ran as quietly as they could on tiptoe up to the corner and then marched smartly into the street. Daniel heard them, turned to look and quickened his pace, as did the other two. They didn't quite get to sprinting pace because Willie had to stop to recover his breath.

'You're puffing just like a little tank engine, totally out of condition, just look at you. I will have to prescribe a course of exercise, with a restriction on the copious quantities of food and drink that you consume.'

'Nowt o't sort.' Willie stopped to take a few deep breaths and to make a few ungentlemanly noises as well. 'It was well worth it,' he said, puffing and laughing. 'Is he still running?'

'Yes.

'Let him go, he'll never speak to us again. How much further's this house we're going to?'

'I think it's about two more streets further up. It's a small smallholding on Badger Hill.'

They walked on slowly, partly to allow Willie to recover and partly to keep an eye out for Daniel Sykes again. They were, however, out of luck on the second item and they didn't see him again that night.

'Here we are.'

'I'm not going in there,' said Willie as he hesitated outside a broken-down ruin which had at one time been an idyllic country cottage. Some windows were broken and boarded up, the remaining whole ones hadn't been cleaned in generations, the front gate was hanging by a thread to the lower hinge, the other being rusted away, the grass in the front garden was waiting for haymaking time and the paintwork looked as if paint had never been invented; in fact, there was a general air of gloom, despondency and dilapidation about the whole place.

'I'm scared, it gives me the creeps. You never know what might happen to you in a place like this.'

Arthur put on a brave face.

'Come on, I'm going in. Are you coming?'

Willie followed on behind as Arthur resolutely strode over the remains of the gate, picked his way along the almost-existing front path and knocked on the rotten front door.

Willie moved right in behind Arthur as what sounded like a giant brute of a dog tried to tear the front door from its frame, barking, snarling and scratching. There then followed a heated exchange between the dog and its master, before the dog was quietened and the door opened to reveal a shabbily dressed man standing in a half-lit entrance hall with doors to left and right, completed by a set of stairs going upwards behind him.

'Who is it and what do you want?'

'Sid Sidebottom?' asked Arthur.

'Who wants him?'

'Arthur Baxter and Willie Arkenthwaite.'

'By gum, the terrible two, haven't seen you in years, didn't just recognise you for a minute. Come on in, won't you? Don't mind the dog, he's a big softy, won't harm you. Just pat him as you pass him to show him you're friendly like. Mind the hole in the hall floor, just follow me, just keep to the right.'

He lead the way into the living room. The terrible two gingerly patted the dog as they walked past it, but all it did was to ignore Arthur and give Willie a big lick. Willie gasped and coughed as the stench from the living room took his breath away. He looked around at his surroundings, there was a general air of filth everywhere. The blackleaded range was blacker than black but not with lead, paper was peeling off the walls in places, there were piles of dog dirt, cat dirt and every other sort of dirt everywhere, the furniture was battered and bruised, and the carpet was half holes and half threadbare. There were three hens wandering around, and Cissy Sidebottom lolled in a chair in filthy clothes, with a cigarette hanging from her bottom lip. There was one forty watt lamp hanging from a flex in the middle of the ceiling – well, not exactly a ceiling, more like religious plaster.

'Sit down, boys, sit down.'

He pushed a mountain of newspapers off the settee on to the floor and made room for them. They both sat down in a fog-like cloud of dust.

'I'll just put the kettle on and we'll have a good cup of tea.'

'No thanks,' said Arthur. 'We've a er, er, meeting to go to and we're late already. We've just come to see if you and your band can play at a dance and Christmas party at the Club on Friday 20th December.'

'By Jove, yes. There's only five of us now, you know, but it'll be all right. There aren't many dances nowadays. I'm sure we can play for you. What do you want, old time or modern sequence? We can do both, a mixture will be best, Christmas melodies as well, we can even have carol singing if you want. We play in evening dress you know. We charge twenty pounds for the night, and only one interval. Mind you, we expect a good free supper and a few drinks to oil the windpipes. Is the piano still okay at the Club, because we need one. I play saxophone, Dennis Shires on trumpet, Maud Lindley on piano, Jack France on percussion and Hubert Shaw on double bass. Not a bad collection, eh? We practise Wednesdays in the band room, for an hour or so, at about eight, if you want to refresh your memories on our talents.'

Sid Sidebottom paused for breath, and Arthur just managed to get a word in.

'That sounds fine, just fine, so that's a deal is it? Friday 20th December, start at half past seven, finish at quarter to midnight, at the Club, is that okay? Good, now we'll have to be going as we're running very late.'

They both rose quickly, but decorously, and took their leave of Sid and Cissy. She had contributed absolutely zero to the conversation, hardly even acknowledging their presence.

*

'Flippin heck,' said Arthur as the cottage door closed behind them.

'Twice,' said Willie. 'What a pong. How the hell does he survive in there? It smells rotten.'

'I thought he was never going to give over talking. I know we agreed to have him and his band, but I wonder what they're really like. I think we'd best go to the band room next Wednesday night.'

'Let's go to the Club. I could murder a quick pint.'

They forgot about Daniel Sykes and joined Eustace and Dick in the Club for a drink.

'Where's Lewis?' asked Willie.

'His missus won't let him out, she won't, she won't let him out. He's got to decorate, he has, he's got to decorate, to decorate, the lounge, poor sod.'

Willie farted and ordered two pints.

'Who's your friend?' enquired Fat Harry of no one in particular.

'We've just been to the dirtiest, smelliest, rottenist, broken-down house in Grolsby,' said Willie.

'You've not been to Cissy Sidebottom's?' asked Harry.

'How did you know?'

'Well-known fact, they've won the Nations Cup for the muckiest house in the free world for the last five years running now. Mind you, his band's still very good. Are we having them at the Christmas party?

'Yes, we are,' said Arthur. 'And, hey, you'd better behave yourself that evening because Sarah Anne's bringing her husband to the party.'

'Aye, I know. Still, I might get her to help behind the bar from time to time.'

He smiled and winked.

'I hope you're going to wear a tie that night,' said Willie.

'Best dressed man that night – evening dress only behind this bar. By the way, Arthur, I shall have to have a lot of assistance for the big do.'

'Daniel Sykes could help you along with her from Number 19,' said Willie,

'By the way, we saw him up there tonight.'

'Did he just go in as bold as brass?'

'No, we ran him a couple of blocks before we gave him up.'

'To tell the truth,' said Arthur, laughing, 'Willie ran out of steam and we had to give up the chase to let him get his breath back.'

Willie decided that it was time to change the subject, and he addressed himself to Eustace. 'Your wife helping with the refreshments at the party?'

'Well, I don't know, don't know, I haven't asked her, not yet, I haven't. She might, yes, she might, yes, yes she might. I don't know, I'll have to ask her, I will, yes, I will. Will you ask her Willie? Will you? Will you ask her? She'll come for you, she will, yes, she will, not for me, no, not for me, but she will for you, yes she will.'

'It's not up to me to ask her, that's your job, you're on the committee like the rest of us.' He had memories of a large nasty-tempered woman that he daren't ask either. 'I'll see if

Thelma will. It might come better from her, one woman to another.'

'Thank you, Willie, thank you. Oh, that is a relief, it is, a relief, she wouldn't have come for me, not for me, no, not for me.' He sighed and sat quietly with his own troubled thoughts.

Willie had walked back into his nice warm and cosy cottage by half past nine. He looked around the neat, clean living room, then he looked at Thelma, and thought about Eustace and his particularly bad domestic circumstances. He walked over to Thelma and gave her a big hug, a squeeze, and finished with a long loving kiss.

'What was that for?' she asked, somewhat surprised at his impromptu action.

'Nowt really, love,' he said. 'Just for you being you.'

It took him a long time that night to explain his action.

*

Considering the very amateurish status of the committee, the whole process of forming the Christmas club and general events so far had gone very smoothly. In fact, they looked as if they would continue to run smoothly, until Arthur enquired of Willie if he had fixed up proper arrangements with the shopkeepers who were going to supply discounted goods at Christmas to the members of the club.

'What do you mean?' asked Willie.

'Have you got them all properly sorted out, who's going to supply who with what and at what price, then who's going to order what from whom and where and why and when and how much and, oh, heck, there is no more questions left.'

'Eh?'

'Is it all under control?'

'Well, er, let's see now, well, er, well, happen, er, yes, happen it is, and there again, happen it isn't, it all depends.'

'Depends on what?'

'On what you mean.'

Arthur was rapidly becoming more than exasperated so he decided to try a different approach.

'Have you, for instance, been along to Freddy Nevershut's to give him a list of what everyone wants on Christmas Eve?'

'No.'

'Have you actually got a list of what everyone wants?'

'No,' said Willie, and belched. 'I haven't.'

'Well, don't you think it's about time we bloody well did have a list then? It was your idea and it's high time you did something about it. We've only just over eleven weeks to go to pay-out day.'

'Er, yes, well, to tell you the truth, I really do not know what to do about it. Do you?'

'Yes, but not right now.' They were just getting ready to play cards in the lunchtime card school. 'I'll come around to your house tonight before we go to the Club. Ask your Thelma to get the coffee pot on about half past eight.'

★

Arthur stood at ease with his back to Willie's roaring fire, trying to get the frosty night air out of his system. He was holding a steaming hot pot of Thelma's coffee.

'Now that I'm comfortable, Willie, let's begin. How many shops have you been into?'

'Let's have a see. Grocers, greengrocers, butchers, toy shop and electrical shop, and that's enough.'

'Well, er, yes, you are probably right, it's enough for you to cope with and it's enough for asking questions of the members.'

'When are you going to ask your members what they want and how are you going to note it down?' Thelma, who had been darning Willie's religious socks and sitting at the side of the fire, intervened using her womanly intuition. 'You can sort out all these problems without doing anything about them.'

'We can?' asked Arthur.

'Yes, it's simple. Just go to each of the shops you have chosen and arrange with the shopkeepers to keep a list of orders from each of your members who calls. Give the members a list of shops they can get discount at, and you've cracked it.'

'Aye, we have, it sounds a great idea to me. Thanks a million, love.'

'It would to you, but we'd have to give each shopkeeper a full list of members so that there were no trespassers, as it were,' concluded Arthur after a heavy thinking round.

'There you are, all settled simply. Why don't you get off to the Club and leave me in peace with my darning.

The terrible two ambled peacefully along to the Working Men's Club discussing the Christmas club and the work they had yet to do for it. The party was now only about eleven weeks away and really, other than talk, they had done precious little about it apart from collect the money each Friday dinner time.

'On Saturday, you'd better get yourself into each of those five shops and tell them to expect a visit from our club members, and to note down their requirements so that they can have it all prepared in time for the big day. Oh, and whilst you're there, just check that the previously negotiated discount level still applies.'

Willie farted.

'Yes, I will,' he agreed.

*

On Saturday morning Thelma asked Willie to help her with one or two of the more arduous household chores, and to take a look at the bathroom which was in need of a fresh coat of paint.

'Sorry, love, got to get around the five shops and prepare them for the onslaught that is to come.'

'But they're all open until six on a Saturday, so you've plenty of time. You can stay home and help me this morning.'

Willie studied carefully and realised he had no good reason or alibi to get him away from the house, so he succumbed to female pressure, pottering about outside when he could escape for a few moments.

*

After a dinner of fish and chips, which was the time-honoured tradition at Number 6 Cutside Cottages, Willie walked into the village and in particular to the emporium of Freddy Nevershut Ogley.

'Third time you've disgraced these humble premises with your presence this year, William Arkenthwaite. It's becoming a habit.'

'Can't resist the overpowering and friendly welcome I get when I do call, can I?'

'Well, now you are here, what do you want?'

'Told you it was the friendly welcome that attracts me.'

'Your Thelma sent you out from under her feet so as to be under my feet, has she?'

'You know this discount for the Murgatroyd Christmas club?'

'Oh, that.' He had been hoping that they had forgotten about it.

'Well, we've about eleven weeks to go now so we are going around telling everyone in the club that wants to buy groceries with their pay-out, to come along and give their orders into you as soon as they can. I'll give you a list of members so that you'll know who to expect. As well as that, we are going to tell them to make sure they tell you they are club members.'

'That's real good of you, Willie, real good. Just what my profits need is all this discount. Real good of you.'

Willie sensed an air of something nasty brewing in Freddy's attitude so, giving the customary belch, he said, 'We can allus go to the co-op, you know.'

'No, no, don't bother, I'll do it, no problem.'

'Are you sure?'

'Yes.'

'Absolutely?'

'Yes, bloody yes. Now go away, I've a lot to think about.'

*

Willie went on his way extremely pleased with his performance, some of which he had been secretly rehearsing for the last few hours. He next called at the butchers, then the electrical shop with the same message, which was received by both proprietors with about the same enthusiasm as Freddy Nevershut had displayed earlier. To all of them the idea had seemed good at the time of conception, but not so good in the grey light of dawn when it came to crunch time.

The last shop to be visited was the toy shop of Herbert Chew. Willie had made the arrangement with him months before, as he had with the others. The problem was that Herbert Chew had the only toy shop in the village, and as such held a total monopoly of the local trade which led him to believe he didn't have to discount his goods to the club. The other problem, and almost as bad as the first one for those trying to set up such a deal, was that Herbert Chew was almost stone deaf. He left the serving in the shop to his wife Agatha whilst he did the paperwork. This deafness did not help matters along when it came to a discussion, particularly when it was one he didn't want to have anyway. It had taken Willie a long time on his first visit to persuade Herbert that they should have some discount, and although he thought Herbert had agreed, he wasn't exactly sure.

Willie opened the front door and entered the old-fashioned, poorly lit shop. An extra loud bell, that was hit by a striker on the door, alerted the entire neighbourhood to his arrival, and he could just hear a female voice coming from the back room at the close of a conversational shout. She shuffled into the shop from the back, her threadbare slippers making a dull scraping sound on the stone flagged floor. Her slow appearance had given Willie time to look around the shop. It was in desperate need of painting. The old dark brown paint was peeling all over and it was crying out to be done again, in a lighter shade, though, thought Willie.

'Hello, Willie, how are you?'

She paused for a cough and a splutter as Willie seized the opportunity for a quick snook up and swallow of the resulting phlegm.

'How's Thelma and the children? Growing up by now, I suppose. Haven't seen them in a long time. Tell Thelma to pop in for a chat sometime will you?'

'No fear,' thought Willie, for Agatha Chew was a scandalmonger *par excellence* and only wanted Thelma to call so that she could extract as much information as possible. This would then be distributed as venomously as possible throughout the length and breadth of the village.

'I've come to see about Murgatroyd's Christmas club.'

'You'll have to see him. He's in the back. Go through.'

Willie walked around the back of the counter and passed from one depressing room to another. It was a typical village store back room, filled with boxes, some full, some empty, reject toys, broken dolls at the dolls' hospital, two chairs in front of a big roaring fire, a small kitchen area, a bench with tools for repairing the broken dolls and an antique bureau full of papers, at which was seated Herbert Chew poring over a set of invoices. He had not heard Willie come in, and almost jumped out of his skin when Willie poked him on the shoulder.

'You daft bugger, what you want to go and do that for? You could have made me have a heart attack.'

'You'll never have a heart attack, you're made of stronger stuff than that. Anyway, how are you?'

'What?'

'How are you?'

'Yer what?'

'I've come about the Christmas club.'

'What?'

'I've – come – about – the – Christmas – club.'

'What about it?'

'About the discount.'

Herbert heard the last word.

'Discount. What discount?'

'The discount of five per cent you said you'd give to club members for their Christmas orders from Murgatroyd's Christmas club.'

'What?'

Willie repeated his small speech, very loudly and very slowly.

'Don't know, you'll have to talk to the wife.'

'She said I'd to talk to you.'

'What?'

'She – said – I'd – to – talk – to – you – about – it.'

'Oh, she did, did she, we'll soon see about that.'

He stormed into the shop where all hell let loose between him and his wife. Willie remained in the back room, standing with his back to the fire, keeping warm and enjoying the row that no one was winning. From what he could hear, however, it was becoming more and more apparent that neither of them was prepared to deal with the matter and as far as they were concerned there was no discount.

The row ceased abruptly and Herbert Chew stormed into the back room.

'There's nowt doing, and that's my final word on the subject and hers as well. Bloody women. So that's it. Goodbye.'

He turned his back on Willie and resumed his seat at the bureau.

'So you're not going to give us the discount like what you promised?'

'What?'

'Oh, nowt. I'm going.'

★

The greengrocers were quite amiable about the discount, but a very disappointed Willie went home and, thinking about Agatha Chew, he walked into his cottage, grabbed Thelma around the waist, giving her a big hug and a long loving kiss.

'What was that for?' she enquired, somewhat taken aback.

'Again, just because you are you.'

Once again, it took him a long time to explain his actions.

Chapter Fourteen

The day of the pay-out and party was drawing nearer and nearer. One last committee meeting was necessary to finalise all arrangements. Before that day arrived, however, Willie had formulated a notice to put up in the canteen, to inform everyone about the arrangements for discounts available to club members.

He had pondered about the wording of it for many a long hour, both at work and in his moments of leisure. He had even smuggled a piece of paper and a pencil into his garden shed one evening in order to write it out. Thelma wouldn't suspect anything as he usually took his hurricane lamp with him in winter into the shed and the pigeon loft when he made his nightly tour to feed the pigeons.

Willie lit the lamp in the back kitchen, carefully pumping it up to the correct operating pressure, or near enough, then took it down the garden and into the shed where he put it down in its usual position on the end of the bench. Having then assessed the mess on the rest of the bench he decided that he had better have a good tidy and sweep down before he could even attempt to write on the paper.

The job of picking out screws, nails and various other remains of months of pottering was going to take at least a good hour before he could start to write his notice. He, therefore, thought it prudent to forestall any intervention that might possibly come from Thelma in view of the length of time he would be missing from the house, so he began to tidy the bench. After a little while he thought of a good excuse to go and get warm again, so he went back up the garden into the house.

He found Thelma sitting in front of the fire, knitting.

'What are you knitting, love?'

'A new cardigan for Josie's birthday, but it's a secret and she hasn't to know about it, so I've got to knit it when she's out or after she's gone to bed.'

'Where is she, then?'

'She's gone with Christine and Pauline to a new youth club they've started at church.'

'But she's a Methodist.'

'I don't think that'll have much effect on Josie. Anyway, it's good for her to get out a bit.'

'Have you a spare, empty jam jar anywhere that I can have, to sort out some of my screws and nails?'

'Yes, there is one under the sink. Don't you think you'd better wait until it's light at the weekend?'

'Aye, you're right, but I'll just make a start and then finish it on Sunday.'

He took the jar back to the shed and put a few screws into it which, effectively, with a little help from a push to one side of the remains on the bench, made an area large enough for his piece of paper. He then swept the dust and dirt in the empty space on to the floor, dusted with a rag carefully placed the piece of paper into the middle of the clean area. He took the pencil in hand with a flourish and a fart, licked the point and stared into space.

After a few minutes, he wrote in big letters at the top of the paper 'NOTICE' and then after a while and under it 'MURGATROYD'S CHRISTMAS CLUB'. He had been thinking about the wording of this poster for days, so he continued to the next line, 'DISCOUNT SCHEME'.

At this point his mind became a huge blank because his thoughts had gone no further than 'DISCOUNT SCHEME'.

The more pressing problem was what to do with the piece of paper to keep it out of everyone's way until he could muster up some ideas to put on to it. He eventually hit on the scheme of emptying the tool drawer and putting the paper on the bottom of it beneath the brown paper liner he had had there for more years than he cared to remember.

Willie emptied the drawer, put the piece of paper under the brown paper and replaced the tools. This had given him the opportunity to clean out the contents and discard one or two broken items that had been waiting to be disposed of for a very long time. In fact, he did himself a very big favour, or so he told himself.

When he got back to the house, Thelma was still knitting.

'I think I'll just go on to the Club for a quick pint.'

Thelma agreed with him because she wanted to do as much knitting as possible, in peace.

'Are you calling for Arthur?'

'No, he's doing some work in the kitchen for Jess tonight.'

'What sort of work?'

'Mending a broken hinge on a cupboard door and that sort of thing.'

'Thank goodness for that. I couldn't quite see him rolling out the pastry.'

*

Willie got washed and changed, then made his way to the Club where the only occupant other than the steward was Philip Perry, or Pee Pee as he was known in the village.

'Hi, Pee Pee, how goes it?'

'How goes what?'

Pee Pee had no sense of humour and was one of those people who believed the world owed him a living. He was a permanent moaner and carried a huge chip on his shoulder.

'How goes everything and life in general?' asked Willie.

'He's full of the joys of spring,' said Fat Harry.

'I'm fed up,' replied Pee Pee.

'Fed up with what?'

'Everything. Everything and nothing.'

'What are you going on about, everything and nothing?'

'Well, I'm fed up with anything and I'm fed up with nothing. I'm just fed up.'

'I am a famous trick cyclist and I'm going to analyse you,' said Willie.

'You're a famous what?'

'A trick cyclist.'

'I think he means a psychiatrist,' said Harry.

'Now when I say a word or few words, you say another word or words, the first thing that comes into your head. Black pudding.'

'Dinner.'

'Very good. Knickers.'

'Mavis.'

'Who the hell's Mavis?'

'Wife's friend.'

'Very good, even better,' said Willie, thinking that he had possibly stumbled into some scandal and thinking he'd better probe deeper.

'I think there's something here we don't know about but that we ought to be knowing,' said Fat Harry.

'No. No, it's nothing like what you're thinking.'

'How do you know what I'm thinking?'

'You only think one way. No, it's just that she wears them modern French knickers. I know, I've seen them on her washing line.'

'A likely story. However, let's get on. The next word is, er, er, bunker.'

'Golf course.'

'Very good, in fact excellent. Now, hole in one.'

'Drinks all round, in the Club house.'

'Mine's a pint,' said Willie.

'Hang on a minute, I didn't invite you to have a drink.'

'You said drinks all round.'

'But that was because we was playing at trick cyclists.'

'Yes, but when you say drinks all round, that's just what it means.'

'I'm fed up.'

'Aye, you will be,' said Willie. 'But thanks for the drink anyway.'

Harry poured the round and then, with a great deal of difficulty, extracted the money from Pee Pee.

'Won't be long now until the big day arrives, Willie, will it?' asked Fat Harry.

'Yes, it's getting here quicker than I'd like.'

'What big day's this, then?' enquired Pee Pee.

'Pay-out day for the Murgatroyd Christmas club.'

'So why's that a big day, then?'

'We're having a big do in here, that's why,' said Willie.

'What sort of a do?'

'A dance and supper, with Sid Sidebottom's Sextipating Cinctet.'

'I think you mean Syncopating Sextet.'

'Yes, that's it, but there's only five of them.'

'Does that alter the spelling then?' asked Pee Pee.

'Eh?'

'I thought he were dead and disbanded.'

'No, still going strong.'

'Can anyone come?' he asked hopefully.

'Not on your nellie. It's strictly members only. Mr Anthony's coming with his wife.'

'So what?'

'Hey, it'll be a good do when he comes, free booze and the like.'

Dick and Lewis walked into the bar.

'Bloody cold, Harry, put some coal on the fire.'

Willie farted.

'That'll keep us nice and warm,' observed Harry. 'Thank you, Willie. If I put any more coal on that fire we shall be in need of the fire brigade, and they can't come tonight because it's half-day closing, so I'm not. Anyway, stand with your backs to it and warm your brains. If you were to make an order to the bar for liquid refreshment I might just bring it over to you. There are two good reasons why I will bring it over to you – I'm short of exercise and I'm fed up of standing here listening to Pee Pee moaning.'

'Are you going to trim the Club room up for the do, Harry?' asked Dick.

'Am I what?' Predictably, he roared, 'Am I hell as like, you can trim your own room and we'll have the artificial tree on the end of the bar as always.'

'Very charitable indeed, very nice of you, a good time is going to be had in here by all, I don't think, with that attitude.'

Harry, who had been walking back to the bar, spun on his heels, charged back and stopped with his nose a quarter of an inch from Dick's. He was purple-faced and about to boil over. Dick, who wasn't given to panicking and took everything in his stride, didn't move but stared straight into Harry's eyes, waiting for the tirade to begin. He didn't have to wait above a split second.

'I'm not bloody paid to bloody put bloody decorations up. The governing committee only pay me a pauper's wage and that's not surprising when you look around and count how many people there are in here right now.

Furthermore, you wouldn't let me join your piddling little Christmas club, so I'm not bloody helping you. Got it?'

He stormed back to the bar.

Dick lit a cigarette and said, 'You're right, Harry, it's not a bad fire you've lit.'

'I can do something right then, can I?' he shouted back.

Willie, Lewis and Pee Pee had been cowering, and pondering whether or not they might have to come to Dick's assistance, or whether indeed it might be best to just quietly go home and leave Dick to Harry's tender mercy. As it happened they were more than delighted when the all clear was sounded.

'Have you got the booking for next week's Christmas club committee meeting in the diary?' asked Willie in a fit of inspiration.

'Yes, that's in all right. Mr One Hundred and One Per Cent put it in after the last meeting.'

'Who's Mr One Hundred and One Per Cent?' asked Pee Pee.

'Arthur 'never put a foot wrong' Baxter.'

'Oh, aye, he's on the ball all right when it comes to efficiency is our Arthur.'

'You related to him?' asked Dick.

'No, why?'

'It was just the way you said our Arthur.'

'Just a term of adherement.'

Fat Harry suddenly brightened up and changed the subject.

'Will Sarah Anne be coming?'

'She'd better be. She is the chairman,' said Lewis.

Harry smiled.

'Good, good,' he said.

Dick looked at him, and an idea crept into his head.

'What about that long dollop Sykes the sod. Is he coming?'

'Well he should be – he's on the committee even though he's a pain,' said Willie.

'He's about as bad as Sarah Anne is good. I think I might ban him from entering the Club again, then get Sarah Anne to come here every night.'

The remains of the evening drifted by with a few more members arriving for a late drink and a convivial atmosphere continuing until closing time.

When Willie got home, Thelma had put the knitting away and was making his supper.

'Anything happened at the Club tonight?'

'Not particularly. Fat Harry murdered Dick, then killed him dead, then shouted at him, but nothing special.'

★

On Sunday morning, Willie was up bright and early, just as it was becoming light and immediately after he had finished his bacon and eggs, away he went to the shed to retrieve his notice. He stared at it for some time, then went for a walk around the allotment and returned to the shed.

He looked proudly at the title, 'DISCOUNT SCHEME', then walked around to the pigeon loft where he spent some time talking to the birds. The next time he returned to the shed he was feeling cold and the lure of the fire indoors was like a magnet to him. He decided that there was only one thing for it – he would have to swallow his pride and ask Thelma to help him with the notice.

He took the paper into the warm glow of the house.

'Any chance of a coffee, love?'

'You'll have to get your own, I'm just a bit busy knitting this cardigan whilst the kids are out at Sunday school. What's that piece of paper you've got hidden behind your back?'

'Well, it's like this... shall I go make the coffee?'

'When you've told me what the paper is for.'

'Well, it's for your idea,' he blurted out.

'For my idea?'

'Yes, you said we should tell the shopkeepers who the members are and the members who the shopkeepers are, so that they can all sort it out themselves.

'Yes, I did. So what's the paper for?'

'For the notice.'

'What notice?'

'The notice to hang in the canteen to tell them who the shopkeepers are.'

'Oh, is that all,' said Thelma, losing interest and putting her attention back into her knitting.

'Yes, well, I've been doing it in the shed, you see.'

'Yes, I see, and?'

'Well, it's like this, you see, I've got stuck.'

'What do you mean you've got stuck?'

'Well, I don't know what to put on the notice.'

'Go and put the coffee on. It won't do you any harm to do it once. Do you know where the kettle is?'

'Yes.'

'Water?'

'Yes.'

'Coffee, sugar, milk, mugs, spoon?'

'Get on with your knitting.'

'Well, go and do it then, there's a love, I could just do with a mug of coffee and I'll do your notice as soon as I've finished Josie's cardigan. I've only got to sew on the left sleeve and the buttons now.'

Willie studied the contents of the kitchen – a rare event. The coffee grounds were in a jar at the back of the cupboard. They weren't used often, and he couldn't think why he fancied a mug of coffee but he did. The trouble was that the coffee grounds got in your teeth, you swallowed some and the remainder made a right mess in the bottom of the mug.

Arthur's missus, Jess, always drank coffee, never tea. She brewed it in a jug then let it settle a while before pouring it through a sieve. They didn't have a sieve but he thought he would try the jug method anyway.

When he finally delivered the mug of not-so-hot coffee to Thelma, he was extremely pleased with the result of his efforts. Even Thelma was full of praise and immediately promoted him to coffee brewer-in-chief, with his promise that he would try to get it hot next time.

'Now, what about this notice?' she asked.

'Well, I've got as far as the title. 'MURGATROYD'S CHRISTMAS CLUB. NOTICE. DISCOUNT SCHEME', and that's all.'

'Sit down at the table with your pencil ready and a piece of writing paper from my pad. We'll make a sort of mock-up before we do the real thing.'

Thelma carefully wrote:

NOTICE
MURGATROYD'S CHRISTMAS CLUB
DISCOUNT SCHEME

in capital letters at the top of the paper, then, in her best handwriting, put, 'The shops listed below have offered a discount on your Christmas orders. Every shopkeeper has a list of members of the club. All you have to do is to give your name in with your Christmas order to get your discount.'

'I think we should ask Josie to do the proper notice with her paint set. She can make a nice coloured poster for you; she's very good at doing that sort of thing. She'll not be long before she's home and you can ask her as soon as she lands.'

'Aye, a very good idea,' replied Willie, and for the third time in recent memory he gave Thelma a big hug and kiss.

'What was that for?'

'Thanks, that's all.'

Willie went out into his garden again. It was dinner time when he next returned to the house having whiled away the time pottering and talking to his pigeons.

'Dinner ready?' he asked of no one in particular.

'Almost,' replied Josie. 'But you'll have to just wait for a few minutes until I've finished your poster so that we can clear away and set the table.'

Normally Willie would have remonstrated that his dinner wasn't ready and that it was half past twelve, but because today Josie was doing something special for him he kept quiet.

'There, now, it's finished, do you want to have a look?'

Willie smiled at her, walked over to her, put his arm around her and looked at his poster. It was bold, brightly coloured, and clearly gave the required message.

'Ee, that's fair champion,' he said and gave her a hug and kiss, then, as an afterthought he said, 'Thanks, love, that's real super.'

The traditional Yorkshire pudding was served and Willie ate his with more than his usual relish, which created more than the usual amount of flatulence. This was followed by roast beef and for pudding jam roly-poly, swimming in acres and acres of custard. Finally, the meal was washed down with a pint mug of tea. Willie then sat down in front of the fire, put his feet on the mantelshelf, and fell into a deep sleep whilst the younger children cleared up and washed up.

*

Wednesday dawned fine and clear and stopped that way until the evening when the Murgatroyd's Christmas club committee was due to convene at the Working Men's Club at half past seven prompt.

They were all there in the bar, on time, except Daniel Sykes. Fat Harry was flirting with Sarah Anne, Eustace was lost in his own little world and Arthur was pacing up and down with a pile of papers in his hands trying to look important. Willie and the others were enjoying a pint and a chat. There was a very convivial atmosphere in the bar.

Arthur brought them all back to reality with an announcement.

'Well, ladies and gentlemen, it his now just hafter half past seven and hi would like you hall to make your way to the committee room so that we may commhence the meeting forthwith.'

'Has he been having elocution lessons?' asked Dick, quietly.

'More like posh gob lessons,' replied Willie.

Dick caught up with Arthur.

'By gum, that were well put, Arthur old mate.'

'Yes, yes,' replied Arthur, his face turning to a broad grin, 'I have been giving hay little private attention to my public delivery recently.'

'I telled thee it were posh gob lessons,' said Willie before relieving his inner feelings rather loudly.

'Can we please get the meeting underway?' demanded Arthur again.

'Are you on a promise or summat?' asked Willie.

'Yes, as a matter of fact I'm on a promise to put up some curtains for our Jess as soon as I can get home. So come on, let's get the show on the road.'

'What show, Arthur? On the road, what show? On the—'

'For heaven's sake, shut up, Eustace.'

The meeting duly sat down, everyone suitably supplied with a drink. Arthur nudged Sarah Anne into opening the meeting.

'Good evening all. Thank you all for coming along this evening to what I hope will be the last committee meeting before we pay out the money and hold the party. We have a lot to get through and so I suggest we begin with—'

'Oh bugger,' thought Willie, 'we're here for the duration.'

'—the item that is customary on these occasions, the reading of the minutes of the last meeting. Arthur, can you please oblige?'

'But hof course, madam chairman. Minutes hof the committee meeting hof the Murgatroyd Christmas club, held hat the—'

He was interrupted by Eustace, who had had a very unusual fit of inspiration.

'Can't we take the minutes as read? Can't we? Take the minutes as read? Can't we—'

Arthur, who was enjoying reading out the minutes to his captive audience, gave Eustace a drop-dead look, but the chairman said, 'Well, yes, I see no reason why not. Does anyone object?'

'Yes, I do.'

They all turned to observe the tall thin figure of Daniel Sykes, who had entered the room very quietly without any of them hearing him.

'Well, you Mafeking well would,' shouted Willie.

'I'll swing for you yet, Arkenthwaite, that I will,' he shouted back in reply.

'You probably will with what I know.'

Before Daniel could reply again, the chairman intervened.

'Look here, you two. Sort out your differences outside the committee room, will you please. Now then, Daniel, it has been carried by an overwhelming majority that we will take the minutes of the last meeting as read.'

'How do you know it's carried by a large majority when you haven't had a vote?'

'Because I am the chairman and I know the feeling of the meeting. Now can we get on? Sit down please, Daniel. I think we should start by asking Willie if everything is all right with the money collection.'

'Yes, Sarah Anne, no problem. We have it sorted out now and it doesn't take us long on a Friday dinner time. Mind you, there's sometimes a long queue at the bank when I go, but I manage.'

'Do you manage to spend the Christmas club's money or your own money when you call in here on your way to the bank?' asked Daniel Sykes.

'I'll swing for you, never mind you for me,' shouted Willie in reply.

Once more the chairman intervened in the dispute.

'Item three,' said Sarah Anne. 'What arrangements have you made, Arthur and Willie, for paying out the money?'

Willie looked at Arthur, who came to the rescue.

'Well we haven't yet finalised the plan hexcept to say that harrangements are hin hand.'

'He's still talking posh gob,' thought Willie.

'Madam chairman, may I be permitted through the chair to ask Arthur Baxter if he is well enough to continue with the meeting as he seems to have a speech impediment, and I was wondering if he should go home to lie down,' said Daniel Sykes as he sat down with a satisfied smirk from ear to ear.

'Don't take the bait, Arthur, ignore it,' commanded the chairman. 'If you don't mind me saying so, Arthur, you've just talked a lot and said nowt. Can you be a bit more specific?'

Arthur stood up.

'Well, madam chairman, we know the party's hon Friday 20th December and we know the bank closes hat half past three hon a Friday. So we, that his Willie and me'll have to be hat the bank just before hit shuts to get all hof hus money hout. Then we'll have to take hit somewhere safe, to look hafter hit huntil party starts, then we'll have to give hit hout hat the party.'

'Thank God posh gob's finished,' thought Willie.

The proceedings were interrupted by Anthony Murgatroyd coming into the committee room, a freshly-pulled pint in his hand.

'Good evening everyone.'

'Good evening, Mr Anthony.'

'Sorry I'm late. I hope you don't mind me interfering in your meeting. It's a good excuse for me to get out for a drink you know. I don't get out often.'

'You are very welcome,' said the chairman, 'and might I say that any contribution you may wish to make to the proceedings will be more than welcome.'

There was a general grunt of approval from all but Daniel Sykes who made a noise a bit like a Bactrian camel with stomach trouble, the meaning of which no one could tell but they all knew it was not a noise of agreement.

'Now, can we get on, please. Arthur, you were telling us about the money.'

Arthur had already decided on the appearance of Anthony Murgatroyd that he had better revert to his normal tongue and give over trying to talk far back.

'Yes, the main problem is how to pay it out.'

'Thank God that Mr Anthony's arrived and the posh gob's gone,' thought Willie.

'If it were me, I would count it before I paid it out,' said Daniel Sykes smirking to himself.

Willie stood up and said, 'One more like that from you and you'll feel my fist.'

'Willie,' shouted Sarah Anne, 'one more like that from you and you're banned, treasurer or not.'

Anthony Murgatroyd intervened.

'Talking about distributing the money, if we give you some envelopes from the mill, why don't you put everyone's pay-out in a separate envelope with their name on the outside, then all you have to do is to get each member to sign for theirs when they take it. Get rid of them at the beginning of the evening and you can enjoy the rest of the party.'

'What a good idea,' said Arthur. 'That'll mean that we can count it out and put it in the envelopes as soon as we get it from the bank, then lock them all in the Club safe until party time. All we need to do is to write the envelopes a few days in advance. Thanks, Mr Anthony.'

Dick's glass was empty so he said, 'Time for another round, I think. I'll just ring the bell for some service.'

'No, no, let me, I'm nearest to it.' Anthony got up and pressed the bell-push which stuck in and would not come out. 'Oh dear, what have I done now?'

'Don't worry, you've only upset Fat Harry,' said Willie laughing.

Sure enough there was the sound of a stampede approaching and suddenly the door opened in three directions at once.

'Who the bloody hell's buggered the bloody bell?' bellowed Fat Harry.

'Guilty,' said Mr Anthony.

'Oh,' said Harry, stopping short. 'Yes, it's inclined to be faulty at times. I'll just fix it.'

He busied himself with the bell-push whilst they all laughed silently at him behind his back.

'Can we have another round of drinks please, Harry,' asked Sarah Anne in her most seductive voice.

'Certainly, my love, anything for you, you know that.' He turned around, having forgotten about his audience, turned crimson around the cheeks and rasped, 'Same again, was it?'

When he had gone they all had a jolly good laugh, but Sarah Anne made a mental note to remonstrate with him later. The chairman then addressed the meeting again.

'Now, the food situation for the party, does anyone know, has anyone done anything about it yet?'

Dick gave a rather loud discreet cough.

'We've asked one or two of the committee wives and a few other women members if they'd help, but we haven't got down to exactly what we're going to have and how much we're going to charge for it. However, I thought it might be best if we could sort it out tonight so that we can say to the ladies that we'll have this and that, then my contribution could be to organise it.'

'That sounds like a very good idea. Has anyone any suggestions for the actual refreshments?'

'Aye,' said Willie, 'Fat Harry's taking a long time with us beer.'

'I mean for the party refreshments,' said an exasperated Sarah Anne.

'Pork pies, cold sausages and piccalilli.'

The chairman ignored him and said, 'Now I think we should have a good wholesome supper. Pork pies and cold sausages, yes. Sandwiches, potato crisps, cakes, trifle, tea and coffee. Does that sound all right?'

'That sounds as right as rain,' said Dick.

'Oh, and I forgot, some piccalilli for Willie.'

'I can get a list of who is going to do what,' continued Dick. 'Now, the big question is how much of what do we need, where shall we get it from and who is going to pay for it all before the night?'

'Well, to deal with the first question first of how much do we want, this depends on how many are coming to the do. Willie, how many members do we have?'

'Well, Sarah Anne, we've got about one hundred and forty-six members, so say about one hundred and twenty, because they'll not all come, then there's their husbands and wives, taking into account them what's not married, and we've got about two hundred and fifty, so that lot wants a bit of catering for.'

Eustace applauded Willie and Willie farted.

'A bit of a squash in the Club room, never mind a bit of catering for – can we cope with so many?'

Mr Anthony intervened. 'Have you actually enquired as to who might be coming to the party?'

'Er, no, not exactly, we just assumed they would all be coming except for a few as Willie has suggested,' said Arthur.

'Well, I suggest that you start tomorrow asking around and get a full list. I tend to believe that most of your members will be here but I do think you should check it out. Now then, about catering. I could ask the works canteen staff to help out, in work time. There is one very important item you forgot from the food list, Sarah Anne, and that is mince pies, which I think the canteen could help with. Dick, please do not think for one minute that I was trying any one-upmanship over your very good organisational abilities. I just thought you could do with the help.'

'Greasy Martha'll not help us out,' said Arthur.

'I'm sure she will if I ask her nicely. If you want I could ask her to make a variety of small cakes and the trifles. She could even cook the sausages and it wouldn't cost you a penny. What you would have to do then is to buy the pork pies, crisps, pickles and get every one of the ladies that are coming to make a round of sandwiches. The only thing that

I've left out is the tea and coffee. If I provide the ingredients can you organise the brewing and serving?

'It shouldn't prove too difficult to persuade Porky Charrington to wait for his money from Friday to Monday for a large order for pies, crisps and pickles, particularly so, if we buy the sausages from him as well. All that remains to be done, and it's a big task, is to organise an army of lady helpers for the night, cutlery, crockery and cruet. Finally, washing up, have you considered that yet?'

'I'll sort out the helpers,' said Dick.

'Ask my wife, Dick, will you please. Ask her please, my wife, please, ask her, Dick. Will you, Dick?'

'Cutlery hand crockery won't be hay problem, there's hundreds of plates, cups, saucers, knives, forks hand spoons from hay collection that's built up over the years from people who have left them to the club hin their wills, or who have been clearing hout their deceased relations' houses. Hi have to say, however, that very few of them match.' Arthur sat back very pleased with his new found accent.

'Posh gob again,' thought Willie.

The chairman rose to her feet and said, 'I think that before we go any further at all, we ought to thank Mr Anthony Murgatroyd for his more than generous offer and to say that on behalf of all the members of the Christmas club, we accept. So we've no more problems left to deal with now, have we?'

'Just one.'

They all turned to look at Daniel Sykes, just as Fat Harry returned with the round of drinks, expertly carried on a tray. Harry managed to rub his leg against Sarah Anne's arm as he walked past her but she ignored him, again making a mental note to have words with him later.

'I think we had better elect a new bar steward,' said Arthur, posh gob forgotten, after Harry had left the room.

'Why?' enquired Lewis.

'Because he hasn't taken any money for the drinks, hasn't asked for it or anything. It's only just dawned on me.'

'Aye, you're right. Happen he's beginning to lose his marbles,' said Willie.

'I think I can possibly quell any false hope or rumour,' said Mr Anthony. 'I paid for the round before I came into the meeting or at least, to be more correct, I arranged to pay for it after the meeting.'

A chorus of thanks ensued, with a polite grunt from the long dollop, as Willie liked to call him.

'Now then, Daniel, you were saying?'

'All I was going to ask was why we should have to have pickles just because of Willie Arkenthwaite?'

Willie belched, stood up hurriedly and began to leave his place at the table.

'Sit down now! Willie! This instant,' screamed Sarah Anne in a very commanding tone. 'For your information, Daniel, the pickles are for everyone. Willie was implicated, as a joke.'

Daniel stared at Sarah Anne, motionless and emotionless.

'Now, it just remains for me to thank Mr Anthony for his more than generous offer of help with the supper, for the drinks tonight and for all the help he has given us so far. Just a minute, we haven't mentioned the band. Is that all arranged, Arthur?'

'Yes, Willie hand hi risked life hand limb to go and book Sid Sidebottom and his Syncopating Sextet. Mind you there are honly five of them, but hall is arranged.'

'Are you all right, Arthur? Are you? You're talking funny, are you? Arthur, are you, talking funny? You are, aren't you?'

'Shut up Eustace,' said Dick.

'I ham talking properly,' he replied.

'As I was saying,' continued the chairman, 'I think that thanks are due to all of us, including myself, for arranging this Christmas club and in particular to the two people who dreamed up the idea in the first place, Arthur and Willie. I think we should all look forward now to the party and to receiving our contributions back. Shall we now adjourn to the bar and close the meeting, or possibly the other way around?'

'There is just one matter I would like to mention to Willie and Arthur before it gets too late,' said Anthony Murgatroyd, 'and that is, I do think that you should warn the bank of your intention to draw out the money and give them a date so that they can be prepared in advance. It wouldn't do to surprise them, would it now?'

'Oh, we have to tell 'em like that we want us brass out, do we? We can't just go and get it then?' asked Willie.

'Well, you could just go in and ask for it and they would be obliged to pay you but it would be better for relations with them if you were to warn them in advance. When you go to pay in on Friday just tell them that you will want to withdraw all the money and close the account on Friday 20th December, then they will have prepared it in advance.'

'Come on, I've supped up, let's get to the bar,' said Dick.

'It's high time you concentrated your efforts on something other than the demon drink. It is the downfall of civilisation.'

'Just like a trip up Mafeking Street.'

Daniel Sykes jumped up and advanced on Willie who hurriedly removed himself to the bar, where he knew that Fat Harry would deal effectively with the long dollop. Anthony Murgatroyd turned to Sarah Anne.

'Whatever possessed you all to elect a man like Daniel Sykes to a committee such as this that always meets on licensed premises?'

'As I remember it, he elected himself in order to see fair play for his fellow men and then tried his best to get us to meet in the church hall. I'll tell you what though, if we do it again next year we're not having him on the committee.'

'If you run into any further trouble with him, tip me the wink and I'll find a good excuse to sack him. He's as big a pain in the mill as he is here.'

When they ambled back into the bar Fat Harry was very hurt to find Sarah Anne in the company of Mr Anthony but she was soon on her own again, and Harry was once again in attendance flitting around her like a mother hen with its newborn chicks.

'Now then, what'll you have to drink, my dear?'

'Nothing, thank you. Harry, come into your storeroom with me.'

Harry thought that for the first time in his life all his birthdays had come together and off he trotted to his storeroom behind the bar with Sarah Anne close on his heels.

'I wonder what them two are up to?' asked Arthur.

'Nay, hold your horses for a minute or two and we might find out.'

They hadn't long to wait, for the two people returned very shortly, Sarah Anne with a big smile and Fat Harry looking as if he'd lost a pound and found a penny.

'Now, I'll just have a whisky and dry before I go home,' said the chairman.

'Well, it wasn't what you thought it was, was it?' said Willie to Arthur.

'No, just the opposite.'

'Are you ready for home?'

'Yes.'

'Let's just go round by Mafeking Street on the way – he disappeared a bit sharp after the meeting.'

'Don't forget I've some curtains to hang for Jess yet tonight.'

'It won't take long.'

'No, I don't suppose it will. Sarah Anne, are you ready? We're going.'

'Not just yet. Dick'll walk me home, won't you?'

'Yes, I will.'

'Okay, we're off. Goodnight.'

'What's up with them two?' enquired Harry after they had left. 'They're early for them.'

'Arthur has a bit of a domestic to-do and Willie's up to no good, and I bet I know where.'

'Where?'

'Mafeking Street.'

'That long dollop Sykes'll belt him if he gets hold of him you know,' said Harry.

'I don't think it will come to that,' replied Sarah Anne.

'I think it might,' mused Harry wistfully.

*

Halfway along Mafeking Street Willie looked at Arthur and asked, 'Well, what are we going to do now?'

'That's a very good question. I don't know either. We might as well go home. I'll have to go soon anyway to give Jess a hand with the curtains.'

They had walked the length of the street twice and not a soul was to be found anywhere, nothing stirred, not even a breeze, it was very frosty and cold.

'We'll just go up and down once more, then if nothing happens we'll go home.'

Willie's front room fire was beginning to have a magnetic effect on him.

Unknown to them they had been observed by two pairs of eyes, and as they passed Number 19 on the way uphill they were not a little startled to hear the door open. They turned to look and found a somewhat buxom, ageing, trying-to-look-young lady in a long flowing chiffon dressing gown. It was gaping and hid very little in certain places. She was leaning on the door post, cigarette in one hand, wine glass in the other.

'Hello, boys,' she shouted.

'Er, er, good evening,' mumbled Arthur.

'Er, yes,' said Willie.

'Are you coming in for a good time then?'

'Er, well, er,' they stammered, both flummoxed.

'Er, well, that is, er, not just—'

They were both rooted to the spot. Neither of them could take his eyes off the apparition in front of them, and both were petrified.

'Come on in, boys, it's a lot warmer in here than it is out there, and I'll make you feel even warmer.'

Willie suddenly remembered his own front room fire. He grabbed hold of Arthur's arm and began to run back down the hill towards the village. Willie's grip was so tight that Arthur had little option but to follow him.

When they had turned the corner at the bottom of the hill and both pairs of knees had turned to jelly, Willie laughed, belched, farted and said, 'Good job I was there to rescue you, Arthur Baxter, from a fate almost worse than death.'

'Yes, Willie, it is. Even the thought of going hanging curtains for Jess sounds not too bad after all.'

'Aye, we're both cowards when it comes to loose women. I think a nice hot mug of tea with Thelma in front of a roaring fire sounds all right as well.'

*

At Number 19 Mafeking Street, Daniel Sykes gave the spare-time love of his life a last farewell fondle and kiss for that night.

'Thanks a million, that was superb, just what those two needed, you couldn't have done it better if you'd tried. I'll never forget the night you frightened off Arkenthwaite and Baxter, me and my shadow.'

With that he marched away into the night without a care.

*

The next day, Thelma met Jess out shopping.

'Was your Arthur in a funny mood when he came home last night?'

'Not especially. Mind you, he did help me put up the new lounge curtains without so much as a grumble or argument now you come to mention it, and it's not like him not to cause a fuss even if he has the smallest job to do. Why, was your Willie in a funny mood, then?'

'He came into our house, gave me a big hug and a kiss, then made us both a pot of tea, following which he sat down with me and talked to me. I'll say he was in a funny mood.'

'I wonder what they were up to last night. I'll get it out of Arthur tonight.'

As the two ladies walked along the village deep in conversation, her from Number 19 Mafeking Street made a point of saying, 'Good morning, ladies,' as she passed them by.

'What was all that about?' asked Thelma.

'I don't know, she's never spoken to me before. Funny that. I bet those two husbands of ours can answer that question.'

'Oh, I don't think they'll know anything about that.'

'Well, I'm putting two and two together with an answer that's about twenty-seven. I'll most certainly get it out of Arthur tonight.'

*

Down in the mill bottom at Murgatroyd's, Daniel Sykes made an unheard-of appearance in the dyehouse. All he did was to walk straight through the room and shout 'Good morning' to Willie and Arthur, with a knowing grin on his face. Arthur grabbed Willie around the neck to restrain him. Willie was rolling up his sleeves and shouting, 'I'll kill the bastard, I will, I'll kill him.'

'Let him go,' said Arthur. 'We've all had our fun out of it and enough is enough.'

Willie gave up the struggle, stared after Daniel Sykes, and mustering all his internal energy he belched as loudly as he could in the general direction of his enemy's disappearance.

'There, that makes me feel better. It's as good as killing him.'

*

Arthur arrived home from the mill to find his tea not in its usual place on the table. Jess was eating her tea and his place was laid but no food was in evidence.

'Where's my tea?' he asked.

'Come sit down here.'

'Yes, but where's my tea?'

'Sit!'

He sat.

'Now, before you can have your tea, tell me what you and Willie know about that floozie that lives up Mafeking Street.'

Arthur's heart missed a couple of beats.

'What?'

'You know what I said as well as I do, and I want an answer before any tea's served up.' She continued to eat hers and Arthur sat in stony silence.

'I've got all night,' she said as she continued to eat her tea.

Arthur was hungry. He wondered if Willie had got his tea or if he was going through the same torture.

Willie was in fact enjoying neck of mutton stew with apple pie to follow because Thelma was waiting to see what Jess had discovered before starting on him.

Arthur did not normally get fed as well as Willie, and he watched Jess devour a slice of cold boiled ham with a tomato. He was hungry. Jess got up to take her dirty plate away, then returned with a piece of currant pasty.

'Come on, let's have my tea.'

'You can have your tea when you've told me what you know about her up Mafeking Street.'

He still sat in silence, watching Jess finish her tea, then realising that he wasn't going to get his he decided to spill the beans.

'Daniel Sykes is knocking her off.'

'I beg your pardon. Kindly do not use such language in this house.'

'Daniel Sykes is knocking her off.'

'Go and wash your mouth out.'

'No, no, it's true, he's been visiting her for months now. Can I have my tea now?'

'Not yet, carry on talking but not in that foul and filthy manner.'

'Nobody knows but me and Willie. We found out by accident, and last night after the committee meeting we went up there to see if we could catch him coming out, because the meeting finished early and we knew he'd have gone up there because he always does after a committee meeting and, anyway, we got a bit of a surprise, me and Willie did, because after we'd walked past a couple of times she opened the front door and came out in her nightdress and said, "Hello boys, are you coming in for a good time?" and me and Willie ran home then and that's the truth and can I have my tea now?'

He sat back and sighed. So did Jess.

'Are you sure that you two haven't been, as you so crudely put it, knocking her off?'

'Certainly not. What do you think we are?'

'Well, based on past performance, in your case particularly – of course, I can't answer for Willie – I won't answer that question. Anyway, if you are telling the truth, what do you want to go spying on Daniel Sykes for?'

'Because he's a big long dollop, a pain in the arse, and there's a lot of needle between him and Willie. Can I have my tea now?'

'You can get it yourself because I am going round to Thelma's to see if Willie's story is the same as yours.'

With that she put her hat and coat on and flounced out of the house, the front door coming to rest with an almighty crash behind her.

*

The Arkenthwaites had just finished a delicious tea and cleared away when the front door received a series of quick hammer blows.

'Who on earth can that be?' asked Josie.

'Nay lass, go and see,' said Willie.

Josie opened the front door.

'Hello, Auntie Jess. Are you coming in?'

'Yes, I am that. Is your mother in.'

Josie, realising that things were not quite right, said, 'She's in the back washing up. I'll go and take over from her.'

Josie took over from her mother who came into the front to greet Jess. Other than the usual if not brusque small talk, Willie had not got down to any serious discussion with Jess.

'Hello, Jess. Are you taking your coat off?'

'Yes, I will. This might take a while to sort out.'

She found it overpoweringly hot in their front room.

'Now, about what we were talking about this morning. I've got it out of him.'

'Have you now? Well, this is interesting.'

Willie's ears pricked up.

'Have you mentioned it to your Willie yet?'

'No, not yet, I was waiting to see what you had to say first. I thought you might have waited until tomorrow.'

'I refused Arthur his tea until he spilled the beans.'

Willie's ears picked up even further, his nose began to twitch and his bald head began to throb. He could sense a lot of trouble brewing. Bluntness was one of Jess's strong points and she didn't back off now.

'I think we should see what Willie has to say about it.'

Thelma had been prepared to mention the matter in her own good time but not just yet and not like this either, but she found it impossible to fight Jess when she was in roaring order.

'Well, so, Willie, what about it then?'

'What about what?'

'Her that lives up Mafeking Street?'

'What, her what's having it away with t'long dollop?'

'So that's your tale as well, is it?'

'It's no tale, it's true. It's been going on months.'

'So what were you and my Arthur doing at her house last night then?'

Thelma began to feel apprehensive.

'We weren't at her house, we were outside it. We thought long tall Sykes were in there but she came out and invited us in for a bit of homely comfort. We decided to decline her offer because we love you two too much for that and, anyway, we thought that long Sykes were in there all the time. Mind you, if we'd thought that long tall Sykes wasn't there we might have taken up her offer.'

'God only knows what good you two would have been to a woman like her. Anyway, at least you're both telling the same tale, so I suppose I'd best believe you.'

'You speak for your own as you find them,' said Thelma.

The atmosphere returned to normal, and after a cup of tea Jess returned home to an empty house, Arthur having gone to the Club early.

Thelma looked at Willie.

'You wouldn't really have gone into that house in Mafeking Street, would you?'

'Gone in! Gone in! You know full well that I would not. Apart from anything else I couldn't cope with a woman like her. I don't know how Daniel Sykes does. To tell you the truth, and don't let on to Jess, we ran all the way home after she invited us in, we were both scared stiff. I bet Daniel Sykes has had a right good laugh at our expense.'

'Never mind love, at least I almost always know where you are.'

'We were just having a bit of fun that backfired on us but, by gum, I aren't half glad I'm not married to Jess.'

He turned to Thelma and, not for the first time in living memory, gave her a big hug and a loving kiss. She, for the first time in living memory, didn't ask why.

Chapter Fifteen

Willie sat motionless, staring into space. Arthur sat motionless, staring into space. The pigeons moved their heads from side to side, staring at Willie and Arthur. It was the next Wednesday evening following the committee meeting, and the flame in the hurricane lamp began to flicker and die.

Willie continued to stare into space. Arthur continued to stare into space. The pigeons continued to stare at both of them, and the flame in the lamp died completely.

'Bugger,' said Willie.

'Hear, hear,' said Arthur.

'Well, that's it then.'

'What is?'

'Well, I'm not filling that lamp again tonight, so we'll have to go to the band room to get warm and to listen to Sid Sidebottom and his Syncopating Sextet practising.'

'Coo, coo,' said the pigeons.

'Shut up,' said a couple of voices.

*

Grolsby Band Club was situated well out of the village. In fact, for a man in Willie's condition, it was a long walk, particularly as it was up a long, steep hill. Many years gone by, in due deference to the wishes of the local community, on suggesting the building of a new band room the people in charge of the project had built it in such a situation so as not to annoy the villagers on practice nights.

In its day it had been a splendiferous building, constructed so that it could seat four hundred people to a band concert, and a brass band as big as could be found could be seated on the stage. Because of this and because of its large bar areas downstairs, not to mention the changing, utility, kitchen and committee rooms, it was still used for all major local concerts and contests even if its general ambience was becoming a little dated. There was no doubt that it would have to go on being used for the same concerts and contests for many years to come because it was the only such building in the area other than the Town Hall. No one in their right mind was going to propose the building of anything like it again, and the acoustics in the concert hall were the best for miles around.

Willie stopped halfway up the hill to get his breath back.

'Hang on, Arthur, till I get right again.'

'It's time you went to see Dr Mitchell to get yourself sorted out because you are going to be in one hell of a mess before long if you don't. You've got responsibilities with Thelma and the children and you could well do to go for a check-up. It's free now, you know.'

Willie had by this time started to recover his breath. The breathing was easier and they set off walking again, only more slowly this time.

'Aye, you're right, it is free now, isn't it. I haven't been to see Doc Mitchell in years but now we've got this newfangled health service I might give it a try – after Christmas when all the excitement's over.'

'You want to go see him now before it's too late.'

'Nay, I'm only a bit overweight, that's all. Nowt that a bit of exercise and a lack of food won't cure.'

'But you never have exercise or lack of food.'

'That's true, so it might be difficult to cure me.'

By this time they had reached the ornate entrance to the band room and Willie was still upright, breathing fairly easily. Because of its popularity, the band room could support its own full-time steward and stewardess. Unlike the Working Men's Club, it had an accommodation unit for the incumbent steward with wife to assist, (as advertised). It was in all aspects much more upmarket than the Working Men's Club, it was far better supported, and the drinks were more expensive. It held a dance almost every Saturday night, sometimes using Sid Sidebottom's Syncopating Sextet, sometimes using other bands. To take an overall view, it was much too posh and much too expensive for Willie and Arthur to use on either a regular or irregular basis. The building was much larger than the largest of Methodist chapels, with big, thick, heavy, double oak front doors sporting long, polished, tubular brass handles which Willie now pulled open. The entrance hall that met them was brightly lit, and warm with the central heating radiators which had been installed recently for the comfort of guests. The bars, for there were three of them, were situated along the left-hand side of the corridor through another pair of big oak doors. The stairs up to the concert and ballroom led off to left and right from the entrance hall.

The terrible two went into the first bar on the left.

'Evening, Stan, evening, Molly.'

'Well, I never did. Well, you can carry me to our house and bring me back again. The terrible two, haven't seen you two in years. How are you both?'

'I'm well, Stan, thank you, but Willie's a wee bit short of puff walking up the hill. As you can see he hasn't found the wind to talk yet.'

'Come to us all it does. Would that my wind pipes were as good as they used to be. Mind, Willie, you're a might young for shortage of breath; still, you're stones overweight and one goes with the other. Of course', continued Stan, 'it's when the shortage of breath becomes no breath at all that you've got to start worrying, haven't you, Moll?'

Molly had just finished serving some other customers, and she came over to them bearing a radiant smile.

'Pardon, love?'

'I was saying that Willie here is short of breath from walking up the hill but, as I tell him, it's when the shortage is permanent that he really has to begin to worry about it.'

'You mean when he's dead?' asked Arthur.

'Something like that.

Molly laughed and said, 'Fools, the lot of you.'

'Anyway, what can I get for you on this most surprising and welcome visit?'

'How much is it?' asked Willie quickly.

'How much is what?'

'How much is best bitter?'

'Penny a pint more than it is at your usual drinking club.'

'How do you know how much we pay?'

'I keep my ear to the rail and my nose to the grindstone.'

'I don't think that was quite right.'

'Probably not, but it's near enough for you two.'

'Well, we'll have two pennyworth just short of two pints.'

Molly laughed again as Stan poured two pints.

'How's Thelma and the children and how's Jessie, Arthur?'

'They're fine, just fine. We're all getting ready for the Murgatroyd Christmas club Christmas party,' answered Willie, who was rudely interrupted by Stan.

'Is it at Christmas?'

'No, it's on Pancake Tuesday. Anyway, as I was saying, that's why we're here, we've come to listen to Sid Sidebottom and his Syncopating Sextet.'

'What on earth for?' asked Molly. 'And anyway, there's only five of them.'

'Because we've booked him and his band to play at the Christmas party.'

'At Christmas,' added Stan.

'And we know there's only five of them.'

'Well, you will not be disappointed for long, for they're due here in a few minutes, it's usually about nowish when they come puffing in. You'll probably hear their van as it tries its best to come up the hill. There'll be much honking, rasping, scraping of gears, backfiring, cursing and verbal abuse before they finally fall into here. It's level odds as to who's in charge, Sid or the van.'

Stan brought the two pints from the other end of the bar, stood one in each hand smiling at Arthur and Willie, took a long slow sip from each glass, handed them over to the two friends and said, 'There you are, club prices. Your club that is, not mine.'

'Dirty bugger,' said Arthur.

'Sorry, you know the rules, we do not allow swearing on these premises. Now, how about paying for your drinks and, by the way, I might let you have our club pints at your club prices next round just for fun, and just once.'

The two friends sat down in comfortably upholstered chairs at an oak table with inlaid tile top to await the arrival of Sid Sidebottom.

'Great pity the Club isn't as nice as this,' said Willie.

'Aye, we should bring Jess and Thelma up here one Saturday to the dance, for a change.'

'Yes, we could,' agreed Willie, which he followed up with a good loud belch, without apology.

'Manners,' shouted Molly. 'You're here again, are you, William Arkenthwaite?'

'Sorry.'

'That is one of the reasons why our club is not as nice as this one,' said Arthur. 'Anyway, whilst we are waiting, what have we to sort out yet for the Christmas club and the party?'

'Well,' began Willie, 'we've got to sort out about getting the money from the bank. About keeping it until eight o'clock at night, about—'

Arthur stopped him whilst he found a small piece of paper to note down the items. He also found a very short, grubby pencil stub.

'Now, start again and let me note it down.'

So as Willie talked Arthur made notes, sometimes adding to the list himself. Finally the list read: 'One – Get the money from the bank, Two – Keep the money until eight o'clock at night, Three – Count the money, Four – Put the money into envelopes, Five – Giving out the money, Six – Discounts from shops, Seven – Booze at party, Eight – Band, Nine – Food, Ten – Decorations at club, Eleven – Arrangements at Club.'

'Well, I think you've made a very comprehensive coverage there, Willie.'

'Eh?'

'I think you've said everything. I've noted down eleven items and we'd best go through them all now very slowly and carefully, one at a time.'

'Why,' said Willie, as he belched.

'Hoy,' shouted Stan.

'Sorry.'

'Well, because it's time we were beginning to make sure we've left nothing to chance. We want everything to go just right, don't we?'

'Oh, yes we do.'

'Right, let's start with item one, drawing out the money from the bank. Have you arranged it at the bank yet?'

'Well, er, not exactly.'

'Don't you think it's about time you were doing it? It was ordered by the committee, you know and you'll be going on Friday to pay in.'

'So I will, yes, go on then, but what have I to do about it?'

'No idea except you must tell the people who serve you at the bank that you want to draw out the entire contents of the account on Friday 20th December at exactly five to four. However, we have a big problem with this money in the middle of all the other big problems.'

'We have?'

'We sure do, buddy, there's all the interest to work out, so on Friday you'd best ask the bank what we shall get as the final figure. After that, we'd better work out what coinage denominations we want.'

'What's that for?'

'So that we can divide the money among the members without us having to go seeking change again.'

'So how are we going to do that?'

'Well, now, let's see. It's easy, but it'll take a fair bit of working out. We'll have to list every member, and against their names all the money they've paid in, then if we can get a total from the bank we can subtract the principal amount and finally apportion the remainder to each member in the ratio of the amount paid in to the total fund.'

Arthur beamed at Willie, proud of his analysis of the situation. Willie was bored stiff and didn't understand a word of it. He had cleaned the wax from his ears with his finger, then deposited the slimy mess under the seat of his chair. Also he was beginning to have the sensation of certain little pressures building up inside his body, when he was saved from further embarrassment by a commotion at the door. A set of drums, covered in their leather cases, was barged in, closely followed by Jack France pushing and the other four members of the Sid Sidebottom Syncopating Sextet carrying their various instruments and music. The instruments were dumped in a heap in the middle of the room whilst the members of the band attended the bar for liquid refreshments.

Sid Sidebottom, pint in hand, looked around and observed the terrible two sitting at a table, watching the proceedings. He walked over to them.

'Glad you two lads could make it to listen to us. We'll not be long, just have the one round, then it's across the corridor into the dressing room where we normally practise. Mind you, if I was you I wouldn't rush, I'd just enjoy your drinks for a few minutes until we get warmed up. It's always a bit on the rough side for the first few bars – it's Maud you know – she needs kick-starting. She's getting on a bit now, as you can see if you're an observant sort of chap, but when she gets going, boy, oh boy, does she get going. Anyway, give us five minutes to get set up and started.'

He and the other members of his band sauntered off with their drinks in the direction of the dressing rooms, then reappeared a few seconds later to collect the pile of instruments.

'Right, now,' said Arthur. 'Point two, looking after the money. First of all, it's obvious that once we collect it we can't leave it alone for one second right up to paying out time at eight o'clock, so what are we going to do with it?'

'Take it to the Club,' said Willie brightly.

'No, I think not, or not until we've counted it and put it in the envelopes. Tell you what, we'll take it to our house, you and me, then we'll get Thelma to come around. Jess can make tea for us, then we'll all count it and sort it. It's a big job as you know, it's bound to take us a couple of hours at least, then when it's ready we'll take it round to the Club and put it in the safe. If we do that, we can go home one at a time to get changed for the do whilst the other one and all those that are at the Club keep their eyes on the safe.'

'You'll have to make arrangements with Fat Harry to keep the Club open for us.'

'No problem, the ladies will be there all the time preparing the supper and the room, so all we have to do is to keep our eyes on it. Mind you, I'll be much happier with it locked in the safe. Anyway, come on, I hear the tinkle of the ivories.'

They managed to get their second pint of the night at a cheaper price than before after a little bit of argument concerning whether or not Stan had been joking at the time of his offer.

'I don't think we'll get the next pint cheap,' observed Willie.

'Oh yes we will, but not here.'

They made their way out of the bar, across the corridor and into the somewhat cooler changing room suite where Sid Sidebottom and his Syncopating Sextet minus one were settling down into their practice routine, playing the music for the Gay Gordons to the tune of 'Scotland the Brave'. The terrible two sat down facing the band, pint glasses in hand, and surveyed the scene.

Sid himself on tenor saxophone and Dennis Shires on trumpet were both red in the face, both puffing merrily away and both concentrating hard on the manipulation of their shiny brass instruments. Jack France was banging happily on his drums without a care in the world, Hubert Shaw was in another world strumming his double bass and Maud Lindley was tickling the ivories just like she had been sitting there for ever. After a short time had elapsed both Willie and Arthur were tapping their feet on the floor in time to the beat of the band and were thoroughly enjoying what was an excellent performance.

Arthur turned to Willie and said, 'By gum, lad, this is good stuff and it'll look even better in evening dress. I'm fair glad we risked life and limb to go to his house and sort it out with him.'

'Yes, we should have a good party with this lot playing.'

They stopped to listen to a further couple of items, then took their leave of the dance band and the band room. Neither of them wanted to go back to the drabness of the Club and leave the luxury of the band room, but neither of them wanted to stay and pay the elevated prices for the ale.

Before they left, Sid Sidebottom asked them if they would like a spot of carol singing at the party, but the subject was left open, to be decided on the night. Sid promised to be prepared, just in case.

'Let's call in on James Richard at the George on the way back,' said Arthur. 'The ale's cheaper there than the band room and we haven't called for a long time.'

'You're right, it's ages since we heard his wit.'

As they approached the George, Willie let out an exclamation. 'Miracle of miracles.'

'Pardon?'

'It's open.'

'What is?'

'The George, it's open and it's only just nine o'clock. It's early, but see, it's lit up.'

'Yes, you're right. Come on, let's get inside before it shuts again.'

The drab interior of the hostelry well reflected its landlord's dowdy appearance. James Richard was leaning on the bar talking to a group of people who nodded to Arthur and Willie.

'How do, lads,' shouted Willie. 'All right, James Richard?'

'As usual.'

The group of people nodded and responded.

'Aye, you look bad, lad. Two pints, please.'

'Not like you to say please, Willie!'

Willie belched.

'I didn't think that'd be long coming.'

'It wasn't long, more short and quick.'

A middle-aged lady left the group of people and walked over to Willie.

'There's ladies here, you know,' she growled.

'Oh, yes, I'm so sorry,' he shouted. 'How do, lassies and lads?'

'I wasn't referring to that,' she bellowed.

'What was you referring to, then?'

'To that horrible noise you just made.'

'Oh, that? That were nowt, nobbut a belch. Anybody can do that, even you.'

'But anybody would apologise.'

'Oh, all right, if it makes you feel any better. Sorry.'

'Thank you.' She turned and walked back to the group.

Willie snooked up as loudly as he could, then, just for good measure, he farted as hard and loud as he could.

James Richard looked at Willie. 'If there's one more episode of that sort, you're barred.'

'No problem, we can take our custom to the Club where they make us very welcome.'

'Rumour has it that you're not welcome, they just put up with you.'

Arthur decided that it was time to change the subject.

'Don't you think that we should sit down and continue our discussion about the Christmas club party?'

'Go on then,' said Willie reluctantly, for he was enjoying doing verbal battle with James Richard.

The more serious side of Arthur prevailed and they found a table with padded seats behind where they would be both warm and comfortable.

'Let's go back to item four, because we haven't discussed it yet.'

'What do you mean?' asked Willie.

'Well, we've got to get the envelopes from the office at the mill to start with, then mark them up with the recipients' names, then put the money in them, then I think we'll get a cardboard box of the correct size to put them all in in alphabetical order. That way it will be easier to locate them to pay them out.'

'You're not stupid are you, Arthur?'

'No, no,' said Arthur, smiling contentedly, 'I pride myself on the fact that I can sort out this type of problem with mental agility.'

'Eh?' asked Willie with a typically blank expression.

'Mental agility. You know, active brain.'

'Oh, aye,' said a completely uninterested Willie.

'Now then, item five, paying out the money.'

'We'll get them to queue up for it,' announced Willie.

'No, no. Well, yes and no.'

'What do you mean?'

'What I mean is that first of all we want to get rid of the money as quick as possible after the start of the do, so whether or not we get them to queue up, or, perhaps we should just walk around with the box of envelopes and hand them out. Yes, that might be the better of the two ways and the easiest. You and me just walk around casually and pay it out.'

'Yes, okay. That's fine by me. Now what are we going to write on the outside of the envelopes, to go back to point four. We shall have to put the name of the member or else we shan't know whose envelope is whose. Then what?'

'Well, what we should do is to put the amount they have saved, then the interest they have earned, then finally the total. That should do it.'

The shadow of James Richard fell upon them.

'Up to your old tricks I see. I thought time might have sorted things out a bit.'

'Can't think what you mean,' said Willie.

'Existing all night on one pint of ale each, that's what I mean. How you expect me to make a living with all this high-speed drinking going on, I do not know. Are you having another round then?'

'You mean it's on the house?'

'Not bloody likely.'

'Nay, then, we'd best be off, hadn't we, Arthur?'

'Yes, best be off, that's right. Goodnight.'

Arthur drained the very last dregs of his drink and got up from the table, closely followed by Willie.

'Well, that takes the biscuit, that does,' shouted James Richard. 'Just what I expected from two such as you—'

He was going to go on, going on and on and on, but what was the use when the two people on the receiving end of his tongue were not there any more.

Outside, Arthur couldn't stop laughing and said, 'I was just going to have another when he came over.'

'Me and all, but never mind, it'll be nice and warm at the Club.'

'No, Willie, thanks. I think I'll go home and have an early night for a change. It's almost ten o'clock and I've had quite enough for one day.'

'Aye, go on then. I'll go and have a mug of cocoa in front of the fire. I haven't seen much of Thelma for a day or two.'

So for the first time in a long time the two friends retired home early and both without too much comment from their respective wives.

*

The following morning Willie was up and about early. He spent more time than usual with the pigeons, he enjoyed an unusually leisurely breakfast and then he waited on the canal bank for Arthur.

'What's up with you?'

'Eh?'

'What are you doing waiting for me, stood standing here? You never, never, ever are early, so why break the habit of a lifetime?'

'I were up early.'

'Why? Did you wet the bed or something?'

'Nay, come off it. I were early to bed last night so I were up early this morning and so I'm here early. Don't worry, it won't happen again in a great hurry.'

'I should hope not, it's more than I can take at any one time. It's a wonder I didn't have a seizure.'

They walked quickly to the mill in the late autumn morning; it was just coming light. During the course of the morning, Arthur attempted to discuss the party arrangements as and when he could, in the midst of the busy schedule of the dyehouse.

When he finally cornered Willie, he said, 'Well, what about item six?'

'I'd rather talk about item seven, my favourite subject, drink.'

'Yes, but we really should talk them through in numerical order.'

'I know, but I don't fancy talking about boring old discounts this morning. Let's talk about drink.'

'Very well. You know I suggested that we could, as a committee, help Fat Harry behind the bar, but if we do we can't enjoy the party, can we?'

'No, we can't, although it would be nice to get around the other side of the bar for a change. It would be free beer all night, and that's never happened before, has it?'

'No, I don't think it has except possibly for VE night and I wasn't here then. Were you?'

'You know full well I was in North Africa enjoying the sunshine. In fact, when I look around here I wish I was there right now.'

'Anyway, don't you think we should ask Harry if he can muster his own troop of assistants, to save us the trouble? I know it will cost the club more to employ temporary staff than it will to use us but I do think they will sell more drink and therefore the club can afford it.'

'Well, yes, I do agree with you but I was looking forward to pint after pint of free ale.'

'Willie, it's supposed to be a party for husbands and wives, no drunkenness, just plain, wholesome clean fun.'

'All right, have it your own way,' said a by now very bored Willie.

'Well, we'd best call and see the fat one tonight to make arrangements.'

*

Willie arrived early at the canteen at lunchtime, just as Greasy Martha was blowing her nose into the bottom of her apron. She took a long drag from a cigarette that was very carefully hidden behind a wooden partition in the kitchen, then turned to face the servery. She gave a start as she saw Willie watching her.

'Don't worry, Martha, I won't let on.'

Although they all cursed her behind her back, most of them had a lot of affection for her.

'How's the arrangements for the mince pies and so on coming along? Oh, yes, and what's for dinner?'

'Thanks. All right. Stew.'

'Eh?'

'You're bloody thick, William Arkenthwaite. What I said was, thanks for not telling, the arrangements for the party is all right and dinner today is sheep stew with boiled potatoes and spring cabbage.'

'Spring cabbage at this time of the year?'

'Well, it's dark-coloured.'

'Come on, come on, get a move on,' came a voice from the back of the queue.

Greasy Martha stuck her head out of the servery hatch and looked in the general direction of the back of the queue.

'Percy Kettlewell, if I hear one more squeak out of you there's no dinner for you. I were just having a quiet and confidential word with my friend, Willie, so you can either piss off without dinner or enjoy waiting until you get served. Got it?'

'What was the confidential word about Martha?' came back the reply, to howls of derision from the rest of the queue.

'That's it, no dinner for you.' She retracted her head into the servery. 'Here, Willie you'd best take your dinner before there's a riot.'

Over dinner Arthur tried to talk about item nine, but to no avail as the others were having none of it. Firstly, they wanted to eat their dinners in peace, then they wanted to play cards without interruption and then it was time for back to work.

On the way back to the dyehouse, Dick asked, 'What is item nine?'

'Don't you know?' asked Arthur, with very well-acted incredulity.

'Why should I know?'

'It's your department, your item.'

'What is?'

'Catering.'

'Catering?'

'Yes, catering. You volunteered to oversee the catering department.'

'Yes, I did, indeed I did, and that were a few weeks ago now.'

'So, is all in hand?' enquired Arthur.

Dick swallowed, opened his mouth, closed it, farted, swallowed again and said, 'Well, I've been a bit busy lately what with the decorating and other things. Well, you know, don't you, so I haven't just got it all sorted yet, but I shall do by the time that the party night comes around.'

'This won't do, it won't do at all, we'd best get it sorted out tonight, everything else's shipshape and Bristol fashion. Club tonight, eight o'clock sharp, all of you.'

'Yes,' agreed Dick, very pleased that someone else was taking an interest in what was to be done, for he hadn't.

'Everyone else?' asked Arthur.

'Me,' said Willie.

'Me,' said Lewis.

'Is Eustace coming?'

'No idea.'

'Best bring him along if you see him.'

'I'll get him,' said Willie. 'Arthur, I've something to do tonight so I'll meet you at the Club.'

'That's all right, so have I.'

*

Willie had had his tea, tended to the pigeons, washed, shaved and spruced up by the time half past seven arrived – early for him.

'What's the big rush?' asked Thelma.

'I'm just going to call at Greasy Martha's before I meet Arthur at the Club.'

'What on earth are you going to Martha Sykes's for?'

'To see exactly what it is she's baking for the Christmas club party.'

'Why you?'

'Because I'm the only one that dare ask her other than Mr Anthony and I think we'll give him a miss on this occasion. He's told her to sort it out and all I need to do is to find out what she's sorting out. She'll tell me seeing that I am her favourite dinner diner, and I'm calling for Eustace on the way.'

'Why?'

'Because we're meeting Dick at the Club as he's supposed to have sorted out party catering and hasn't, and so we are going to.'

'So what use is Eustace at such a gathering?'

'None.'

'So why take him along?'

'The exercise will do him good, and anyway, it's not safe to leave him with the dragon for too long – she might burn him to death with her fiery breath.'

'Is she helping with the party?'

'We're not sure, but not if we can help it.'

'Well, if she is, keep her as far away as possible from me and Jess. Anyway, get gone if you're going. As Josie's staying in, I'll wander around to see Jess for a while.'

*

Willie waited a few seconds outside Eustace's front gate, then, plucking up courage, he walked up the short front path, and after a further few seconds followed closely by one very deep breath he grabbed the brass knocker in his hand and crashed it heavily against the plate.

She opened the door. She looked at Willie.

'Good evening, Mrs Ollerenshaw, is Eustace ready?'

He got his spoke in first.

'Ready for what?' she rasped.

Willie decided it was no good messing about with this nasty woman.

'To go to the Club, he should have been ready and waiting for me.' He looked straight at her. 'Why isn't he?'

She was a bit taken aback by this onslaught.

'I don't know anything about it; he hasn't informed me of his intended movements.'

She turned and bellowed down the hall. 'Willie Arkenthwaite's here to collect you. Are you ready?'

Eustace came out of the back kitchen.

'Yes, er, no, er, are you going to the Club, Willie? Are you? Going to the Club?'

His dear wife interrupted, saying, 'Get your coat on and get off with Willie. See if I care whether or not you stop in to look after me.'

'It's a very important meeting we're having about the Christmas club party,' said Willie.

'What Christmas club party?' she demanded.

'Hasn't Eustace asked you to help with the catering, as the wife of a prominent committee member?'

'The first time he's prominent will be the last. Are you still wanting helpers?' She turned on Eustace. 'Why haven't you mentioned it to me?'

'I did ask you, my love. I did. I did. I asked you, I did.'

'You didn't.'

'I did.'

'Never. You never asked me. Not at all. You daren't. You're too scared. You're a coward.'

Willie decided he could easily be a coward too under the circumstances. However, he decided that this was not the time for cowardice, so he said, 'We need to know if you're helping or not. We've got this meeting tonight to sort out catering and we have to have an answer. So what's it to be?'

She wasn't used to being talked to like this by anyone and it held her a little bit nonplussed.

'I don't know. I don't think so. If I change my mind I'll let you know, you'll always be able to find me a job, won't you? Anyway, when is it?'

'Friday 20th December, at the Club. Eustace'll have to help and that's why we asked you along with all the other committee wives.'

'Who says Eustace will have to help?'

'We do, the committee, he's a member so he's got to help.'

'Well, I'll see, I might come, there again I might not. I'll let you know.' She turned to Eustace. 'Have you got your coat on yet? Come on, Willie's waiting for you.'

She got hold of Eustace, who was struggling to get his second arm into the sleeve of his mackintosh, and forcibly assisted him through the front door.

'And don't waken me when you come home, if I'm in bed.'

By the time they had walked a few hundred yards along the road, Willie had recovered his composure and Eustace had managed to get his mac on properly.

Eustace spoke. 'I hope she doesn't come to the party, I hope she doesn't. Can't stand her at the do, annoying everybody, I can't, I can't, can't stand her at the party. Can't stand everybody and their cousins being there with her bawling and shouting at them as if she owns the place. It's not on for the others, Willie, it's not, Willie, it isn't, it's just not bloody well fair. I haven't asked her to help, I haven't Willie, I haven't, I know I said I had but I haven't. Can't stand the woman, I can't, no more, can't stand her. I used to be able to, but not now, can't stand her. I hope she doesn't come, she'll cause nothing but trouble if she does, nothing but trouble.'

The two mates ambled slowly along to Greasy Martha's house. Willie said nothing, he couldn't, for he couldn't stop Eustace moaning and groaning about his dearly beloved.

'Hang on, Eustace, shut up a bit, we'll have to call at Greasy Martha's.'

'Oh, why, where are we? Willie, what have we come this way for? I hadn't noticed we'd come around by Ashbourne Road. What have we to call at Martha's for, Willie? What for?'

'Because I want to have a word with her.'

Willie knocked, or more like hammered, on the front door. There were shouts from inside of, 'All right, don't knock the house down, I'm coming.'

The door was opened by Hector Sykes, otherwise known as Horrible Hector.

'Hey up, Willie, Eustace, what can I do for you two at this time on an early December evening?'

'Now then, Hector, is your Martha in? We've just called to have a few words with her about the Christmas club party.'

'Have we, Willie? Have we? Called to have a few words about the party, have we, Willie?

'Well, at least it proves he's listening if nowt else,' said Willie under his breath to Hector.

'Aye, it does, but it's a great pity when you come to think about it, isn't it.'

'What is?' enquired Willie.

'Why, him, and her what he's married to as well – you'd not like her for a daily companion and a nightly comfort, now would you?'

'Not likely, I'd run a mile.'

'So would most men but not him. Anyway, come along in, Martha's in the back.'

So they followed Horrible Hector into the cosy back room where there was a hot blazing fire, and Martha was sitting in a rocking chair by the fireside knitting.

'Hello, hello. What's this, then?' she asked.

'Well, I thought it best if I called to see you and get to know properly about the Christmas club party, seeing that it's impossible at dinner time, even if I am your favourite customer. You see, we have a committee meeting at the Club in about half an hour and that is only to talk about party catering arrangements.'

'You've left it a bit late, haven't you, to start making arrangements.'

'Well, Dick Jordan was supposed to be sorting it out, but it seems he hasn't.'

'Never sort anything out that lad on his own. I've known him all his life, he never could, he never has and he never will. Be a good help to you, mind you, if you tell him what to do. Why don't you both sit down.'

Willie had been standing with his cap in his hand, rolling it around and around. Eustace had been standing, just vacantly standing. They both sat down on the settee and Hector resumed his fireside chair opposite Martha.

'Now,' began Martha, 'to start with, I don't want it broadcasting to all and sundry that I am helping you out of my own free will, only that Mr Anthony has made me bake some mince pies, with the emphasis on 'made'. The fact that I'm going to bake whatever you want for the supper, using the mill canteen and its ingredients, is another matter between you, me and the gatepost. It'll be no problem, because Mr Anthony has asked me to help you and to do whatever I think necessary for you to have a bloomin' good night, and, on the other hand, I have my rotten reputation to maintain in the canteen. All you need to tell your committee is that Mr Anthony has made me do it and you all know there's nothing I won't do for the Murgatroyd family.'

'That's all right, absolutely smashing, thank you. You can rely on me to spread the word as how you've been forced to do it.'

'How about you, Eustace?'

Eustace was still in another world, dreaming of ways to legally dispose of his wife. Problem was, he couldn't manage to live with her and he certainly couldn't manage to live without her.

'Eh? What? Oh, yes, er, what was it you wanted to know? Sorry, I was thinking about something else. What—'

Martha continued talking. 'No problem there then, is there, Willie?'

'It doesn't look like it, mind you it never does.'

'Right. Now then, as far as I know, you want sausage rolls, mince pies and trifles for the party, all of which I can make fresh in the canteen on Thursday and Friday, ready for Friday night, if that is all right with you. I shall want some help. Will your Thelma come along and give me a hand? I suppose she thinks the same things of me as everyone else around here but if you explain that it's all a big act, and she's to keep quiet about that, do you think she'll help me?'

'I'm sure she will, I think she knows you're all right anyway without me having to tell her. Don't worry, I'll make sure she helps you.'

'So, is that all right then? How many am I catering for?'

'Well, we're not right sure and that's something we have to settle yet but we think about one hundred and eighty to two hundred.'

'That's all right then. If Thelma will come to the canteen on Thursday afternoon, I'll stay back, and by the time you finish work we'll be all about done, leaving happen just a bit to do on Friday afternoon. What are you going to do about the rest of the food?'

'We're going to finalise that at the Club tonight so I can't tell you just yet, but I'll let you know as soon as I do. Anyway, thanks, Martha.'

'Still messing about with the pigeons, Willie?' asked Hector.

'Oh, yes, always will. Nice and steady is pigeons.'

'Hey, what's up with him then?'

Hector turned to look at Eustace who was whimpering to himself.

'Oh, nowt, it's just the dragon, she's been having another go at him and he's wondering what to do about her. Not that short of either divorcing her or putting her in an early grave there's much he can do. Mind you, if it were me, I'd kill her till she were dead, then murder her, following which I'd take her life from her. But then she'd come back to life again, she's that sort of a woman.'

'Mmmm, it's a mess for him, a real mess.'

'Come on, Eustace.'

'Eh? What? Where are we going, Willie?'

'To the Club, come on.'

They both got up and Hector came with them to the front door.

'Don't forget, Willie, mum's the word,' shouted Martha from the back. 'And Willie, I think you're wrong, it's not her that wants murdering and killing.'

Willie walked down the street laughing. Eustace followed, still whimpering.

★

Arthur had also left home early that evening but he had headed straight for the Club. When he arrived it was deserted except for its cheerful and grossly overweight steward, who, as Arthur entered, chimed up with, 'Hail the conquering hero comes, sound the trumpets, beat hell out of the drums.'

'Shut up.'

'Thank you, music lovers, it's nice to know that my happy thoughts are much appreciated. Why are you here so early?'

'I come specifically.'

'Is it catching?'

'To have a word with you about the bar for the Christmas club party.'

'All arranged, squire, no problem, you and the little engine and others appointed by you two are doing it.'

'Little engine? Who's the little engine?'

'Little, fat, bald head, belches, farts and throws snot a lot.'

'Oh, that little engine. Yes, we were but we've come to the conclusion that our help will probably be needed elsewhere and therefore I've come to ask you if you can get hold of an outside crew to help.'

'That's a bit gross, isn't it? Dropping a thing like that on a bloke after all this time and all these committee meetings that you've had. There was me thinking I were going to have the pleasure of your company behind the bar that evening.'

'Sorry, but we've only just realised.'

'All right.'

'What?'

'All right. All right. You know it's okay.'

'Eh? What?'

'Well, I decided that it would be bloody hard work for me, towing with a bunch of amateurs like you lot. I've done it before for other functions and there's no pleasure in it, I can tell you. Where's this, Harry? Where's that, Harry? How much is this, Harry? This won't work. How do you do that? It's just not on. I was going to have a word with you to see if it were in order for me to use my usual crew, and seeing that it is, I'll get them organised. Well, actually, I already, have in anticipation.'

'Good. I know it will cost more to get hired staff, but the Club should be able to sell more ale to make up for it if customers aren't queuing all night waiting for us.'

'True, true, and anyway my crew don't cost a lot. Free ale all night and ten bob out of the till before they go home. No problem.'

'Is the meeting room free?'

'When?'

'Now.'

'Yes. Why?'

'The committee are coming to finalise one or two details about the party.'

'Is Sarah Anne coming?'

'Yes, or even maybe.'

'Go put the heating on, will you? Hey up, it smells as if one of them might be here now.'

A far distant belch was heard followed by the door opening to reveal Willie and Eustace.

'I was just saying to Arthur, we smelt you coming – you can't creep up and surprise us like that you know. What the hell is that you've fetched with you? Quick, Arthur, pull up a chair and let me pull a quick pint before he expires. My God, you're one committee member here in body but not in spirit tonight.'

Arthur carried a chair to the bar. Fat Harry downed the pint in one long swallow.

'That's better.'

'I thought you were pulling that pint for Eustace.' observed Arthur.

'No, not likely, it were to help me get over the shock. Anyway, what on earth's up with him?'

'He's had a bit of trouble with the wife,' said Willie.

'Only a bit, it looks like a maximum sentence job to me,' said Harry, laughing.

They ushered Eustace into the chair. Harry pulled another pint which they gave him and which he also downed in one long swallow, immediately handing them back the glass.

'Another, please.'

They stared aghast at his expressionless face. Harry poured yet another pint which they gave to Eustace and which he drained in one again. This time, as he lowered the glass from his lips a faint flicker of a smile crossed his face.

'I think just one more, please. Yes, just one more, just one.'

'Who's paying?' ventured the steward.

'I am,' said Eustace.

'I think it's time I had one,' said Willie. 'I can't stand all this excitement.'

By the time the remainder of the committee arrived Eustace was well into his fifth if somewhat slower pint, but he was beginning now to giggle and talk a lot. Sarah Anne was enjoying flirting with Fat Harry who was more than enjoying it.

*

Having given Josie her instructions about the younger children, Thelma went round to visit Jess.

'Here, throw your coat over that chair. Have you brought your embroidery? Good, I'll just get my knitting. They're gone for the night. Arthur went off early to talk to Fat Harry – I don't know his other name – about staffing the bar at the party.'

'Yes, Willie went off early too, to collect Eustace, then visit Greasy Martha to find out what Anthony Murgatroyd had asked her to bake for the party.'

'Do you want a rum and blackcurrant?'

'Oh, yes, please.'

'Well, I don't see why we shouldn't, they do. Now, what about Eustace and his dragon, as they know her?'

'Well, I don't know. I can't say that I like the woman though.'

The evening passed with the pulling to bits of Fat Harry, Greasy Martha and Eustace. Thelma was home and in bed, long before Willie appeared.

★

Meanwhile, down at the Club, after a bit of slap and tickle between Sarah Anne and Fat Harry, which he was loving and she was enjoying just a little bit, Arthur once again managed to assemble the committee in the meeting room.

'Now, there is just one item to discuss and that won't take much of your time. Almost everything is under maximum control except the catering and that, I think, we have now under control also.'

Arthur stopped as loud snoring came from Eustace.

'Someone thump him please,' said Arthur.

'Madam chairman, may I interject?'

'Pardon?'

She looked at Daniel Sykes.

'Who the hell invited him?' asked Willie, who then produced a well-timed belch.

'To continue, without interruption, if I may.'

'You may.'

'Madame chairman, it is farcical that we have one member of this committee fast asleep at a vital meeting. I appreciate that his contributions to this whole affair have been less than zero but I do think that he could refrain from sleeping at a meeting, and I do think that he should immediately be given the sack.

'I think that you will be in a minority of one on that issue. I agree the situation is far from ideal, but for the moment it is as good as it can be.'

'Well, I think that it is ridiculous.'

'Please now, carry on, Arthur,' said the chairman.

'Yes, thank you. Willie and I realised that although we had covered most aspects of the arrangements for the party, the catering was not coming along just as it should be. The reasons for this I will not divulge, but suffice to say that tonight we have addressed one or two of the problems.

'Firstly, the bar. As you know, it had been agreed that we would all lend a hand behind the bar on a rota system so that Fat Harry did not get overloaded and to save the Club the expense of hiring extra staff. However, on reflection, we came to the conclusion that it would probably be better all round if Harry engaged a crew of helpers and then we could all spend our time with other aspects of the party. Harry would not then be frustrated trying to teach a lot of raw recruits at a very busy time, and, as well as that, we could all enjoy the party much more than if we were behind the bar all night. So I came along early to have a chat with Harry and it's all agreed. The Club will run its own bar without interference from us.'

'Excuse me. Sorry I'm late again.'

They all turned to welcome Anthony Murgatroyd who had entered the room quietly and unseen.

'Why is Eustace asleep?'

'Well, Mr Anthony, he's had a bad barney with his wife, so now he's blind drunk and asleep. Best place for him at the moment, I think,' said Arthur.

'Yes, probably, you are right. Please ignore me and continue.'

Arthur resumed.

'So now, to food catering. We were aware that Greasy Martha was baking mince pies and possibly something else, but just exactly what, we did not know, so Willie and Eustace called at her house earlier this evening to ask her and I will ask Willie now to explain, rather than Eustace.'

'Yes, well, me and Eustace went on to Greasy Martha's house. Mind you, Eustace didn't listen to her because he was in a tizz over the dragon.'

'Excuse me interrupting again, but who's the dragon?' asked Mr Anthony.

'Eustace's wife. And the word is a bloody good description of her. Anyway, Martha says she's making sausage rolls, trifles and mince pies, but she's only making them because Mr Anthony's told her she has to and not to help us lot out.'

'So what else do we want?' asked the chairman.

Dick took the floor.

'Pork pies, crisps, sandwiches, cakes, tea and coffee. I have ordered the pork pies from Porky Charrington's butchers, and the crisps from Fat Harry to give the Club a bit of trade. Harry's promised us a bit of discount from them, but I bet it will be a little bit, knowing him.'

'Excuse me, yet again. I would just like it to be put on record that I didn't force Martha to bake the various items, I asked her to. I also thought that I'd asked her to bake the cakes. I will check that out first thing tomorrow morning and if she isn't intending to make the cakes I'll make sure she does.'

Willie at this point made a mental note to add cakes to the list. He was going to tell Thelma about the list and also that Martha wanted her help.

'So that leaves tea, coffee and sandwiches,' said Sarah Anne.

'The tea and coffee present no problem whatsoever facilities for brewing up, plus a more than ample supply of cups and saucers even if not exactly all matching. All we need is milk and sugar. Dick, can you attend to that list if I try to work out how much of each we want?'

'Yes, Miss, no problem.'

Sarah Anne pulled her tongue out at him.

'We can order the milk through the Club steward, then all I have to do is to buy the other items from Freddy Nevershut's.'

'Well, now, that only leaves the sandwiches. Plates again are no problem, there's a mountain of them in the kitchen. If we ask Mr Bun the baker—'

'Mr who?' asked Willie.

'You know, old Trapps the baker, to make us some bridge rolls, two for each person should be adequate, then when we get this party of ladies organised, and I intend organising them next week, half a dozen of us can get the sandwiches put together on Friday teatime whilst the rest of them dress out the Club.

'Now, that just leaves us with costs. We have pies, crisps, coffee, tea, sugar, milk, bread, butter and sandwich fillings. We'll have to reckon up how much a head that's going to come to, then there's the band, the Club room and any other incidental expenses we might come across before the night.' Arthur paused to draw a fresh breath. 'So, all in all, we've a lot of reckoning to do yet. Mind you, I've one suggestion that might just answer the problem. We banked all the money in a deposit account, but up to now we've no idea how much interest we've earned. The members don't know it's on deposit, or that they're going to get back more than they put in, so why don't we use the interest to pay for the party? I believe I did suggest this course of action at a committee meeting a few months ago.'

Daniel Sykes rose to address the gathering. 'I do not often lavish praise on members of this committee, but I must say that I think this idea put forward by Arthur is a most excellent suggestion and to be thoroughly recommended.'

'If you are short at the end of the night, I'll make up the difference,' said Anthony Murgatroyd. 'But what happens if you have some left over?'

'A week's holiday for me and the wife in the Channel Islands,' shouted Willie before he belched and farted with overexcitement.

'Who is? To the Channel Islands? When Arthur? When Willie? Who is?'

'For heaven's sake go back to sleep,' barked Daniel Sykes.

'Might I suggest you wait and see what happens on the night,' said Mr Anthony.

'Right,' said the chairman. 'That's it then. It's downhill all the way from here to the party. Sixteen days to go. Good luck, everybody. If we need to meet again before the night we will have to do it as and when required. Thanks for your help, all of you. Please enjoy the party and we'll have a debriefing meeting on the first Wednesday after Christmas, here at half past seven. Thank you all, and good night.'

With the exception of Daniel Sykes they strayed back into the bar to share a convivial pint or two, and by the time that Fat Harry called time, Eustace was too alcoholically paralysed to support his own weight. He therefore fell down before he got up, to fall down again, to go home.

Arthur looked at Willie, who reluctantly said, 'Go on then.'

Anthony Murgatroyd had a better suggestion.

'Let's bundle him into the back of my car and we'll run him home, though I doubt very much that he wants to go home. But he'll have to.'

'Are you sure you don't mind?' asked Arthur. 'He's not very good, you know, and could easily be very sick.'

'It's not far, I'll drive steady.'

When they arrived outside Eustace's house, the debate began.

'What are we going to do with him now?'

'Well, the last time we brought him home in a state like this, we hung him on the door handle, hammered the knocker and ran like hell,' said Willie. 'So let's do the same again. As soon as we get him out of the car, you get gone, Mr Anthony, and we'll deal with him.

But the best-laid plans of mice and men, and so on... Eustace refused to get out of the car, and among the four of them they made a substantial amount of noise trying to move him, so much so that they disturbed those whom they were trying not to. None of them had seen the dragon approaching down the front steps, dressing gown, curlers, harsh slippers, hairnet and all.

She startled them by rasping, 'What state is he in?'

'Not good, Mrs Ollerenshaw, not good,' said Mr Anthony, 'and just at this precise moment he is refusing to leave my car.'

'Don't worry, I'll get him out. Come out of my way, man!'

She then realised that although she didn't know who the driver of the car was, perhaps it might be prudent to be a little more polite to him in future. Eustace, left ear first, was soon in a heap on the pavement, but it still required the combined resources of all four of them to get him into the house and slump him into an armchair in the back room. Mrs Ollerenshaw thanked them profusely.

Anthony Murgatroyd waited for Willie and Arthur to give them a lift home.

'I'm not surprised he's in that state, I've only met her briefly just now for the first time, but if I were married to her I'd be quite prepared to murder the woman on a continuous basis, and the furnishing of the house is typical of her, cold, stark, bleak and uncomfortable.'

'Yes, he is as he is, but she makes him worse,' said Willie. 'I hope she doesn't come to help at the party. Anyway, he's not the only one that doesn't want to go home tonight, I've got something to tackle Thelma about.'

'What's that?'

'Oh, it's nowt really, nowt at all.'

*

'Thelma, love,' he said as they were getting into bed, 'I've got a favour to ask you. Will you go and help Greasy Martha do the baking for the Christmas party?'

'Will I what?'

She sat up and looked at him.

It was late that night before Willie finally secured an agreement and went to sleep.

Chapter Sixteen

It was party day minus one and Thelma, as requested, made her way to the mill canteen at half past one to help Greasy Martha bake for the do. She hadn't been to the mill before, and Mrs Anthony had allowed her time off from her cleaning job to help Martha, though Mr Anthony, being the good and benevolent man he was, had told his wife to pay Thelma for both Thursday afternoon and Friday, as she was on mill business, as it were.

Thelma walked into the penny hoil to find George Schofield beaming at her.

'You've come to help Greasy Martha with the baking.'

'How do you know?'

'It's my job to know everything. All movements in and out of here, I have to know them all. It's strategic planning, you see, most important job in the mill I have, full of responsibility.'

'Where's the canteen, please?' said a very unimpressed Thelma.

'Seeing it's you, I'll take you over there. I wouldn't do this for just anyone, you know, but come along with me and we'll walk over there. It's on the top floor of the low building over there, next to the office block.'

They ambled over, chatting away, and climbed the stairs to the first floor. George opened the door of the servery to let Thelma in, to be greeted by, 'What the hell do you want?'

'I've brought Thelma over.'

'Show her in, then bugger off.'

Thelma began to wonder why she had let Willie talk her into coming along to help Martha. George Schofield began to wonder what sort of an afternoon Thelma was going to have helping Martha.

But Thelma was very soon put at ease for, as soon as George was out of earshot, Martha said, 'Come on in, Thelma, and make yourself at home. You can hang your coat up over there on that hook.'

Martha pointed to a row of hooks on the wall by the sinks, and whilst Thelma was putting her pinafore on Martha continued talking.

'Now, I know you'll have heard nothing but bad about me and you've just seen a good example of it, but it's all a big act really that over many years I've developed into a fine art, especially for this lot here. I don't remember by now how it all began, but I'll tell you this, I enjoy it. The fouler, dirtier and nastier I become, the better it is. But away from here I'm a different character, and you'll see a different side of me whilst you are here helping me. But if anyone comes in, the other side will come out again in a hurry, so just be warned and don't be alarmed.'

'Yes, Willie has told me many times of the way you carry on in here.'

'I've no doubt you've both had a good laugh about it. I treat Willie just the same as all the rest of them, but much better if no one's looking.'

'Yes, I know that as well.'

'You'll also have heard that Anthony Murgatroyd has ordered me to bake for the party.'

'Yes.'

'Well, that's not true either. He asked me if I would help and there's nothing I wouldn't do for the Murgatroyd family. You work up at the house for Margaret, don't you? How do you like it up there?'

'Oh, I like it very much. She's a super lady to clean for and she looks after me very well. She often helps me a bit when none of her golfing friends are there.'

'It sounds as if you and me are going to get on very well together and, I'll tell you this, I don't normally allow anyone other than the Murgatroyds in here, but you are very welcome. Well, we'd best get on, we've almost a thousand items to prepare, but I'm well on with it already. The list is sausage rolls, mince pies, trifles and cakes. I've already baked six hundred mince pies, made big squares of robin cake, so they'll cut up, ice, decorate, and we'll put a layer of jam into some of them. The pastry's made for the sausage rolls but they're to fill and bake yet, and we've got to start on the trifles. So, where do you want to start? I don't mind.'

'Well, I don't mind either – you say.'

'Sausage rolls, I think, then they can be baking whilst we do the trifles and decorate the fancy cakes.'

So they set to work with a vengeance, and by the middle of the afternoon the sausage rolls were all baking, the trifles had their bottoms in, the custard was boiling, and footsteps were heard approaching.

'Right, Thelma, I don't know who it is but watch this.'

The door began to open.

'What the bloody hell do you—'

She stopped.

Margaret Murgatroyd looked at Martha with a wide grin and said, 'Hello, Martha, I see you've not improved with keeping.'

'No, and I don't intend to. Come in, won't you.'

'Hello, Thelma, I've just popped down to bring you a couple of bottles of sherry to put on the trifles.'

'You're almost too late but I think we'll manage to shove it in somehow. Thanks,' said Martha.

'Do you want a hand with anything whilst I'm here?'

'I don't think so, unless you want to cut those big squares of robin cake into fairy cake-size pieces. But no, let's ice them first. There are four big squares, so we can have vanilla, orange, lemon and strawberry. The icing sugar's in there, as are the little bottles of colouring.' She pointed to a cupboard. 'And you can mix it in that basin that's in front of the cupboard.'

So whilst Thelma kept her eyes on the boiling custard and Martha more than liberally laced the trifles with sherry, Margaret mixed and spread the icing. By the time the mill hooter blew for the end of the day's work there was only the synthetic cream to mix for the top of the trifles, plus the big squares of cake to cut up and decorate with nuts, cherries, hundreds and thousands and anything else that could be found.

'How are you going to get all this food to the Club tomorrow?' asked Margaret Murgatroyd.

'The one thing the brains of Britain haven't thought about,' laughed Martha. 'Just like a committee of men. Still, it's best kept here until late tomorrow afternoon, out of harm's way.'

'I'll ask Anthony if he can arrange the van to take it round.'

'It'll smell of nowt to do with catering,' observed Martha.

'Yes, but, it's only a short journey. It will be all right, there won't be time for it to get contaminated. What time will you be here till tomorrow, Martha?'

'Till the van comes. No problem.'

*

Later that same evening, Sarah Anne did a walk around the houses of the various lady helpers, just to check that they were still all right for making the sandwiches for the big job on Friday evening. She called at Cutside Cottages and got Thelma's 'yes'. The same from Jess Baxter, Kathleen Jordan, Norah Armitage and Brenda Sykes. She had asked Thelma's advice on exactly how many helpers they actually required, and it was agreed they could avoid asking old dragon Ollerenshaw. Mind you, if she did turn up they'd have to find her something to do. So it was all agreed: four o'clock at the Club tomorrow, armed with pinafores and, of course, best hats.

Meanwhile down at the Club, the menfolk, including a very yonderly Eustace, were engaged in a heavy bout of drinking. Even Daniel Sykes was breaking the habit of a lifetime, standing at the bar with a glass of orange juice and being in good humour with everyone. The ambience of the gathering was shattered by Fat Harry.

'Don't you think that you collection of gormless idle lumps should at least be starting to look for the decorations and bunting before closing time arrives?'

'Aye, happen you're right,' said Willie.

They all made their way, as best they could considering their alcoholic state, down the stone steps into the cellar to search for the string of flags, bunting, streamers and Christmas decorations that hadn't seen the light of day for years and years.

'I know where they are,' exclaimed Arthur. 'They're in that cupboard over by the far wall. Mind you, I don't know what else there is in there, so let's get it open and have a look.'

They pulled out all the trimmings they could see and began to carry them upstairs.

Willie said, 'Hang on a minute, it's a bit dark in this corner, there might be summat else in this cupboard yet. Has anyone got a flashlight?'

Dick, being the nearest to the top of the stairs, was despatched to the bar to locate one. When he returned, they shone its meagre light into the back of the cupboard.

'Well, I'll go to our house and back again,' exclaimed Willie. 'Just look here, there's this old set of fairy lights what we had before the war, you know, what fit over the King's picture at the end of the Club room. Let's take them upstairs and find out if they work.'

'We shall have to change the plug by the look of things,' observed Arthur. 'They've changed the wiring in here from two pin to three pin since this lot were last plugged in. Do we have a three pin plug?'

'Go and ask Fat Harry,' said Daniel Sykes.

'You go and ask Fat Harry yourself,' said Willie.

Daniel retained his composure and said, 'It's no good me going to ask, he'll do nothing for me.'

So Arthur approached Harry to see about a plug.

'A plug? A plug? What do you think this is, Woolworths? Yes, of course, I have a three pin plug, here you are. Can you change it or would you like me to come and do it for you?'

'No, it's all right, thanks, I think we can manage.'

'So, do you want to borrow a screwdriver now then?'

'Yes, please.'

'I just knew you would. I did, I knew you would. Here.'

He put the screwdriver into Arthur's hand. Arthur arrived back at the Club room to find everyone gasping for breath and evacuating the room, as Willie had farted yet again. He stayed out in the corridor until the dust had settled, then he went into the room, changed the plug and connected the lights to the electricity.

'Absolutely amazing!' said Lewis as the lights came on. 'It's unbelievable.'

Arthur agreed, saying, 'Yes, it's far more than could be hoped for. Anyway, let's hang them around the King's picture like we used to. Now, Eustace, we need an extension lead for up here. There should have been one in the cupboard with the lights. Can someone go and fetch it, please.'

Willie returned with it a few minutes later.

'It's nobbut a two-pinner, you know.'

'No, I didn't know, but I should have done. Best go and ask the steward for both another three pin plug and a three pin socket.'

'We haven't a cat in hell's chance of getting that.'

'Oh, give it here, I'll sort it out myself.'

So Arthur went again to see Fat Harry who agreed, after a little persuasion, to get a new plug and socket the next morning, fit it on and test out the lights in good time for the party.

The remainder of the evening was taken up with drinking, putting up the streamers, drinking, putting up the flags, drinking, putting up the bunting, drinking, getting the room ready for the party and drinking. They got all the card tables and trestle-tables they could find and arranged them around the perimeter of the room, along with the chairs, which left a very nice area in the middle for dancing. The low stage for the band was in one corner of the room next to the King's picture. Fortunately, the club's one and only honky-tonk piano was on the stage already and so that wasn't to move.

'Willie! Do you think we should have the piano tuned?' asked Arthur.

'Nay, it's only an old honky-tonker, do you think it's worth tuning?'

'Well, I expect that it's a matter for debate but let's go and have a pint and ask our fat friend.'

'Well, lads, you're in luck and make no mistake. It was tuned about three months ago for Susie Stomachache's dancing class and furthermore, and this will amaze you, it was tuned by none other than that master of the musical ear and beer belly, Ivor Ivory.'

'Well, to start with, who on earth is Susie Stomachache?'

'Her what runs the dancing classes, always moaning about her guts of which she has more than her fair share, and everything else. You know her, her father works in Murgatroyd's carding department. Just to give you another clue, she never eats one fish when two will do.'

'Oh, I know who you mean now, eats a bit like a hungry cannibal, a bit of a pain,' said Willie.

'Has one and is one. You'll of course know Ivor Ivory.'

'Oh, yes, he's been tuning pianos round here since the early seventeenth century. Don't know his real name except it's Ivor. Does he work for himself or somebody?'

'Yes,' said Harry.

'Well,' said Arthur. 'we're as ready as we're going to be so I reckon we'll go and get an early night, ready for the big day ahead. What say you, Willie?'

'Yes, okay. We'd best take Eustace home though on the way.'

*

'Your missus coming to help tomorrow, Eustace?' asked Arthur.

'I hope not. I do, I hope not. She'll make a good do into a bad one if she does. She will, Willie, she will, she'll make a right good do into a right bad one.'

He became very quiet and retreated into his own little world.

'What shall we do with him now?' asked Willie.

'Oh, let's lean him over his front gate and leave him there. We don't want a confrontation with the dragon.'

Chapter Seventeen

'That's it, they've got me, I'm going fast. Help, Help.'

Thelma sat up in bed with a start, it was pitch black.

'Whatever's the matter? What's happened?'

She was half-asleep, coming more awake by the second. She fumbled for the light switch. In so doing she hit Willie who was sitting up in bed waving his arms about and jabbering wildly.

'What'd you hit me for?'

'It was an accident. I was trying to find the light switch and still am for that matter.'

Eventually she grabbed the swinging pendant that Willie had already hit several times, and switched on the light. Willie was sitting up, calm now, with gallons of sweat pouring out of him.

'Now, whatever is the matter?'

'I must have been having a nightmare. It was those pound notes, they had me, they were wrapping themselves all around me and starting to strangle me.'

Thelma laughed out loud.

'It's not funny, it's nowt to be laughed at.'

'It is and it isn't. Never mind, this time tomorrow it will all be over and you will be able to relax. Anyway, you've nothing to worry about, you've only got to get the money from the bank and pay it out.'

'Aye, but it's a big responsibility.'

'Well, here's another responsibility. Go and make me a mug of tea seeing that you've wakened me up.'

Willie put on his dressing-gown and slippers before going downstairs to make Thelma and himself a mug of tea, following which they both fell into a deep sleep.

*

'I'd a nightmare last night, all about pound notes that were strangling me,' Willie told his mates at morning break time. 'And what were more horrible were that Thelma made me get up and brew up for waking her up.'

'Happen it's an omen,' said Lewis.

'What's one of them?' asked Willie.

'It's like warning you of bad times to come.'

'Nay, I think it's more like a bad worrying dream about what we have to come later today,' observed Arthur. 'We've quite a big job on this afternoon. Yes, we have that.'

'What time are you going?' asked Dick.

'Two o'clock from here, three o'clock at the bank.'

'Does Mr Anthony know you're both skiving off work?'

'Oh, yes, he does that,' said Willie. 'He's been very helpful as we all know. Have these women got the supper sorted out?'

'Yes, they have that. I'll make sure they have it all ready on time,' said Dick.

'Sarah Anne will, you mean,' said Arthur.

'I don't know what she thinks she's doing interfering like that in what I was doing.'

'But you weren't, were you! Or else she wouldn't have.'

Further argument was forestalled as it was time to start work again. On his morning tour of the mill, Mr Anthony stopped with Willie, just to reassure himself that everything was all right and that both Willie and Arthur were all right for going to the bank.

*

Although Willie was early at the canteen, Sarah Anne had beaten him to it and she saw him coming.

'Change of staff today, Willie.'

'Eh?'

'Your Thelma's in charge.'

'Nay, I'm not, I'm only helping Martha.'

'Have they finished tonight's food?'

'Almost, Willie love. Martha's just put the cream on the trifles and we've then just got a bit of final decorating to do after dinner, then we're all ready for off to the Club.'

'Is it real cream?' asked Willie, his mouth watering.

'You know better, it's sympathetic, but it tastes good. It's that sweet powder you mix with milk and get cream.'

'I wish it were real cream straight from the cow – it used to be lovely, did real cream. I wonder if we'll ever be able to get it again, ever.'

'Oh, I'm sure we will, sometime before long now. They're beginning to relax some of the final rules about food and I don't think it'll be long before we can get such luxuries again,' said Sarah Anne.

'What's for dinner? I'm starving.'

'That sounds more like my Willie.'

'Fish,' said Martha. 'You know full well it's fish. It's been fish every Friday since Mafeking was relieved.'

'Don't mention Mafeking.'

'Why?'

'It's a long story,' said Thelma.

'So why ask me the same question every Friday when you know the answer?'

'Nay, well, I only wanted to check. You might have changed it, then I would have to think about it before I could eat it.'

'The day you have to think about anything before you eat it will be your last. I don't know how you put up with him and his table manners, Thelma.'

'Oh, and what, pray, is wrong with his table manners?'

They turned to look at Thelma, then at Martha.

'Well, he does grunt and squeak a bit you know.'

'Yes, I suppose he does, but that's my Willie.'

Rather yours than mine, said Martha to herself.

The conversation was ended abruptly by the growing murmur of complaint, from further down the queue, about the speed of service.

Despite the experiences that lay ahead Willie dined like a king, as usual, whilst Arthur picked and poked at his food in a more sombre mood, his mind on the task ahead.

*

At two o'clock, Arthur and Willie placed their cards in the time clock on the penny hoil wall and clocked out.

'Big day today,' said George Schofield from his warm seat in the penny hoil. 'Taking your assistant with you, are you, Willie? Going to help Willie, are you, Arthur? Yes, well, you both need help so if you help each other along the way, it will be almost as good.'

'Almost as good as what?' demanded Willie, his hackles beginning to rise.

'Almost as good as if I come with you to help the pair of you.'

'I think we can manage,' said Arthur.

'You probably can, of a fashion.'

Willie was about to launch another tirade when Arthur said, 'Come on, we've got to get to the bank. We haven't time to stand around here talking to the lower echelons of society.'

'Lower what?' asked George.

'Echelons.'

'Yes, that's what I thought it sounded like.'

They left him thinking, and both went home to get changed.

★

They met up again at Arthur's house, on the way to the bank.

'Where's Jess?' enquired Willie.

'She'd better be at the Club helping to get it all set up for tonight, or helping Thelma to make sandwiches or something.'

'Hey, I hope they've managed to get the van for Thelma and Martha.'

'I think they will have, they were going to sort it out all right. I had a word at the mill garage and all was merry and bright.'

In front of the Grolsby branch of the Northern Counties Bank, Willie, as was his ongoing custom, emptied his nostrils into the gutter at the side of the road.

'You filthy bugger,' said Arthur.

'Well, it was the last time I've done it every week up until now so I wasn't going to miss doing it today. One windy day it blew all over a car that was passing.'

'Good job it wasn't the co-op horse.'

'Aye, you're right there, old Dodson the drover would have got off his cart and killed me.'

'Now, then, Arthur, are you ready?'

'Yes, lead the way, let's get on with it, troops to the fore, onward Christian soldiers.'

Willie looked at him with a withering look.

They entered the magnificently appointed hall of the bank and joined a queue at one of the counters.

'Mr Arkenthwaite, sir, good afternoon, you'll not be paying in today,' said the young, spotty-faced individual that Willie had got to know quite well over the last twelve months, and who, after a time, had realised that beneath the noise and the smell there was a warm-hearted human being, and had really quite taken to him eventually.

'You've actually remembered then?' Willie questioned him with a smile.

'How could we forget, sir, when the entire staff of the bank has been up all night counting and guarding your money.'

'Give over, you've not been.' Then he laughed. 'One up to you, young 'un, still it is your turn. Now, give us us brass and we'll get out of your hair. This is Arthur by the way, Arthur Baxter, my chief assistant.'

This time it was Arthur's turn to give Willie a withering look.

'Good afternoon, Mr Baxter, it's a pleasure to meet you, sir. However, I'm afraid, gentlemen, that I cannot give you your money.'

'Can't give it us? What do you mean?' screamed Willie in a violent mood change.

'Mr Sharples, our dear manager, wishes to have a word with you.'

'Is there a problem?'

Both Willie and Arthur were getting to little panic stations.

'Yes, sir, I would imagine so. However, probably only a large one. I'll just let Mr Sharples know you've arrived.'

Little panic stations were rapidly turning into big panic stations.

'Please come this way gentlemen, Mr Sharples will see you now.'

They walked into the oak-panelled office. Horatio Sharples stood there, a smile on his face, his arm outstretched in welcome.

'Come in, Mr Arkenthwaite, come in. Oh, there are two of you. Fetch another glass, Brushwood, there's a good chappie. Well, well, it's taking-out day, and I thought you might like to have a glass of sherry with me to celebrate your success and as a thank-you from the bank for your trade. I would also like to add that if you're going to run again next year, and as I understand it there's no way you can't, the bank will be very happy to accommodate you.'

Brushwood returned with two more glasses which he put down on the desk.

'Only one glass, thank you, Brushwood, I only asked you for one glass.'

'Yes, Mr Sharples, sorry.'

He picked up the glass and looked longingly at the sherry decanter.

'Well, Brushwood?'

'Yes, sorry, Mr Sharples,' he said and he went out of the door.

Following a bout of awkward small talk, they thanked Mr Sharples for his generous hospitality and told him they'd best go to the counter to get the money.

'Oh, there's no need, it's all here, counted and bagged, all the money you've paid in plus the interest. Do you know what you're going to do with the interest?'

'Well, we thought we'd pay for the food for the members' Christmas party out of it,' said Arthur.

'What about the tax on it?' asked Willie. 'Someone told me we had to pay tax on the interest.'

'Well, strictly speaking, it's unearned income and therefore subject to income tax, but we at the bank do not deduct basic rate tax at source like they do at a building society. You will have no means of deducting it, so I am of the opinion that as it's for use at a social gathering, I would risk a non-event and ignore the matter, if you get my drift.'

'Yes, I think I do,' said Arthur.

'I don't,' said Willie.

'Anyway, isn't it time we were away, Willie?'

'Aye, give us us brass and let's get going.'

They thanked Mr Sharples for the sherry, then walked quickly to Arthur's house with the money in a big blue cotton bag which had to be returned to the bank later.

★

Jess was home when they arrived, and made them each a steaming hot pint mug of tea before they counted the money. She gave them an up to the minute report on the fact that everything was in order at the Club, that Thelma had arrived with Martha with the food in the works van and with a very handsome young driver, that the Club was now cleaned, cleared and decorated for the occasion, and that the whole of the Club end of the arrangements were in first-class working order.

'Good. Has Fat Harry been helping you?' asked Willie.

'Yes, he's spent most of the afternoon flitting about flirting with all of us, but yes, actually he has been a great help to us.'

They laid out the money on Arthur's dining room table to count it.

'Exactly right, not a penny to the good. Where are the envelopes, Willie?'

'They're, they're round at our house,' he said with a grin. 'I'd best go and fetch them.'

Over the last few nights, the two friends had met at Willie's house, carefully named each of the envelopes and then inserted into each one a small slip of paper detailing the amount due.

Willie soon returned and the correct amount of money was put into each envelope, the envelopes were sealed and put into Arthur's box in alphabetical order. By the time they had finished it was five o'clock, Thelma had arrived and was helping Jess with the tea.

'What's for tea? I'm starving.'

'Is that the only question you ever ask?' enquired Jess.

'It's usually the only question worth asking.'

'Well, the answer is, wait and see.'

The table was soon laid and, to Willie, a light snack of sausage with baked beans, bread with thinly spread butter and fruit cake for afters appeared.

'How's supper looking?' asked Willie, without a thought for anyone's feelings.

Thelma looked at him. Jess looked at him. Arthur looked at him. Willie observed the three staring faces and realised that he might just have put his foot in it regarding the size of the tea, so he decided that a diplomatic comment might be best.

'No, like, I was just running through the arrangements in my head for tonight and we'd heard about everything else except supper. So, how's supper looking?'

'All right,' snapped Jess, wishing that she hadn't asked them to stop for tea, and certainly deciding that she wasn't asking Willie again, ever.

'Fine, just fine,' said Thelma.

'Good, excellent,' said Willie, who proceeded to eat his tea, being very careful not to make any rude noises whilst eating, and even more so to contain his innermost feelings after he had finished, for, as he was well aware, Jess would not approve of his outcomings and he had upset her enough already.

Tea over, Arthur and Willie set off for the Club with their box of envelopes. Arthur had already changed into his best three-piece grey suit and the plan was for Willie to go home to get changed as soon as the money was safely in the safe. They were very pleasantly surprised by the decorations in the Club. The ladies had put up miles and miles of streamers whilst the Christmas tree was in its place of honour with its lights lit.

'See, it's right champion,' said Willie.

'Yes, it's a credit to the ladies is this. Now come on, let's stash the money in the safe before anything happens to it.'

Arthur produced the safe key and they unlocked it with some difficulty. They were about to lock it when Arthur decided that it might be a good idea to oil the lock, so he went in search of the mythical oil can, rumoured to be kept by Fat Harry but never before produced.

'Harry, can we borrow the oil can please, just to oil the safe lock – it's a bit stiff after all these years of no use. The hinges wouldn't say no to a drop either.'

'Yes, it's here. No, it isn't, it's – it's, er, nowhere. Let me see now, last time I had it were, now let's see, I haven't had it since, nay, I don't know the day when. Sorry, can't help.'

'Have you got an oil can at home, Willie?' Arthur asked on his return to the office.

'Oh, yes, a couple.'

'Bring one with you, will you, when you've got changed, and in the meantime we'll just push the door to, turn the handle and I'll sit guard until you return.'

'Haven't we time for a quick pint before I go home to change?'

'Under the circumstances I have but you haven't. You'd better go home, straight home, do not pass go, do not collect two hundred pounds, and on your way out please call in on the fat one and ask him to deliver me a firkin of his best ale, under the circumstances.'

Willie addressed Fat Harry from a safe distance. 'Hoi, you.'

'Yer what.'

'My good and kind friend, Mr Baxter, wishes it to be known that he would welcome a pint of your best bitter served by your own fair hand, in the Club office, now, immediately if not sooner.'

With this he made a double acceleration out of the bar. Fat Harry walked around to the office and stared at Arthur sitting primly in the chair at the side of the safe.

'For what is the reason, Mr Baxter, sir, for why you finds it impossible to get off your fat idle backside and enter the noble portals of my bar for in order to get your own pint of ale without me wearing out my body and soul carrying one round here for you?'

'Because we've got all this money in the safe and we can't or daren't lock it until he returns with the oil can. Seeing that I daren't leave it, I asked Willie to ask you if you would mind bringing me a pint whilst I sit here.'

'Okay.'

Harry was no sooner gone than he had returned with it.

'Thanks.'

'No problem for you, it's Arkenthwaite that gets at me.'

'Oh, he's all right. Take no notice of him.'

'I don't.'

*

Willie arrived home to find Thelma dressed and ready for the party.

'By gum, you look super, just like a millionairess. Remind me to take the oil can back to the Club with me, we daren't lock the safe because it's stiff and we can't find the club oil can. By Jove, I wouldn't want to live at Baxter's, I aren't half hungry. Supper looks good. Club looks good. I'd best go and get changed. Arthur wouldn't let me have a drink until I get the oil can there because he's having to sit and guard the money.' But Thelma was laughing.

'What's up?'

'You are, you haven't stopped talking since you walked through the door. Now go and get changed and I'll come back to the Club with you. I'll get the oil can for you out of the kitchen and put it in a bag.'

'Thanks, love. I'll go and get changed.'

So, arm in arm, Willie and Thelma walked slowly to the Club in their best Sunday outfits looking every bit as if they were in charge of the evening to come, and as if they were very much in love with one another.

*

'Where on earth have you been?' Arthur demanded of Willie.

'Been home to – you know full well where I've been, and by the way, here's the oil can.'

He took the oil can out of the bag he was carrying. Thelma had gone to inspect the final layout of the food, that she had missed earlier.

'Well, go on then, oil the lock seeing that you have brought the can.'

'Right. Yes. Okay.'

Willie proceeded to squirt the oil into the keyhole.

'There, that'll do.'

Arthur opened the door of the safe then tried the lock half a dozen times, found it to be working well, shut the door again and locked it. As a last precautionary check he tried the handle several times to make sure it was locked, then he put the key in his waistcoat pocket, and in a jovial mood went off to get a drink and join the rest of the party. Willie went to get Thelma and Jess so that they could all have a starting drink together to get the evening away well.

'Won't be long now,' said Arthur. 'All the happy smiling punters will be here, starting in about half an hour. It's about time. Oh, I spoke too soon.'

A very smart Sid Sidebottom arrived, accompanied by his sextet minus one. He was decked out in full morning dress complete with striped trousers and tails.

'Evening, folks. Thought I'd put the best clobber on seeing that it's a special occasion. In the Club room, are we? Good, we'll just go and get set up. By the way, is Eustace Ollerenshaw coming tonight?'

'Yes, why?'

'Well, I've just passed him a couple of hundred yards up the road, looking very smartly turned out, but being tried to look even smarter by the ugliest woman you ever did see.'

'Oh, is the dragon coming, then?' asked Willie.

'If that's her, and no doubt it will be, then yes, the dragon's coming. Have you prepared a special dish of fire for her supper?'

'Bugger,' said Willie, and farted.

'Willie!' screamed Thelma.

'Sorry, love. It was directed at her.'

'Who?'

'The dragon.'

'You've no need to do that to her.'

'Yes I have, for Eustace's sake.'

'Well, yes, for him we all feel sorry.'

'Best go get the band set up.'

'Oh, aye, Sid, you go and get on with it, don't let us hold you up with our idle gossip,' said Arthur.

The chairman and her husband were next to arrive. She played up to Fat Harry but he didn't take the bait, although he hoped he might later.

'Eustace and his wife will be here shortly, I think,' she said.

'What do you mean, you think? What's happening to him now? Let's have the next news bulletin.'

'Well, the dragon's just giving him a lecture outside the front door about staying sober. Anyway, you can ask him yourself, here he is now.'

A very smart Eustace walked towards them in his best black trilby, best grey woollen overcoat and best grey worsted three-piece suit, accompanied by his dear wife. He greeted them with a smile; she greeted them with a face like a quarry bottom.

'Hello, Willie. Hello, Arthur. Hello, Harry. Hello, Jess. Hello, Thelma. Hello, Sarah Anne. Hello, everybody. How are you all? Are you? It's cold outside. Very cold. Isn't it? Do you all know my wife, Joan?'

The smile left his face at this point.

'Pint, Eustace?' asked Arthur. 'And how about you, Joan?'

Joan was just about to say that Eustace would have a lemonade, when he said for himself, 'Yes, please, and Joan would like a dry sherry, please. A dry sherry, Arthur, thanks. I'll just go and take my coat off, I will, my coat. Can I take yours, Joan?'

She removed her coat, hat pin and hat, which he took away to the cloakroom.

Arthur ordered the drinks but conversation was a little bit sparse.

'Now, what can I do to help?' asked Joan.

The other seven were dumbstruck. Willie wanted to belch but daren't. Fat Harry turned away and escaped into his little back room for a laugh. Sarah Anne was the first to recover enough to speak.

'Well, actually, Joan, there's nothing to do, it's all done. The only thing we've overlooked and a job that does want doing is that we want someone to sit at the door to act as welcoming hostess, along with my husband who is going to act as host. The object is to welcome all our guests, to make them feel at home, and to show them where the cloakrooms and the bar are. Also, you have to look out for gatecrashers.'

'Fine, that suits me just fine. Just make sure all of you, that Eustace does not drink too much. Come on then, let's get to our post, the visitors will soon be arriving.'

'Bit of good quick thinking, but why didn't you put her on car park duty?' asked Willie.

'Now, now, Willie.'

'Thanks, thanks a million, thanks again, Sarah Anne.'

Eustace had by this time rejoined the group.

'I'd buy you all a drink if she'd let me have any money. I didn't think she'd go like that. I didn't. I thought there'd be a big argument, I did, a big argument.'

'Method in my madness,' said Sarah Anne to herself as she quietly went behind the bar and into Harry's back room where she closed the door, then hugged and kissed him for quite a time.

'By gum, I enjoyed that. But I thought you hated my guts.'

'Let's just say it's party night and I'm here to party. If I can think up a good excuse to get rid of him later I'll come back for more. But beware, this is only for party night so make the most of it.'

As it was getting near the arrival time of the bar staff, Sarah Anne came back into the bar and bought Eustace a pint, the others having dispersed in different directions to see to other pressing matters.

Chapter Eighteen

The band was tuning up, the bar staff were in position, the host and hostess at their posts, Willie and Arthur were parading backwards and forwards keeping their eyes on this, that and nothing in particular; the three ladies, Thelma, Jess and Sarah Anne, were making sure that supper was fully prepared, and Eustace was steadily drinking and drinking as people bought him yet another pint.

The time was twenty-five past seven. Joan walked over and, as well as strong words, gave Eustace a sharp crack around the head.

The first guests started to arrive for the party, the band struck up with a quickstep and by quarter to eight the event was in full swing. The atmosphere in the Club was warm and friendly, the bar was doing a brisk trade and the party was going like clockwork.

At quarter past eight, Arthur and Willie entered the Club office to retrieve the money. Arthur produced the safe key from his waistcoat pocket, put it into the lock and it would not turn.

They tried turning it, forcing it, removing it and putting it back in again. They tried it in different positions, gently moving it in and out at the same time as trying to turn it, all to no avail.

'Problem,' said Arthur.

Willie belched and asked, 'What are we going to do now?'

'Panic.'

'Then what?'

'Nay.'

'We'd best fetch Harry.'

'Aye, go and get him, but quietly.'

So Willie walked behind the bar and tugged Harry's sleeve.

'Hey, come here a minute with me, will you?'

'Shut up and go away – can't you see I'm busy.'

'Come on now, please, it's a matter of life and death.'

'What on earth's the matter?' asked Harry.

'Please, Harry, just come in to the office, now.'

So Harry reluctantly followed Willie into the office.

'This had better be good. So, what's up?'

'We can't open the safe,' said Arthur.

'Try unlocking it.'

'We can't.'

'You locked it. So what exactly's the problem?'

'The so and so key won't turn.'

'It did turn a couple of hours ago.'

'We all know that, but it won't turn now.'

'Here, let's have a go.'

Harry knelt down in front of the safe, took the key from Arthur, inserted it into the lock and tried to turn it. Once again it would not turn.

'Well, now, here's a problem and no mistake.'

'So what do you reckon we should do?' Arthur asked him.

Willie also asked, 'Have you any suggestions?'

'Police job, I think; they'll know where there's a locksmith.'

'Can I go and ring nine, nine, nine?' enquired Willie eagerly.

'Fat lot of good that'll do. Just go down to the phone box and ring the Police station. Better still, run round there, you'll nearly be as quick as telephoning.'

*

So Willie ran out of the Club and around the corner to the headquarters of the Grolsby constabulary, the nerve centre of local crime and punishment, manned by one solitary sergeant on night duty, with a back up of two constables out on patrol. They also had at their disposal, for emergencies, two bicycles and a squad car at headquarters in the town eight miles away. It was into this hive of activity that Willie burst at half past eight to find Sergeant Crabtree sitting in the constabulary chair in front of the constabulary fire, fast asleep. The very act of Willie banging on the doors as he entered, and of knocking on the desk top, awoke Sergeant Crabtree from his slumbers.

'Now, now, what's going on? What's all this noise about? Oh, it's you, Willie, a very rare honour to have you in here. What's the matter?'

Willie explained the predicament.

'Well, now, there's a turn-up for the books. What are we going to do? I can't leave the station unmanned, now can I? Hey up, I know, the other two'll be back in a minute or two for their supper, then I'll come with you if you'll just hang on. In the meantime, come around here, stand with your back to the fire and warm your brains.'

Willie stood there enjoying the warmth on the bottom of his back and the backs of his legs, chatting to Sergeant Crabtree about this and that whilst the Sergeant assembled his tools and paraphernalia for the job.

'It's a little-known fact that I'm an expert safe-breaker, so I'll bring the tool bag along and see what I can do.'

Laurel and Hardy, as the two constables were known throughout the village because of their build, soon arrived back at the station. They were instructed to remain at the station until the sergeant returned, and he and Willie then set out for the Club.

*

Arthur and Harry were both beginning to get worried about the length of time that Willie had been away. They were about to send out a search party, consisting of Thelma and Jess so as not to alarm the revellers, when they heard a commotion in the bar. Sergeant Crabtree appeared, followed by Willie, followed by a crowd.

The crowd was trying to get into the office, making it impossible for anything to happen in any way whatsoever. The sergeant, having been trained to take command of situations, took control of this one.

'Now then, ladies and gentlemen, there's no panic, just a small problem, so please go back to your party.'

With one almighty push he shoved the party-goers out of the office and closed the door behind them, leaving just himself, Arthur, Willie and Fat Harry to sort out the doorlock.

'Keep watch on that door, Harry, if you please – no one to enter under any circumstances. Now, let the dog see the rabbit.'

He knelt down in front of the safe, tried the key, withdrew it, got out a bunch of skeleton keys from his pocket, selected one from the bunch and inserted it into the lock. He slowly turned it backwards and forwards, at the same time moving it sideways, carefully moving the internal levers of the lock out of the engaged position. He tried to turn the door handle several times, when suddenly it moved one sixteenth of a turn, allowing him to bring it to the open position after another bout of slow key manoeuvring.

'There you are. Fetch me a pint, Harry, please.'

'With the greatest of pleasure. However, no drinking on duty you know.'

'Shove off and get me a pint.'

'Yes, Sergeant.'

'By the way, Harry, don't lock this safe again until you've had it repaired. The handle's locked in against the lock when it's locked. Have you had it locked and opened recently?'

Arthur looked at him and said, 'Well, yes and no actually. We oiled the lock because we knew it hadn't been locked for a long time, tried it with the door open, found it all right, so we put the money in and locked it.'

Sarah Anne opened the office door and peered in.

'I said nobody in here,' said the sergeant.

'Hang on, Sarge, she's in charge,' said Willie.

'What do you mean, she's in charge?' asked an incredulous Sergeant Crabtree.

'Sarah Anne is the committee chairman and therefore she's technically in charge of the money,' said Arthur.

'You'd best come in then, lass. You've had a near do with that safe, you almost didn't get to pay the money out tonight.'

'Why, what happened?'

Willie related the whole story in a few choice words, and Fat Harry came back with the sergeant's pint, plus three more.

'Where's mine?' asked Sarah Anne.

'I'll go and get you one in a minute,' he said with a twinkle in his eye. 'But first of all, I must just say that years ago, and I mean years before the start of the war when I was a member here and not the steward, I remember they had a lot of bother with this safe. They locked some important papers in it and couldn't get them out. There was all hell to pay at the time I seem to remember, something to do with the Club deeds. They couldn't get them out of the safe, they were locked in, just the same as tonight. They had to get a locksmith to unlock it. It's all coming back now. They told them never to lock it again until they had had it mended, but it looks like it never got mended.'

Anthony Murgatroyd popped his head around the door.

'Evening, Mr Murgatroyd, sir,' said the sergeant.

'Good evening, Sergeant Crabtree. Is everything all right?'

'It is now, sir, it is now. However, I suggest the Club gets its safe lock mended as soon as possible.'

'By the way,' said Fat Harry, 'has anyone seen the Club deeds in recent times?'

'Not tonight, Harry, not tonight. We'll sort that matter out after Christmas. Let's get back to the party now,' said Arthur.

*

Willie and Arthur entered the Club room, clutching the box of envelopes, and there were loud cheers. The band stopped playing and the Christmas club members crowded around the terrible two in order to retrieve their money.

'Right, queue up in orderly fashion. We've got them in alphabetical order so it won't be any trouble to find your particular envelope.'

Willie handed them out as Arthur sorted them. The operation lasted all of five minutes before it was completed.

Willie and Arthur went to find their respective wives to take them for a drink. Arthur ordered four whisky and waters.

'We don't want whisky,' said Jess.

'Shut up, woman, and get it into you. Willie and me are ready for a relaxing drink and you two can jolly well join us.'

They had just taken their glasses in hand when cries of, 'Speech, Speech. We want Willie. We want Arthur,' came floating across the bar from the club members who had congregated around the band.

Dick came through to the bar and escorted them around to the rostrum. The band struck up with 'For he's a jolly good fellow' whilst the crowd sang and cheered.

'What are we going to do?' asked Willie.

'I don't rightly know. You go first.'

'Nay, I'm no good at this sort of thing. You're much better at it than me.'

'Well, go on then,' said Arthur with a superior look on his face. 'I had actually prepared a few words.'

Arthur mounted the stage and managed to squeeze himself in, between the piano and a big drum.

'Ladies and gentlemen, friends, fellow members of Murgatroyd's Christmas club.' He stopped for breath and to collect his thoughts. 'Well, we've done it.'

Loud and prolonged cheers came from the audience.

'This has been a first-class team effort right through the twelve months, and it has all worked out as planned. I would like to point out that we have gained a small amount of interest over the year on the money we banked and we decided to use it to pay for part of tonight's party so that we did not need to charge you for it. There was not enough to pay for the whole of the party, but through the generosity of the ladies of the committee, that is, committee members' wives, the Club committee, but more importantly, Anthony and Margaret Murgatroyd, we have managed to give you a free do.'

Even louder and longer cheers from the audience.

Arthur continued, saying, 'I would like especially to thank Anthony Murgatroyd for his major financial contribution and also for his physical help, particularly with the supper. Two members of the committee deserve special mention, Sarah Anne Green for her tireless devotion and total impartiality to the job of chairman and, finally, our little friend with the big heart, enormous appetite, gargantuan thirst and double, treble, quadruple indigestion, who has worked his clogs off for you all, Willie Arkenthwaite.'

Cheers and shouts of, 'We want Willie, we want Willie,' resounded around the room.

Willie tried to hide but could find nowhere to go and was picked up by the crowd to be carried shoulder high around the room. Sid Sidebottom had a problem – what sort of music to play to accompany the revelry. He had no time to make his mind up as events were passing him by, so he shouted, 'See the Conquering Hero Comes'. He raised his baton and they played as well as they could with a long since played piece. Willie was carried in a big circle for a considerable time before they would put him down again.

When the noise finally subsided, Anthony Murgatroyd mounted the stage and found a tiny space between the drums and Sid Sidebottom. He called for order.

'Ladies and gentlemen, I think we should all be very grateful to the whole of the committee who have worked so hard on your behalf. I also think we should thank the ladies of the committee for their hard work in preparing for us such a magnificent supper. For those of you who haven't seen it yet, as I have, it's a feast fit for a king. So I ask you all to join me in three cheers for the committee, hip, hip.'

The Grolsby Working Men's Club had not heard such uproar and cheering in many a long year, and it was several minutes before Arthur could attract the attention of the crowd again.

'Now, for one or two serious bits. Is everyone familiar with the discount scheme operated on our behalf by various shops in the village? Has everyone ordered their various items from these shops ready for collection on Christmas Eve? If by any chance any of you have yet to order, it's not too late, and you all know which the shops are that have joined in the scheme.

'Secondly, and more importantly, supper is served, so before you all rush into the supper room, thank you all for joining the club, we have enjoyed running it, and a very merry Christmas to you all. Just one thing, we will be open for business again after the first of January, if any of you want to join again.'

He got down from the rostrum to great applause and a tidal movement towards the supper, then he got back again with a lot of difficulty as he met the band getting off. He banged the big drum loudly and shouted for quiet.

'I was just thinking – so that we do not break with tradition we should allow Willie to be first in the supper queue. I know that he is the treasurer and that at any do, family holds back, but he is always first in the dinner queue so I think we should let him and Thelma head up the queue tonight. Any objections?'

There was once again a lot of shouting which Arthur took to mean no objections, and at the same time both Willie and Thelma were propelled into the supper room at the head of the crowd with all their friends following, except for Eustace and Joan. A heavy hand was held on Eustace's shoulder, preventing him from getting up.

'What's all this about a discount scheme?' she shouted in his ear.

Eustace screwed up his eyes and gave her a sheepish smile.

'Hello, my love, do you want a drink?'

'A drink? A drink?' she shrieked. 'When you've had more than enough for everyone at the party. Now, what's all this about a discount scheme?'

Eustace looked at her, tried to focus his eyes, then slurred his words.

'Why don't you sit down here and let me get you a drink.'

He indicated a non-existent chair somewhere near him, with an unsteady wave of an uncontrollable arm.

'What about the discount scheme?'

'Which discount scheme, my love?'

Supper was becoming of secondary interest to many of the party-goers who were gathering around to listen to Joan and Eustace.

'What do you mean, which discount scheme? Don't you know anything about it?

'No. Can I have another pint please, Harry. What will you have, Joan?'

'Nothing, and neither are you. Get up off that chair, I'm taking you for your supper.'

She gave poor old Eustace a smack with her fist across his back, knocking him off his chair and on to the floor. He picked himself up, dusted himself down, and very meekly followed Joan into the supper room.

⋆

Willie and Thelma were receiving right royal treatment at the hands of the supper room staff. With their being first in the queue, there was no worry of what might have been eaten by those who had gone before, and at the end of the table Willie, with a groaning plate, had only one complaint which was that the plates were not big enough. Willie, Thelma, Arthur and Jess sat at a table near to the food-laden buffet and began to enjoy eating their supper. Willie was trying his best to suppress an overwhelming desire to relieve his body of all manner of internal pressures which were building up. They had just nicely started eating when they were disturbed by the noise coming from Joan Ollerenshaw as she dragged Eustace towards the supper buffet.

'Why didn't you tell me about the discount scheme? I bet you didn't know anything about it. I reckon you never heard them talking about it. You were probably asleep at the meetings you went to. I don't know why you bother going to these meetings. I can't understand why you ever got elected to the committee. Were you absent the day they gave brains out? I think—'

The whole of the supper room had stopped eating as the tirade continued.

Thelma nudged Jess. 'Come with me a minute.'

They got up and Jess followed Thelma over to Eustace and Joan. As they got near, Thelma whispered, 'You grab her left arm and I'll take the right one. We'll have to grip tight on her.'

They carried out their plan, much to Joan's surprise, as they gripped hard on to her arms.

'Now then,' said Thelma.

'Let me go,' shouted a very shocked Joan, struggling.

'Oh, not just yet awhile. Now, you are disturbing our party and you're making a laughing stock of both yourself and Eustace.'

Thelma turned to Eustace. 'Go and sit down with Willie and Arthur.'

Joan was still struggling, but the two ladies held on to her with grim determination to finish what they had set out to do, whatever that might have been.

Thelma continued, 'I'm not surprised that Eustace didn't tell you about the discount scheme. For a start, he probably didn't understand it properly, and secondly, he wouldn't dare tell you about it because you'd probably only go off at the deep end at him.'

Joan remained silent, fuming and wriggling. Jess took a turn.

'We heard you say you didn't know why he'd got elected to the committee. Well, I'll tell you why. He wasn't elected because of his ability, he was asked to attend by Arthur and Willie so that they could look after him of an evening, like they do during the day at work. They both think a lot about him, as do Thelma and me, in fact, a damned sight more than you do.'

Joan said nothing. She had given over struggling and held her head bent, just staring at the floor. Thelma took the lead again.

'You've been causing a disturbance at the party that we've all put a lot of work into to make it into a very nice evening for everyone, and if we hear any more of it we're going to throw you out.'

'You've no need to worry on that score – I'm not stopping here where I'm not wanted. You coming?'

She looked at Eustace. Before he had time to answer, Thelma answered for him. 'No, he most certainly isn't, he's staying here to enjoy himself. At least he'll enjoy it as well as he can now you've ruined it for him. We'll drop him off on the way home. No doubt he'll be well and truly drunk out of his mind by that time and I don't blame him. In fact, we'll probably help him get there, and if I hear one word about you having taken it out of him later, me'n Jess'll be round at your house to sort you out once and for all.'

Joan removed herself from the party, quietly with head bowed. The throng in the supper room applauded Thelma and Jess as they returned to their table. They walked back arm in arm.

'I'm shaking all over,' said Thelma.

'I'm sweating, shivering and shaking,' replied Jess.

Eustace stood up to vacate his seat and began to walk away.

'Where do you think you're going?' asked Arthur.

'Going? Me, going? Going to the bar, to the bar, that's where I'm going, to the bar.'

'Sit down and I'll go and get you some supper.'

Arthur grabbed another chair, then grabbed Eustace, making him sit down.

'I'll get you two girls a brandy each,' said Willie. 'I reckon you deserve it.'

'I reckon we need it,' murmured Jess.

Eustace began to talk to all of them at the same time.

'Thank you. Thank you. I don't know what I'm going to do now, I don't, but thank you anyway. I don't know what for, but thank you.' He belched, screwed his eyes up, stared at nothing in particular while trying to focus properly, then started talking again. 'I'm very sorry for belching. I'm also very sorry I put you to all this trouble. I am, very sorry, but I don't know what I'm going to do now I don't.'

'Well, I do,' said Thelma, who was fed up listening to him. 'First of all, you're going to have a good supper, as much as you can force into you, then you're going to drink as many cups of coffee as you can drink, then you're going to go to the bar and get drunk again, then we're all going to take you home when the party's finished.'

'But I don't want to go home, not to her, no, not to her. I don't want to go home.'

'But you'll have to go home eventually, later.'

'Yes, I know, but I shan't want to, I shan't.'

*

When Willie went to the bar Anthony Murgatroyd followed him.

'Your girls did a sterling job on Joan Ollerenshaw, she's been asking for it for more years than I care to remember. What are you going to do with Eustace now?'

'Best thing to do is to get him paralytic.'

'I don't disagree.'

'There's just one problem – she never let's him have owt, he has nowt, he's skint and I can't afford to get him drunk.'

Anthony Murgatroyd caught Fat Harry's eye and gave him a big, white five pound note.

'Now, then, Harry, that is for the use of Eustace Ollerenshaw. Let him get drunk on it. Let Willie and Arthur and their wives have one each from it and yourself, but it's mainly for Eustace. Let him be happy in drink.'

'What's all that about?' Harry asked Willie when Anthony Murgatroyd had left.

'Have you not heard about the big row in the supper room between Eustace and Mrs Eustace, or the other way around. She nearly killed him with her mouth, it was like the third world war starting. Anyway, she's gone home, he's having his supper, and that brass's for him to drown his sorrows. I'll bring the others back later for their free drink, and don't tell him where that brass's come from for his bout of heavy drinking.'

Eustace thanked Willie yet again when he returned to his supper table. Most people had by this time finished their suppers and were slowly drifting back to the dance floor. The band had eaten enough for themselves and several others, the bar staff had taken the opportunity to have a bite, but the poor old steward had been left looking after the bar, without food.

'Good supper, Harry,' observed Dick when he went for some drinks.

'How the hell should I know?'

'Not had yours yet then?'

'Call yourselves mates. You come in here year in, year out, you reckon to be my pals, but when it comes down to it I can get lost, I can. Poor old Harry, let him starve, feed everyone else but ignore the steward. No recognition for all the help I've given.'

'Oh, for heaven's sake, shut your gob and go and get yourself fed.'

'Thanks, I will.'

He ambled off towards the supper room, leaving his temporary staff with the bar. On the way he had a thought. He changed direction towards the music and searched for Sarah Anne Green. He innocently asked Daniel Sykes, 'Have you seen Sarah Anne Green anywhere?'

'Why? Are you going to have your wicked way with her this party night?'

'No, and furthermore, I will not smack you in the gob on this party night. How's your lemonade?'

'Have you met my wife?' asked Daniel. 'My dear, this is Fat Harry the Club steward, whose charm and effervescent wit I have often told you about after our committee meetings.'

Harry was somewhat taken aback at the sight of a most beautiful, well-groomed and very presentable lady who gave a radiant and very genuine smile as she shook his hand.

Harry stuttered, 'How, how do you do, pleased, yes, pleased I am to make your acquaintance.'

He spied Sarah Anne in the distance, made his excuses and escaped to her. She was dancing with her husband Bill, when she saw Harry standing at the edge of the dance floor beckoning to her. She stopped dancing and came over.

'What is it, Harry?'

'I haven't had me supper. Everyone else has but me. I've been left out in the cold. Your oldest mate and you've all ignored me.'

Sarah Anne told Bill to go dance with Thelma as she had a small problem to sort out, then she took Harry by the arm and walked him towards the supper room. As it happened, there was plenty left and they filled two plates which were taken discretely into Harry's little back room. Behind a locked door, she fed him a giant supper, then amused him and herself in several other ways.

Eustace was enjoying, or enjoying as much as he could because of the state in which he found himself, an excellent supper under the gaze of four pairs of watchful eyes. Willie brought him a pint at the same time as he delivered the brandies to the two girls, and his and Arthur's pints.

When Eustace had eaten the last crumb and the pattern from the plate, Arthur asked him, 'Do you want some more, Eustace? Or some coffee?'

'Yes, please, Arthur, some more. Yes please, and some coffee, please, yes, some coffee, please, and some more supper, please. Where's Joan gone?'

Thelma answered him, 'Home, I hope. Anyway, give over worrying about her tonight and enjoy yourself instead.'

'Yes, but what is she going to do when I get home? What is she? I didn't understand about the discount scheme, I didn't Thelma, Jess, I didn't. She'll kill me, she will, it'll be horrible, it will, horrible. I don't want to go home, I don't, not tonight, no, not tonight, not ever. I don't want to go home.'

Fortunately, Arthur returned with his plate of food and Jess fetched him some coffee. He tucked into the food with gusto.

Thelma said, 'Don't worry, Eustace, we've already had words with Joan about treating you properly.'

'That'll only make it worse that will, worse, much worse.'

'Now you've finished your supper let's all take you for a drink,' said Arthur.

So they all five returned to the bar, put Eustace on his bar stool, and had their next free drink after some argument with the temporary bat staff in the absence of Harry. They then left Eustace to the tender mercy of Harry when he emerged from the back room very indiscreetly, accompanied by a very guilty looking Sarah Anne, who tried to creep quietly back to the dance floor without being noticed by the crowds around the bar. The remainder of the evening passed with everyone enjoying the festivities, the dancing and the party.

★

At midnight, everyone that was left at the party gathered around into a big circle to sing 'Auld Lang Syne'. Arthur went to get Eustace but left him when he saw the state he was in.

'Has he drunk all that brass?' he enquired of Fat Harry.

'Every last drop and some more of mine.'

'Ah, well, never mind. Come and enjoy the festivities on the dance floor.'

So Harry joined the big circle. Sarah Anne, Bill, Willie, Thelma, Arthur and Jess were pushed into their own small circle in the middle of the bigger one. The band struck up and the crowds surged back and forth, squeezing the small party at every rush forward. Fat Harry positioned himself so that he could squeeze Sarah Anne as often as possible. When the music had finally stopped and the crowd had settled down a little, eagerly awaiting the next happening, Anthony Murgatroyd walked into the middle of the three couples and, waving his arms in the air, he called for silence.

'Well, ladies and gentlemen, that's it, I am sorry to say. I know from looking around that you have all thoroughly enjoyed yourselves, as have Margaret and I.' He shook the hands of the six people around him in the centre circle. 'I just want to thank you all for a most excellent evening. You have done more than you'll ever know for comradeship and friendliness at the mill, and I have thoroughly enjoyed being a part of it even if I did foist myself upon you. Are we on again for next year?'

'Yes,' came a chorus of three voices.

'Good, then it only leaves me to bid you all good night, and to wish you all a very merry Christmas and a very Happy New Year.'

The cheering started and went on and on, then the band started to play a selection of Christmas carols to round off the evening. The whole of the party stood and sang as long and loudly as they could. When the band finally stopped the revellers shouted for more and more, and it was only Fat Harry's insistence that they all go home which eventually persuaded them to do so.

Thelma went to get Eustace's coat whilst Willie tried to stand him upright. With Arthur's help he eventually succeeded, then with Thelma's help they managed to get his scarf, coat, gloves and hat on. It took all four of them to get him to the door, but as everyone was shouting goodnight to their friends, actually leaving the Club took some little time.

*

Walking Eustace home took a little longer than it should have done. It took all four of them to get him there, some pulling, some pushing, at times picking him up, at times stopping him from singing. When they finally arrived, a hurried conference took place as to who was going to knock on the door.

Eustace, having recognised his own house, was protesting that he didn't want to go home. The conference came to an abrupt end as the front door opened and Joan stepped out.

'Bring him in, will you please?'

'But we usually leave him out here,' protested Willie.

'Please, just bring him in and come in yourselves. Please.'

They looked at each other then, with telepathic agreement, they ushered Eustace inside, still protesting that he never wanted to go into that house again and that he would go home with them for the night.

Joan motioned them into the back living cum kitchen cum dining room where there was a meagre fire burning. Willie was heard to remark later that that was the first and last time he'd ever seen a cold fire. They sat down on the hard chairs and surveyed the cold, unwelcoming atmosphere.

Joan carefully removed Eustace's outdoor clothes, hung them up, then led him back into the back room.

'Why haven't you hit me? You haven't. Hit me, you haven't. Why not?' Eustace asked her.

Joan looked at the four silent people, then began to talk. 'Now look, I don't know how to say this, but I came home boiling mad as you can imagine, but then I got to thinking about things. You two ladies stood up for my Eustace tonight.'

'That's more than you've ever done.' Jess got a quick one in.

'Yes, I know. Anyway, as I was saying, you two stood up for him and it's made me realise just what good friends he's got, and just how bad I've been with him.'

A tear was seen to roll down her face. Eustace stared at her disbelievingly.

'So, I want to thank you ladies for what you did to me tonight, from the bottom of my heart. I want to thank you two gentlemen for being such good friends to him for all these years when I haven't been and, finally, I want to tell you that you've no need to worry about Eustace coming to any harm again, by me.

'Now, I have said all that, and believe you me it's taken some saying. I would like you all to go please as it's been a very different night for me which hasn't turned out quite as I expected it to do. In fact, it's eventually turned out much better. I would also like to think that next year, perhaps, if you will have Eustace on the committee again, and I hope you will, that I can play my full part in helping you ladies with the party.'

An uncomfortable silence followed. Arthur was lost for words. Jess was getting ready to tell Joan to get lost. Willie wished they could go as he wanted to fart, daren't, and was having extreme problems containing himself.

Thelma was the one who spoke first. 'Yes, yes, we'd love to have you help us. In fact, we'd love to see more of you during the year, providing, of course, that you're all right with Eustace.'

'You've no need to worry any further on that account. I know they all call me the dragon but that will be a thing of the past, although I assume the name will stick – they usually do.'

The four friends got up to go and made their way to the front door.

'Goodnight, and thank you very much,' said Joan.

'Yes, thank you, thank you, Arthur, Willie, thank you. Thank you for everything, and I mean everything. Especially thank you to Thelma and Jess. Thank you, yes, thank you all.'

Because of his state, Eustace would have gone on all night, but as his guests disappeared he gave over talking and turned around to face a smiling Joan who helped him inside, gave him a pint of tea, and then helped him to bed.

⋆

'Well, I'll go to our house,' said Willie, the first to speak, after much belching and farting.

Jess was the second. 'Nay, you'll not. You'll go to ours and have a pot of tea. You've nowt to rush home for.'

So they sat at the Baxters' house until well into the night, talking and drinking tea. Willie summed it all up.

'Been a bloody good do all round, it has.'

'Yes, you're dead right,' said Arthur.

'Here's to next year,' said Jess, and Thelma agreed.

Willie felt yet another overwhelming urge to belch. He got up to go to the bathroom but could contain it no longer.

'Willie!' screamed Thelma.

'Take him home,' said Jess.

⋆

If Arthur and Jess had stood a while on their doorstep after Willie and Thelma had departed, they would have heard yet again the call in the still night air: '*Willie!*'